Vardo Path

Vardo Book 1

Adam Fox

Foxes' Retreat

Visit the author's website at www.adamfoxauthor.co.uk

Published by Foxes' Retreat Ltd, Ashbourne, United Kingdom.
Visit the publisher's website at www.foxesretreat.com.

Book Cover by Adam Fox, Zain Ali, Sienna Arts
Editing by Manda Waller www.mandawaller.co.uk

1st edition 2024 (1.0.2)
ISBN (print) 978-1-7384340-2-2
ISBN (e-book) 978-1-7384340-3-9

MAP

Part I

It is said that Henry de Ferrers, castellan of Leadestre, was awarded 'All the lond that may be ryden aboute bitwene the rysyng and the settyng of the sonne upon the day of mydsumeres,' that land being known as Roteslund.

- George Villiers, Duke of Bochinghehamscire

Chapter 1

She sat up in bed, soaked with sweat, her blonde hair stuck to her face, her mobile on the bedside table, blaring and buzzing. She fumbled to silence it, leant forward, sobbed once.

"God help me," she gasped. What was happening to her? This was the same dream, three nights in a row. Maisie flung her duvet back and swung her feet off the bed. Which was when she noticed the blood. Blood on her sheet, by the pillow. A patch the size of her palm.

"What ...?"

And then she noticed the pain. Her shoulder. She craned her neck to look. Could see blood on her nightie, and realisation struck. In her dream, she had slammed into the door jamb. The splintered oak frame had ripped her shirt, her skin. In her dream.

"Not possible," she breathed, her mind in turmoil. If she was someone who swore, she thought, now would be the time. As the pain increased, she yelped, "Ow, ow, ow, damn it! Ow!"

Holding her shoulder, despite the stinging that her grip engendered, she stepped to the tiny en suite bathroom. Clicked the light on. The extractor fan started its annoying clatter. Still not fixed. She glanced at herself in the mirror. Good grief, she looked terrible. Shadows ringed her cornflower-blue eyes, puffy and red-lined from lack of sleep. Hair a complete scarecrow. And blood on her shoulder. She stripped off her nightdress and turned on the shower, stepped in when it ran hot. The water cascaded over her slim form, pooling red around her toes. She tried to wash, but was afraid to touch her shoulder again, so settled for a thorough rinse instead.

As she dried herself, she tried a tentative pat on her shoulder; the towel came away spotted with blood, but not as much as expected. The pain was receding. She rubbed condensation from the mirror and craned her neck, peering at the wound. She couldn't really tell with the smears across her reflection, but it seemed like it was fading.

"Like the dream," she mused, shaking her head, trying to remember the details of that ... it was also fading. Her nightie lay crumpled on the floor, the blood still staining it, drying to a dull brown. She shook her head again. Walked back to her bedroom and surveyed the disaster zone that was her clothes drawers, her wardrobe. She wasn't, she'd readily admit, the tidiest of people, and her dirty laundry storage area was usually her bedroom floor. She pulled out clean underwear.

Dressed in bra and knickers, she hurried downstairs to the kitchenette. The first aid box was under the sink. She located a broad adhesive bandage and some antiseptic cream, and went to the mirror in the tiny living room to look at her shoulder again. The cut was gone. The pain was gone. She dropped her head to her chest in despair, sobbing again.

"I'm going mad," she said to herself. And wished once again that Tamsin was there. Wished that the zany northern girl was still in her life. Tamsin would know what to do. She'd be all practical and amazing and ... but she wasn't there.

The words, unbidden, rang in her head: "All you care about is God and how you appear to Him, you self-centred cow!" Tamsin's last words to Maisie, as she'd slammed the door on their shouting match. Three weeks ago. Or was it four? She sniffled, tears welling.

"You're not self-centred," she whispered to the girl in the mirror. "Tamsin was a cheating narcissist, and you're best rid of her." She couldn't smile, though. Emotions were still too raw. She grabbed a tissue from the box on the mantelpiece and blew her nose, popping her ears.

"Maisie, get the Alcomber report to me by one," said Laurence Coleman, calling across to her as she pushed through the double glass doors to the office reception.

"Good morning, Mr Coleman," she replied, not gracing him with a smile.

"One o'clock, and not a minute after." He scowled, punctuating his reply by slamming his office door.

Maisie dropped her bag behind the reception desk and gripped the back of her chair, leaning her weight on it and trying to hold the tears back. Life as a trainee accountant wasn't really shaping up to her expectations. If she'd wanted to be a receptionist, she'd have applied for that position. Instead, her co-workers and boss expected her to fulfil multiple roles. Accountant's assistant. Report collator. Office gopher. Receptionist. And cleaner. All at once. She had noticed on her first day that some of the male members of staff, ostensibly her junior in terms of education, age and ability, didn't end up answering the phone, cleaning the kitchen area or emptying the wastepaper bins.

With a sigh, she set about her day. Coffee. Emails. Answer the phone. Fix the damn Alcomber report that some idiot financial analyst had formatted with their thumbs. The spreadsheet's numbers and layout soothed her mind as she coaxed it into the correct shape. Time passed.

"You coming to Savrano's at lunchtime?" Gemma's brash voice made Maisie jump. She glanced up from the report. Fiddlesticks! Almost one o'clock.

"No, sorry. Got to get this report done for Himself."

"You never come out." Gemma pouted, flouncing away. A wave of relief washed over Maisie. The very last thing she needed right now was a noisy café with Gemma and her friends. They were OK, but she had, frankly, no interest in the latest so-called reality TV show. Or, any TV show, come to that.

Finally, the formatting on the report was correct. She saved it, pressed send and headed for the door. She needed some space to think. "Cathedral," she muttered, heading towards the ruins.

Chapter 2

Steig watched and waited as the last of the gawkers, do-gooders and friendly neighbours departed along the driveway into the valley, below the poplar trees. Only the police forensics van remained parked outside the farmhouse. The sun was almost on the horizon, casting a golden light on the land. With a sigh deeper than usual, he turned and walked into the house.

The burgundy front door used to have a slim, leaded-glass panel set into it. Now it boasted a tall, narrow hole, jagged glass reflecting at the edges. Inside, the smell was worse than he thought possible. Cloying, a stink of tar and ash and a sickly smell of burnt paint. The staircase was gone, or at least, the lower half. The fire had destroyed the living room, the pictures and antique maps now charred and curled. Rows and rows of books on the bookshelves he had made, now so much fluttering black strata of carbon. Every surface – the walls, ceilings, carpeted floors – were sticky with a layer of bituminous, stinking soot.

He found the forensics guy, a weasel-faced man with a balding pate, fingerprinting a window handle, where the arsonists had opened it from the inside.

"What do you think?" he asked. More to be polite, to show respect to the man for working after hours, than for conversation.

"Looks like they smashed the glass in the door, squeezed through, then opened the window to take things out. I'm looking for prints but ..." He shook his head, tutted. "I'm not seeing anything. Gloves, probably. Sorry."

"It's OK." Steig was getting sick of people being sorry. He'd only been back half an hour. "In your experience, how often do burglars torch their target afterwards?"

The forensics weasel straightened up, pushed his glasses up his nose, and glanced at Steig, then looked away.

"In twenty-five years of doing this job, I can count those situations on one hand," he said, his tone muted, gentle.

"So, I've really pissed someone off?"

The man smiled, but it held no mirth. "It does rather seem that way, yes."

As the evening dimmed and cooled, Steig closed the gate at the end of the farm drive, in the shade of the trees, after the forensics weasel left in his van. He sighed again at the gate latch, ripped from the post and hanging by the padlock. He fished in his wax-coat pocket and came up with a length of baler twine. Farmer's super glue, he called it. Smiled to himself at the silly joke. Tied the gate closed. Trudged back up the drive to the blind-eyed house, but couldn't bring himself to enter. Instead, he walked through the farmyard, where the echoing barns and empty loose-boxes paid testament to the lack of friends, workers, family. He leant on the gate to the lower paddock at the far end of the stacking yard.

"Beckett! Comeaarrrhhnn!" he shouted, elongating the words, seeing the big piebald carthorse's ears twitch. Beckett threw his head around and pranced in a pirouette, dreadlocked mane flying as he cantered up the field, huge hooves flinging up divots of earth in his wake. "You're tearing up your dinner!" Steig called, grinning, as Beckett arrived, puffing like a pair of bellows, warm and whiskery.

"Yeh. But apple," the big horse replied, using his nose to search Steig's long wax coat.

Steig pulled out an apple from his pocket; there were always apples, and Beckett knew it. Beckett's breath was warm with grass scent, like a mown lawn; as he crunched the apple, the scent changed to mingled grass and fruit. Steig let himself relax. He was home. He rubbed the horse's broad face up into his tangled forelock.

"What did you see last night, lad?"

"It was dark."

Steig chuckled. For all Beckett was unique in his ability to communicate with Steig, he was often obtuse. Pig-headed. Blunt. Probably, Steig supposed, because he himself was obtuse, pig-headed and blunt, and Beckett's speech was a figment of his imagination.

"What did you hear, then? Smell? Feel?"

"Men came. They made smashing noises. They talked quietly. Then they left."

"Did they come near you?"

"I stayed at the bottom of the field. I didn't like their smell."

"What did they smell like?"

"Like Norman the travelling man."

"And you don't like Norman?"

"No."

"What, even when he gives you an apple?"

"He only ever gives me a bit, always eats the rest. He smells greedy."

"Huh. Alright." Steig gave the horse a scratch behind the ears, which Beckett leant down into, sighing in appreciation. Soon, grey scurf from the horse's hide covered Steig's fingertips. "That's enough now. I need to get some rest." He left the horse by the gate, walked across the stacking yard to the open end of the barn, where the vardo sat.

He approached with trepidation. The vardo caravan's door was open, ajar. He could see the damage to the door frame where persons unknown had splintered it. A fine patina of fingerprinting dust made the jamb sparkle in the dim light. He climbed the curved wooden steps and pulled the door open, expecting a tumult of destruction.

"Actually, could be a lot worse," he muttered. There was a gap where the stove used to be, but the thieves had removed it cleanly. The chimney remained, dangling from the curved ceiling. Everything else was much as it should be. The bed was made. The cupboards shut, and when he opened them, he found their contents as expected.

He reached for the hurricane lantern hanging by the bed and lit it, allowing the warming diffuse yellow glow to lift his spirits. He remembered what the old travelling man, George Boswell, had said to him the previous summer: "If you've got your wagon, an' your 'orse, you got all you needs." Remembering that made him think that really, he was lucky to have this, and chasing everything else was pointless.

"I'm going to go mad if I don't get out of here," he muttered. He sat on the ledge seat and tried to take stock of his life. It all felt too big.

Reckon if you think it's too big, y'need to make it smaller, a voice in his mind told him. He shook his head, peered around. Hearing voices now. Definitely going mad.

But. Smaller, simpler. Was it that easy?

With the house uninhabitable, and the vardo's stove gone, Steig fell back on his old habits, kindling a small cooking fire on the concrete stacking yard. It was well away from the hay barn with its flammable contents. One building on fire was enough for the year. For a lifetime. But he found the kettle still in the pan box, under the back of the wagon, along with the fire trivet and the frying pan. He brewed a mug of tea and fried up a couple of eggs. Ate the runny yolks with a slice of dry bread made moist with butter. Or some vegan analogue to butter that Geoff and Shelly had come up with. Shelly, with her long dark hair and expressive dark eyes and flashing smile, vegan in an earnest, gentle way. Geoff, with his working hands and that ridiculous ruffed white cotton shirt he wore down the pub. Steig smiled, almost chuckled. Whilst people like them existed in the world, it would be OK. But as close as the three of them were, he didn't feel like he fit in. Oh, they would be down here tomorrow, full of help and love and hugs, their words and support welcome. He could almost map out the conversation in his head: *your house isn't habitable, we have a big bed, come stay with us.* But he wasn't sure that was a long-term solution, tempting though it was. Or even a short-term solution. *Make it smaller,* the voice in his head had said. Smaller. The vardo was about as small as he wanted to go. And the world? The lanes of Olde Breotonlond. Maybe into Europa. One small patch of roadside verge at a time. The idea held more appeal than any other he could conjure up.

Chapter 3

During the war, the Luftwaffe had bombed the cathedral, along with most of the rest of the city. The new cathedral, built in brutalist style, was not a favourite spot for Maisie. However, the city had also rebuilt a section of the old site. It had become a quiet space within the walls and sightless, unglazed windows of the original structure. Open to the elements, it put Maisie in mind of a church crossed with one of the ancient Hellenic sacred groves. Sometimes she half expected Pan, or Apollo, or Zeus himself to put in an appearance, as she sat in quiet contemplation. Of course, she would have liked Jesus to put in an appearance, or at least, answer her prayers. Or even give some sign that He was listening. But no. Nothing. She was alone.

Today was no different. She felt more isolated, with the breakup with Tamsin, the weird dreams, the lack of sleep, the unmotivating, awful job. Without hiding her face, slumped on a bench in the old cathedral ruins, she cried. Silent tears rolled down her cheeks, hot salt droplets landing on her hands as they knotted together in her lap. The terrible emptiness that always enveloped her was getting worse.

You need to do something about this. Had she said that? Had she thought that? But yes, she needed to do something. Anything but carry on.

Her lunch hour was almost over. She wiped her eyes on her sleeve and stood, pulling her duffel coat tight about herself, and headed back to the office. As she left the cloister, a poster on the diocese noticeboard caught her eye.

"Launde Priory – Christian Retreat: Connect with Jesus," said the headline.

"Launde Priory? Well, that might be an idea," she thought out loud. She had worked at the accountancy company for the best part of a year and not taken any time off. "Hah," she scoffed. Maybe that was half the problem? Her employer owed her three weeks' holiday. At least. Probably.

She resolved to look up the retreat, and book the time off, as soon as she got back to the office.

"The sooner, the better, Maisie, my girl." She smiled to herself. The first smile she'd managed on her face for weeks.

Chapter 4

"Good as new, that." George sat back on his haunches on the floor of the vardo. He wiped the battered, rusty Queen Anne stove's top with a rag, removing the last crumbs of fire cement left over from sealing the chimney.

"Yeah, just the job. Thanks again for getting it sorted so quickly." Steig was leaning in, nursing a mug of coffee, his back to the morning. Mist still lay in the valley; a distant cockerel put up a call as Eos, goddess of the dawn, threw her pink and orange paints against the sky.

"Are you off today, then?" the old travelling man asked, eyes sparkling as he glanced up at Steig.

"I am. Going to head down to ... well, I don't know. South, or something like that. I fancy Gaul or Iberia. Somewhere different."

"Well! Fair old way, that." George looked about the vardo. "You've got just about everything, including the kitchen sink." He gestured at the washing-up bowl wedged under the shelf seat. "Just be careful not to overload the running gear. And just the one horse?"

"I'll be careful, yes, George. You worry too much. And Beckett will manage. We aren't in a rush to get anywhere. Well, 'cept off here."

"Aye, well, reminds me, gorra get on up to the site at Spallinge, see a man about a dog." George struggled to his feet. He climbed down from the wagon, taking care to hold on to the door frame as he navigated the steps. He wiped his hands on his trousers, leaving a sparkle of fingerprinting dust on them, grimacing in distaste. "Terrible business, that," he muttered, shaking his head. Steig turned away, hollowness in his heart. George clambered into his battered car and started the engine, stuck his head out of the window and, with a wave of his arm, shouted, "Kushti bok!" Safe travels.

"Kushti bok, yersen!" Steig shouted in return, his voice echoing back from the empty buildings.

Steig loaded the last few items into the vardo. Some woodworking tools. A tin of paint. A spindle-backed chair. He repacked the pan box from the cooking fire, then fetched Beckett in from the field. Tied him up to a ring set in the barn wall opposite and set about grooming the scurf and mud from the horse's hide.

The sun did its best to burn off the low mist as it pushed into the azure expanse of the sky. Beckett dozed, one rear hoof poised, giving an occasional swish of his tail at flies.

"You're serious, then?" Geoff's modulated voice was a pleasant baritone. Steig's neck prickled with goosebumps. Damn him. He turned, gave a sheepish grin, watched Geoff approach at his usual easy lope through the stable yard.

"Yeah, I'm gonna take the summer off. See where I get to."

"You know you can always stay with us? You're welcome to. You know that, right? More than welcome. Shelly says, too." He was closer now. Steig could smell his scent, not sweat, more ... earthy. Though at least Geoff was in a normal T-shirt, not the frilly affair reserved for Saturday nights. Geoff reached out, and Steig leant into the hug. Geoff pulled him close. "It's a fucking awful thing, what those wankers did to your gaff," he said, his voice carrying a heartfelt timbre, resonating in Steig's own chest.

"Yeah, well. It's made me re-evaluate my life choices a bit," he replied, grinning. "I appreciate the offer, I really do, and it's been a wonderful few months. But ..." His voice broke, the sudden emotion catching him by surprise, a constriction banding his chest. "Shit, I'll miss you guys." He hugged Geoff tight, wrapping his arms around the taller man's back. Geoff reciprocated.

"Shell's gonna be sad."

"Yeah. And me. But." He looked Geoff square in the eyes. "I need to do this for me."

"I know, I know." He laughed, but it sounded hollow. "A part of me wishes I were going with you."

Steig clicked his tongue, and Beckett took up the pace, swinging into a gentle trot, lifting his feet well up as he was fresh for the day. His metal-shod hooves rang clear on the tarmac of the sleepy country lane. The wheels of the vardo rumbled behind, the harness jingled a merry cadence.

On the road again. Steig didn't know if it was the right thing or the wrong thing. His mind said to fix the house, work harder, do more. His heart said to make it smaller. Take the summer off. His heart had won. But this course of action filled him with trepidation and excitement in equal measure.

A couple of miles into the journey, he and Beckett approached a small village with a solitary road junction. Next to the junction was an old well, fed by a natural spring, hidden back under the trees on the right. Few people knew of it, but Steig did. There was a magical, gentle air about the place. He had an idea that its spirit of place, a genius loci, was benign. He didn't fully understand the Old Ways, but he subscribed to the view that if you sat and listened, you would hear. You just had to give it time.

Beckett, however, was of the firm opinion that this spirit of place smelt evil and had teeth. For Beckett, whatever lived in the well was to be avoided.

"I got you, lad. Don't worry."

"I can smell it. It's bad. Don't want to go that way."

Beckett took a quick step to the left, towards the grassy edge of the road, away from the well. Steig was ready, caught him with the rein, held him with a gentle voice, stopping him from pulling the whole wagon up the steep verge and into disaster. As they were almost at the junction anyway, he allowed Beckett to roll on through, taking a smooth left-hand turn.

"Tell you what, Beckett, we'll go this way, shall we?"

"Yeh."

"South, you say? Fine idea."

As soon as Steig relaxed the hold on the reins and they were beyond the well, Beckett sprang forward, the wagon lurching and rattling behind him. As he gained distance from the spring, his ears came forward again, pricked to the surrounding sounds. He relaxed, and the cadence of his trot steadied. Steig relaxed as well, into the curve of the wagon at his back, and let Beckett lead – he knew the way down this road, into town. No more surprises for a few miles.

"Town. What are we even doing here?" Steig asked. Beckett flicked his ears. He wasn't a fan of built-up areas either. Steig shook his head, wondering at himself. He had never felt comfortable in towns, surrounded by people, on trains, buses, in shops. "The sooner we're out of here, the better, hey lad?"

They rolled through the centre of the town, past the local shops and bijou cafés, past the supermarket, past the library. They circumnavigated a mini-roundabout and headed out along a narrow lane boxed in by post-war semi-detached housing. Beckett's hoof-sound echoed back from the blank faces of the buildings. People were out at work, children at school. No one around. Ghost town. The road started a slow climb to the first of many hills out from the Catmouse Vale, towards Broc and the Leefeilde Forest.

As the hill's incline steepened, Steig jumped down from the ledge, onto the verge, grabbing the wheel chock from its holder as he did so, just in case they needed to stop. He clipped the reins onto the top of the saddle to keep them from falling and tangling in Beckett's legs. He walked with him, on the verge side, at his head, murmuring encouragement as Beckett heaved the weight of the wagon up the slope. At the steepest part, Steig grabbed the breeching strap where it looped onto the shafts and lent his weight to the task. As they crested the hill, they were both sweating. They paused at the brow, looking out over the land arrayed beyond; the rolling green fields, sparse fluffy clouds and the far smudge of the forest on the horizon. Steig took off his old wax coat and used the bottom of his shirt to mop his face.

"You'd best lose some weight and get fit, laddo, if these hills are like this all the way through Roteslund," he said to the horse.

"You could lose a few kilos, too," Beckett replied.

Rude, Steig thought. But accurate. Too long he'd been languishing in a dreamer's kingdom. There was a definite strain to his muscles; he could indeed do with losing weight, toning up.

As lunchtime approached, Steig felt they should push on, though the pull-in at the top of this hill was one he had used before for an overnight stop, in the small copse on the left. "Put a bit more distance between us and the gadjo, hey lad?"

Going down was almost as hazardous as climbing up the hill. Five or six turns of the brake wheel, crafted by Steig from an old horseshoe, were enough to apply a gentle braking action. The breeching strap was taut over Beckett's rump, and the horse leant back against it, tucking his rear legs under him against the weight of the wagon. His titanium horseshoe pins dug into the tarmac like a rugby boot's studs into a muddy pitch.

Lazy insects buzzed in the uncharacteristic afternoon heat as they arrived at a long, broad section of the lane, in the Chaterflu river valley. The verges were level, the grass long and plentiful.

"This'll do, lad. Come a-left." Steig steered with rein and voice, and Beckett pulled the wagon, slowing as it bumped over the cambered edge of the road, onto the verge. He came to a halt four-square, in the lee of a small sycamore tree.

Chapter 5

On reflection, thought Maisie, the whole retreat business wasn't quite turning out to be what she had in mind. Launde Priory was pleasant enough, in a, well, priory sort of way, but it wasn't exactly five stars.

Ascetic would be an accurate description of the rooms. Which, she supposed, was the point. But couldn't you get in touch with God and still have a comfortable cushion to sit on instead of this cold, hard, straight-backed wooden chair? And carpets! What was wrong with a carpet?

Not to mention mealtimes. Yes, the refectory was old and historic and was where the Augustinian monks had sat a thousand years ago, probably on the same hard wooden benches, to eat their daily bread. But would installing heating have been so difficult?

Day three of fourteen. There she sat, on her uncomfortable wooden upright chair, with her slippered feet on the cold unyielding flagstones, resting her elbows on the tiny wooden desk in her tiny stone room. She gazed out of the leaded window through the warped ancient glass and watched the sheep grazing the vast swathe of countryside.

Just as she thought that there must be a better way to find God, God answered her prayers. At least, that was how it seemed. She'd never received an answer to a prayer before, and yet there it was, as clear as day. A gypsy carriage emerged from the woods at the edge of the parkland. An enormous black-and-white horse pulled it at a leisurely pace along the road right in front of the priory, and away up the hill. As far as Maisie was concerned, it might as well have had a neon sign hovering over it with a huge arrow pointing down, saying "Answer From God".

Quick as thought, she discarded her slippers, pulled on her sensible flat-heeled shoes, grabbed her duffel coat and messenger bag and swung out of the door in a flurry of hope.

The morning's journey, since pulling off from the overnight in the Chaterflu valley, had been hard on both of them. Steig's hands had gained blisters from pulling on the breeching. Sweat flecked Beckett's flanks.

This last hill was long and steep, so Steig didn't stop to take in the majestic view of Launde Priory resplendent in its parkland. Once at the apex, the track narrowed between hedges and ended at a cattle grid. They arrived at an opening leading onto the grass, under a small group of ancient oaks. It had a welcoming feeling about it, and as the hour was past lunchtime, he decided they had done a full day's work. This would be their overnight pull-up. Plenty of firewood, shelter under the trees, level ground and abundant grass for Beckett. Steig wasn't too fussed about who owned the land – they would either ignore him, or come along and piss and moan at him. Occasionally, a farmer or landowner would just come to visit and drink tea. Steig preferred that sort of visit, but he never assumed.

Beckett managed a last heave, pulling the wagon off the road and into the parkland, into the lee of the trees. He untacked the horse and put an old blue sweat rug on him to wick away the moisture so he didn't catch a chill in the freshening springtime breeze. He pegged out the chain and rope to tether Beckett. The horse's ears swivelled, and he turned to look down the road through the sheltering trees whence they had come.

"What's up, lad? Someone coming?"

Beckett continued watching the road through the trees. Steig could see a pair of sensible shoes, and the hem of a long blue skirt or dress, standing on the road beyond the trees. The branches of the oak obscured the rest. He shrugged. Time for tea. He started wandering around the oak trees, picking up fallen wood. Oak trees tended to die by degrees and shed entire branches. Steig found one that was movable and dragged it back to the camp in front of the wagon, where he set about it with a battered orange bow saw.

The mystery feet hadn't moved. Now he was closer to the road, he could see they belonged to a young lady in conservative clothing. Skinny. Blonde hair to below her shoulders. She had wrapped herself in a yellow duffel coat and was holding it closed with both arms around her sides, a tatty messenger bag slung across her front. She seemed perplexed. Worried, perhaps. Steig wasn't sure. He concentrated on the woodcutting, the job at hand, and after a few minutes got a fire going and the kettle hung on its hook. He settled himself, with the kitchen box open and a mug at the ready, watching the fire, the kettle.

"I saw you going past the priory," the woman stated in a gentle tone. Steig looked up from the fire. She had taken tentative steps towards him, and stood now in that same posture, hands wrapped around herself, at the very edge of the camp.

"You can come near the fire. I don't bite."

"Oh! Thank you. It's not that. I was just ... I thought ... I ... I don't know why I'm here."

"Are you looking for an existential debate or are you just lost?" Steig gave a half-smile. He didn't feel like company, but there was no need to be too blunt. He knew he could be very to the point.

"I'm not lost. Well, not physically lost. Spiritually, maybe ..."

"I can't help you with spirituality, I'm afraid. I have tea though, if you'd like some?" He pulled another mug from the kitchen box.

"Er ..." The woman took a step back in alarm, but after a few seconds appeared to come to a decision. She took some steps closer and took the proffered mug. Steig hauled himself up and fetched a wooden folding chair from the cratch at the back of the wagon, unfolded it, and set it by the woman.

"Steig Sturluson," said Steig, holding out his hand.

"Maisie Hanson." She shook his hand, her grip gentle, her hand warm and smooth. "Pleased to meet you." She gave a small curtsey, holding the hem of her dress to one side.

Maisie sat on the folding garden chair, wrapping her skirt around her legs, and keeping her feet flat on the ground. She watched the gypsy busying himself with the tea.

He was lean, dark-skinned, and appeared a little older than she was, maybe forty. Clean-shaven, brown hair down to his collar. He was well groomed, like he cared about his appearance. Her eyes roved downwards. The most worn, brown long wax coat she had ever seen, its sleeves almost falling apart in places. A tattersall checked shirt, dark greens on cream, of the type favoured by countrymen. Tan moleskin trousers above heavy black leather boots. His hands were calloused and rough. Working hands. But clean.

The kettle was a huge, fire-blackened thing, which he lifted with ease. He poured the boiling water into the mugs and set the kettle into the embers at the edge of the fire. The kitchen utensils were in an old, worn wooden box that had once been painted green and gold, but was now faded with age. Steig took a teaspoon and stirred the teas before scooping out the teabags. He flicked them into the fire, where they hissed, before drying out and flashing to ash.

"Sugar? Milk?"

The question startled Maisie out of her watchful reverie.

"Milk, please."

He fished around in the old green box, produced an individual portion of milk and deposited its contents into the mug, giving it another vigorous stir. He handed her the drink. She read the words on the mug.

"What does 'kushti bok' mean?"

"It's Romani. Means good luck."

She couldn't think of anything else to say for a moment, so settled, watching the fire, cupping her tea in her hands. Steig also sat; he seemed to be lost in contemplation, though when she risked a sidelong glance at him through the steam from her tea, his pale blue eyes met hers with a piercing stare. She dropped her gaze back to the flames.

"So, what is it you want, Ms Hanson?"

Maisie looked back up at him and was about to answer when the gypsy carried on – she realised almost too late that the question was rhetorical.

"You were at the priory – on some God-bothering retreat, I presume? And you saw this romantic notion of a retreat from a retreat rolling on by, and you thought, what, there's a message from God?"

She felt the heat rise to her face, lowered her eyes to the fire, nodded, mute. Steig's voice changed, like he realised he was being harsh.

"I'm sorry to tell you, but I'm not your answer. This" – he gestured at the carriage, the horse munching the grass nearby, the fire and kettle – "isn't a message from God. This is me trying to run away from society. And you see a holy message where I see my home. You wouldn't stop someone as they walked up to their house and ask them to help you find God? You wouldn't knock on a random door in a street and ask if they had the answer, would you?"

Maisie was trembling now. An overwhelming sorrow was rising from her belly and pricks of tears started in the corners of her eyes.

"I'm so sorry. I see now I've been foolish. I'll leave you to your home. Thank you for the tea." This last, at least, she delivered with a wan smile, as she put the empty mug down next to the worn wooden box. She made to get up, gathering her hems.

Steig watched the sorrow and stress, most likely embarrassment, wash over the woman. He'd done it again, been too blunt. When would he ever learn? What could he do to soften this for her? He didn't want company, but he didn't like to be unkind, either.

As she stood to depart, he blurted out, "Before you go, come and meet Beckett."

"Oh, no! You think me petty and ill-mannered. And a 'God-botherer.' I'll go."

"Sometimes when I speak with people, I am too forthright. I am, let's not put a shine on this, difficult to get along with. But I see you have questions, and you are looking for a way through life, and I should not be so judgemental. And to a gadjo, this way of life is sometimes so different and romanticised, but I forget that. So I'm sorry, truly sorry, to be so difficult. Beckett is much more forgiving, and easy to get along with." Steig stood and rummaged in the cupboard inside the wagon door, pulling out a couple of carrots.

"He'll mug you for a carrot. But gently. Come, see." He held out the carrots for Maisie, who reached over and took them with an uncertain, tentative look on her face. Steig walked over to Beckett, who had focused his full attention on the carrots the moment Steig had reached for them.

Steig walked up to Beckett and placed his palm on the horse's broad face, rubbing from his nose up to his poll, the point between his ears. Beckett leant into the rub. As Maisie came near, his attention went to her. First a general sniff. She smelt of dust, books and indoors, he thought. After the sniff, he used his prehensile lips, and followed her arm down to the carrots clutched in her hand. As his rubbery lips smacked and snitched with gentleness along her sleeve, she let out a small squeak and pulled her arm back.

"It's OK, he's just working up to snatching the carrot. Just hand him one end and let him bite it off. He'll have half at a time."

Maisie held out one carrot, and Beckett closed his mouth over it, biting it in half with a slow crunch of his front teeth, then set about chewing it. Maisie fed him the other half. The second carrot followed the same course as the first.

"He'll be your friend for life now. He likes a scratch behind the ears, and under his mane on his neck, if you don't mind smelling of horse."

"I don't mind. He's wonderful. Huge and hairy and warm, he smells of candle-wax and log fires and summer rain." Beckett was nudging at her duffel coat pockets and messenger bag with his broad nose, hoping for more carrot. He was sure he could smell mint in there, too. Maisie placed her hand on his face like Steig had done, and rubbed. Worked her way up to his ears, scratched in the crease behind them. Beckett leant into the scratch like it was the best thing in the world. Which to Beckett it was, after carrots.

"I'll leave you two to get acquainted. Kettle's on, if you fancy another tea."

Maisie shone a huge smile at Steig, her blue eyes bright. "Thank you! I'll just carry on talking to Beckett for a bit, if that's OK?"

"Of course. Just mind your toes. He's sometimes careless where he puts his feet. He'll wander off and eat grass if he gets bored."

Steig left them to it, Maisie whispering into the horse's ear, one arm around his wide neck. Her other arm reached up to scratch behind his ear, her face buried in his shaggy, dreadlocked mane. She was standing on tiptoe to reach. Beckett had his head resting on her shoulder, the bottom of his jaw lying on her back. Steig smiled – it was a Beckett hug – and set the fire to burning hot again.

As the afternoon faded into early evening, Maisie walked back into the campfire's radiance. The light was dwindling, and the fire cast a warming yellow luminance onto the front of the vardo. Steig watched her approach. "How's that, then? Good?"

"He's very, er ... calming, you're right. Thank you."

"I've made a stew. Travelling folk call it an ish. Bit of everything. Vegetables, that is."

"I'm not vegetarian."

"Oh, wish I'd known that. I left out the pheasant and rabbit that I trapped earlier."

Maisie pulled a horrified face, casting around for the carcasses. He grinned.

"Got you."

"Oh!" She coloured red.

"So, has God delivered your message? Or answered your question for Him?"

"I still don't know. I mean, you're right, what you said earlier. I wouldn't just walk up to someone's house and knock on the door. But this is all so … so …"

She cast around for a word, gesturing with her upturned hand at the wagon and Beckett on his tether, the warm cooking fire.

"Romantic? Mystical? Idyllic? Try it on a winter's night when it's snowing and blowing a gale and your horse can't get any forage for the ice and the firewood's just run out. Not so fun then."

"I suppose. But of course, it's late spring. The weather is lovely. So, I'll go with idyll."

"Fagh. You're a gadjo, alright."

"Gadjo? You used that word before. It doesn't sound complementary at all."

"Gadjo. Non-travelling folk."

"You say it with such … disdain."

"No, not disdain. Um, impatience? I don't know."

Steig used his jacket sleeves pulled over his hands to lift the cooking pot from the trivet over the fire, and set it on the grass by the side. He ladled out two bowlfuls of vegetable stew and passed one to her.

"I don't do the whole grace thing, but feel free, if you wish."

"Dear Lord, I thank you this day for our food, and for the company of Beckett and Steig. Amen."

"Do you really believe in God?"

"It's a matter of faith."

"That's a simple answer. Huh. Theology." He looked at her, right into her eyes. "I have a real problem with organised religion. Individuals should be free to believe what they want, so long as it doesn't hurt other people. But when an organisation tells you what you can and can't do with your life ... well, it puts me right off."

"Well, perhaps we should talk about something else, then. Only, er, not politics." She smiled, then. Steig laughed.

The fire burnt down whilst they chatted; they settled in to eat, and to drink more tea. Steig fetched a lantern and lit the wick. It cast a yellow glow that suffused their faces, augmenting the light from the fire.

"So, Steig, what of you? How is it you're here and now?"

His face darkened, troubled thoughts tumbling through his mind. He gathered himself. Took a breath.

"Well. It's been a difficult few years. I was between four walls ..." He paused at Maisie's confused expression. "It means housed. And then I had a run in with ... some people, and ... well ... I had the wagon sat there, and Beckett languishing in a field, and I thought, to hell with it all. Why not just run away? So, I did."

"What are you running away from? Living in a house?"

"Ah, not really. I suppose, well, everything. Society. Responsibilities. Family. Work. Fairly cowardly, no?"

"No, sounds like you would need a lot of courage to do that."

Steig stared into the fire, taking his time to consider this.

"Yeah, courage or cowardice. One of the two. Given enough time, I suppose I'll discover which it is." They both stared into the flickering flames, lost in their private thoughts. After a few moments, Steig looked up again. "And what about you, Maisie? What brings you to Launde?"

"Oh, I don't know. Even less to tell. My father's a vicar, so I grew up in a rectory, raised a Christian. I went to school in Middeltone and studied classics at Waruic. Obviously, everyone wants a classicist in their organisation, so once I had a degree I had to start at the bottom again. I spent five years working in an accountant's office in Coventreu, until one day I thought, I can do this better than they can, so now I'm a trainee accountant. Though I'm finding it terribly dull. I'm not sure it's really for me, but I don't know what else to do."

"And Launde? The retreat?"

"Lost my way a bit. Had a troubled relationship." She paused, gulping a breath. As if she were re-living a harrowing moment. "Now I don't have anyone, not even a cat, and I feel like God has abandoned me as well. So, I went on retreat to reconnect."

"How's that going?"

"I'm sitting by a campfire in the middle of a field, drinking tea. That's how it's going," she said, though she was smiling.

Steig smiled as well, but then stretched and stood up. "I've an early start tomorrow. I'd best turn in. Are you going to be OK getting back to the priory?"

"Oh yes. I have a torch, and it's just down the hill. Really. I'll be fine. Thank you for a wonderful afternoon and evening, and the stew, and the tea. I wonder, will you be here tomorrow?" She fumbled around in her tatty bag and pulled out a small flashlight.

"No. As I said, early start. I'm going to Stirwood. I'll hang around there for a couple of days, then head further south."

"Oh." She cast her gaze down. "I'd like to see Beckett again. And you."

"Well, you could always come along for a bit, if you have time ..."

As soon as the words floated from his mouth, Steig cursed himself internally; this wasn't what he was looking for, saddling himself with a God-bothering gadjo. But the words were out there.

"OK, perhaps I will do that." She flashed a contemplative smile.

As Maisie's torchlight disappeared through the oak trees and onto the lane, Steig heard Beckett moving around on his chain.

"Ha. You left yourself open to that one, didn't you?"

"Shut up, horse. She'll have forgotten by the morning. All that God stuff she's into will distract her." I hope, he added under his breath.

Chapter 6

The twin thumps of Beckett's front hooves striking out onto the yielding ground, one after the other, roused Steig. He opened his eyes to a gentle morning light, taking in the curving deep-red paisley-patterned material lining the inside of the vardo. Beckett, he guessed, had just hauled himself to his feet. The sound of him shaking off the dust of the night cemented this supposition, the rope pulling the end of the chain with a faint tink. And finally, a long pee, the horse's flow cascading loud in the still air.

"Argh, Beckett!" Grumbling, Steig threw off the quilted cover and stumbled to the front of the wagon, down the carved wooden steps, half pulling on a pair of old blue jeans. He relieved himself against a nearby tree, just as Beckett's flow dwindled. He looked around. The day was shaping up to be clement, the mist and dew already burning off the surrounding grassland. A heavy, deep scent of pollen and tree sap permeated the air.

"Ha. Mornin', horse. Good sleep?"

"Yeh. Nice under this oak. No dryads. Got any mints?"

"No mints. You're addicted. Get some grass. Long way today. Stir-wood."

Beckett gazed back at Steig through his tangled forelock.

"What about oats?"

"No! Grass!" He pointed at the lush greenery around the horse's hooves, doing his jeans up with his other hand. Beckett huffed a deep sigh and pulled generous helpings of the plentiful grass into his mouth, chewing with resignation.

"And don't colic," warned Steig. "You're a pig."

"Are you talking to Beckett?"

Steig spun around, startled, fumbling for his belt buckle. Maisie.

"Bloody hell! You scared the shit out of me! You shouldn't creep up on people like that!"

"I didn't creep. I walked. The grass is soft. Good morning, Mr Sturluson." She curtsied.

"Heh. Mornin'. Going somewhere?" He indicated Maisie's ruck-sack, stout walking boots. Confusion marched over her brow.

"You said ... last night ..."

Damn it. Steig cursed under his breath. She hadn't forgotten. He reached into the wagon for a T-shirt.

"I didn't expect you to take it seriously. It was just idle banter."

"Oh." She looked crestfallen, like Steig had thrown a switch, her sunny disposition of a moment ago clouded over. Steig swore again, under his breath.

"Look, come and sit. I'll get the yog on. We'll have a cuppa."

He finished dressing, busied himself around the camp, got the fire kindled up from the embers, and filled the kettle with water from the container under the vardo.

As it boiled, he took a deep breath and addressed Maisie, who was sitting quietly on a log, fiddling with the toggles of her duffel coat.

"Look, I know I said last night you could come on part of the journey with me, but I don't know if it's a workable idea. I don't really do people, and it's not like there's much room in the vardo."

"I can sleep under the vardo," Maisie retorted, "but if you don't want me around, I guess I understand."

"You can't sleep under it. That's where dogs sleep. It wouldn't be right."

"I can get a tent. I can sleep in a tent. In fact ..." She stood upright, squaring her shoulders. "In fact, it's a free country. I can camp where I like. Well, within reason. Your horse, your way of life, has changed my outlook. I need to do this. I know you don't 'do people'" – she made air quotes – "but you'll just have to manage."

She shouldered her rucksack, and headed off the way she had come, back to the priory.

Steig glanced sidelong at Beckett. "You two are conspiring."

"What? I didn't say anything."

"You know what. Bloody horse."

Stirwood, an old woodland that was part of the Leefeilde Forest, was a vast swathe of dense trees so dark it cast a constant twilight under the bough's cool shade. Steig regarded it with equanimity, as it loomed dark on the horizon.

Beckett was into his stride, trotting along on the level. The vardo's pump-up tyres made a soothing, deep rumbling noise. In counterpoint to this, the clatter of hooves, the squeak of harness and the creak of the bow-top's stringers punctuated their progress.

The worst of the hills were behind them, dealt with in the morning since leaving Launde Priory. Now they were approaching Stirwood itself, and what had been a smudge on the horizon was a great green wall, a mile or two ahead.

Maisie hadn't reappeared. Steig didn't know if she had called it a day and gone back to God-bothering at the priory, or if she was casting around for a tent and rushing to catch up. Well, he wasn't going fast, but she'd have to use her wits to work out where he had gone. If she was clever, she'd search for the hoof marks on the tarmac. Especially downhill, where the skidding of Beckett's road-nails created a distinctive pattern. Though there had been several junctions, and the way to the woods wasn't straight. If she just followed the lane, she'd end up in Ledecestre. Well, at least she'd find a camping shop there. He chuckled to himself. Beckett's ears flicked back.

"Leave me alone, horse. I can laugh if I want to."

"You don't have to justify your mirth to me. But go on, admit it, you like her."

"I do not. She's a royal pain in the backside. Feckin' gobshite townie."

"Oh, now, that *is* harsh. Just because she's a gadjo doesn't mean she's a gobshite."

"Yeah, yeah. Just cos *you* have a soft spot for her. Bloody nag. You'd sell your own granddam for a scratch."

"True enough."

"Heddup, then."

"I *am* hedding up."

The pair worked their way along the lanes and settled into the lee of Stirwood. They turned onto a smaller track running alongside the ancient forest, bounded by the scroll of green countryside on the left. It fell and rose, then fell again to Redlinctune, its church spire just visible in the distance.

On the right, the wood cast a blue-grey gloaming upon the land, deepening to an impenetrable wall of grey-green bark and leaves. Under the edge of the woods, the grassy verge was spacious and level.

"This'll do us, my lad."

Beckett pulled the vardo off the road and came to his usual square halt, steam rising from his haunches in the cooler air under the trees.

The first flush of absolute fury, or the nearest equivalent that Maisie would allow herself, was fading as she descended the long hill to the priory. Who did that scruffy gypsy think he was, telling her where or when she could walk the lanes?

By the time she arrived back at the priory, tail somewhat between her legs, she had formulated a plan and was determined to follow through with it. Really, she had not thought about sleeping arrangements at all. Steig was pleasant enough when he was being pleasant, but then he was so blunt! And where had she thought of sleeping? In his bed? Oh no, not with him, surely? She gave her subconscious mind a gentle ticking off. That would simply not do! Not that she was averse to men … memories of Tamsin's taunting words to her played back in her mind. "You just want to have your cake *and* eat it. Life doesn't work like that!"

She breathed out a sigh. So, sleep on the floor of the wagon? What had he called it? A vardo, that was it. There wasn't room to stretch out. So, a tent was what she must procure. And bedding.

She staggered back up the hill to where she had met Steig the previous day. Her rucksack, now stuffed with borrowed tent, sleeping bag and ground mat, had doubled in weight, the straps digging into her shoulders. Standing up had been an effort, the whole thing threatening to pull her over backwards.

Arriving at the top of the hill, she found, of course, that the wagon was gone. Beckett was gone. Steig was gone. All that remained was some horse dung deposited on the edge of a neat circle of grass that Beckett had eaten down to bowling green short. And the black charcoal remains of the fire, still warm but no longer hot.

"Oh, bother!" she exclaimed, resting her pack against the bole of an oak, letting the huge roots hold up the base of the rucksack for a moment. She engaged her brain. They wouldn't go back past the priory, and Steig had said they were going to a place called Stirwood. She pulled out her phone. No signal. Of course, no signal.

She looked around again, at the grass and the road. The grass had hoof prints on it, and marks from the tyres of the wagon. But on the road, these marks disappeared.

"Oh," she wailed, tears brimming in her eyes. Then she remembered her resolve, reached down inside herself and stood up, shouldering the heavy pack. "Best foot forward, Maisie, my girl."

She set out along the narrow road, which linked remote farmsteads. The hedges on either side, tall hawthorn and blackthorn, masked the countryside beyond; she glimpsed it occasionally at gateways to fields. A broad rolling swathe of green pastureland. Bouncing spring lambs and their patient mothers. The greensward dotted with copses and small woods. A looming band of older woodland on the far horizon. Was that Stirwood? It had the right feel to it. Cow parsley, elderflower and buttercups peppered the verge.

She constantly swept her gaze over the road surface and the verges, looking for any telltale sign the wagon had passed that way. She found occasional well-defined hoof prints in softer patches of pitch. Beckett's feet were so large they were unmistakable. As she got her eye in and saw more and more of them, she realised there were always a pair of holes in the tarmac, one on either side of the hoof. He must have a nail protruding from his shoes.

"I do hope they aren't coming off. How does one go about fitting new shoes if you live on the road?" Another conundrum. She'd ask Steig. When she found them both. She re-shouldered her pack and marched on.

At every junction, she would look for the hoof marks that would tell the story of Beckett's passing. Sometimes she saw none and had to guess; if she didn't find a mark within two hundred paces of the junction, she would work back and try the other way. One crossroads led her back and on to the next road three times, before she finally picked up a sign of the enormous shoes that Beckett wore.

All the while, on this convoluted pathway, the woodland on the horizon loomed closer. It must be Stirwood.

The last of the hills were behind her now. She walked with an exhausted stagger along a straight roadway on the high escarpment before Stirwood. The sun had just set, and she realised she wouldn't catch up with Steig that day. With a curse and a cry, she shrugged off the heavy pack and searched around. There was a copse of trees just off the road, a flat sheltered patch of grass next to it; this would have to do.

Chapter 7

Steig paused to catch his breath, enjoying the warm, late morning air. He listened to the swirl of birdsong, turned to the sun, let it warm his face. Bending to grip the branch, he continued to drag it out of the edge of Stirwood and alongside the vardo. It would do for the day and the following night. And he would stay another night. It was a lovely spot, tucked in against the woods, with fine views over the rolling hills to the south towards Redlinctune.

As Steig was about to cut the branch with the bow saw, Beckett's ears swivelled, and he stretched his neck to peer around the vardo and down the farm track. He gave a low rumbling whicker of greeting.

"What you got, lad?"

"Someone coming."

"Not that bloody Maisie again?"

"Yes. And you like her."

"Huh." He carried on cutting the firewood.

"Well, at least you're still here!" came the exasperated cry from the lane. There Maisie stood, sweaty and red in the face from exertion, dwarfed by an enormous rucksack that was topped with a tent strapped sideways over the whole. She had found herself a stout branch to use as a walking staff and was leaning against it as if she was about to collapse.

"You have no idea," she panted, "how far I have walked, and how hard it has been. Why didn't you wait for me?"

Steig didn't have an answer. He looked away, concentrated on the bow saw, cutting the logs.

Maisie set up her tent along the lane from the vardo, with the fire between them. She could see the wagon, and the fire, and Beckett tethered out, further along, from her bedroll.

Her stomach rumbled, a reminder that the meagre rations, chocolate and biscuits that she had brought with her had run out that morning. She pulled her boots on and went to the fire.

"Is there anything I can do to help? Collect wood? Cook?"

"Did you not bring your own food?" He rolled his eyes.

Maisie's face burnt with shame. She dropped her head. "I-I didn't have time. I ate it already."

"Ah, well. OK. There's a pheasant there needs skinning and jointing," Steig said, giving a casual wave to a bundle of light dun feathers lying in the grass beyond the fire. "Shot it this morning. It's dinner, if you like." He turned his gaze up to her and she saw his face soften. "Or you can chop the veg? Skinning them can be feathery work, if you're not used to it."

She felt queasy at the thought of dealing with the pheasant. But also, starving. "I'm happy to chop vegetables, if you show me where everything is."

Steig fetched a tiny wooden cutting board, a sharp, ancient kitchen knife, its edge curved from years of honing, and a bag of vegetables. He placed a heavy, blackened iron pot on a trivet made from an old horseshoe that sat on the edge of the fire.

"Just chop what we need, straight into the pot. I'll sort the meat."

As she chopped, she watched him, fascinated despite herself. He was deft, slipping a small knife under the bird's feathers, under the skin. He pulled it back to expose breast meat, shiny like iron, with a yellow ochre stripe of fat down the middle. He pulled further, and the legs popped out, their muscle and sinew straining against the sudden exposure. Her stomach and her heart warred with each other.

Four accurate, sure cuts. Four chunks of meat. He tossed them into the pot, added a glug of oil. The meat spat and popped as it browned.

Her stomach won. "Oh, that smells amazing. Here, I've done some carrots." She looked up at him from her spot beside the fire. At least he was smiling at her.

After dinner, the rich stew mopped up with chunks of two-day-old bread, Steig settled back in his chair. His feet were to the fire, his face to the setting sun, catching the last of its rays. Despite Maisie's presence, he was at peace. She was quiet. Happy to read her bible or write in her journal. Not constantly asking questions or talking for the sake of it. Also, she spent a fair amount of time grooming Beckett; the big horse was, of course, delighted with that arrangement. Steig drifted off, daydreaming, content.

The next moment, he jolted up, quite awake. Something had roused him. There was an ethereal quality to the air, the deep amber of the sunset shading into russets and golds, gilding the leaves at the edge of the forest. Peering into the trees, he gave a start; a figure stood some way within the shade, side-lit by the setting sun, which cast along the edge of Stirwood. An elderly woman, in a green hooded cloak, white hair visible, but features shrouded by the fall of the sunlight. She held a tall, straight staff in her right hand.

"Seek the gateway of Heracles, Traveller Steig of Roteslund. Seek the Wayland." The voice resonated as if from inside his head.

He scrambled to his feet, knocking over his mug of tea, which hissed into the embers of the fire.

"Steig? What?" exclaimed Maisie, startled, looking up from her journal.

He peered again into the woods; nothing but trees, and bracken, and leaves.

"Now I'm seeing things. Fuck. Did you see that? Hear that? Some woman in a green cloak, holding a staff?"

Maisie shrugged, nonplussed. Scanned the gloaming. "I didn't hear anything."

"She said, 'Seek the gateway of Heracles'."

"Heracles?" Maisie asked.

"I don't know. She said ..." Steig concentrated, playing back the encounter as best he could in his head. "She said, 'Seek the gateway of Heracles, seek the Wayland.' Or something."

Maisie shrugged again. "What's a Wayland?"

"It's the river. South of here."

Chapter 8

"Are we going to Redlinctune, then?" Maisie asked the next morning, as she pushed the last of the tent into its bag and strapped it to the top of her rucksack.

"Well, no. I'm heading south. Hah. I was heading south, anyway. Maybe now I'll go a different way ..."

Steig continued to tack Beckett up, as the horse stood, waiting, in front of the wagon's curved wooden shafts. The brass bound tips of the shafts were resting on the ground, on either side of Beckett's rear hooves.

Maisie pursed her lips in exasperation. "You can't stop me coming, you know. You might as well have the good grace to accept that."

"It is, as you said the other day, a free country. But things are getting weird. I don't know if it's you, or me, or something else, but ... I'm uncomfortable." Beckett put his ears back and swished his tail. Steig looked at him. "You're uncomfortable, too? Just ... just come a-back, now." Steig pressed his hand on the horse's chest and Beckett took a tentative step backwards, then another, and reversed into the shafts. "Good lad." Then, sotto voce, "We'll be away in a minute."

"Can you at least take my pack on the ... cr-cratch?" Maisie stumbled over the unfamiliar word. She hoped that learning some of the gypsy's words would help, but all she had so far was yog, the fire, and cratch. And vardo, of course.

"It's not a luggage rack. It's for hay."

"It's empty, apart from a folding chair. There's no need for hay. Look at the grass!" She gestured. Steig glanced at the long, fecund grass, and sighed.

"Fine. I'll take the tent and stuff on the cratch."

He continued to buckle up a series of straps that held Beckett in the shafts, which he had lifted to fit into the harness. Maisie stood for a moment, waiting, before coming to the realisation that she would have to heave her enormous pack into the cratch herself. Huh, she thought. Fine. I can do that.

She teetered on an upturned plastic milk crate whilst balancing the huge pack half on her shoulder, half on the wagon. Then heaved it onto the wooden rack. The vardo wobbled on its suspension, but the pack was secure. The acute angle of the contraption held it still, a pair of small chains at the sides keeping the rack in place at the back of the wagon.

When Maisie returned to the front, she found Steig was walking all around, peering into the grass.

"Did you drop something?"

"Checking for rubbish, tat, anything left that shouldn't be left. The gadjo have nothing better to do than criticise when we leave rubbish. Also, who wants to leave rubbish?"

Maisie checked the ground around her feet.

"You can understand their concern, though. You see all sorts of rubbish around gypsy sites."

Steig unbent himself from looking at the ground and stood still for several seconds. There was palpable anger radiating from him, just from the set of his shoulders. He turned to glare at her, resentment or fury clouding his face. She wasn't sure which.

"'Gypsy' isn't a word you should use."

"Why on earth not? You're a gypsy, aren't you?" she asked, bemused.

"If I was Black, would you call me a ... uh ... would you use the N word?"

Maisie gasped. "Of course not! Why would you think that?"

"Well, to some travelling folk, that's how gypsy is. It can be a racial slur against the Roma people. So I, and most travelling folk I've met, prefer 'traveller' instead." He shook his head, as if weary of the conversation, and turned to continue looking for stray rubbish. After a few seconds, he turned back. "Also, I'm not Roma, so even if it wasn't difficult for me, you shouldn't use gypsy to refer to me."

Oh dear, thought Maisie, the day hadn't quite got off to the right sort of start.

Steig lifted the last of the items into the wagon: the kitchen box, packed away tidy, the plastic milk crate, the old wooden chair he had sat on earlier. He unclipped the curved wooden steps and slid them inside, almost to the bed, where they fit against the bench seat. The fire had spent itself, just a thin wisp of smoke rising. He kicked dirt and ash over it. Finally, he turned to Maisie.

"What's your plan?"

This question startled her. "I don't have a plan. Other than to come with you."

"Are you walking?"

Oh, that again. He hates me, she thought. "If you wish, of course I can walk."

Steig let out a long sigh, pushed his hand back through his hair. His exasperation was apparent, but the earlier anger seemed to have dissipated. Maisie didn't want to walk. The march of the day before had stretched her, and she wasn't sure she'd make it more than a mile today, even with the rucksack being transported for her. Her blisters had blisters. But she would not ask to ride in the wagon. Steig had already made it clear she wasn't welcome. Especially in the wagon.

"OK, here's the deal," started Steig, looking directly at her with his piercing blue eyes. "You ride on the wagon with me. On the front ledge, or just inside the door. You help with the hills, that means you get down and help Beckett with the pulling. And if a downhill is steep, we'll both be walking there, too. You'll help when the ground's rough, like pulling off here." He waved his arm towards the edge of the lane, which was rutted and muddy. "I don't do stop-start, so if you need a pee, now's your chance. We'll be off in a minute."

Maisie breathed out a sigh. She hadn't realised she was holding her breath; she offered silent thanks to God.

"I'm ready now. I had a ... um, a pee, earlier."

Steig nodded once, had a last scan around.

"Give a push, now, let's get off here."

He led Beckett by the bridle in a wide circle that had the horse stumbling and straining over the rough ground. Maisie pushed the wagon from behind, a faint smell of wood smoke and paint reaching her from the pan box. The vardo rocked, water containers sloshed and cups chimed like bells somewhere inside as the motion shook them. But then they were on the lane, pointing back the way they had all come, and the wagon came to a halt.

"Get on!" came the shout.

"OK," squeaked Maisie, skipping to the front, where Beckett stood holding the wagon against the slight incline, leaning into the collar of the harness. She hauled herself up, using a metal stirrup that was attached to the suspension, and settled herself on the comfortable ledge on the right-hand side of the vardo. It was a long way up, and she had to cling on; the structure of the wagon rocked as Steig led Beckett along the farm track and towards the country lane she had turned off the previous day. Stirwood loomed, implacable, to their left. Maisie peered into the woods, trying to see more than a tree's depth, where the light faded to layers of greys and mossy greens. A shudder ran down her spine; it wasn't a forest she had any desire to explore.

As Beckett got into his stride, Steig picked up the reins and climbed with agility over the shafts and into the doorway of the wagon. He settled himself onto the left-hand ledge, one leg dangling, the other resting, just touching the shafts, the reins loose in his left hand. The wagon rumbled and creaked, but the road, now gravelly, was getting easier. Once they turned onto the metalled country lane, the going was almost calming, and the noise reduced to a gentle rumble from the tyres. The creaking of the leather harness, and the bright ringing percussion of Beckett's shoes on the tarmac sounded a merry counterpoint.

He kept his usual eye out for traffic, for the cadence of Beckett's stride, for changes in the road surface. It was a slow way to travel, and the wagon was running heavy with his worldly belongings. The more he could do to make life easier on the running gear and harness, and on Beckett, the better. George had made a fair point, back at the farm.

He took a sidelong glance at Maisie. She was dozing, lulled by the movement of the wagon and the noise of the horse's shod hooves. Braced onto the shelf, leaning into the curve of the canvas top. Much like he was, in fact. She'd used a couple of Rom words, and if he didn't know better, he would have thought she was enjoying the lifestyle, such as it was. She had thrown herself into helping with the hills, that much was certain.

They approached the village of Nortone; it was a raggle-taggle of houses along the lane they were trotting up. The country's main east-west highway, carrying heavy, fast traffic, bisected it. Steig ignored the turning through the village to the huge junction, with its slip roads and chevrons. Instead, he carried on until he came to a cutting that led to a farm access track, snaking under the trunk road through a short tunnel. There was a solid farm gate chained closed across the lane. Constructed from galvanised steel, the gate was shiny, new, and immovable.

"Hoo, standing now, Beckett." The horse had his ears back; he didn't like the traffic noise from the road above them.

Maisie stirred when they halted, and she nodded towards the gate. "Are we going through there?"

"Yep. Here." Steig patted his coat until he found a pocket that jangled with keys. He fished a small bunch out on a leather keyring with an oak leaf motif. He spent a second counting through the keys and selected the right one. "Hop down and unlock that chain, can you? There are two padlocks on it. It will be the brass one with an *S* engraved on it."

Maisie frowned, then shrugged, took the key, and stretched down from the seat. Standing, she took a moment to arch her spine to ease her muscles, then walked to the gate, still twisting her back. She spent a minute fiddling with the chain, and with a clatter, she had it unlocked. She pushed at the gate. It stuck halfway on the uneven ground and she had to tug and lift it, but eventually had it wide open.

"On you go," Steig commanded.

"Don't like the noise," Beckett grumbled back, ears flicking as cars and lorries hurtled past above them. He pulled the wagon forward with a lurch.

As they passed Maisie, Steig called down, "Lock it again, then catch us up."

Maisie nodded and once they were through, Steig heard her scrape and heave the gate closed again. As Beckett walked at half-speed, Steig could hear the chain going back on, and then the drumming of Maisie's boots as she sprinted to catch up. She swung up on the right-hand side of the wagon, windswept and bright-faced.

"You could have waited," she remonstrated.

"The exercise will do you good," said Steig, grinning.

"Huh. You can do the next one. Also, how come you have a key?" She handed him back the keyring.

"I've travelled this way before. Tis a simple matter to add your own padlock, if you have the equipment."

"How?"

Steig just grinned, flicked the reins and clicked. Beckett changed up a gear, and they pulled out of the far side of the tunnel into more open countryside, another tiny lane. The noise of the main road faded behind them.

"Welcome to Leadestrescire," he declared, making a sweeping gesture with his right arm. Laid out before them, the land was like a tree-studded green patchwork jigsaw. From their elevated position, they could see for miles. On the far horizon, small copses, woods and greening fields met the billowing white haze of cumulus clouds. "Beautiful, is it not?"

"It's certainly ... expansive. Rural. Green. Yes, it is beautiful."

Steig shook his head. He couldn't work Maisie out. She seemed all gung-ho for the life on the road one minute, and all uncertain the next.

"There's a spinney up there a ways. We'll pull up for lunch" – he pointed at a small group of trees on the top of a distant hill – "and have a bite to eat. Beckett can have a drink and some grass. We'll see if we want to stay there tonight or push on."

"We? Whatever happened to *I'm* doing this, *I'm* going there?"

Steig was confused for a second, then embarrassed. He concentrated on the road ahead. What was going on? She was still a gobshite gadjo, still in the way. Still tagging along. Beckett's ears flicked again.

"Be quiet, horse."

Maisie looked at Steig in confusion.

"What did he say?"

"You be quiet too!" he quipped, but with a slight smile on his face. "Heddup, lad."

Beckett put a bit more effort into the hill up towards the spinney.

At the top of the hill, they pulled onto a patch of level ground in the lee of the woods, at the mouth of a T-junction with an even smaller track. A broken, canted sign declared it to be Crackbottle Lane. Steig took in the spinney. More like a strip of trees; you could see through from one side to the other. It straggled off over the brow of the hill and thickened up into a proper wood, growing from copse-dom as it marched over the countryside. The fields on either side were a fresh tilth, the red-brown earth tinged with the fuzz of green as the crops pushed through.

Maisie hopped down and stretched, arms reaching skywards; she cast around with her eyes, and Steig saw her face brighten.

"I'll fetch some wood for the yog," she said.

"Good plan. I'll get Beckett watered." He was bemused. Yog. There it was again – like she was embracing the lifestyle. "What do you think, horse?"

"Don't ask me. You never listen to my advice, anyway."

"True."

Steig fetched water from one of the five-gallon plastic containers slung under the wagon, in its metal frame. It was an addition that wasn't traditional, but came in very handy. He sloshed the water into an equally modern plastic bucket that lived on a hook next to the water containers when not in use and held it up for Beckett.

"There you go, my friend."

The horse slurped water past his bit, using his big lips to slosh it around in the bucket.

"What do you think, then? Stop here? Or go on?"

"It's nice here. There's a meliad in the woods, but she smells alright." Beckett's ears swivelled back and forth, and he snorted down his nose.

"Well, we can go on, if you like, after lunch?"

"I'd like some grass. Or mints."

Steig laughed. "OK, we'll stay here. I'll untack you." He set about unstrapping the breeching and traces, and walked Beckett out of the shafts, which fell with a thud to the ground. Unbuckling the tack without ceremony, he dumped it down in a tangle. Finally he pegged Beckett out in his usual manner, and the horse set about the long, sweet grass with enthusiasm.

Maisie returned from the strip of trees, hauling a substantial, dead ash branch. The far end dragged on the ground; she had mud on her hands. The fresh air had added a flush to her face, and her smile telegraphed excitement.

"You seem to be getting into the spirit of this?"

"It's wonderful! I feel ... alive!"

Steig wasn't convinced. Still. Tea. He broke the dead branch up and kindled a fire on the grass.

"Aren't you supposed to dig out a square of grass and build the fire in a hole?"

"You'd think so," agreed Steig. "But when I go to old sites year after year, like up on the edge of Sarisberie plain, all I see is little squares of dead grass. The weekend warriors leaving a mess as usual. I think it kills the roots. But make a small fire on top of the grass, or even a big fire, and a couple of months later, it will have grown back."

"Weekend warriors?"

"Yeah. We did some stuff, way back, when the government banned the Ambesberie Stones solstice celebrations. Organised walks from all over, through June. People would come out from the towns at the weekends to join in the fun. Weekend warriors."

"Oh. I see."

It was clear that she didn't see. Steig thought back to those times. A different epoch, almost. Back before the world went sad and mad, back before his own difficulties. He sighed and put the kettle on.

As it grumbled and steamed, waiting to boil, they sat, Maisie engrossed, reading her old black leather-bound pocket bible. Steig daydreamed, staring into the middle distance, listening to the birdsong, the chomp of Beckett's eating, and ...

Something moved in the strip of woodland. It was large and indistinct, seemed to shimmer and fade in and out of perception, like a distant heat mirage on a blistering day. He looked again, but all he could see was woodland. Greens and browns, stands of hazel with their tufted straight boughs, beech trees tall and sparse and majestic. Ash, all rough bark and spindly leaves just peeking through, always the last. Not much in the way of understorey.

He thought about what Beckett had said. A meliad, in the woods. Beckett rarely named the spirits he saw. They were, as far as Steig could tell, just things of tooth and claw that the horse worried would get him. Of course, they never did. They were just ... just what? Imagined threats? Genii locorum, spirits of place, the feel of a thing, nothing more?

There! Again, the flicker of movement, gone when he looked. He heaved himself to his feet and walked over to the edge of the wood. Maisie was deep in her bible studies, didn't look up. Beckett flicked an ear but carried on munching. Nothing imminent was worrying the horse.

He stood still, silent, before the cathedral-like heights of the beech trees. Slowed his breath. Cleared his mind. Closed his eyes. *Listened* with his heart, a trick an old woodsman had taught him years before.

There was a movement, heard at the edge of perception, a rustle, as of small animals in the undergrowth. A sudden smell of turned earth and leaf mould, musty like sandalwood. The birdsong dimmed, hushed. He opened his eyes.

The meliad was standing before him, inside the line of the trees, out of his reach by an arm's length. He stopped breathing, frozen in place.

She was at once a young, elongated, dark-haired woman with quick eyes and an angular, pointed face, and simultaneously, an old and wrinkled creature, nut-brown of skin, with a twisted back and gnarled hands. Her dark black eyes regarding him with equal parts wariness and amusement. Steig squinted, and she resolved into the younger self, wearing a royal blue robe, with a lighter blue dress flowing out underneath.

"Well met," Steig said, his voice tentative. Bloody hell. Here he was face to face with a supernatural being and he comes out with "Well met". Embarrassing.

"Well met, yourself, Traveller Steig of Roteslund."

"Thank you for the gift of your wood for our fire." He bowed his head.

"Your travelling companion didn't ask. She just took."

Fear trickled down Steig's spine, raising hairs. "I apologise. She is new to the life, I'll make sure she knows to ask, next time."

The laughter was a dry rustle, like a playful gust of wind in the tallest branches of a silver birch tree. As she laughed, her teeth showed – they were long and pointed. Then she stopped laughing, sobered, and stared into Steig's eyes with her own dark pools of black.

"She will ask, or maybe she won't come out of the fidh again."

"My Lady, I will ensure she is polite in the future."

"Very well. To business, for I tire of this. You must make your way to the place where the Wayland crosses the Devana."

"Devana? What ..." But already, the meliad had flickered from her young self to her older self, to a memory, to a whisper, to a breath ... and was gone.

"Are you talking to the trees?"

Steig spun around, startled. Maisie was standing a few paces from him, holding her bible in one hand, down by her side, a steaming mug of tea proffered in the other.

"I made you a tea."

"Thank you. I was ... I just had the oddest thing happen."

"What?" she asked, her face open and bright.

"Come, sit by the yog. We need to talk."

Maisie's stomach plummeted as they settled by the fire. "A chat, by the yog," he had said. Oh no. She was just beginning to enjoy herself, this glimpse into a different life. Now he was going to abandon her. She just knew it. She did her best to put on a brave face. He wasn't even looking at her. Staring into the fire. Oh, this was bad.

"So, the oddest thing just happened," he started, then stopped, as if he were unsure what to say.

"Do you want me to leave?"

"What? No!" he blurted. He looked at first confused, then embarrassed. "I mean, no, I'm not talking about us. I mean, you. Well, not directly. Something odd just happened to me."

"What, then? Tell me. Please."

"There's a meliad in the woods."

"The Meliae, the ash tree spirits?"

"Yes. I think. I met one, just now, in the wood."

Maisie wasn't sure if he was mocking her, making things up to make her seem foolish. With an edge of caution in her voice, she asked, "You met a tree spirit, in the woods, just now?"

"I said that, didn't I?"

"Are you taking drugs?"

"What? No! I know it sounds odd, fantastical. I can hardly believe it myself. But Beckett saw it. Didn't you, horse?"

Beckett continued eating, but gave the smallest two flicks of an ear.

"Oh, he's not saying anything *now,* of course."

Maisie was sceptical. Did Steig think tree spirits were real? It was clear he could read her face because he exclaimed, "Look, you believe in God, right?"

"I have faith, yes."

"Well, this is the same, surely? Like saints or something?"

"Faith doesn't require proof, that's sort of the point."

"Fagh. People say if your senses are sharp enough, you can see magical things. Well, I'm feeling pretty sharp today, I can tell you. Oh, and another thing. She said you took the wood without asking. And she had teeth. Lots of sharp, pointy teeth. You need to remember to ask before you take wood. And say thank you."

Maisie was worried. Steig was raving. Asking the meliad's permission for fallen wood?

"Listen to yourself. You're not making sense."

"Yes, I know. Don't you think I'm aware how crackpot this sounds? But there it is. Beckett saw her. I spoke to her. It's as plain as day to me. She said, 'Go to the place where Wayland and Devana cross.'"

"Wayland? The river? What's a Devana?"

"I guess she meant the river. As for Devana? No idea." Steig seemed to curl in on himself then, hugging his knees, staring into the fire, which was putting up fitful sparks.

Maisie dug out her mobile phone, pressed a button to turn it on. After a few seconds it chimed, the electronic sound almost alien in the environment they were in.

"No signal. What is it with this county?"

"It's rural, is what."

"It's not that rural. I mean, there's a farm just over there." She waved her arm in the general direction they had come, where a farmstead roof showed above the hedge line in the valley. "I've not had a signal since I left Launde Priory. That's why I gave up and turned it off. I was going to look up Devana, but it will have to wait, I suppose."

"Where Wayland and Devana cross ..." mused Steig. "Wayland is a river, so is Devana a path? A road? A bridge?"

"Did your 'tree spirit' say anything else?"

"She said ..." He concentrated, brow creasing, remembering the conversation. "She said, 'Don't take wood without asking or she'll trap you in the forest forever.' Only she used the Gaelic word, fidh, for forest."

Maisie's head snapped up, and a real pang of fear raced across her belly.

"She actually said that?"

"Yeah." Steig's face clouded with woe. "Seriously, ask before you collect wood, and make sure you say thank you."

"Be polite to the trees?"

"Yes. Always."

Maisie thought; his world, his rules. I can live with that. "OK," she said, uncertain. "I'll be polite. I can do that."

Steig smiled, shook his head, started preparing some vegetables for a stew. Maisie watched him working, chopping carrots and onions on the tiny wooden chopping board, frying them off in a blackened iron pot over the fire.

She glanced along the small verge side they were on. The wagon behind them. Beckett pegged out further along. There was room for her tent, in front of the wagon, on the far side of the fire. But she recalled what Steig had said about the meliad: "It had lots of sharp, pointy teeth." She didn't like to admit it to herself, but part of her was fearful.

The afternoon and evening progressed with no more supernatural apparitions. Beckett had worked his way through his section of verge and Steig moved him along to a fresh stretch. Steig walked into the deeper part of the woods during the afternoon. He returned with more firewood and no sightings of anything untoward or unusual.

As dusk fell, Maisie looked up from her journal, in which, Steig noticed, she had been doodling aimless spirals. She had seemed lost in thought, her eyes half closed.

"Steig ..."

"Yep." He was looking into the fire, also defocused, trying to decipher the Devana riddle. It sounded somehow familiar.

"I'm scared to sleep out here."

"Oh." He didn't know where this was going. Well, he had an inkling. "And?"

"Can I sleep in the wagon tonight?"

"You mean swap? I-I guess." He wasn't keen on tents but could appreciate she might be nervous on the side of a road like this.

"No, not swap ... oh ..." She turned her face towards the fire again, a flush of red sweeping her face.

"Oh. Um. OK. If you want." What was he doing? He didn't need her in his wagon. Hang on. In his bed? Surely, she didn't mean ...? Bloody hell. He stood up, set off at a brisk walk out of the firelight. He needed a pee anyway, he told himself.

"Goin' for a pee," he cast back over his shoulder.

He walked up to Beckett, who was dozing. One hind hoof lifted, resting. Beckett raised his head, saw it was him, and went back to dozing. Steig leant against the horse's side, feeling the warmth of his hide, inhaling his waxy, horsey smell.

"Hey, horse."

Beckett snuffled around to Steig with his nose, seeking mints or carrots. Finding neither, he returned to dozing. While he ruminated on Maisie, Steig scratched the horse's withers and the base of his mane.

"Ooh yeah, that's nice, do some more," muttered Beckett, twisting up his lips into an involuntary curve.

"Silly old horse. What am I going to do about that woman?"

Beckett remained silent. Steig carried on grooming him for a bit, then walked further out into the darkness to pee in the hedge.

When he came back to the camp, Maisie was trying to read from the light of the fire. She sat twisted around in her seat, peering at her bible, which she was holding perilously close to the flames. He fetched the hurricane lantern from inside the wagon and lit it. Pushed a road iron into the ground next to Maisie and hung the lantern from it, where it cast a dim but serviceable yellow light onto her book and face.

"Thank you," she whispered, looking up at him, face glow-lit and soft, and then turning back to her book, abashed.

"Any words of wisdom from the prophets?"

She giggled. "No, they are surprisingly silent on the subject of local deities and weird quests."

"Well, I'm worn out, gonna turn in."

Steig didn't say, "Goodnight." If she were going to sleep in the wagon, she'd say it then. He didn't say, "See you in a minute." Last thing he wanted was to invite her, give her any idea that this was something he was keen on.

Stumping up the steps, he left his boots just inside the door and lit the other lantern, which he hung on its usual hook near the bed. He looked at the narrow bed that filled the width of the back of the wagon, cupboards underneath. Then he looked at the floor – barely room to stretch out. Horse-drawn wagons, he mused, are not huge spaces. They didn't need to be. He lived life outside, for the most part.

Stripping off, he left his clothes in a neat but crumpled pile and climbed into bed. He reached out and turned down the wick on the lantern. He left it just burning, as was his habit, so that he could turn it up at any moment, without fumbling for matches. Staring up at the curved ceiling, which the fire lit with a wavering light, he tuned into the sounds. Fire crackle. Breeze soughing the trees above. Owl in distance. Beckett shifting his weight. The rustle of a page turning. He slipped into a light, fitful sleep, dreaming snatches of forest, fragments of an old, weathered face with deep black eyes. All the while, a susurration of treetop branches was murmuring, "Devana, Devana, Devana ..."

At some point, in the dark and the still of the night, he felt Maisie climb the steps, making the wagon rock slightly. Heard her taking off her boots, the whisper of a layer of clothes, felt her get into bed with him, felt her skin, bare in places, cool from the night air, against his skin.

"Goodnight, Steig."

A whisper, almost silent.

"'Night, Maisie," he managed, through layers of dream.

Chapter 9

Maisie woke by degrees. She was comfortable in bed for the first time in quite a few days. The bed in the priory had been hard, lumpy and cold. As for the tent, her ground roll was meagre and thin, allowing any twigs and stones under the tent to push through into her back.

This bed was soft, deep and supportive with a warm, heavy eiderdown. She opened her eyes with a start, recalling the previous day's events. She was in Steig's bed. She held herself immobile and let her eyes glance around, stilled her breath and listened.

Steig's gentle breathing sounded from somewhere near her right ear. She could feel his warmth along her right-hand side. She could smell his smell, not unpleasant, mingled with the odours of wood smoke and horse.

The curve of the wagon's roof was close, almost touching her forehead as her breath misted in the cool of the morning. Light flooded in through the tiny window at the back of the wagon, just above the bed, revealing ornate curlicues of gold leaf on the wooden lattice.

Slowly, so as to not disturb the slumbering Steig, she slid out of the bed, just touching the floor with her tiptoes before she completely lost her balance. She grabbed at the edge of the tiny table next to the bed and eased herself into a standing position. She was still wearing her underwear and a white cotton slip, the cool air goose-bumping her arms and legs. Quick as she could, she shrugged into her clothes. She rubbed morosely at the front of the dress, which was looking very grimy in places. Turned and saw that Steig was awake, and watching her with an amused smile.

"Mornin', Ms Hanson." His voice was soft and deep.

"Good morning, Mr Sturluson." She managed an embarrassed smile before bobbing a quick curtsey and bolting for the door.

Outside, she found the morning dew-laden and fresh. The sky was a deep pink gold to the east, a dull battleship grey coming from the west, in a band of low cloud. Her breath steamed in curling plumes. Beckett gave a gentle nicker of greeting. He was standing four-square, his water bucket resting on its side. He kicked it, a flick with his front hoof, so it rolled towards her.

"Did you run out of water?" She pulled her boots on without doing up the laces and walked over to him. The bucket was full of horse dung. She looked at the bucket, and at Beckett. "Yuk. Why have you done that?"

"Accident. Can I have some water?"

"Of course." She picked the bucket up, emptied the dung into the hedge, and went to rinse and refill it. Only as she struggled back with the almost full bucket did she realise Beckett had spoken to her. The bucket slipped from her fingers, landed with a thud. Water splashed up her leg, soaking her dress.

"What did you say?" she enunciated.

Beckett flicked one ear back, regarding her with equine innocence. She sighed. Hearing things. Seeing things. The world was going mad, and she was being swept along with it. She picked up the bucket and plonked it in front of the horse at the edge of his circle.

"Don't spill it. Or poo in it. Disgusting." She turned her back and paused. Opened her senses to the land, the spinney, the lane. Everywhere was silent, still, as if waiting. She breathed in through her nose, then out through her mouth, deep breaths like on her yoga sleep tapes. The feeling of imminence was almost tangible.

"Tea," she mused, going to the remains of the fire and poking at it with some twigs, like she had seen Steig do. Fanned it with her hand. Eventually got down on all fours and blew onto the twigs, then coughed and spluttered as she inhaled a cloud of ash and smoke. Finally, the embers glowed, and the twigs caught. She built up the fire and started the kettle to boil.

"It's like you were born to it," said Steig in a wry tone. He was clothed, leaning in the vardo's doorway, a slight smile on his lips.

"I'm getting the hang of things," she said, smiling up at him, pushing her unruly hair back from her face.

The morning was busy with breakfasting, tending to Beckett, ablutions. Steig said nothing about the previous night. His feelings were a confused jumble. He was adamant that she was an unnecessary distraction, despite what Beckett said. In her turn, Maisie didn't mention anything, either. As if everything was normal. Though she seemed preoccupied with some deep thoughts. Steig shrugged. It wasn't really his problem. He continued putting Beckett's harness on. Beckett was taciturn for a change.

After breakfast they set off, heading south, into the lowering cloud and a freshening breeze. They had taken up their accustomed positions on opposite ledges at the front of the wagon. Steig looked up at the greyness, frowning. Winter was a distant memory. The spring equinox had passed, but wintery showers would surely be a feature for a while yet.

"Looks like the weather's turning. A front pushing through. Hopefully, we can park up before the worst of it hits, but it can be pretty boring sitting in the wagon all day. You got any other books?"

"I'll manage, thank you."

Steig glanced at Maisie; she had been acting funny all morning. Sort of distracted. Surely it wasn't because they had shared a bed? Nothing had happened between them. Quite the opposite.

"What's bothering you?"

"Your horse talked to me this morning."

"How do you mean?"

"He apologised for pooing in his bucket and asked for water. Verbally."

"Ah. Well, sometimes he speaks to me. So ... maybe we're both imagining it?"

"I'm right here, you know," called Beckett, as he trotted up a slight incline.

Steig grinned at Maisie. Her face split with such a broad smile it was almost a caricature.

"Well. That's put both of us in our place, hmm?" He chuckled.

"Yes, it has!" She laughed, but then her face took on a thoughtful cast. She held up the fingers of her left hand and bent each back as she ticked off. "So. Run away with a traveller in a vardo, check. Weird Heracles voice from the woods, check. Talking horse, check. Tree spirit, check. Mystery quest that no one can understand, check." She stared down at her left hand, frowned, then turned the thumb of her right hand upwards. "God moving in ineffable ways, check. What's next?"

From the top of the escarpment that they crested, Steig could see the rain sweeping in from the right, from the west, in a vertical band of grey, blotting out all before it.

"Next? Biblical rain."

The storm rolled in, plunging them into a twilight world of stinging precipitation and squalling winds. They abandoned the ledges at the front of the wagon and shut the bottom half of the split door, Steig leaning on the door and driving Beckett through the opening. It wasn't the best or safest way to drive, as it made jumping down to assist Beckett less instant. Also, looking behind to check traffic was difficult. But the road was quiet and level, so it was a calculated risk Steig felt worth staying dry for. The rain beat a percussive drumming on the roof of the wagon, drowning out all other sounds. Maisie had scrambled back into the wagon as the first deluge hit. She looked out in awed wonder at the downpour, the rain sheeting the road surface, Beckett stoically walking into the teeth of the tempest.

Steig realised Maisie was leaning against him, a gentle pressure where they touched. He could feel her warmth through his coat, and smell the smoky smell of her hair, with a faint undercurrent of shampoo. Since the doorway was narrow, it was natural they would crowd together. He realised he didn't mind the intimacy. If that was what it was. It was pleasant. Comforting. Companionable.

She was still a gadjo, still a pain in the backside. But like the pain in his rear he sometimes had after a long drive, sitting on the shelf, it was a pain that, somehow, seemed worthwhile.

Beckett whickered, a rumble of mirth. Steig smiled. Yeah, alright, horse, you might have the right of it.

They rolled past the edge of a sprawling village, Alcatone. Rolled past the mere, a small lake on the left, then turned right at the Fox Inn, an imposing, whitewashed public house. The pub was shuttered against the weather, and the outside lights at the door shone in the gloom of the day. They rolled up a narrow road between two small housing estates, new builds, all tiny rabbit-hutch boxes. Each one stamped out from the same mould, the same brick, the same four windows, the same doors. Each had the same bare tiny handkerchiefs of gardens, all waterlogged as the deluge sheeted from the roofs.

"I'd sooner die than live in a box like that," Steig muttered.

"I live in a box like that."

"Really?"

"Yes. It seems far removed from here."

"Do you like it?"

"It's home, I suppose. It's where all my books and clothes and things are."

"Does that make it home?"

"I don't know. They say home is where the heart is."

"And where is your heart, Maisie Hanson?"

Maisie looked thoughtful, wistful. Sad.

"I don't know. But I suspect my heart isn't in the house I own." She brightened. "I'll think on it and let you know."

Beckett continued to plod through the downpour, shaking his head as rivulets ran into his eyes. Steig steered him carefully, mindful of the poor visibility and narrowness of the road.

"There's a ford through a stream down here somewhere, with a pull-up next to it. We can stay there. It's alright for an overnight."

"How come you know this countryside so well?"

"I grew up here. Truth be told, I've never really been anywhere else."

As they left the village behind, the road dipped down to the ford and the stream. The rain had swollen it to a torrent, which spread out over the road. Beckett stopped, his front hooves inches from the rushing water. Steig leant out of the doorway.

"Heddup lad, gayyorrn!" he shouted.

"Nope. Scared. Can't move," came the strained reply.

"Here, Maisie, hang on to these." Steig passed the reins to her. "Just keep it gentle, left and right, easy. Keep your little fingers out, just three fingers on each. Like this." He demonstrated, holding each rein between three fingers and a thumb.

Maisie took the brown leather reins, her touch at first hesitant. Steig opened the door and jumped down from the wagon and into the deluge. He walked up to Beckett and took the reins under the horse's chin.

"Come on, lad, it's not deep. I got you."

"Still scared."

"I know. It's safe, here, look." Steig stepped ahead of Beckett, standing in the water, which covered his ankles. "See, it's only ankle deep."

Beckett took a step into the stream, then struck out with his hoof, making a tremendous splash, testing the depth. Another step, then two, and his hind legs were in it, the churning water now covering his shins. Steig felt the water rush into his boots as he went in deeper, but this was a metalled ford. There was a depth marker at the side that showed the water in the middle was less than twenty centimetres deep. Though still it tugged at his legs, letting him know it had power.

Steig led Beckett, still complaining, through the ford and up the other side, where a grassy space on the right opened out. Beckett, muttering, hauled the wagon onto the grass, with Steig walking at his head.

"Here you go, lad, well done." He turned to Maisie who was standing in the wagon doorway and called, "That's fine right there!"

She jumped down, put the chocks on the wheels, and came to help with Beckett, the rain darkening her hair and plastering it to her face in an instant.

"There's a waterproof rug above the pan box. Go get it; he'll be cold in the wind."

By degrees they untacked the horse, pegged him out, put the rain sheet on his back. Steig lit the Queen Anne stove, using the store of dry logs stacked next to it. All the while, the storm broke over them; the wind picked up. The wagon rocked, and the rain beat against the tarpaulin like a thousand demented drummer monkeys. Beckett stood, head down, tail to the weather, waiting it out. Steig shut the bottom, then the top doors, and glanced at Maisie. The downpour had soaked her blouse and dress through, her skin was blue and she was shivering. He wasn't in a much better state. He frowned at the feel of the damp and wet that had soaked through his ancient coat.

The wagon heated quickly with the fire, and the windows became opaque with rain outside, condensation inside. Steig fetched a towel.

"Here, get out of those clothes and get dry before you get hypothermia."

Maisie hesitated for a second. Steig could see her thinking it through, coming to the rapid conclusion that this wouldn't be anything he hadn't seen before. She took the towel, stripped off down to her underwear, and vigorously rubbed her skin dry, warming her bare legs by the wood burner.

Steig stripped off his sodden jumper, jeans and T-shirt. He wasn't wearing any underwear. He shrugged, and took the towel from Maisie, who seemed fascinated by the misty view out of the back window.

When he was dry, he stood, letting the heat from the fire warm his skin. The space they were standing in, in front of the fire, was tiny, barely room for them both. He was aware of the heat from Maisie's body as she warmed up. He hung their wet clothes and the towel on a short clothesline that ran along the ceiling by the wood burner, from the front of the wagon to above the bed platform. Droplets of water from his jumper hissed and spangled as they landed on the stovetop.

It was a ballet, a study in not touching each other's skin, but it was impossible. The space was too small. She wanted to be near the fire; he tried to reach around her to the cupboard for more clothes ... as they touched, his arm and shoulder brushing her bare back, a shock of electricity ran through him. Maisie took a gasp of air and turned to look at him, inches from his face.

"Sorry ..." he muttered.

"Steig ..." she whispered, placing her hand on his chest, her touch tentative.

They stood, looking at each other, both frozen in place, unsure, irresolute. The noise of the storm seemed to recede.

Steig was very confused. The proximity to this gadjo was doing something to him. Something unexpected. A tightness in his chest, where her hand warmed his heart. A flush to his face. He looked at her and saw a pinkness to her cheeks as well. Her eyes, a deep blue, were receptive, her pupils huge and black in the dim light. He shook his head; tried to think straight.

"I'm gonna get into bed, try to warm up a bit."

He shuffled around her and climbed up onto the bed and under the eiderdown, which was cool and heavy and slightly damp on his skin.

"Can I ... can I warm up, too?"

"Yeah, I think so."

Maisie hesitated for a heartbeat, then climbed into the bed next to him.

"Ooh, it's chilly ..." She shivered.

Steig reached out, put his hand behind her shoulder, pulled her close.

"Here, I'll warm you."

"Why, thank you, Mr Sturluson," she replied, a bubble of laughter in her voice.

"Ew. Your underwear is sodden."

"Hang on." She wriggled around, and was soon naked, slim, warm, and lithe, lying in Steig's arms again. The duvet pulled up to her chin.

"Is that better? Warmer?"

"Yes, thank you," she replied with a smile, and snuggled into his shoulder.

The wind continued to rock the vardo from side to side; the rain continued to beat a dissonant rhythm on the curved roof. Steig listened to it for a while, allowing his body to relax and warm up, her skin touching his, long and even down his side.

"One of the best things about living in a wagon is the joy of being ensconced whilst the elements tear at the world outside," he stated.

"Mm, 's poetic ... 's warm n' snugly ..." came the sleepy reply. She burrowed her face further into his shoulder, and as he held her gently, he realised she was drifting off to sleep.

He sang, sotto voce, barely a whisper, barely audible over the cacophony of the rain:

"It was there last week you'd a rabbit hutch house,
Curtains drawn so comely-o.
But tonight, you lie in a goose feather bed,
In the arms of the raggle-taggle gypsy-o."

"Traveller-o," a murmur from his shoulder. He smiled and shut his eyes.

Maisie woke to the sound of gentle rain on the canvas. The duvet wrapped her, her nose peeking out; the curved roof above her a comfort, an enclosure. She patted out to her right but found the bed empty – Steig was gone. She sat up, careful not to bump her head. No sign. Door ajar. He had lit the lantern, and it cast a warming glow about the wagon. The fire was hot, burning with a fierce crackle. She glanced at her wristwatch. Still early evening. They had slept through half the afternoon. She felt warm inside at the decadence of it.

She slipped out of bed and dug around in her rucksack for dry clothes – the ones on the line were still drying off. Her last set of fresh underwear. She had a pair of blue jeans tucked away. They would be more suited to this life, she suspected. Harder wearing. Wagon-living involved more manual labour than she had expected. She pulled them on. A yellow cotton short-sleeved shirt was the only clean top she had ... it would have to do. Her duffel coat was damp, but serviceable; she didn't have another one, so that was that. She shrugged into it and, pulling her cold, damp walking boots on over bare feet, stepped out onto the ledge.

She could just make out Steig through the early evening gloom. He was standing next to Beckett, who was tethered on the far side of the little green space they had stopped on. They both looked over, and she waved. Steig waved back, gave Beckett a rub on the forehead, and started over to the vardo.

"How are you feeling?"

"Much warmer now that I'm dry, thank you."

"I'll put the kettle on. Come on, there's no need to be out here."

"Is Beckett alright?"

"Yeah, he's fine. Bit damp, but warm enough."

"I'm just going to ... to pee."

She walked away through the rain, towards the field gate opposite, embarrassed. Why was she embarrassed? They had just been naked in bed. Not that he had hardly touched her, just held her ... Oh ... she kept forgetting, he thought her a nuisance and a God-botherer. Oh, now she was squirming with embarrassment. Oh dear.

When she climbed back up the wagon steps and slipped inside, Steig had prepared some sandwiches – cheese and onion – and a mug of steaming sweet tea. She realised she was starving, took the plate, and began wolfing the sandwiches down, slurping tea between bites.

"Mm, so tasty, thank you." He was grinning at her. "What's so funny?"

"Nothing. I'm just enjoying your enthusiasm for a simple sandwich."

Through the evening, as the darkness outside deepened, they relaxed into each other's company. Maisie found the lack of a need to chatter a blessing. She was comfortable in the calm of the vardo. She wrote a paragraph in her battered yellow journal about the storm. He was reading, she noticed, a history of Breotonish folklore. He had a tiny, varied library on a shelf at the back of the bed platform. It included a dictionary and a couple of classics, and several odd reference books. There was one on folklore, also some on plant medicine, bird recognition. Country stuff, she supposed.

They drank many mugs of tea and ate some plain biscuits that had been hiding at the back of a cupboard.

"We'll re-provision in a couple of days," commented Steig, when she produced the packet, dusting it off, and raising an eyebrow. "There's plenty of veg and we're good for bread tomorrow."

There it was again. "We". "Couple of days". He wasn't expecting her to disappear anytime soon. She felt herself going gooey inside. Good grief!

"You'll sleep in here tonight?" It was a question. "Bit damp to put up a tent."

"Yes, thank you, if that's alright?"

"Of course. Do you mind my nakedness? I don't really do bed clothes, pyjamas, stuff like that."

She felt herself colouring red from her toes to the roots of her hair. Turned her face away.

"Sorry," he said. "I didn't mean to embarrass you. I can stay clothed. It's no problem."

"It's not that. Oh. You're fine. Stay however you are comfortable. I'll ... Oh! If ... if you don't mind, I'll wear my pyjamas."

"Of course I don't mind."

In the end, Maisie stared at the wall whilst Steig stripped and got into bed. He turned the light down to a glimmer as she changed into her pyjamas, still facing the wall.

"No peeking."

"I wasn't."

She glanced over her shoulder at him as she pulled on her pyjama bottoms. He was grinning, staring at her with those deep blue eyes.

"Well, not much."

"Oh!"

Chapter 10

The next morning dawned bright and clear. The storm had spent itself in the night. After a breakfast of coffee and porridge oats heated through on the stove, Steig set about cleaning the driving harness. The leather was wet and stiff after the soaking of the previous day. He sat on the old wooden spindle-back chair in front of the vardo. The tack cleaning box, full of leather unguents, cloths and utensils, was open before him. Steig soon had lengths of brown leather harness, all unclipped and unbuckled, draped over his knees.

Maisie sat in the vardo's doorway. The morning lacked warmth. Her breath puffed into white vapour, and she heated her back by the Queenie stove. A gentle grey smoke tumbled from the chimney above the curve of the wagon's roof.

Beckett plumed clouds of steam into the air, munching grass and searching for the very last sweet fresh shoots in his patch. He looked up with a start, towards the ford and the stream, then spun and backed away, his ears flat on his neck, the chain clinking as it stretched out. He came to rest, backed into the far hedge, the collar hard against his ears, the rope and chain taut and straining.

"What's up, horse?" Steig stood, harness and the open pot of leather-dressing falling to the grass, forgotten. Maisie froze in her place, eyes darting between Beckett and Steig.

"Naiad. Bitey one. Don't like it."

"Well, that's charming, that is. I don't bite. Well, not much."

Steig turned towards the voice, a voice that was distinctly nasal; Maisie craned around the edge of the vardo to look.

The creature that walked out of the stream had that same duality of vision that Steig remembered from the meliad. If you squinted, you could see one and the other. Here, a young man with an unkept mane of sandy hair and a scraggly wisp of beard, a narrow brown face with a thin-lipped leer. His eyes were like the muddy depths of a hillside stream in spate. He dressed in ragged tan animal furs, patched and stitched with dark leather, and carried a spear longer than he was tall, tipped with a broad sharp-edged point made from white animal bone.

The other, that which Steig suspected was its true nature, was a creature of fluidity and motion, with ill-defined edges that did strange things to his vision. It shone deep blue, green and purple, shifting with iridescence like a jackdaw's wing; but the features were indistinct and ever changing. It exuded the essence of deep water, hard rain and something more intense. The suggestion of endless blue, the pulse and push and power that had tugged at Steig's feet when he waded the ford.

As the naiad walked towards the camp, Beckett gave a loud, deep, resonant snort, the sort horses reserve for things that are utterly terrifying.

"Please halt," asked Steig, holding up his hand, "and allow me to calm the horse, lest he flee."

"Oh, if you must." The naiad rolled his eyes, gesturing for Steig to attend to Beckett, then turning to regard Maisie. He leered, opening his mouth in a toothy smile. Steig took in the rows of sharp pointed teeth, similar to the wood spirit, but then jogged to Beckett, worried he would uproot the peg or snap the rope. Behind him, he heard the naiad speak.

"Well hello, Maisie Hanson. You're far from your home and your God, are you not?"

"Yes, I am far from home. As for my God, I think you'll find he's right here!" came Maisie's reply, delivered, Steig thought, in a far more even tone than he would have managed. "And I'll thank you for keeping your tongue civil."

"Ho, Steig, she's a feisty one, no? A fine fish to land; not so cold, eh?"

"Leave her be, naiad," he called over his shoulder, as he approached the horse. "Beckett, come on ..." He tugged at the rope, and the horse moved forward an inch, slacking the chain.

"Don't like him. Fur prickling. Scared."

"I know, but come now, hold hard. You're alright here?" He rubbed Beckett's face with the flat of his hand, long even strokes. Beckett snorted again, but didn't uproot his peg or break the rope. He remained motionless, at the limit of his range, ears still back, and his eyes rolling, showing their whites.

Steig turned to regard the naiad. He had now solidified in what Steig was coming to think of as the human form; you would be hard-pressed to say he wasn't human, but anyone meeting him would find him unsettling. As Steig was indeed finding him. He walked back towards the wagon, all the while his back-brain was sending messages of alarm and distress, suggesting immediate flight.

"What is it you want, river naiad?"

"River, eh? So grand! Oh, I bear a message, is all." Again, he leered at Maisie, some drool dribbling from between rows of sharp razor teeth and over those thin, bloodless lips.

"Let's have it, then."

The naiad let out an exaggerated sigh, and turned back to Steig, leaning on the spear, giving him his full attention.

"The message is thus: 'Opus es pro Khôra.'"

There was a pause as Steig waited for more. When none came, he asked, "Is that the whole message?"

"Aye." The naiad's gaze was supercilious.

"Who asked you to deliver this message?"

The naiad drew himself up and sneered at Steig. "Oh, asked, was I? Nay, I was told. Ordered. Like a servant." With that, he turned away and fractured in the air. As Steig watched, he became ethereal, slicing into a reflection of himself, as if seen in the ripples of the stream. Returning to the other form, Steig thought, fascinated.

As the naiad put its now ill-defined foot into the water of the ford, the whole dissolved into the idea, the essence, of the flow of the stream, and was gone.

Maisie had grabbed a pen from the holder on her journal the moment the ... the *thing* had spoken in Latin and scribbled it down. But in actuality, "Khôra needs you" was plain. She wrote the Latin phrase down anyway, so they had it as the naiad had uttered it. Then, after a moment's hesitation, she detailed the entire event as best she could in a few lines of text. Just in case. She already felt like she wouldn't believe her memory later.

Steig returned to Beckett and was coaxing him back from the far hedge. The horse had his ears down flat on his neck, showing what Maisie now recognised as worry or fear, but relaxed when Steig produced something from his pocket and offered it up. The horse nibbled whatever it was and then mugged Steig's pocket for more. Mints, Maisie thought, smiling.

"He'll be fine, so long as there are mints." Steig came back to the front of the vardo. "How are you?"

Maisie thought for a moment. How was she?

"I'm ... OK, considering what we just witnessed. I mean, we both saw it, right?"

"What did you see?"

"I saw a man with *far* too many pointy teeth, with clothes that appeared prehistoric, and a spear, who had something very odd about him. He definitely made my flesh crawl. And then I saw him ... dissolve into thin air, just as he touched the water. Like a reflection in a pool or a stream. What about you?"

"Yeah, the same. I could kind of see behind the man to this watery thing, like an afterimage, that faded out as he started talking to us."

"I didn't see that."

"No, it was as he was walking out of the stream. The meliad had the same look about her. That duality."

"Was the meliad dressed the same?"

"No, she was in a blue cloak, and her 'other'" – he made quotes in the air with his fingers, brow creased – "was an ancient, gnarled, green-brown thing, I suppose, like an old tree."

"So, we're talking actual spirits of place? Genii locorum?"

"It's kind of looking that way. Come on, let's get tatted down and tacked up. Find a hill."

"What?"

Steig gawped at her. "What, you *want* to stay here? Next to a stream that has an active, fairly unpleasant spirit in it? What if it returns and brings along Ginny Greenteeth and her grendylous?"

Maisie was intensely curious about whether these creatures were independent beings, or manifestations of a greater power. But she also assumed the naiad could come back at any moment, day or night, with his teeth and his spear. So ...

"You make a very good point," she said, nodding. "Yes, let's get shifted, away from the brook."

Between them, they tatted down the camp in a matter of minutes – the chairs, kitchen box, tack cleaning box; all were thrown into the wagon. Maisie helped with tacking Beckett up; she was working out where things went, but copied Steig. As he did one side, she would replicate the buckles and hooks of the breeching, trace, swingle, on the other. Since Steig had pulled the tack apart for cleaning, it all needed to be reattached. There was a lot of leather, and it was still stiff. The cleaning would have to wait.

"Are there more mints?"

"Hold still, horse. Maisie, like this, see, loop through the back." Steig demonstrated, attaching the end of the reins to the bit in Beckett's mouth.

"Got it."

"OK, we're all set, I think. One problem."

"What?" Fear prickled her nape.

"We need to go back that way." Steig pointed at the ford. "This road doesn't actually go anywhere, it just peters out after a mile or so."

"Oh. Well, it's only a couple of metres of water, right? We can get through that. Quickly?"

"Yep. I'll lead Beckett."

So, in a repeat of the pull-on, Steig led Beckett, whilst Maisie held the reins, seated on the ledge. The vardo made a wide circle on the grass, bumped down onto the road, and approached the edge of the rushing stream.

"Not going in there again." Beckett exhibited a stubbornness that Maisie was recognising, lurching the wagon to a halt, his hooves inches from the water.

Steig let go of the reins and waded into the ford, water again filling his boots. Maisie squeaked. What was he doing? She was in sole charge of Beckett and the vardo. Uncertainty welled in her chest, and she gripped the reins tighter.

"Beckett! Fancy a mint?" Steig called from the far side of the ford, waving a tubular packet in the air. The horse almost leapt forward, splashing through the water to get to the sweets. Steig, laughing, backed away until the wagon was through the water and Beckett had to lean into the collar to pull it up the far side. Steig gave him a mint and skipped up onto the shelf opposite Maisie.

"You could have warned me."

"You did fine. Here, shall I drive through the village, or would you like to?"

"Maybe I could drive later?" Her face flushed with excitement at the thought of driving the vardo. Steig glanced at her with an odd look in his eye and took the reins.

"Heddup, lad," he called, and Beckett took up the pace.

They rolled back the way they had come. Past the industrial units, past the rabbit-hutch housing estate, and past the whitewashed pub. At the junction, they turned right, south, down Main Street.

The character of the village changed. The houses were more substantial, built from cream or dark red-brown stone, some with thatched roofs, some of a grey slate.

"I always think this village is weird every time I come through here," Steig muttered. "It's mad. Some of these houses are huge. I mean, who lives in a place like that?" He gestured at a building on the right, set back from the road. It had a broad cream gravel driveway snaking up between manicured lawns, ending at an imposing front door set into the expansive light stone facade.

"Looks like a vicarage."

"Pfff. Church has all the money, then."

Maisie frowned at him. "They don't, anymore. I grew up in a place like that. I can tell you; they are draughty, cold, lonely places to live in, and the plumbing doesn't work."

They rolled on, Beckett walking with a steady gait, past a small village green, and the war memorial cross. Past a stone church, set back in a tidy, manicured graveyard, yew trees lining the approach. And past the village primary school, all blue railings and modern low-rise classroom units.

On the ironstone wall around the graveyard there was a black-and-white sign which stated "Museum". It had an arrow pointing up towards the school.

"Gosh, look." Maisie waved at the sign. "Do you think they know about Devana?"

"Worth a try, and I need to change my shoes, anyway. They are disgustingly squelchy."

The museum turned out to be in a sizeable blue-green corrugated tin shed at the back of a grand stone house, sandwiched between the church and the school. Despite the contrast with the stone buildings, it looked interesting and modern. As they pulled into the gravel car park, they could see an entire class full of children straining at the windows opposite, watching them. Maisie waved, smiling. Some waved back.

"You go on in and see what you can find out. I'll get my feet dried off and sort Beckett out," said Steig.

Maisie slipped through the white painted door, her eyes taking a moment to adjust. The room beyond was serene, reminiscent of a church. Its bare wooden floors showed a high sheen, and smelt of polish. The blue-grey-green colour scheme continued in the architrave and ceiling joists. The airy space contained display cases arranged tastefully, filled with artefacts and information panels.

An elderly lady with white hair and a pink cardigan was sitting in a chair, reading a book – it was a murder mystery novel – and glanced up at Maisie over half-moon glasses.

Maisie saw her eyes sweep over her, taking in the disarrayed hair, the dirty dress, the unlaced boots, covered in mud. Saw the lady's mouth turn down at the edges and a frown crease her forehead.

"I'm so sorry," Maisie started, breezily, smiling her best sunny smile. "It's been quite the morning. I know I look a state. I was camping, you see, and got caught in yesterday's storm!"

The lady's face softened.

"Oh, you poor thing. It was a terrible downpour."

"It was. But we're all well, so that's alright." Well, apart from the riddle, the river naiad, the meliad, and the talking horse. "I was after some local knowledge, actually. If it's not too much bother?"

The lady inclined her head. "Of course. What would you like to know?"

"We have been given a riddle to solve. A silly thing, I am sure, but we have been asked to find the place where the Wayland and Devana cross? It's sort of an orienteering thing."

"Like a team-building exercise?"

"Something like that."

"Well. Wayland is easy. That's the river. We're right on the edge of the Wayland valley, to the south of here. Devana ... that sounds familiar. A Roman road, I think?" She put down her book, having folded over the corner to keep her page, Maisie noticed. Terrible habits, some people had. But best not to judge, not just yet. "Now then ..." She walked with slow, careful steps to a map that took up a fair proportion of one wall. It was large scale, and showed Alcatone in the centre, with all the land around, for twenty miles or more in each direction. "Look here, young lady ..." She pointed to the map with one thin, bony finger.

Under the lady's arthritic digit was a fine dotted line, arrow straight, with the inscription "ROMAN ROAD (course of)" written alongside. "That is Via Devana, a Roman road that runs from Deva in the west to Camulodunum in the east. Deva, we know now as Cestre, and Camulodunum is Colecestra. Of course, there's not much left of the road these days. But you can find traces here and there. Look, here, at Metorne, it crosses the Wayland." She pointed out the next village along the valley, and Maisie saw that the dotted line of the Via Devana did indeed bisect the convoluted folds of the Wayland River.

"Bingo! Thank you! That, I think, is just the clue we need!"

"Oh, it's a pleasure to be able to help. I do hope the weather holds for you."

Maisie took her leave of the old lady and returned to the vardo. Rounding the side of the building, she stopped in astonishment. An entire class of seven-year-olds surrounded the wagon. They were asking questions of Steig and taking turns to pat the patient horse on the nose. Steig was standing, looking very uncomfortable, next to Beckett, who was wearing a head collar over his bridle, tethered to a drainpipe. The form teacher, a no-nonsense woman in her forties with brown hair, stood nearby with a smile on her lips.

Maisie eased through the diminutive throng to Steig. "I have found the place where Devana crosses Wayland," she murmured in a conspiratorial whisper. Steig visibly brightened.

"Well, I got my spare shoes on." He indicated a pair of very tatty trainers. "So let's go!"

Maisie turned to the children. "Well, everyone, I do hope you have enjoyed visiting with us, but now we must be on our way!" The form teacher smiled, started shepherding the children back towards the school gate.

Maisie rummaged in the cupboard inside the door, where she had seen the same large-scale map that the museum had on their wall. She folded it out and showed Steig the Roman road, the river and the crossing point at Metorne.

"Oh, OK. I think I know roughly where that is. It's a bit south of my usual stomping ground. We can park up tonight on Craweho Hill. It overlooks the valley." He tapped the map only a couple of miles away from Alcatone.

The sun was well on the way to sinking to the horizon by the time they pulled on at Craweho Hill. It cast a soft, golden hue over the landscape. Craweho was a broad, gentle, rounded hill, right on the edge of the vast swathe of the Wayland Valley. The valley spread out before them to the south, two miles across, and stretched away east and west, to the distant horizons. Its floor was a flat patchwork quilt of fields, bounded by hawthorn hedges and small strips of woodland.

The river itself was only visible by the meandering line of trees and hedges, the water hidden by the density of the growth.

Maisie helped with the pull-on and set-up of camp. It was, she realised, the third time she had helped with this, and already it felt natural, the rhythm of the day, like doing the washing up or setting the table for dinner. She helped untack Beckett and peg him out, and Steig showed her how to check if the horse was sweating enough to need a rug, to stop him getting a chill. The run from Alcatone had been easy and slow, so no, he didn't need coddling.

Collecting firewood held a frisson of excitement at the thought she might meet a meliad or dryad.

Of course, she was especially careful to ask and thank them for the wood when collecting the fallen branches. She didn't meet a genius loci, a spirit of place.

"We need to have a chat about where all this is leading," commented Steig, as she unloaded her armful of firewood by the fire.

"All what?" She could feel herself reddening and cursed her open mind. Steig smiled at her again, but with that odd quirk in his eyes. Simultaneously, laughter and sadness appeared to touch his face.

"You know. This so-called quest that actors unknown have instigated around us."

"Oh, yes. That."

"So. We know one certain thing: the genii locorum, or someone or something that has power over them, want us to go to this point where the Roman road and the river cross."

"Yes, that seems plain."

"We'll gloss over the whole 'spirits of place exist, and we can see them' part, for now, or I think my head will explode."

"Agreed."

"So, we know that, but why? Why there? Why us?"

"I don't know."

"Not a clue? Any news from Him upstairs?"

Maisie stared at the ground. She was, it was clear to her, having a crisis of faith.

"I ... I don't know. Please don't ask me about God. I just don't know."

"OK, well ... I guess the other question is, do we go on to the crossing point tomorrow, or avoid it at all costs? Or do we go on foot, just walk down there, check it out? Or ride Beckett? What is it that makes it so important we go there? And what is Khôra?"

"My guess? And this is only a guess. We'll never know anything until we go there. So, we can go, or not, depending on whether we want our curiosity sated."

"You know what curiosity did to the cat, right?" Steig's eyes were sober as she tried to read his face.

"Oh, come on. We're in the middle of nowhere. I can't see a single snake or brigand for miles! It's not like the countryside is actively dangerous." As she said this, she realised her statement might not, in the strictest sense, be true.

"Very well then, we'll head over there tomorrow."

Maisie averted her gaze as she organised her thoughts for the next thing she wanted to say. It was so difficult. But ...

"I'm going to sleep in the tent tonight." There, she had said it. "It's lovely, sleeping in the vardo" – lovely sleeping in your arms, she wanted to say – "but you need your space, and I have a tent, and ... and you didn't want me to come along anyway, so I don't want to be in the way. And I'm not soaking wet today!" She gestured at her dry clothes. Steig looked at her again with that oddness of gaze. But he smiled, nodded once, and didn't say anything else, just set about dinner, cutting vegetables.

"We should try for Nail Soup one day. It's usually a success, though you need a busier path than this one." He pointed with the kitchen knife at the lonely stile, the long straight green lane.

"Nail soup?"

"It's a folktale, as well as a meal. I'll tell it you, sometime."

"So much I don't know about you, Mr Sturluson."

"Like what?"

"Oh, you know, stuff ..."

She felt embarrassed. Again.

Chapter 11

The road from Craweho to the Wayland–Devana confluence took them through the village of Metorne. They rumbled over a small brick bridge spanning a brook in the centre of the village. Maisie thought of the naiad, almost crossed herself, but held back.

"We should stop here and get provisions." She pointed at a blue-fronted shop set into the yellow-brown stone that seemed to be the ubiquitous building material in use, if it wasn't modern brick. The shop doubled as a post office and had "Village Stores" sign-written in white along the frontage.

"OK. I guess we could get some bits and bobs. What would you like?"

"Coffee. Bacon. Fresh bread. I'd kill for a croissant. Real milk, too."

Steig smiled. "OK. Though milk won't keep. Hoo now, Beckett." He put gentle tension on the reins, and the horse came to a standstill.

"Don't forget the mints. I love mints," Beckett muttered under his breath.

Maisie jumped down, slipped the head collar on over his bridle and tied him to the drainpipe next to the shop frontage. "We won't forget the mints. But you must be patient, and wait here, and not wander off."

Beckett regarded her with deep liquid brown eyes, from under his raggedy dreadlocked mane, and flicked his ears. Which Maisie thought was Beckett for, "Of course I'll be well behaved. What do you think?"

The route out of Metorne village saw the architecture change. They left the ancient village centre, with its stone walls and roofs made of thatch and slate. Passed through the outskirts with the ubiquitous rabbit-hutch new builds, then larger, brick-built semi-detached houses standing opposite open countryside. Finally, they were in the sweep of green again, leaving behind the cars and houses and …

"No signal! Again! How is that possible?" Maisie wailed, waving her mobile phone in the air in frustration.

"You should just forget about your phone. Live in the moment. Experience things, listen with all your senses, be present."

She sent Steig a suspicious glare. "All very well for you to say, Mister Zen Buddhist. I suppose you don't even own a phone?"

"What would I charge it up with if I did? Plug it into the ground, use 'earth energy'?" He grinned.

She heaved a theatrical sigh. "Of course, as usual, you're right. I don't need to be on my phone. I'll … look at the paper map, then. So quaint."

"If we were travelling rapidly enough to require super-fast navigation devices, we'd be travelling too fast. I mean, I have a sextant and a wind-up fob watch. What more does a navigator require?"

She regarded him with a critical eye. Was he joking, or did he really have those items? She examined the map. "The turning should be along here on the right in about a mile."

Steig settled back into the curve of the vardo, waved the whip in the air, clicked his tongue. Beckett flicked his ears, and stepped up the pace into a fast trot, his shoes striking a ringing tone. He held his head up, his ears pricked, ready for adventure.

The turning, when it came, was anticlimactic. A tiny lane on the right, little more than a bridleway, crowded in with nettles, thistles, the hedges pushing in, unkempt. Steig peered in at it, a frown creasing his brow.

"If we get stuck in that, it will be a challenge. Are you OK to hold him a minute while I have a gander?"

"Of course." Again, she jumped down with the head collar. Steig clipped the reins onto their hook on the saddle.

"You be good. We're on a road here," he said to Beckett. "Just stand still and behave for Maisie, OK?"

The horse flicked his ears to say, "Yeah, yeah, whatever."

"All OK?" Steig asked Maisie.

"Yes!" She flashed a bright smile in return. That smile was lovely. But ... No. Enough. Get back to the job in hand. He grabbed a branch from the hedge and used it to beat a path through the nettles. The overgrown track was not as bad as it first appeared, opening up almost immediately into a reasonable path – rutted in places, but perfectly passable. He walked along for about a hundred metres. The track opened out to a wide, level patch of grass next to a small farm bridge. The bridge, made from railway sleepers and girders, stretched over the river. A pull-up that couldn't have been more idyllic. He made his way back to the road. Beckett and Maisie were in deep conversation.

"Still OK?"

"Yes, we were just discussing theology."

"Theology?"

"Yes, the theory and study of the nature of God and religious beliefs."

"I know what theology is. What does Beckett think?"

"He has a horse-centric viewpoint."

"Yes, I do," said Beckett.

The vardo squeezed into the gap between the hedges; the hawthorn scraping down each side of the tarpaulin sounding preternaturally loud. Steig led Beckett, and Maisie clung to the edge of the bow-top as they wobbled and lurched along the uneven track. Once in the clearing by the river, surrounded by trees and hedges, it felt as if they had entered another realm. No sound of traffic reached from the road. The sun broke through the low cloud and warmed their faces. The river, down a steep bank where it cut into the valley floor, flowed serenely on towards the distant sea, passing under the bridge, and curving away in a series of gentle sweeping bends.

Maisie once again marvelled at the rhythm of life on the road, as she helped untack Beckett and peg him out. She went to collect firewood, checking in with the local dryad. Beckett said he could feel its presence. She didn't see it. But she asked its permission and thanked it, as she had done with the previous woodland.

Another thing she was realising was that you could pull on to these tiny pocket handkerchiefs of land and no one seemed to notice. And if they noticed, they didn't mind or say anything.

"How does it work then, if you pull on somewhere and the locals don't like you?"

"Well, I find if I'm well out of the villages and off the busy roads, you don't get any bother."

"You've never had any trouble?"

"Well, yes, there's always occasions when things don't go to plan. But people see the vardo and get all misty-eyed about Olde Breotonlond. Or something. Daft, really."

"What about landowners?"

"I usually get along OK with them. If you're travelling a couple of miles a day, the locals all get to know you, see you don't leave a mess. That helps a lot."

"Oh, I see, because you're so slow, people have time to realise you're OK before you arrive?"

"Er, I suppose. I don't really give it much thought. If someone really doesn't want me on their land, I'll probably move. The police hardly ever get involved, which, to be honest, suits me down to the ground.

In my experience, the presence of the police makes any situation more dismal."

Steig set the big cooking pan over the fire and filled it with water, dropping in the chicken thighs they had bought at the village shop. He added onion, carrot, wild garlic and celery, some herbs, salt and pepper. Soon the broth was bubbling away, and the meat was falling from the bone. He fished the bones out and threw them in the fire where they charcoaled and flashed to flame. Then he shook out matzo-meal onto a wooden board, added flour, and broke in an egg. He poured in a touch of cooking oil, and a spoonful of the broth, then mixed the whole with his hands until he had small round balls of dough, which he dropped into the pot.

He pulled the pot off the heat, leaving it in the embers at the side of the fire, and put the lid on. Then noticed Maisie watching him, fascinated.

"What?"

"You made that seem easy. Were they dumplings going in?"

"We got so much stuff at the shop – too much, really. I needed to cook it up or it will go off. No fridge, see?"

"Yes, sorry, I got a bit carried away."

"Anyway, it's a treat, chicken soup with kneidlach."

"Knaydlatch?"

"Jewish dumplings. Give it ten minutes, then we can have a bowl."

After dinner, Steig wandered over to Beckett and gave him a groom, sweeping the dried sweat and scurf out of his fur where the harness had worked up a lather. The horse leant into the brush with appreciation.

"Oh yes. There. Harder. That's nice."

"You're so silly, Beckett," exclaimed Maisie, walking up to the pair of them.

"No, I'm a horse."

"Yes, you are that. So, tell me, horse. How does the river feel? Any bitey things?"

Beckett took a second to think before replying.

"Not ... bitey. Old. Sleeping. And far away."

Maisie visibly relaxed at this news.

"So, a river spirit, but ancient, somnolent, and somewhere else."

"Yes, what I said," agreed the horse.

She turned to Steig. "I think I'll put my tent up again tonight, see how I get on. If that's OK?"

"Yes, of course. Why would it not be OK?"

Maisie gave him an exasperated glance, her lips pursed, but didn't reply.

The borrowed tent was spacious, designed, she guessed, for four boy scouts or guides. Her sleeping bag, at least, was the right size for her. For one person. She arranged herself at the back of the tent, the canvas close over her head as it sloped down, reminiscent of the vardo roof. She enjoyed sleeping in the vardo. Really enjoyed it. Was that because she liked to be close to Steig? Or because of the comfort? Or the security? A combination, she supposed. She mused on these thoughts, trying her hardest to not muse on Steig himself.

She woke with a start at … what? Two o'clock in the morning, the luminous hands on her wristwatch announced. Cold. Uncomfortable on this thin ground mat. It was, as her grandmother used to say, as dark as the inside of a black cat. She listened – not a sound outside, no owl, no Beckett, no sound of Steig's gentle breathing in her right ear … Urgh. Get back to sleep, woman. She closed her eyes …

The dream came again. Beyond the smashed door frame, she's reaching for the key, that curious geometric bronze key. A familiar shape. She can't quite reach it. It glows with an inner blue light. She stretches out her hands, but it's too far. Something is pulling at her, holding her back. She struggles against invisible bonds, slaps away hands, claws, that hold her. She needs to get rid of her clothes; they are getting in the way. She tugs them off, throws them down, reaches again, teetering, tiptoes, taller, further, stretching … Then she's flying, her stomach fluttering, the key looming closer.

CHAPTER 12

Hitting the surface of the river hurt her more than she could have imagined. It slapped her side, and she shrieked, once. She ducked under, then came back up winded, with a mouthful of frigid water. It was night dark, the river deep and cold. Her breath caught in her throat, gasping, gulping. Staying afloat became her sole focus. Too deep to touch the bottom. Then that which she could not understand drew her ever onwards. She kicked with bare legs, swam hard with the current. It was a compulsion, a necessity, a need. She couldn't think, couldn't understand, only feel. Felt drawn to this point. She upended herself, legs flailing as her ears and nose filled with freezing water, eyes open to blackness. She descended beneath the swirling dark waters.

The pressure changed in her ears, though she could see nothing. It was pitch-black and colder than thought, deathly cold, like a knife. She reached out with her hands, felt mud, rock, weed. She was at the bottom of the river, the current dragging her.

Her hand brushed something hard, electric. She grabbed for it, whatever it was. Small. Heavy. Angular. She held fast. It was trapped in weed, in dense mud.

Her chest spasmed, pain spreading. She couldn't let go of the thing. Her anchor. She had to breathe! She couldn't. Blackness, darkness, all around her, freezing. She was going to die, this night, in this river, and she didn't understand why. Her thoughts faltered as she breathed in the muddy water. Consciousness fled from her like crows before a storm.

Steig woke with a start, from a dark dream of drowning and death, the image of Maisie, pale and unmoving, naked and blue on a shoreline, etched in his vision. He opened his eyes to the dark of night. A still, moonless night, inside the wagon, all calm. What woke him? There! A splash from the river. Was that a shout? A gasp? More splashing?

Fearing a naiad attack, or worse, he threw back the quilt and stumbled to the door. Looked out through the open top half. The night was still, quiet. The eastern sky was lightening almost imperceptibly. Dawn was coming but was some way off yet. Beckett was awake, looking towards the river, but unmoving.

He listened again. Splashes from the river. Another gasp or cry. Softer. He jumped the steps, navigated the detritus of the camp hearth by the predawn glow, ran to the bank. The river stretched away, dark and foreboding, swirling with currents. There! A head, an arm, splashing. Then they submerged, a pair of legs upended, leaving only ripples. Maisie? Swimming?

"Maisie!" he shouted.

No answer from her tent. No time, if it was her. And if not? What if it was a trick? No time.

He dived, aiming for the point where he last saw the legs, almost at the next curve of the banks. The water was terrifyingly cold, halting his breath in his chest. He rallied, plunging onward, a strong front crawl to reach the spot, gasping air at every other stroke. Then he stopped, treading water, and the current carried him. His foot brushed against something. Something soft. He dived without thought, reaching, fumbling in the dark, searching. Snagged that soft thing – a leg, an ankle, foot upwards, not moving. He grasped with both hands, heaved against the water, felt movement and they floated free with the current. He worked his way along the leg to the torso, grabbed around the waist, kicked for what he hoped was the surface, his chest burning with the desire to breathe.

They broke the surface, a crescendo of splashing, his arm around her waist. Maisie! He held her with one arm under her chin, her neck arched back. He struggled, breathing deep, ragged breaths, swimming on his back, blowing water from his face, heading for the nearest shore. Her limp, lifeless body lay on his, cold, unmoving. The current carried them onto a beach of shingle and mud.

"Maisie!" No response. Her face was pale blue in the weak, dim light, hair plastered to her cheek, eyes closed. He felt for a pulse. She was holding a ball of mud in both hands, heavy, weed-wrapped, disgusting. She had clamped her hands into it over her groin. He found a pulse, faint, at her wrist.

He pushed on her chest, hands overlapping on her sternum; she vomited out river mud. He forced his thumb and forefinger into the corner of her mouth and cleared the airway of weed and slime. Another push on her chest. Another ejection of muddy water and mucus from her mouth. Another heave. Still no breath.

He held her nose and put his lips to hers. Not how he had hoped it would happen. Had he hoped? No time for that. Blew hard, filled her lungs, saw her chest rise, saw her chest fall. Repeat three times? Five? He couldn't remember which it was supposed to be.

He checked her pulse again. What the hell was that ball of mud? No time. Her pulse was weak but there. Breathing? He held his cheek near hers. No breath.

"Maisie! Come on! Fuck's sake! Breathe!"

Another five breaths, then. One. Rise, fall. Two. Rise, fall. Three ...

She coughed, and vomited river water, mud and snot, up and into his mouth, just as he was about to give her a third breath.

He spat it away. She coughed again, taking deep, tearing, ripping lungfuls of air. He collapsed next to her, in the soft gravel and shingle. They were both covered in river mud, slime and her snot. He laughed, whilst also gasping for his own breath. The aching cold was bone deep.

Now Maisie at least was breathing, but unconscious, naked and soaking wet. Steig couldn't lift her and carry her back to the wagon. He wasn't going back into the river, even if they could struggle against the current and the cold. The land route was up the steep shingle bankside, a near vertical climb, and over a barbed wire fence, then a hundred metres of field. He left her in the recovery position on the beach and ran back to the vardo, fetching as many clothes as he could carry. Grabbing a towel and blanket, matches and paraffin, he dashed back to Maisie. She was shivering, terrible tremors and shakes running through her body. Her skin was blue as she lay on her side, with her hands still clutching the ball of mud. He dried her by parts, wrapping her in the blanket as he went. Then got himself dressed and set about building a fire on the riverbank. The river had deposited plenty of wood on this curve over the years, and most of it was dry from higher up, so it burnt fiercely. After a few minutes, the heat was intense enough that Steig shifted Maisie back from it. The blanket was steaming, and her shivering had stopped.

"Maisie. Wake up."

Her eyes snapped open. She let out a whimper and shook, spasming, her face a mask of abject terror. Steig knelt and hugged her to him. She sat up to move into his embrace, then looked with confusion at her hands, holding a ball of river weeds and mud.

"It's OK, Maisie. You're safe. Here, let go of the ball."

"It's not a ball. It's ... I don't know what it is."

"Even so. You need to get some clothes on, and I can't dress you if you're holding it."

She nodded, and relaxed her grip on the ball, pulling her fingers from small holes in the sides of it. Steig busied himself with her hands and fingers, drying them vigorously with a towel, then bundling her into one of his tattersall shirts and an old thick cable-knit jumper that smelt of Beckett and wood smoke.

"I ... I drowned, didn't I?"

"No. Maybe. I don't know. I pulled you from the river by your feet."

"I owe you my life, don't I?"

"Don't be silly. Anyone would have done that."

"No, they wouldn't. In the dark, in the cold. Only you."

"Fagh."

Once Maisie had warmed through and recovered her strength and dignity, Steig assisted her up the bank of shingle, and over the barbed wire fence. She insisted on bringing the thing, balled in river weed and mud as it was, with them; Steig wrapped it in the towel. The dawn was breaking around them, birds singing, as they walked back into camp. Beckett was snoozing, one hind hoof resting.

Steig poked at the campfire and got the kettle on, while Maisie changed out of his jumper and shirt into her own clothes. She came and sat by the fire, warming herself against the chill. A shiver ran down his spine; his bones still ached from the dunking, and he too was glad of the fire's warmth.

He didn't want to push her for answers, but he was burning with curiosity as to the circumstances that led her to be drowning, trying to retrieve the weird ball. And it was a weird ball. He had unwrapped it from the towel and started pulling the weeds from it. Underneath, there was an angular metallic ... thing. Twelve sides. Just smaller than his fist. Each side had a hole in it and it had knobbles at the vertices. What its purpose was, he could not fathom.

"Any idea what it might be?" he asked, his tone casual, as he poured hot water into a pair of mugs.

She glanced at the metallic thing. "No idea. A relic? Something religious? When I found it, I couldn't let go. I didn't *want* to let go. Even though I knew it would kill me, that I would drown. Complete mind control. I don't know if it's good or ... or evil." She became thoughtful, her eyes taking on a defocused cast for a second. "I've seen it before."

"What? This thing?" He gestured at the bronze ball. "Where?"

"You'll laugh. Well, maybe you won't. I had a recurring dream in Coventreu. Before I went to the priory. In the dream, I was fighting, smashing a door, to get to ... to one of them." She took another furtive glance at the bronze object, as if beholding it all at once would cause it to disappear. A tremor shook her body.

"I'm not laughing," Steig said, his voice soft. They sat in contemplative silence for a minute. "So, how did you ..." He waved his hand in the air, trying to find the words. "How did you ... come to be in the river? How did you find it? Know where to look? You must have dived to it, in the dark."

Maisie screwed her face up, on the verge of tears or despair, and wailed, "I don't know!" She took a deep, ragged breath, and in a more even tone, said, "Sorry. I don't know. And that scares me. I was asleep. In bed. In my sleeping bag, at least. In the tent. Weird dreams. Next thing I know, I'm jumping, naked, into the river. And there's this urge to get this ... thing. I sound crazy."

"No, you don't." Steig sipped his tea. "Well, no crazier than everything else that has happened in the last few days." He smiled. "Hey, we got bacon, right? I'll fix breakfast."

He cooked up bacon, eggs, fried bread, mushrooms, tomatoes, all in one large cast-iron frying pan. Served it up to Maisie on a chipped white china plate and added a mug of fresh coffee.

"Here, this will set you right for the day."

"Thank you."

Her smile was like a sunbeam, and something shifted in his heart. He felt it and, he realised, he didn't mind. He'd see where it went. No hurry.

He served up his own breakfast, along with his own mug of coffee, and settled on his chair by the fire.

As they ate in silence, barring the occasional sigh of enjoyment from Maisie as she mopped up her egg with the bread, Steig watched the weather. The morning had dawned misty, and oh, so cold. Now, though, the sky was clear, and the air was heating from the sun's radiance. He knew enough of physics to realise, therefore, that the fog that was coalescing around them and their camp was something other than natural.

He put the kettle back on to heat, even though they both had full mugs of drink. He considered cooking some more food as well, but held off. He'd been mistaken before.

As the mist shrouded the orb of the sun above them and dropped them into a chill greyness, Maisie shifted her weight, glancing around. Ah. She had noticed.

"Steig?"

"It's OK. I think I know who's coming." Well, he thought to himself, all the other faery tales are coming along. Might as well expect this one as well ...

Maisie let out a brief squeak of alarm, wide-eyed as an elderly woman in a green cloak, white hair cascading out of her hood, leaning on a long carved wooden walking staff, materialised next to the yog. Steig stood and bowed to the woman with care and respect. She stood watching, her lip quirking upwards, her deep blue-grey eyes twinkling with amusement.

"Kushti divvus, Bobe Elka. Welcome to our yog. How may I be of service?"

The woman nodded, a curt, sharp movement in response.

"Sturluson. Kushti divvus. We have much to discuss."

She said this in a formal manner, and he could detect the strain it took, and heard a hint of Lincoliscire underneath.

"Please, be seated." He offered her his chair. "Tea?"

"Aye, tea would be grand. Thank you."

As she spoke, her accent broadened. Without a doubt, Steig thought, Lincoliscire. She took the chair and seated herself at the fireside. As she sat, she muttered some words in what Steig recognised as Old High Romani, waving her staff like an overlarge wand. The mist dissipated with unnatural rapidity, the sun once again warming their faces. Steig glanced at Maisie, who was watching everything with eyes like saucers. But she was also exhibiting a reasonable level of control and steadfastness. He set about the kettle, dunked a teabag in a mug, added two heaped teaspoons of sugar and a slice of lemon. He passed it to Bobe Elka, who took it with solemnity and a bow of thanks.

"Maisie, this is Bobe Elka. Bobe Elka is sort of the Fairy Godmother for travelling folk."

Maisie's mouth opened, but she thought better of uttering anything, and closed it again.

"Well now. That's an interestin' take on me place in life. I'll remember that. Hah! I like that. Fairy Godmother."

She cackled, a long high-pitched sound, uncomfortably reminiscent, Steig thought, of fingernails scraping down a blackboard.

"Now then, we must talk. First off, I'm sorry for 'aving dragged you all across the scires by way of me machinations, like."

"The naiad?" asked Maisie.

"Oh aye, lass. Alcatone Brook naiad's a nasty bit of work, I 'ad to threaten 'im." Again, the cackle.

"And the meliad, at Crackbottle Spinney?"

"Aye, she owed me a favour."

Maisie's face darkened. "And the weird dreams in Coventreu?"

Bobe Elka had the grace to look embarrassed. "Aye. Sorry."

"So, last night? Did you try to kill me by drowning?" Maisie's voice rose in pitch and volume.

"Eh? Ooh, nay, that weren't mine, lass, nay. I was hoping you'd find the clavis, right enough, but didn't expect you to jump in the river stark nongo in the middle of the night, did I?"

"So, if it wasn't you, who, or what, was it?" asked Steig, his tone flat.

"Buggered if I know! I'm not all-seein', y'know!"

The cackle was wearing on Steig. He stared into the fire for a few seconds, collecting himself. Looked up at her. "Was it you that … caused my problems at the farm? The fire? Little push to see me on the way?"

Bobe Elka stared straight back at him, her face sombre.

"Nay, lad," she said in a voice soft with compassion. "That weren't nowt to do with me. And I'm right sorry it 'appened, like. I caught up with you at Stirwood." She took a breath, the twinkle returning to her eyes. "Still, you got the clavis. That's the important bit. I can turn the lock and we can all go to Khôra together."

She finished this with a flourish of the mug, spilling some tea into the embers, where it spat and hissed. Steig sat down next to Maisie and put an arm around her shoulders in what he hoped was a supportive manner. She leant into his side. He could feel her trembling.

"Khôra. Opus es pro Khôra. Tell me about Khôra," he said.

"It's right there. Look, far side of the bridge!" She pointed with her staff at the sturdy farm bridge over the river. It was a simple structure, and the grassy track ran over it, leading to a pair of fields, one planted with winter barley, showing green over the rusty brown of the soil. The other was pasture. Ash and hawthorn grew all around the edges. He couldn't see anything unusual in the bridge, or the fields, or the track. He shrugged.

"It's a veritable cornucopia in there, lad. You know what cornucopia is, aye?"

"It's a magical goat's horn that overflows with fruit, grain, nuts, anything you need," offered Maisie, pursing her lips.

"Aye, that's the one! Fruit trees allus in fruit all season long. Food grows everywhere, year round. Weather's allus warm, like."

"Who lives there? What sort of place is it, politically?" Steig asked.

"Oho, so many questions. Let's see. Gatekeepers, them as live there. Sorta like elves, I s'pose you'd say. And there's a bunch of other peoples, an' all. Dryads and suchlike. It's peaceful, never seen no chingaro, no arguments, like."

"Why are we needed there?"

"Don't know. It was a message I got in a dream. Dream's the only way out sometimes. You're needed though, mark my words. Though I've not been back in ..." She lost herself in thought for a few seconds. "Not been back for, well, ten years, I suppose. Misplaced the clavis, see?" She waved her staff at the odd metallic knobbly ball. "They made this bleedin' bridge and dislodged it into Wayland, and she's bleedin' sleepin', somewhere down Spallinge way, lazy cow. No use to any bugger down there. And I thought to me sen, what I need is a strappin' mush what can assist, like. Only nowadays there ain't many as can *see*, if y'know what I mean. So, I chose you, by way of you *seein'*, an all." She waved her hand at Steig.

"What is the ... clavis?" asked Maisie. "I mean, that's Latin for key, plain enough."

"There you go then, dear. No flies on you. It's a key for a gateway to Khôra. You put it in the lock, turn it, like, and there you are. Them gatekeepers call 'em dodecaclavis by dint of havin' twelve sides."

"How does it work?" asked Steig.

"Dunno. You just turn it, like, and it opens the gateway. No idea *how* it works. Something they druids or Heracles or ... whatshisname ... Hephaestus, come up with. One of them lot. Probably."

She stopped talking, closed her eyes for a moment. Steig realised he could see her edges, a bit like the meliad. She was so ancient, bits of her were out of focus on this plane. She had an air of terrible age and deep fatigue.

"Do you need to rest, Bobe?"

"Aye, I do, lad. I've travelled far today, by yog, it fair takes it out of me."

She rubbed at her forehead, pushing back the hood of her cloak. A faded, circular birthmark peeked from her hairline.

"Please, rest on the bed in the vardo. We'll tat down and we can be on the way this afternoon."

Bobe Elka nodded once, then heaved herself upright, resting her weight on the staff, and hobbled to the vardo steps. She pulled herself up and disappeared inside. The door shut with a thud.

"Are you insane?" Maisie stage-whispered, anger and worry tingeing her voice, eyes like saucers, her grimace showing teeth.

"No. I thought it would buy us some time to discuss our next move without her listening. Come on, over here on the riverbank, by Beckett. She won't be able to hear us. Probably."

Grumbling, Maisie stood up, and walked with a slight limp to the riverbank where the flow of the water had hollowed a natural beach. Her ankle and calf had finger-shaped bruises on them from Steig rescuing her. Her body ached from swimming – well, drowning – and the cold still permeated her bones. Her ribcage was incredibly tender from, she guessed, resuscitation. She had bruises on her lips and nose, too. And her brain was ... well, it was a whirlwind of uncertainty. She shuddered at the sight of the water, swirling and dark. It would be a long time before she could bring herself to go swimming again, even in a bathing pool, let alone a river.

Beckett ambled over at the limit of his tether. Maisie leant on one side, and Steig on the other. They both scratched and groomed him with their hands, and Beckett twisted his lips almost inside out with the overload of pleasure. The horse's skin and fur were warm and wonderfully greasy to the touch. Maisie took delight in the layer of grey, greasy horse-scurf on her fingertips. It felt real, elemental, vital.

"So. Khôra. Over there." Steig nodded at the bridge.

"Magical kingdom full of elves and faeries, or a field next to the river Wayland." Maisie's eyes danced with some of their old mischief.

"Simple question. Do you want to find out which? Or do we refuse and run screaming for the hills?"

Maisie considered the options. On the one hand, she had her life. Trainee accountant. Empty, cold rabbit-hutch house full of dusty books. A godhead that wasn't answering her calls. On the other hand, a chance to see a magical kingdom, mythical creatures, real adventure. Really real adventure, not stuff she would just read in books. And, of course, she'd be with Steig. If she went back to her rabbit hutch, that would be the end of that. He would continue "running away", whatever that meant, and she would be all alone again.

"If we go over there" – she nodded her head at the bridge – "how long will we be gone?"

"No idea. If it's just a field and all this is some sort of an elaborate joke by the Travellers' Fairy Godmother, then we'll not be gone long. And having met her, that isn't beyond the realm of possibility. But conversely, it might be a while. Weeks? Months? Forever? It is, as they say, a known unknown."

"Forever?"

"I don't know how this works. But Bobe Elka has said the same – she doesn't know how it works. And she's the Fairy Godmother. So basically, we're all screwed. Potentially. It might be just a simple thing to come back any time we want."

"A gamble," rumbled Beckett.

"Quite. What about you, horse? You been following this?"

"Not really. I was eating. This new place ... do they have mints?"

"Yes, lad, they have mints. And apples, by all accounts."

"Oh, well, I'm in, then."

Maisie took a deep breath.

"I've made my decision. I'm in, too."

Steig appeared ... pleased, Maisie thought.

"Well," he said, "I wanted to run away. And this seems to tick all the boxes. So, I'm in, as well."

Bobe Elka reappeared at the top of the vardo steps as Steig cooked lunch – piles of bacon and sausages. He was using the last of the perishables, so the cook-up was sumptuous.

"Summat smells grand!" Bobe Elka declared, hobbling down the steps.

They ate their meal on the riverbank, watching the swirl and swift of the currents. Early swallows skimmed the surface, picking off flies and dazzling the three of them with their aerial abilities.

After lunch, Steig and Maisie set about finishing tatting down the camp, striking Maisie's tent, and tacking up Beckett. Bobe Elka busied herself cleaning the last of the mud from the dodecaclavis. She revealed a bronze dodecahedron with holes in its surfaces and knobbles on its vertices. She lifted the hollow object, her fingers slipping through two holes to hold it in one hand.

By early afternoon, they'd completed all the preparations. Steig put the fire out and climbed up onto his usual spot on the left-hand shelf. Maisie was on the right-hand shelf, and Bobe Elka sat on the wooden spindle-back chair, in the open doorway of the wagon. She held the clavis on her lap.

"How do we do this, Bobe?" asked Steig.

"You roll forwards, slow, like, over the bridge. I'll turn the key. Don't stop or falter, just keep going, slow, like."

"Did you hear that, horse?"

"Yeh, just keep going."

"Good lad. Ready, Maisie?"

"Yes. Ready!" She smiled at Steig. He could see excitement in her eyes, but also a smidgen of trepidation.

"Heddup, lad."

The wagon rolled forwards towards the bridge. Bobe Elka again murmured words in Old High Romani, holding her hands over the dodecaclavis like a scrying crystal ball. A faint blue glow, similar to Cherenkov radiation, emanated from the hollow within the dodecaclavis. The fabric of the veil between the worlds ripped asunder. To Steig, it sounded like a sheet of newspaper being torn. The hairs on his neck stood up in goosebumps as a literal rift in reality opened at the centre of the bridge. It resembled a hole with ragged, glowing blue edges, the full width of the track, and high enough to encompass the wagon.

Beckett's ears were back, and they could hear him muttering imprecations. Despite the unusual circumstances, he remained resolute, walking forward with methodical steps. Through the rift, they could see very little. A silvery mist, again tinged with blue violet light, shrouded everything. Steig watched in astonishment as Beckett disappeared into the foggy blue silver shroud. Then he felt it wash over them, a clammy, electrostatic otherness. A moment of disorientation, a sideways slipping sensation. He shut his eyes.

Part II

Moreover, a third kind is that of the Khôra, everlasting, not admitting destruction, granting an abode to all things having generation, itself to be apprehended with nonsensation

– Plato, Timaeus, 52a-b

Chapter 13

The sideways-shifting electrostatic shiver passed, and the blue-tinged mist dissipated. Maisie took a sharp breath – the air was frigid and rank. She coughed, gagging as it caught in her throat. Her grip on the shelf seat was already white-knuckle tight, but it involuntarily increased a notch. The road they had been on, which ended at two farm gates leading onto green fields, surrounded by woodland and hedges, had transformed. Now it was a fork in a road, but the road was of a dirty grey mud, stones and lumps making the vardo shudder and heave as Beckett pulled them stolidly along. The trees were gone – where they had been, stumps and dead wood remained. The hedges were bare and empty, as if autumn had just been. Instead of lush grass, there was only mud, bare soil, occasional weeds and sparse marsh growth. She twisted around and looked behind them, along the line of the wagon's side. The river was there, but a sludgy, turgid thing, nothing like the free-flowing, deep, strong river she had almost met her end in.

“Hoo up, Beckett, hold hard, we’re here,” said Steig, his voice sounding unnatural in the still air.

“Don’t like this,” complained the horse.

“Well, I know I’ve been gone a while, but ... I’m right worried, I ’ave to say.” Bobe Elka put the clavis down on the floor of the wagon and stood up, holding on to the doorframe for balance. She looked left and right, craning her neck. “It looks the same, but different. Best we gerralong to the ostiarius’ house. It’s left ’ere, Steig.”

Steig had a pensive air about him, and didn’t speak. Instead, he clicked Beckett forward, adding a shake of the reins. They rolled slowly, bumping over the stony track, onto the left-hand roadway. The land was flat and, with the trees either fallen, dead or dying, they could see for a fair distance. Not a soul was about. No birdsong. No wind. The air was as still as death. Eugh, thought Maisie; that smell! Like rotting vegetation, rotten eggs, something putrid. She wrinkled her nose in disgust.

“Was there a war?” Steig asked, his voice muted in the still air.

He waved his hand at a blasted tree trunk that seemed to have shattered under some extreme impact. Grass and mud churned up in places as if the land had seen heavy bombing.

“Nay, not that I heard, like. I’m gobsmacked, I can tell thee.”

Beckett was having to work hard with the mud, which had become deeper in places, though the roadway underneath seemed solid enough and at least it was on the flat. Steig kept him steady, collected, a gentle pressure on the reins holding the horse's head in toward his chest; this was their "driving through danger" position. Beckett knew Steig was there for him, and vice versa.

"You OK, horse?"

"Yeh. OK. Muddy."

"Good lad. Keep going."

He turned to Bobe Elka, who had taken her seat again with the movement of the wagon.

"How far?"

"Should be just round the next corner."

Steig glanced at Maisie. She was silent; her face achromatic, and her knuckles showed white and purple where she was gripping the shelf edge.

"Maisie?"

She jumped, startled.

"Yes?" There was a tremble in her voice.

"It will be OK. We're OK." He tried his best smile. Hoped it wasn't coming out a rictus. She smiled back, but her grip on the shelf remained rigid.

As they rounded the corner in the road, there was a high, grey wall to their right. It was stone with a stucco plaster cladding, Steig thought. It stretched along the road, and back from the road, making an extensive rectangular enclosure. He could make out a pitched, red clay tile roof beyond the wall, above a row of evil-looking black metal spikes that lined the wall's apex. A gateway stood close to the corner. The gates, heavy, wooden, bound by black iron straps, were also topped with spikes.

"Someone doesn't want uninvited guests," he commented.

"That weren't like that afore. Bloody 'ell," muttered Bobe Elka.

They rolled to a stop.

"Maisie, hold the reins, please. I'll go knock."

Whilst Maisie did as she was asked, with trepidation on her face, biting her lip in worry, Steig jumped down. His boots, barely dried from the ford, sunk into mud that almost covered them. He squelched to the gate and banged on it with his open palm.

"Quis est?" came a shout from inside. A male voice, Steig thought.

"Amicis!" Maisie shouted back. Steig gave her a quizzical look. "He asked, who is it? I said friends."

Steig nodded and walked back through the tenacious mud to Beckett. A small hatch set into the gate at head height opened, and a brown, open face with a broad smile and deep, round, brown eyes regarded them.

"Salve! Momento," he said, in a resonant voice, and the hatch shut again.

The gate opened, after much muttering and the sound of a barricade bar being withdrawn. The man with the brown face was huge. Tall, muscular, solid, dressed in a simple dark tunic and leather sandals that laced up onto his calves. A substantial leather belt held the tunic at his waist, and from this belt hung various pouches and what Steig took for a long knife in a bronze scabbard.

"Salve!" he said, again, and gestured that they enter. The gate let on to a stone-flagged courtyard next to the house, with lean-to stock and storage buildings against the walls.

Steig nodded thanks to the man and led Beckett, then lent his weight on the breeching. Together, they pulled the wagon into the enclosed space. Steig chose a spot away from the house, on the far side of the yard, out of the way, and circled around slightly before stopping Beckett, so that the vardo faced the house, whose entrance also let into the courtyard.

"Right, lad, this is important. No talking to strangers, got that?" he said under his breath.

Beckett flicked his ear, twice. Two flicks for yes.

"Good lad. I'll see about some hay. Because there's bugger all grass around here." Beckett pawed the ground once, his shod hoof leaving a mark on the heavy flagstones. "We have apples and carrots. Don't worry. Hay first, you need the fibre."

Steig looked across at Bobe Elka, who was standing by the gate with the dark-skinned giant and Maisie. Maisie was in conversation with the man; Bobe Elka seemed impatient. The man said something, a hand gesture toward Beckett, and a nod. Maisie started over towards them, as Bobe Elka and the huge man disappeared into the house.

"What's occurring?"

"Calix said that the 'house spirit' would help with the horse. I think that's what he said. He speaks Breotonish, but I spoke to him in Latin, too."

"Calix, hmm? And house spirit? A hob, you mean?"

"You may call me that, if it pleases you, sire."

The wheedling voice came from a half-height doorway in the end wall of one of the lean-to buildings. Steig had assumed it was for a dog or chickens. The owner of the voice was a diminutive, hairy creature. Steig thought how true to form the stereotypical drawings of hobgoblins had been, if this was indeed a hob, or hobgoblin, a house spirit. He was a lean, wiry thing, hands and feet fractionally too large, a mean narrow face, elvish, pointed ears, and a thatch of greasy brown hair poking out from under a dark-brown leather skull cap. His clothes were of leather and cloth, buckled and strapped together in patches and pieces, in shades of brown and black and grey. His feet were bare, hairy and dirty.

"Very well, hob. How should we address you?"

"I am known as Kord."

"Do you have hay for the horse?" He wondered at Beckett, then – he seemed unusually relaxed, given the proximity of the hobgoblin.

"Aye, sire."

The hob disappeared, moving with such rapidity that Steig barely saw him go, but for the kicking up of grit from the ground. He was back in a heartbeat, carrying a well-stuffed woven net of hay bigger than he was tall. He jumped up and attached the net to a ring set into the wall next to Beckett's face.

"Was there anything else, sire?"

"No, thank you, Kord."

"If you need anything in the yard, sire, I will be here."

"Is the yard your domain? Not the house?"

"Oh no, sire," the hob said with a guttural laugh. "Vilicus should skewer me if I sets foot in the house. More than my gizzard's worth." And he was gone. There one second, gone the next.

"Huh. Hobgoblins. Who knew?" He smiled at Maisie, who was standing with her mouth wide open. "Best shut that or you'll be catching flies."

Her mouth opened and closed a couple of times, then she managed, "Hobgoblin?" with a squeak.

"I'm just rolling with it, for now. Did you see how fast he moved? Pretty fantastic. I mean, Beckett pulled us through a magic portal. It can't get any weirder, right? You OK, horse?"

"The hay smells funny. But it's OK."

"You OK with the hob? You didn't seem surprised."

"Saw him watching us coming in the yard. Seems OK."

Maisie scoffed. "Oh, well, that's fine then. The talking horse has vouched for the hobgoblin." Her voice was high and brittle, like she might descend into hysterics at any moment. Steig put his hands on her shoulders and held her at arm's length, looking into her eyes. He shook her shoulders gently.

"Hey. We're OK, right? Magical kingdom full of elves and faeries, remember?"

In reply, she pulled him to her and snaked her arms around the back of his neck, and clung on tight, burying her face in his hair, holding him in the embrace. Steig didn't really know what to do. He hadn't been expecting that. So, he patted her back, hugging by degrees.

"I'm OK as long as I have you," she whispered.

"We'll be OK. We have each other," he replied. Though he wasn't sure if that was strictly true.

Beckett seemed content with his hay net, though Maisie tied him to the ring to stop him from wandering. Steig was watching her.

"Just in case," she said with a smile.

Calix emerged from the house and beckoned them to follow him. Steig checked with Maisie again.

"OK?"

"Yes, let's see the illustrious ostiarius."

"Ostiarius?"

"Gatekeeper."

They walked up the steps to the house, and Steig realised they were almost touching. Almost holding hands. Almost leaning on each other. His thoughts were still in turmoil, yet he was becoming increasingly happy in her quiet, understated company.

They left the chill air of the yard and, beyond the heavy scuffed wooden doors of the house, found themselves in a warm, open hallway with a floor of terracotta tiles overlaid with woven rugs. Tall, thin leaded-glass windows let in daylight. Steig slipped his boots off; they were caked in mud. He tapped Maisie on the arm and pointed down at her feet. She coloured a deep pink and removed her own filthy footwear.

The floor was heated. He had a dim recollection from school of some sort of Roman underfloor heating system that was thought advanced for the period; well, it certainly made for warm feet. Calix led them through the hall and into a smaller room off to one side, where Bobe Elka was sipping a cup of something steaming. She was sitting on a pile of cushions on the floor, at a squat table. She was deep in muted conversation with a robe-clad figure who stood as they entered.

Well, thought Steig, Bobe had said the gatekeepers were like elves. That was an understatement. The woman who stood before them, a smile touching her lips, was the personification of elven kind. Tall, slim, androgynous. Long, straight white hair held from her face with some sort of tiara or crown, a band of silver set with a single, substantial emerald. Below the crown, a heart-shaped face, bright green eyes, high cheekbones, a wide mouth. She had long, elegant, pointed ears pushing through her hair.

She turned to Maisie, and bowed, holding her white silk robes out in a curtsey.

"Inventor Clavis, honoured guest. Welcome. I am Ostiarius Lavinia Angita né Danann," she breathed in a sibilant whisper. Turning to Steig, she added, almost as an afterthought, "You also are welcome."

"Thank you. I have many questions," said Maisie.

"Please, be seated. Let us talk."

She gestured to the cushions on the far side of the table. Calix arrived with a lacquered tray laden with cups and a plate of tiny pastries. Steig sat at the table, feet flat on the floor, sitting almost on his heels, resting on the cushion. He took a cup from Calix, nodding thanks. Inhaled the steam coming from the drink. It smelled like mulled wine. He took a tentative sip. It was something alcoholic, sweetened with honey.

He looked around the room. One wall held a window that opened out onto the courtyard, where they had left Beckett, who was working his way through the hay. Kord had found a crate to stand on and was grooming him, working a brush through his mane and hide with care. He had already cleaned Beckett's legs of mud. As he groomed, he was also removing the harness in sections. With each section, he disappeared for a fraction of a second, then returned with the leather cleaned and shiny, to be reattached. Beckett remained stationary, passive, eating, while the hob removed and cleaned and replaced his tack, piecemeal. The hob brushed sections of Beckett's hide whilst that part of the tack was off. It was the most peculiar way to groom a horse and clean the tack, but the entire process proceeded at such a pace, Kord had it almost completed between the second and third sips of Steig's drink.

Steig continued to look around the room as Maisie and Lavinia made their initial forays into conversation. Heavy dark blue drapes covered most of the walls – insulation, he guessed – and where the walls were bare, they had been rendered with rough plaster and white-washed. Set into one wall was a cubbyhole that contained a figurine and a shallow bowl holding an offering of fruit. Steig guessed this was an altar to the house spirit. He wondered if that might not work, when the spirit was as corporeal as the hob grooming Beckett.

Maisie was confused. The ostiarius had said "honoured guest" and shown her deference, and all but ignored Steig. She sipped her drink in an effort to buy time; inhaled the aroma of cinnamon and alcohol. Hot mulled wine. The cold weather outside made this warming drink welcome. The underfloor heating was startling, as well – though it warmed her feet in the most delicious way.

Looking around at her host, she tried not to stare. But really! An actual elven queen! Maybe not a queen, but ... Remembering the illustrations in Steig's folklore book, and her own childhood books, the ostiarius certainly had all the elven attributes.

As she sat, demurely sipping and looking around through her hair, she replayed the greeting the elf queen had given her, that title. Inventor Clavis. Finder of Keys. What did that mean? It sounded like an honorific, the way she had said it ...

"What would you ask me?"

The question brought Maisie out of her reverie. She had so many questions, though. Where to start?

"Your title, ostiarius. You are a gatekeeper? Bobe Elka said the gatekeepers were ... like you. And what is it that gatekeepers do?"

"I am a gatekeeper, yes. I care for the people who use the Wayland gate, as you have just done, though you are the first travellers to pass through here in many years. When I greet them, I make sure that they have all they need for their travel in Khôra. I offer them shelter and sustenance, and advice, if I can. That is the function of the gatekeeper."

"An' to keep out the riffraff, an' to keep the gobshite Gratadei from diggin' the clavises up!" added Bobe Elka.

"Riffraff? Gratadei?"

"Another function I fulfil is to protect Khôra from interlopers who wish to do us harm, or to use the dodecaclavis for ill."

Maisie's eyes widened. "Does that happen a lot?"

"It is happening more often, yes. We have had to hide the claves, in some instances. My people are active in patrolling the lands, more than ever."

"Who are your people?"

"My people are the Tuatha de Danann."

Maisie filed the name away – she would look it up later. Look it up? She'd ask around. Or something. It sounded Celtic. Maybe Steig's folklore library referenced it.

"And the Gratadei? Grace of God?"

A troubled look passed over Lavinia's face. "They are a recent threat to us. For the last ten years they have subverted the clavis network. They are sucking the energy that protects the country from it. This is why our once benign utopia looks like a war zone."

Maisie nodded. "It has broken the cornucopia."

"Indeed." That same smile again quirked Lavinia's lip. "We need someone to help us fix it. Someone who can find the missing dodecaclaves. Someone who can fight back against the Gratadei and deny them access to Khôra."

Something shifted in the pit of Maisie's stomach, and she tasted bile as her gut twisted in alarm. Finder of Keys, she had called her. Oh no! She looked over at Steig, but he was busy examining the furnishings and watching Beckett through the window.

"You can't possibly mean me? Inventor Clavis? Oh, no! Don't be ridiculous."

Bobe Elka cackled loud and long. Maisie winced.

"Ha! She does mean you an' all, girl!"

Maisie glanced at Steig for support. He was watching in bemusement. He shook his head, shrugged. Oh dear.

Lavinia continued, "You must be aware you have a gift. I understand from Bobe Elka you located the Wayland clavis in deep running water, in the dark of early morning?"

Something snapped inside Maisie. "I almost died! And that was some ..." She searched for a suitable expletive. "Some bloody dream-manipulating ... sorcery!" she finished, slamming her cup down on the low table, and struggling to her feet from the cushions. Steig stood with fluidity, she noticed, that trick he had when sat on his heels. He was infuriating, too. She headed for the door at a half run. Steig caught her up, jogged alongside her down the hallway. Yes, he was infuriating, but ...

Pulling their boots on, they let themselves out into the darkening afternoon. As they slipped out, Bobe Elka and Lavinia appeared at the reception room door. Calix also arrived from further inside the house, a frown on his face and a tray of refreshments in his hand. Maisie slammed the door behind them. She rarely allowed herself anger like this, but she felt betrayed, used. By whom? Bobe Elka? Lavinia? Khôra? How could a country betray her? As she thought it, she realised that was exactly what could, and did, happen, all the time. To millions of people.

"Come on. I need some space. Can we sit in the vardo?"

"Of course. We can get the stove on, have a cuppa."

They walked down the steps and towards Beckett and the wagon. There was no sign of Kord, but Beckett had a fresh hay net and there was a metal-bound wooden pail of water within his reach.

"D'you want to pull up here tonight, or shall we find somewhere else?" Steig said in a guarded tone.

"Well, it's getting dark. And spikes on the walls ... seems like there might not be so much of the sweetness and light Bobe Elka promised us, in this world of plenty. I'd feel safer in this compound, dreary though it is."

"Suits me. Kord?"

"Sire?"

Maisie jumped. The hob was right there, in front of them, as if it had materialised from thin air.

"Is there a stable or stall that Beckett can stay in tonight? I'm presuming that it's OK to stay?" asked Steig.

"It is not my place to say whether you stay, sire, though Vilicus said that if you decide to stay, the horse will need to be stabled. So, I have prepared a stable for him already."

"Vilicus? You mentioned that name earlier?"

"It means housekeeper," suggested Maisie.

"You are welcome to stay. It is the function of the ostiarius to provide shelter to gateway travellers." Calix spoke in his deep baritone, and Maisie jumped again, as she had not heard him approach. "Vilicus has prepared rooms for you both."

"That's very kind," replied Maisie, her earlier anger abating somewhat, "but we'll stay in the vardo for now. I have things I need to discuss with Steig."

"Of course. If you wish for food or drink to be brought to you, please ask the hob. He will be obliged to assist."

Steig bowed to the huge man. "Thank you, Calix. Kord, please settle Beckett into his stable. Beckett, you OK?"

Maisie saw Beckett flick his ear twice. He was OK. She felt a warmth in her belly for the heavy horse.

"I'll get the kettle on," she said, and with nimble steps slid into the wagon, where she set about lighting the Queenie stove. She could hear Steig and Calix murmuring together. Felt a slight movement as Kord unhooked the traces from the front of the wagon. The noise from Beckett's shod feet clattered away on the flags as Kord led him to a stable further along the yard.

The wagon lurched as Steig climbed the steps and came in. He reached for the lamp and lit the wick. The afternoon was getting dark much more quickly than Maisie had expected.

"I know you're not OK, so I won't ask if you are. Just know that I'm on your side. This is all new to me, too. Let's have a cuppa and settle for a bit and try to work out what to do next."

Maisie gazed up at him, from where she was kneeling by the stove. His face was lit by the yellow glow from the lamp. She felt that warmth in her belly again.

"Whatever happens, I'm glad I'm with you and Beckett."

Steig poured the boiling water from the kettle into two mugs balanced on the tiny table next to the Queenie. He preferred being outside by a yog, but the chill weather, accompanied by a light drizzle, and the oddity of being in a compound, put him off the idea. And he wasn't sure how their host would react if they started a fire on her flagged yard.

"Here you go." He passed a mug to Maisie, who was sitting next to him on the bench seat opposite the stove.

"Thank you." She smiled and cupped the mug in her hands, then blew steam from the tea. The light from the lamp caught her eyes, and they shone.

"So, I had a quiet word with Calix," Steig said. "He says we can stay here as long as we want. There's some sort of Hellenic thing going on, means you must be hospitable to guests."

"It's called xenia. With an *x*. Safe harbour overnight, food, drink, that sort of thing. It's built into ancient Hellenic culture, as commanded by Zeus."

"Yeah, xenia, that's what he said. So, we're OK to stay here for a bit, is what I was getting at."

"OK."

"So, there's no need to rush off, or fret that we might outstay our welcome by a day or two." He frowned, ran a hand through his hair. "What I'm trying to say is, we have time to ask questions, and plan, not shoot off all half-cocked."

Maisie smiled. "That reduces the pressure somewhat, doesn't it?" she said.

"It does. So, what I suggest is, we spend tonight having a bit of a think about what we want to ask, and then tomorrow we set up a meeting with Ostiarius Lavinia nay whatever-it-was."

"Ostiarius Lavinia Angita né Danann."

"Yeah, what I said. Meet with her and get answers, see if we can make sense of it all."

"And what about my honorific, Inventor Clavis? Like I deliberately jumped in the river and almost drowned, all on my own?"

"Yeah, she seemed to think that was a good thing, right? Finding the clavis?"

"It's the method through which I found it that worries me. I don't want a repeat performance."

"You and me both, we're agreed on that."

They sat in silence for a few minutes. The stove cast a warm glow from its open front, and the windows fogged with condensation. The rain became more insistent and started a gentle patter on the tarpaulin.

Maisie glanced up at the curved roof.

"I'll never tire of that noise."

Steig smiled, settled back in the seat. It gladdened his heart that she noticed things like that. Most gadjo would be so intent on their lives they wouldn't take the time to just be.

Maisie reached across and under the bench seat, pressing into Steig's leg as she did so. He felt her warmth. He felt a renewed surge of emotions. Confusion. Worry. Was that ... fear? He enjoyed having her around, though. Was that so bad?

She straightened up, holding the dodecaclavis.

"Bobe Elka must have left it under the seat here. Seems careless?"

"She said herself she lost it in the river. I'm not entirely convinced by her, I have to say. Something off. I mean, don't get me wrong, she's the real deal and all, just ... well, I don't know if she has our best interests a hundred per cent at heart."

"When she appeared out of that mist. You knew she was coming, didn't you?"

Steig gave a slow nod.

"How?"

"I've met her before. Seen that mist before. Did a bit of research. It's called kathalyog, means 'going gently by fire'. She can travel from campfire to campfire, maybe through time as well. Sort of like a Roma version of the clavis, I guess."

"So she can travel where she wants, so long as there's a yog?"

"That seems to be the case, yes. By all accounts, she is old. And I feel the Tuatha de Danann and her don't always see things in the same light."

"Oh! I was going to ask you what that is. Lavinia's people, the Tuatha de Danann?"

"It's Celtic. It means Danu's people. Danu being the proto-goddess of the pantheon of Èirinn, such as it is. I think they are associated with the daoine sidhe, who are the fae folk who supposedly live in the earth mounds scattered across Èirinn."

"Elves and faeries," breathed Maisie, her eyes shining in the lamplight.

"Yes. I mean, you saw Lavinia, right? If there was a textbook on this sort of thing, she'd be right there on page one." Steig considered his tea for a moment, blew the steam from its head. "Another thing that confuses me," he said. "We have ancient Hellenic custom, like xenia. Fair enough, Heracles built Khôra, but then, everyone speaks Roman? And Breotonish?"

"Latin. But yes, it's one to add to the list of questions. Along with how this works." She held up the clavis, peered through its inert innards. Reached into her bag and pulled out her yellow leather-bound journal and opened it at a blank page. Took a pen from a holder sewn onto the leather binding. "So, I shall start the list," she muttered.

"I'll go check Beckett and see if I can find the kitchen door. Ask for some food."

"Great, I'm starving!"

Steig lit the other lantern against the deep darkness outside and left Maisie to her journal. With his stockman's coat on and a broad-brimmed wax-cotton hat against the rain, he headed in the direction Beckett had gone. Around the corner, he found a block of stables, with a couple of draught horses, enormous broad brown beasts, standing docile in their stalls. They watched as he passed and went back to munching hay. In the third stall he found Beckett, rear foot resting, eyelids drooping. The stall was spacious and clean, with a deep bed of straw and a substantial pile of hay. Kord had wedged a wooden pail in the corner, full of clean water.

"All OK, horse?"

"Yeh. Sleepy."

"Good lad. Ride out in the morning?"

Beckett's ears pricked up. "Adventure? Yeh."

"Always. Night, then."

A flick of the ear; his eyes were already closed.

Steig continued along the back of the house until he came to a door that was ajar, from which emanated the steamy heat and noise of kitchens everywhere. He banged on the door with the flat of his hand, and instantly a tiny, hairy hob, shorter and more slender than Kord, appeared. They looked up at Steig, gave a startled squeak, and disappeared again. Steig chuckled to himself. And wondered who they had been expecting.

The door swung open further and a tall, severe-looking fae woman in a russet tunic presented herself.

"Salve." Said in that sibilant whisper he was recognising as fae. Faery. Elvish. Whatever she was. Tuatha de Danann.

"Er, hi. Hello. Um. Vilicus?"

"Yes, I am Vilicus. How may I assist you, Traveller Steig of Rotes-lund?"

This took Steig aback for a moment. Then realised that Vilicus had probably heard his history from Bobe Elka, or more likely her staff had "overheard" Bobe talking with Lavinia.

"Calix mentioned we could get some food brought to the wagon in the courtyard." He pointed back the way he had come. "Would that be possible?"

"Yes, of course. I shall send hob, directly."

"Thank you."

She bowed and glided back into the kitchen. The door slammed.

"Huh. OK." He turned and walked back, lantern lighting his way, casting a circle of dim light, pushing back the grey dark.

Steig had just climbed the steps to the vardo and closed the door against the chill air when there came a gentle knock. Maisie, who had been writing in her journal, gave a start, eyes wide.

"It's OK." He pushed open the door again; there was Kord, balancing a huge tray of dark wood in one hand, his other hand raised to knock again. The tray was crowded with two covered plates, a steaming jug and a plate of cold meats and cheeses. Along with cups, cutlery, linen napkins. Steig took the tray and put it on the bed – the only flat space large enough for it. "Thank you, Kord."

"Sire," and he was gone.

Maisie had watched the whole delivery from the seat. As Steig closed the door, she stood and stretched.

"How's Beckett?"

"Like a horse who doesn't have to be tethered out on a verge. He's got a huge stable and a deep bed and more hay than he knows what to do with. Heh. He'll go soft, if we're not careful."

"You found the kitchen, then?"

"Yep. Met Vilicus. She's fae like Lavinia. Knew all about me. Think they might have a bit of an eavesdropping problem. Or maybe they talk to each other telepathically. I dunno. Makes my head spin. Let's see what we have for dinner?"

Maisie lifted the domed silver lid from her plate, revealing steaming vegetables, slices of roast meat, potatoes and gravy almost spilling over the sides.

"Wow! Roast dinner!" Maisie grinned up at Steig through the rising steam.

The jug contained more of the mulled wine, hot and fragrant. Steig poured out two cupfuls.

"Do you think there might be too much food here? We'll save the cold stuff for breakfast, perhaps?"

"Yes, I think I'll just about manage with this tiny plateful," she said with a laugh, waving at her overloaded dinner plate.

A hush descended on the wagon, just the sound of the gentle rain on the roof, as they sated their hunger.

"Gosh, I hadn't realised how starved I was!" exclaimed Maisie, as she mopped up the last of the gravy with some sourdough bread they had found hidden away under another linen napkin.

"Yeah, it's been quite the day. How's the list?"

"Well ..." She returned her plate to the tray and sat next to Steig, who was still finishing his food. She opened her journal book and read. "We need to know what the clavises really are. How they work, what their parameters are."

"Parameters?"

"You know. What makes them tick, what opens the gateway, stuff like that."

"OK. What else?"

"Well, why they think I'm some sort of Keyfinder General? That's a top question."

"Agreed. Also, I'm interested in the relationship between fae, hob, human ... any other mythical creatures around here."

"Apart from talking horses?" she asked with a smile.

"He's not mythical."

"Unusual though, you must admit."

"I suppose."

"Anyway. I have already written 'Get list of mythical creatures' as a question, so that covers that. Also, Gratadei. Bobe Elka said they dig up clavises. Clavisum. Clavii. Claves. They sound like a group we need to know about."

"Do you have a note to ask why us? All the weird shit like dreams and messages from the Meliae? I mean, notwithstanding Bobe Elka's fairly obvious hand in it all. 'Scuse my language."

"Your language is fine. Shit, fuck, bollocks. There, see?"

Steig stared at her in astonishment, then burst into laughter.

"Oh my Goddess, Maisie is a sweary potty mouth!"

"Well, I'm not, thank you very much. But occasionally, maybe one or the other of us will feel the need to express ourselves verbally in the strongest possible way. I just thought I should practise."

She paused, a faraway look in her eye. She glanced down at her plate, then back up at Steig.

"You said 'Goddess'. I thought gyp ... travellers were strongly Christian?"

"Mostly, yes. Not me."

She regarded him with an even stare; her face was open and guileless. One eyebrow twitched upward. He sighed.

"OK then, I don't really know, alright? But I hold more store by what I can see and feel around me – trees, nature, rivers, the sun and moon – than some invisible beardy bloke sitting on a cloud, commanding from afar."

"Invisible beardy bloke?" Her eyes were dancing, mischievous. "You won't get into heaven referring to Our Lord like that."

"Your lord, not mine."

"Well, yes, about that. I'm not sure he's mine so much anymore. Seeing and feeling, as you say. We've seen plenty in the last couple of days that flies in the face of the church's teachings, don't you think?"

"I was never one for those teachings, but from a purely theological standpoint, yes, I think you're right."

Steig collected the cold meats and cheeses and the remaining sourdough into a linen napkin and stored it in the cupboard. He put the rest of the crockery and cutlery back on the tray and took it outside. The rain was still coming down, but there stood Kord, as if he had been waiting and listening for movement.

"Hello, Kord. If you can return this to the kitchen with a message of our thanks?"

"Of course, sire. Do you require anything else?"

"No, we're fine, thank you."

"Goodnight then, sire." And again, gone, with a rapidity that tricked the eye, thought Steig. Only carrying a tray laden with crockery. Another mystery.

He backed up the steps and shut the door on the dark, wet night. Turned to find Maisie already in bed, the covers pulled up to her nose.

"Oh! I see. We're sharing the bed, again, then?" he asked, with what he thought was obvious mock exasperation.

"Oh! Oh, no, I'm so sorry, I thought ..." She started to get out of bed, a bare foot and calf waving around seeking the floor.

"Don't be daft. I'm pulling your leg."

He grabbed her foot and gave it a gentle tug. She squeaked. Slipped back fully under the covers.

"You had me worried. I wouldn't relish sleeping in the tent in this rain, in the courtyard."

"Flagstones. Very hard bed. Difficult to get the pegs in. Best stay here," he said, smiling, as he undressed.

"Steig. Behave. We're sleeping together for warmth and safety."

"Obviously." He clambered over her covered form and slipped under the covers on the far side of the bed. "Shove over."

"Ooh, you're cold. Freezing!"

"So, whatever happened to 'sleep together for warmth'?"

Steig reached out to the lantern and turned the wick down to a guttering dimness.

Chapter 14

Getting out of the bed in a vardo without disturbing the other occupant was a skill that Steig had not practised overmuch. Using a combination of hand-holds and careful foot placement, he eased from beneath the duvet, placing his toes on the wooden floor. He felt grit and dirt. It could do with a sweep out. But later. He dressed as silently as he could, without turning the lantern up. A series of steady snuffling snores emanated from the duvet, where Maisie slumbered.

The sun, or what stood in for the sun, was stealing a dim glow into, he presumed, the east. Another set of questions for their esteemed hostess. With an overabundance of care, he placed a log onto the embers of the fire in the Queenie and closed it back up – it would stay in through the morning, keeping the chill off. He snagged some of the sourdough and cheese from the cupboard, shoved it in his coat pocket. Then slipped down the steps, taking care to move evenly, so as to not rock the wagon. And was away, toward the stables.

Beckett was awake, his stable immaculate, no sign of any muck, and with hay and water already refreshed.

"Mornin', horse. Up for a ride out?"

"Yeh. Boring in here. Those two are dullards." He swished his tail at the draught horses in the stalls next door.

Steig found Beckett's harness, spotless and smelling of leather-dressing, hanging on a series of hooks in a small tack room next to the stables. Once Beckett had his bridle on, Steig led him out of the stable. He grabbed a handful of mane at the base of Beckett's neck, and the reins, and vaulted on board with a grunt. Then swung his leg and his weight so that he was lying along the horse's neck, sat up and settled on the horse's back. Kord appeared and looked at Steig with what passed for hobgoblin astonishment.

"Does sire require anything?"

"Good morning. I would like you to open the yard gate so I can ride out."

The hob wrung his hands, pulled a face that contorted his features into a worried knot. "I is not s'posed to touch the gate, sire."

"Well, I do not wish you trouble. Who can open it?"

"That is my duty," came the baritone of Calix, who had come out of the kitchen door, presumably at the sound of Beckett's shoes on the flagstones. "Though I would advise caution at riding alone in this country."

"Noted, Calix. Thank you, my friend. I'll take my chances. I want to see a bit more of Khôra before we get side-tracked, engrossed and bamboozled, sitting with your mistress, the ostiarius."

"As it pleases you, Steig. I will open the gate."

The huge man walked with a light, fast step, and was at the gate with the barricade removed and one leaf open before Beckett arrived.

"I'll be an hour, two at the most."

"Very well." Calix contorted his face almost as much as the hob's, worry lines etched on his forehead.

"Heddup, lad." Steig gave a dig with his heels and Beckett sprang forward, cat-leaping over the threshold of the gate and into the muddy lane. Steig was ready and had a handful of mane to hold on to, then used his weight to spin Beckett to the right and away along the track, transitioning into a steady trot. He heard the gates closing behind him. His face split into a cheerful grin. "Steady, Beckett, we got an hour or so of this mud before we turn. Watch for holes and stones."

A flick of the ear. Beckett knew his job. He trod with care, reading the surface, dropping to a walk in deeper mud, picking up the trot where the going became firmer. After a few minutes, Steig noticed blades of grass appearing. The green was bright and almost unnatural amongst the sea of muddy grey slurry that covered the road. He relaxed into the ride, feeling the warmth of Beckett's hide under him; he loved riding like this – at one with the horse, warmed and connected, feeling every muscle moving in Beckett's broad back.

Cresting a small rise, he pulled up. The valley swept away and hazed into ochre foothills and taller grey-purple almost-mountains. The land continued in the same hue of grey for a half a mile, but then verdant growth feathered the edges. In the middle distance, the land was at least the dull green and brown associated with winter crops in Breotonlond. So, thought Steig, all was not so blasted in other parts of Khôra.

They'd come to a fork in the road. By habit, he took the left-hand path, the road less travelled. Indeed, that was the case here. The median strip was growing over with mosses and sparse, dead grasses. Less travelled, also less muddy. He applied gentle pressure again, and Beckett picked up a gear, striding into a gentle canter that covered the ground with a rhythmic cadence. The wind whistled past Steig's face. The movement added a slight freshness to what was otherwise stale air, but it remained sour.

They cantered down a gentle incline, and between scrubby thorn bushes, descending into a lonely, marshy, scrubby woodland. The track became narrow and difficult, forcing Beckett to slow.

Picking their way between dense thorn bushes at a walk, they arrived at a small lake, inky black and still. The remains of an ox-bow nipped off from the river. Crooked, bare blackthorn bushes pressed in on all sides. Once they had stopped, the oppressive stillness encroached again.

"Don't like this. Nope." Beckett backed up from the pool, throwing his head around, prancing and plunging. His front feet churned the ground, his haunches tucked under him, ready for flight.

"Hey, hey, hey, you're OK, I got you." Steig lay forward along Beckett's neck. He stroked the horse's shoulder, tried to calm him, all the time scanning the water and keeping hold of the reins.

"It's wrong. Need to go. Scared!"

Something stirred in the water.

The top of a head, green and slimy with weed and mud, broke the surface. Two large, round, dark-green eyes followed, but no more of the face appeared. It rested at the pool's centre, creating no ripples. Beckett stopped his prancing, transfixed. Steig regarded the creature with interest. What was it? It could do them no harm, all the way out there? And so small?

Only when he realised he was being sucked into the gaze of the thing did he try to break away his regard. He struggled to move his head but was unable.

Panic set in as he tried to blink.

Couldn't.

Finally, he held up an arm in front of his eyes and the hypnotic glamour fell away. The thing's many arms were feeling their way out of the pool. Long, grey-green, glistening tentacles quested towards Beckett's hooves.

"Beckett! Time to go!" he shouted, digging his heels in.

The thing's eyes had Beckett paralysed in place. Quick as thought, turning his head away from the mesmeric eyes, Steig threw the reins, whipped off his coat and flung it over Beckett's face. He held the coat by the collar so that it hung over the horse's eyes. Beckett reacted in an instant, reared, shied from the encroaching tentacles, pirouetted on the spot. The coat flapped, just about held in one hand as Steig grabbed for reins and mane with the other, wrapping his legs as far under the horse as he could. He was hanging on for, he suspected, his life. Beckett leapt away up the narrow track, back the way they came, at a flat-out gallop.

The path through the thorn bushes was narrow and tortuous. Beckett was in a panic and the thorns were sharp; they plucked at Steig's legs. He tried to duck away from the worst, tried to steer Beckett along the actual path. In his blind terror, Beckett wasn't listening, taking his own line, crashing past bushes and overhanging branches. Steig ducked and lay as flat as he could, felt a branch scrape his arm, knew it would be bad, concentrated on hanging on. He was lying almost prone, arms around the horse's neck, head down. Beckett kicked and swerved as he careered up the track. Another branch crashed into Steig's knee, pushing him back, almost unseating him. Pain shot up his leg, and he cried out.

They erupted from the sparse woodland into the dreary but oh-so-lacking-immediate-danger plains, and up again to the slight rise. Steig sat upright and tried to regain control over the horse. Beckett listened, slowed to a canter, then a trot. Steig steered him to the right, back towards the Wayland crossing and Ostiarius Lavinia's villa.

"Well done, lad. You OK?" Steig wheezed out, straining lungfuls of the dead air.

Beckett was heaving, his flanks frothed with sweat, flecked with blood from blackthorn scratches. Steig looked at his own arms and legs. Blood was streaming from a laceration on his left arm, where he had been holding on to Beckett's mane. His right knee was bleeding through his jeans. The pain was building. Oh, how foolish did he feel?

"Yeh," managed Beckett. "OK." He slowed to a walk, still throwing his head, still showing the whites of his eyes. "Nasty smelly thing, that was."

Steig barked a laugh.

"Yep, you can say that again. Bit different from the ones in Roteslund, hmm?"

"You sneak out. Like some sort of thief! And come back covered in blood! And Beckett, he's a complete state! What the hell were you thinking?"

"But ..." began Steig.

"No. Don't say anything." Maisie held up her bloodstained hand, silencing him. "It was rhetorical. You're so ... damned irresponsible! Headstrong! Stupid! Thick-headed!"

"Um ..."

"No! I don't want to hear it. Oh, for goodness' sake, hold still."

"Stings!"

"Good. Bloody ... bloody well serves you right. Idiot." She dabbed the square of gauze over his arm, where a deep, jagged scratch bled a last few smeared drops of bright crimson. She dipped the gauze into the pot of astringent wash Vilicus had provided. Apparently, it was a ward against the poison in the blackthorn. Steig's arm had swollen and turned an angry red around the cut. She finished washing the wounds and laid more gauze over them, then bound them proficiently with a self-adhesive bandage that she had found in a first aid box under Steig's bed. Although marked "Veterinary Use Only", she felt it would suffice.

"Take your jeans off."

Steig looked at her, looked at the house hob busy at the grate lighting the fire in this reception room, shrugged and slipped off his jeans, wincing as he did so. Maisie sucked air through her teeth and shook her head.

"Stupid, stupid, stupid. Oh, my word. Hang on, I'll need tweezers."

"But—"

"But nothing. There's a blackthorn sticking out of your knee. It needs to come out, and the wound washed, or you'll get sepsis."

"It's just a splinter!"

"Shut up. Oh, do hold still." Maisie used the tweezers from the same first aid kit, heavy-duty things for horse wounds, she guessed, and pulled the thorn from the side of Steig's knee. She examined it, wiping the blood from it. It all seemed to be there, which was a relief. She had seen the result of ordinary blackthorn on her father's hands after gardening. This stuff, according to Vilicus, was worse because the grendylou poisoned the area around its pool, and the vapour sat on everything. Hence the warding tincture. She sluiced the wound with the acrid stuff. Steig tensed up. At least he had stopped trying to speak.

"There," she declared, adding more gauze, and wrapping a veterinary bandage about his knee. "Now let's go see how Beckett is faring."

Steig tried to stand, but staggered when he put weight on his leg.

"Here. Lean on me." Maisie offered her arm.

Steig gave her a look. "I'm not an invalid."

"I beg to differ. But have it your own way." She marched off toward the stables. Oh, he could be such a ... she searched for the right words. Self-centred, egotistical, righteous ... She shook her head, hoping fervently that she hadn't made an awful mistake marooning herself here with him.

Favouring his leg, Steig hopped, clumsy from the pain, and made his way to the stables. Maisie was already there, of course. He cursed himself for being too proud to accept her help. Kord was washing Beckett down with warm water from a huge bucket. Calix watched, concern clouding his face. Beckett stood with his head down, water trickling from his forelock and pooling all around his hooves. Kord had washed most of the sweat and foam from him and was using a sweat scraper made from leather and wood to remove the last.

The hob had shaved a few small spots of hair around Beckett's chest and front legs, where scratches and minor cuts showed through.

"How is he, Calix?" asked Maisie, as Steig arrived, puffed for breath.

"I'm OK," mumbled Beckett, though his tone was morose.

Maisie shot a glance at Calix, who merely grinned.

"We get talking animals occasionally in Khôra. It's normal for us," he said, smiling at her surprised expression.

"Oh! Well, that's one question answered, I suppose. So, Calix, how is he?"

"I am not a veterinarian, but I believe he will be alright in a few days. We checked and cleaned all his cuts, as you can see, and applied the ward tincture. Hob has been very thorough."

"And I thank you so much, Kord and Calix, for your help."

"It is not a problem." He turned to Steig, who was recovering his breath and leaning against the doorframe. "How are you, Steig?"

"Hello Calix. I'm OK, I think."

He held his head up as he faced the four of them. They were all looking at him like they were expecting more. An apology? An admission that he had been foolish? He knew it was a stupid thing to do. Saying it out loud wasn't going to change that. Fagh. He turned away, colouring and feeling as depressed as he had in some time. He hobbled towards the vardo, raising his hand in farewell as he went.

Climbing the wagon steps was not easy. In the end, he went up on all fours, like a dog. He felt about as low as a dog, one that had been soundly thrashed and was quivering with its tail tucked firmly between its legs.

The Queenie was out, radiating the last of the residual heat from the embers. He didn't have the energy to relight it. Shaking his head in despair, he crawled up to the bed and hauled himself under the quilt, favouring his arm and knee, which were throbbing in time with his heartbeat. Closing his eyes on the day, he reflected on the stupidity of his actions. He buried his face in the pillow, trying to blot out the world.

Chapter 15

Maisie watched in astonishment as Steig limped away, towards the vardo, an arm raised in farewell. She glanced at Calix, who looked on with a grim face. Only Kord seemed uninterested, diligently washing and sweat-scraping the rest of Beckett's flanks.

"Ostiarius Lavinia would like to speak with you when you are ready."

"Oh, yes, I suppose she would. I'm ready now. Thank you, Calix." She searched in her tatty messenger bag, checking she had the yellow notebook. It nestled there amongst the other books, her pocket bible, pens and general bric-a-brac that littered the bag. "Lead the way."

Calix showed her into the same reception room in which they had met Lavinia. The ostiarius was waiting, seated at the same table. This time, Bobe Elka and Steig were conspicuous by their absence.

"Ah, Maisie. Good morning." Lavinia stood up and gave a sort of half bow, half curtsey. She still wore white silken robes, though she had now braided her hair. It hung in a thick white plait down her back.

Maisie curtsied in return, unsure of the formalities. She covered her confusion by fussing around at her bag and seating herself. She pulled the yellow notebook out and placed it on the table. Calix returned with a tray laden with drink and food. The aroma of fresh coffee made Maisie's nose twitch. Real coffee! She had assumed this land existed as a snapshot of Roman times, but she must be mistaken. And were they ...? Oh, my. Actual croissants. Her mouth almost fell open, and she salivated. Lavinia chuckled with deep mirth.

"Go ahead, help yourself to coffee and pastries. I understand from Elka these are a favourite of yours?"

"Well, yes. Thank you." She took a cup of steaming coffee and a couple of the delicate croissants. "How is it that you have coffee?"

"We are in a parallel world, in Khôra; but there are, um, a few gateways that open regularly. We have had coffee since the seventeenth century. Though I and other ostiarii have found it an ... acquired taste." Her expression lost its levity; concern clouded her features. "How are Steig and Beckett? I understand from Vilicus that they had a problem with a grendylou, and some blackthorn bushes this morning?"

"Beckett is fine, thank you. Steig's cuts will hopefully heal rapidly, thanks to Vilicus and the tincture, or ward, or ... whatever it was she supplied. But I think Steig is very embarrassed. He may take some time to come back to himself."

"Well, please pass on my regards, when next you see him."

"I will." She put down her plate of croissant, re-arranged her knees, and stared directly at the ostiarius. "I have a number of questions; I wonder if you could answer them?"

"I will do my best, of course."

Maisie opened her notepad. Here goes, she thought. Either the questions would annoy their host and she would cast them out into the dreary landscape to fight the grendylou, or ... they wouldn't. Actually, in thinking this, she remembered xenia, and realised it would be unlikely that their host would expunge them. But, best to tread with care.

"Why did you call me the Inventor Clavis, the Finder of Keys?"

"Let me tell you first some history." Lavinia settled back. It seemed to Maisie this would be a long answer. "For two and a half thousand years or thereabouts, Khôra has existed as a place that is a sanctuary to all travellers who use the clavis network. It has also become a home to those races who choose to live here, away from the world of men."

As she paused for breath, her green eyes sparkling, Maisie asked, "The daoine sidhe, the grendylou, Tuatha de Danann?"

"Amongst others. Khôra extends across all of Europa and much of Mauretania. Parts of Araby. It is home to many people."

Maisie nodded. "All the mythical beasts and fae of folklore." She inhaled, eyes wide. "What about dragons?"

"No dragons. You asked about your honorific. So. Ten years ago, after centuries, millennia of peace, an organisation – who call themselves Gratadei – invaded us."

"Grace of God. You mentioned them yesterday."

"Indeed. They subverted the clavis network, which was already suffering severe degradation. They stole claves, used them for their own ends, and killed some ostiarii. It was, and still is, a dark era. Their actions forced us to hide the network, or what remained of it. The Gratadei dug up claves, moved them, took them. We, in turn, hid ourselves."

“Which is all awful. But what has this to do with me?” Maisie wrung her hands in fearful anticipation.

“There are some amongst us who can see, if not the actual future, then maybe a path through the tangle of possibilities. The Fates foretold your arrival, with the Wayland clavis. It was they who called you Inventor, Finder. You have the gift, as some very few do, a natural gift by birth – with what you would call magic, elemental powers, the supernatural. As you so ably demonstrated the other morning, you can find lost keys.”

Maisie had suspected that might be the answer Lavinia would give her, but could not accept it.

“The Fates? Don’t be ridiculous. I’m not special, nor do I have magical ability. I’m a Christian, for goodness’ sake!”

“Even so, you found the clavis, in the dark, at the bottom of a river.”

“OK. Well, what of it? It makes no sense.” She shook her head. “I get it. It’s a joke, right? This whole thing is a ruse. Is Steig in on it?”

Lavinia smiled. She was infuriatingly serene. Maisie was sweating. Her neck was wet, her palms clammy, and her ankles prickled.

“There is no joke. It is true we asked Bobe Elka if she would facilitate your arrival. Unfortunately, she seems to have taken a rather … how shall we say … a rather hands-on approach. Though, of course, not without results. And no, Steig knows nothing about this. He is a simple travelling man, nothing more.”

Maisie bridled at this, sat up straight, and looked Lavinia square in the eye.

“He’s not just a simple travelling man, thank you so very much.”

“He almost got himself killed by a grendylou this morning.”

Maisie turned her gaze away, chin in the air. Lavinia's tone was hurtful, almost snide. Her eyes brimmed, but she held back the tears. Damn that man and his idiotic, impulsive foolishness. She composed herself, replayed the conversation so far in her head. She felt Lavinia wasn't being completely frank with her.

"What are you hoping I will be able to do? What do the ..." She scoffed. "The Fates foretell?" She mentally kicked herself, almost unable to believe she was talking like this.

"A simple matter. Find the missing claves. Disable and dismantle the Gratadei. Restore the network to its previous strength. Restore the spirit of Khôra, heal the land."

Maisie's mouth went dry. "*That*'s what you call a simple matter? Do you understand how insane that sounds?"

Lavinia shook her head. A sorrowful air clouded her eyes.

"It is a challenging task. I would not expect you to do this on your own. There is a force of Fae warriors ready to assist you in physical matters. We hope to assemble an entourage to support your baser needs – sustenance, clothing and so forth."

"Hold on a minute. Warriors? Physical matters? You mean, fighting?"

Lavinia cast her eyes down, her face grim.

"I am sorry. It is indeed much to ask, but you are our last hope. We must stop the Gratadei. They are killing the land, exploiting the people both here and in your world. Yes, there will be fighting. Yes, it will be dangerous." She stared into Maisie's eyes. Reached out and took both her hands in her own. Clasped her fingers in a vice grip of emotion. "Please, we need your help."

Maisie pulled her hands away. Her stomach was in freefall, as if she were falling backwards into a black abyss. "I need some time to think."

Again, Lavinia took her hands, entreating her, her face stern in warning.

"There is so little time. As soon as Beckett is able, you must leave. The Gratadei are looking for you. They have spies everywhere. You need to blend in and travel without fuss. You must get to the Ostiarius Principale at Mediolanum as quickly as you can. Only she has the full map of the clavis network, and only she knows where to search for the missing claves."

"Mediolanum? You mean Milano, in Calabria?"

"Yes. That which you know as Milano is where the Ostiarius Principale resides. That is, the town of Mediolanum in Khôra is in the same location as the city of Milano in Calabria."

"How on earth are we going to get the vardo to Calabria?"

"Ah. Of course. You don't yet know."

Maisie was becoming, in short order, exasperated, then annoyed.

"What don't I know?" she snapped.

"The gods built Khôra to travel quickly. It is much smaller than your world, and so points are closer together. Mediolanum is seven miles away."

"Seven? Seven miles? What? How can that be? Calabria is a thousand miles from Breotonlond!"

"It is true. You can travel at your leisure and be there in a day."

Maisie was losing the thread of the conversation. The thrum of her heartbeat, drumming in her ears, masked all else. A tightness spread through her chest and she gasped for breath.

"I need to go now. I need to think. I'm going to the vardo." She shook her head, trying to clear her thoughts. "Please have some refreshments sent over in an hour or so, if that would be possible."

Lavinia bowed her head with a smile. "Of course."

Maisie stuffed the unused notebook into her bag, stood up, wobbled a bit, then found her feet and strode away, back to the hallway and the door to fresh air. Fresh-ish air.

She closed the vardo door behind her and slipped off her boots by the stove. The rain drummed a gentle patter on the curved roof. Steig was under a ruck of duvet, invisible beneath the bedding. The stove was cooling; she set to rekindling the fire. Once it had caught, she slipped off her coat and hung it on the hook by the door.

"Steig?" she called in a half whisper.

"Not here," came the grumpy retort.

"We need to talk."

"Go away."

Maisie clenched and unclenched her fists a couple of times, felt the sinews crack; she ground her jaw, the anger rising. And then fading.

"We need to talk. We need to either get back to the real world, heaven knows how, or go to Milano, which, apparently" – her voice rose into a shaky laugh – "is only seven miles away."

Steig peered out from his duvet nest.

"Milano?"

"Yes. Milano. Calabria. Seven miles. Looks like topology's gone mad. Or scale. Or something."

"What the fuck?"

"Indeed. Also, there's a bunch of religious zealots searching for me with murderous intent, and we have a fighting force of elves at our disposal."

"A fighting force of elves? Like in a role-playing game?" Steig sat up, a worried smile playing over his lips.

"Oh! The grouch rises from its pit!"

"The grouch is feeling pretty sorry for itself and is very embarrassed and also in pain. So much pain." He pulled a face, using both hands to lift his knee so he could sit sideways on the bed with a leg dangling. "Hang on. Murderous intent? Like, they want to kill you? What? Who?"

"Gratadei, apparently. I think Ostiarius Lavinia is being somewhat economical with the truth. But she seems to think we're in deep ... deep trouble, and we need to get to Milano to meet up with the head gatekeeper. So that we can find the missing keys. So that I can find the missing keys. Apparently, that's my role in this little quest."

"You're definitely giving it a fantasy roll-playing-game slant."

"I've never played them. My father wouldn't allow it. Bible studies all the way."

"What about your mother? You never mention her."

Maisie's felt herself falling, unhinged, inside. Her face crumpled into tears as she stood in the wagon, and she hid her face in her hands.

"Oh shit. Sorry, sorry, sorry ... hey, come on ..."

She heard Steig jump down, heard him suck in a sharp breath at the pain of using his leg, but then he had his arms wrapped around her. She snuffled into his shoulder.

Between the sobs, she choked out, "She left when I was quite small and I … I can't remember what she looks like!"

A searing pain filled her chest. Her ears roared with her heartbeat, and she descended into great heaving sobs, with snot and tears mixing down her cheeks. Steig held her close, rocking her from side to side. She clung to his jumper. Everything else outside their embrace seemed to recede.

After a minute, she looked up. Mucus strung from her nose to Steig's jumper.

"Sorry. Ew. I'm all snotty."

"Yes, you are. Here." He held out some tissue. She blew her nose, wiped her eyes. Tried her best to regain some composure. "I'm sorry I mentioned your mother. I didn't know."

"It's OK. I'm feeling rather fragile at the moment. Guess it tipped me a bit."

"Did you manage to ask any of the questions we listed?"

"No. I got as far as Keyfinder General and went all to bits."

"OK." Steig's brow furrowed. "Should we go back and try again? I can come with you if you don't mind me hobbling along?"

She smiled up at him.

"I don't mind. Yes, let's do that this afternoon."

Chapter 16

Calix entered the room, carrying a tray of tasty pastries and hot drinks.

"Ostiarius Lavinia will be with you in a few minutes."

"Thank you, Calix." Maisie smiled.

Steig and Maisie loaded their plates with pastries, some form of small tart with a meat filling, and filled their cups with the warm spiced wine from a tall jug. Steig bit into a pastry. It was delicate, yet warming, filling, delicious.

"I really appreciate the food here. Very wholesome," he mumbled through crumbs and a full mouth. He slurped some wine to wash down the pastry.

"You have crumbs down your front." Maisie's eyes twinkled with mischief.

"Huh." He began brushing them off, but then Lavinia arrived with a sweep of her robes and a nod to each of them. Steig thought she was a bit flustered. The unflappable ostiarius, flapping? This couldn't be good.

Maisie went to speak, but Lavinia held up her hand.

"I have received urgent news. The Gratadei are searching for you, Maisie. They will be here within the afternoon. But a group of neraides, er, Hellenic elves, are passing through, returning from the far west. They will travel with you and use their, er, special skills to protect you. But you must be ready to depart as soon as they get here. They will not wait."

Steig bridled. "I can hardly walk, and Beckett is a mess."

"Even so. You must leave, or we will all be in danger. You must travel to Mediolanum. The neraides will guide you. Vilicus will provide you and Beckett with a potent medicine. That will help."

"An' I'm comin' too, apparently." Bobe Elka's broad Lincoliscire accent filled the room. She stood at the doorway, leaning on her staff. "Tis an ill wind, an' all that."

Maisie's face lit up. "Bobe Elka! I thought you'd deserted us!"

"Nay, not me, lass. I was away for a bit, like, by yog, but I'm back. Sounds like you got in a right scrag with the grendylou, eh, Steig?" She cackled.

Steig winced. He hadn't, to be fair, missed that laugh. And then a terrible thought occurred to him. "I have a question, if I may?"

Lavinia nodded. "Ask with haste."

"We are presumably going to be travelling towards Mediolanum, to find the chief ostiarius?"

Lavinia inclined her head. "Yes, as I said to Maisie this morning."

"So, where are the Gratadei based?"

"Mediolanum."

“And how many roads are there, between there and here?”

Lavinia had the decency to look abashed. “Just one, for the first half of the journey.”

Maisie jumped up, threw her hands in the air in exasperation.

“How on earth are we supposed to avoid them, then? Shouldn’t we be heading in the opposite direction?”

“The neraides will cast a glamour around you for the first hour of your travels. Then you have options for different roads, through the Mockminnis woods, or up into Silentoak. Either of these routes will afford you the opportunity to hide for a day or two. Then you can join the main Autissiodorum highway, and over the Fenis mountain pass to Mediolanum.”

Maisie and Steig looked at each other. Maisie bit her lip, her brow furrowed. The plan definitely didn’t convince Steig. It sounded way too simple. But what other option did they have?

With Kord’s help, and much remonstrating from Beckett, who was sore and, more importantly for him, committed to eating the enormous pile of hay in his stable, they tacked the horse up and reversed him into the vardo’s shafts. Maisie and Steig tatted everything in the wagon down in double time; the hob’s assistance and the lack of an outdoor hearth made this a rapid job.

Bobe Elka took her usual seat in the wagon’s doorway, overseeing the packing away and the tacking up like a reigning monarch.

“What should we do with the clavis, Bobe?” asked Steig.

"You can hide it away in that priest hole y'have at the back, can you not?"

Steig was aghast. "How do you know there's ...?"

"You forget, I'm mostly Rom, me. Got me own vardo in an orchard up Lincoliscire way. You know that tho', don't you? Nosin' around me 'istory up Chirchedele, eh?" She grinned up at him. Infuriating. But it made sense. He had researched her story in the university's Roma library at Chirchedele. He had found quite a few references to "travelling gently by campfire". References to the old, white-haired, green-robed traveller woman who passed through, often stopping for tea, or a bowl of soup.

Steig opened the cupboard door under the bed, pulled out boxes of supplies, tools, bedding, spare driving harness. He uncovered the back wall. Half in the cupboard himself, he pressed just *so* on two corners, and the back wall hinged out, revealing a space that ran the width of the wagon. The clavis fit neatly into one corner, nestling up against a couple of long parcels wrapped in oilcloth. He shut the compartment again with a snap, but not before Bobe Elka had got down on all fours next to him and had a nosey around.

"Oy, Steig, you fogle! What you got there, then?" Her grin was as broad as he'd ever seen it.

"Let's hope we don't need to find out. Otherwise it will be grief all round. Keep it to yersen?"

Bobe Elka's grin subsided. "Aye, you 'ave the right of it. No chingaripen 'ere."

"What are you two doing under there?" Maisie's query at their backs made them both jump like schoolchildren caught in a nefarious act. They reversed out and Steig repacked the cupboard, completely covering the back wall.

"Just, y'know, er, packing stuff in safely ..." he muttered.

Bobe Elka silently showed her toothy grin and went back to her chair.

The neraides, when they arrived, must have done so in stealth mode, thought Maisie. One minute everyone was busy getting Beckett tacked up, the wagon tidied and packed. The next minute, half a dozen elves were hanging around, languorous, unapproachable. They were tall and skinny, like Lavinia, but had more ... well, pointed features. Substantial ears. Long black hair, either flowing free or braided. Their gender was difficult to determine. Dark-skinned, so yes, Hellenic, just as Lavinia had stated. They clad themselves in a range of dark greens and browns – jerkins, trousers, capes, all with intricate fastenings and findings.

They were armed.

Some carried swords, knives. Some had enormous wooden bows and quivers of arrows. One carried an ancient rifle slung over their back, hanging from a leather sling.

"Steig?" she queried. He was strapping a curved kukri knife, in a plain brass-bound leather scabbard, onto his belt.

"Yeh? Oh, yeah, uh ... I figured if there's extreme prejudice around the corner, best not be a complete pushover?" Bile rose in Maisie's throat. The shakes were coming on. She wobbled a bit, then leant against the side of the wagon's front cupboard. Steig took a step closer, handing her something wrapped in an oily yellow cloth. "Here, put this on your belt. At the very least, it will help when wood collecting."

She cradled the package, then unwrapped it.

It was a long hunting knife, with a grey bone handle.

She pulled it from its well-worn black leather sheath. It had a burnished silver-black blade, hefty and sharp.

"I don't know how to use it."

"You won't have to use it. Steig's law. You have the knife, so you won't need it."

"Like taking an umbrella, and then it doesn't rain? Only, um, higher stakes?"

"Exactly." He hugged her – a brief, one-armed affair – across her shoulders. It lifted her spirits. She undid her belt and looped the sheath through it, fastening it again. It felt weird. And it got in the way. Every time she moved, the hilt brushed against her hip. But, and she supposed this was the point, she felt protected by its presence.

After half an hour of rushed preparation, Maisie thought they had everything. Kord and Vilicus had arrived with a mountain of supplies – packages of all shapes and sizes wrapped in beeswax paper.

"It is all travel ready – it will keep. Nothing is perishable. And here ..." Vilicus passed a stoneware pot with a wax sealed lid to Maisie. "This is a potent medicine for Steig and Beckett. Put it on their cuts every night for a week. Every night, without fail."

"Vilicus, thank you so much. When this is all over, hopefully we will be back, and I can repay your generosity."

"You will be back. And that simple act will repay my hospitality, and that of the ostiarius," the housekeeper replied.

“I don’t understand.”

“She means,” piped up Bobe Elka from her grandstand seat, “if you make it back, you will ’ave broked the Gratadei, an’ that will be the test of it.”

“Oh.” She felt that tipping inside her again. If they make it. The big if. Oh dear. She swayed again, caught herself, reached for her resolve, and tried once again to keep her welling tears from falling.

Steig was down at Beckett’s head, talking with the lead neraida. What she assumed was the leader. He glanced up at her as she leant against the doorframe.

“Maisie, a moment? Introductions.”

She climbed down over the shafts and stood with Steig at Beckett’s head.

“Pheoreth, Maisie,” he introduced her to the elf. She certainly had the bearing of a leader. Tall, even for the neraides. Her jerkin and cloak were fastened with elaborate clips and buckles. Haughty. Looking down her elegant nose. Maisie smiled; Pheoreth didn’t smile back. Well, she thought. Just rude.

“Er, OK. And that’s Thonwen, and Morwen. I think they’re twins.” Steig pointed out the elves as he spoke. “Andion, Wenlor, and, er ...” He pointed at the last neraida, waving his hand in circles as if that would help his memory.

Pheoreth sighed, rolled her eyes. “Kansreth. Are we ready, Steig?”

“Yes. Sorry. Oh, Maisie, can you lead him out?”

Of course. Steig could hardly walk. Maisie pushed aside the tide of annoyance at Steig’s earlier stupidity and self-indulgence. Now was not the time. Especially not in front of Pheoreth. “No problem,” she said with a smile.

"Thanks. Are you OK walking with him for a bit? Just until we get going?"

"Of course," she replied, her voice lacking enthusiasm. The mud on the road was thick, grey, gelatinous ... she had her stout boots on, but even so. Steig limped to the stirrup step and hauled himself aboard, settled on the shelf and took up the reins.

Beckett's ears swivelled back and forth, tracking all the elves, Steig, Maisie.

"It's OK, Beckett, I've got you," she whispered.

"Thanks. Bit scared."

"We'll be on the way in a minute. I'll be with you, OK?"

"Yeh. OK."

The going was terrible. Deep, muddy, horrible. Maisie looked down at her legs as she hauled at the breeching strap next to Beckett's heaving, sweaty flank. The stuff was so sticky; it was like treacle. Only less tasty. She knew; some had splashed into her mouth a minute ago, as Beckett had put his huge hooves down in a liquid puddle of the stuff. Ew.

But they were making progress. Most of the time it wasn't so deep, and Beckett pulled the wagon, if not with the usual ease, at least without requiring help. And the ground was becoming firmer and less sticky. Oh, what she wouldn't give for a bath. A hot, deep bath, with scented crystals and salts, and shampoo, and ...

"Hand here ...?" gasped Beckett. He had hit another patch of deep mud.

“Sorry, here, got you.” She heaved again on the strap, lending her weight to the task, her boots slipping in the grey ooze. One of the neraides came to help, and although they were slight of build, she could feel the change in speed as they pulled. Maisie guessed they had more than average strength. She tried a smile, but the neraida looked away in disdain.

After half an hour, and the final pull up a gentle rise, the land opened out before them. Maisie’s breath caught in her throat, and not just from the foul air. Green! Actual greenery was growing, a faint fuzz in the distance. It felt like it had been so long since she had seen anything but grey mud; it was a shock.

Steig called to her. “Hey, Maisie, we should be OK, now we’re on the level. Come, rest.”

She swung up from the roadway onto the shafts, scraped her boots off on the edge of them, letting her feet dangle over the ledge. Dollops of mud fell to the roadway in pattering splats. The road here was hardening up, and the wagon rolled much more easily.

Steig smiled at her, though his eyes were serious. “Thank you. I couldn’t have done that. I really appreciate it.”

She felt a surge of warmth; she had helped pull Beckett through some of the deepest mud and urged him with a gentle voice. She smiled back, slipped off her boots and tucked them inside the door. Really, they needed a good clean, but that would have to wait until they stopped. Grasping the doorframe, she swung up and around and inside, past Bobe, who took up most of the doorway. Bobe Elka was dozing, her eyes closed, her face slack and a series of gentle snores punctuating the other sounds of travel.

Maisie stripped off her filthy jeans and put on her long blue dress, looping the belt and knife around her hips. It felt out of place, odd; but she did feel safe. She hopped up onto the bed and looked out of the back window. Two neraides were loping behind the wagon. They seemed alert, looking left and right, and behind. Nothing else to see, just blasted trees and scrubby bushes to the flat horizon.

She looked ahead, through the open door. The plain stretched a mile or so ahead, with forests smudging the land on either side. These, she guessed, would be their hiding places. The plain then rose to a series of gentle foothills and a range of truncated peaks.

Two more neraides were on either side in front, also alert. So, the elves were making a protective ring around them. She wondered, had the elves cast the glamour? Was it working? Could you tell from inside? She couldn't see anyone on the road ahead, but then, maybe the Gratadei had a glamour of their own.

Steig drove Beckett with care; thought about what Lavinia had said. If the Gratadei were coming for them, they would surely use this road, which headed to the centre of this world, the town of Mediolanum. The sooner they left the road and hid in the hills or the forests, the happier he would be. Sitting duck didn't even come into it. Running away wouldn't be an option. Stealth was their friend. He hoped the elves' glamour was solid.

When he'd spoken earlier to Pheoreth, she had said the plan was to hare off into the woods at the first opportunity. As if reading his thoughts, the neraida at the front left dropped back to a brisk walk beside Steig. It was Pheoreth. He reappraised her; androgyny was a trait shared with Lavinia, but the hair was dark, almost black, long and straight. Her ears were far more acute than Lavinia's, ending in sharp points. Smooth, dark, Hellenic skin. And deep brown-black eyes, set in a long, thin face. All sharp and angular, matching her body. She carried a wooden longbow over her back, and a quiver of arrows. A short sword at her belt.

"We take the next right, by that bush ahead, you see?"

"Yes, got it." He nodded.

The road split, the right-hand path little more than a farm track, but when Beckett turned onto it, the vardo ran easier. It was hard packed, possibly paved under the dirt. Old Roman, Steig suspected. It wasn't straight, but they were in a magical kingdom. So, new rules? He had no idea.

The road followed the contours of the foothills, winding in and back along a ridge, affording them a view over the plain to their left. As they ran into the beginnings of a light woodland, Steig spotted movement on the road they had left, a mile distant. It was a convoy of small trucks, or four-wheel-drive pickups. Pheoreth reappeared at Steig's side.

"That is the Gratadei. They will send a scout up here when they get to the junction. Andion and Thonwen have hidden our tracks, but we must now get off the road. Pull in here." She pointed at a widening of the track where there was a grassy area. "We will use the glamour to mask us."

"Just like that? In plain sight?"

"In plain sight. Yes. That is how the glamour works."

He did not feel confident, but pulled the wagon onto the grass as far as he could. The overhanging oak branches scraped the tarpaulin. Maisie stuck her head out of the door, as Bobe Elka woke up with a start.

"What are we doing?" Maisie asked.

"We," Steig replied, winding the wheel brake on tight, "are hiding. In plain sight."

Maisie stared around in horror at the proximity of the road, the dense forest on one side, the scrubby bushes on the other.

"Pheoreth thinks they will send a vehicle up here to check for us; she will use the glamour," continued Steig. "I have a parallel plan."

With Maisie watching in confusion and Bobe Elka laughing, Steig pulled all the items out from under the bed again. He extracted one of the long packages, placing it onto the bed before closing the hidden compartment and repacking the cupboard.

He unwrapped the package with reverence, revealing a long, matt-black hunting rifle. He grabbed two magazines; stuffing one into his back pocket, he pushed the other into the slot under the action, where it clicked home. He pulled the bolt back, checking the breech, before slinging the rifle over his shoulder on its strap.

Pheoreth appeared at the wagon door, her eyes growing larger at the sight of the gun. But then she nodded.

"That is a sound plan. I suggest you take a position in the treeline with a wide field of fire. If I give the signal, do not hesitate. Take Maisie with you."

"What? Wait, what? What do you mean, signal?" Maisie's voice rose in panic.

Steig grabbed her shoulders, his gaze level with her eyes. "Come on. Focus. We're hiding in the woods. That's all. It will be fine. Breathe."

She took a shuddering breath, then another. Some colour returned to her cheeks.

"OK. We're OK, right? Just ... hiding in the woods."

"Yep. Come on. I saw a suitable spot as we pulled on." He let himself down to the sparse grass by degrees, wincing. Maisie jumped down next to him. "Beckett, just stay still, OK? Like that time in Hameltune, remember?"

"Yeh. Hameltune. There were mints, after."

"And so there will be. But first, silence. Don't move a muscle, no matter what happens. OK?"

"Yeh."

"Come on," he called to Maisie over his shoulder, setting off at a fast limp into the treeline. He heard her following. A few yards past the end of the wagon, he sank down behind a fallen tree. There was a notch in the trunk where a branch had snapped, making a natural crenel from where he had an unobstructed view over the whole track as it passed the clearing. A scraggy stand of hazel provided limited cover. He hoped the glamour also extended this far, though he had no idea how to tell.

One of the neraides – Andion, Steig thought – took cover behind the log as well. He was carrying a long gun of uncertain vintage, but he handled it well and gave them a broad grin as he pushed the bolt home and made ready. He winked at Steig, the gesture incongruous given the circumstances. Steig grinned back, shrugged, and sat with his back to the tree. Maisie was next to him. He could feel her warmth where she leant against his side. She was shaking. A vehicle's engine in the distance was getting louder. He turned to her.

"Hey. We're OK. Just stay still. Keep your head down." He gave her what he hoped was a reassuring smile, a supportive touch on the shoulder.

"I'm terrified."

"Concentrate on your breathing. Stay down, don't move."

He lay down and wriggled so he could see around the end of the tree, looking along the ground. A dark-green pickup truck, of the type favoured by rural farmers and Mauretanian adventurers, hove into sight at the edge of the clearing. It swung around in a tight arc, churning up the ground with its oversize tyres, and stopped, pointing the way it had come. It was twenty-five yards from the fallen tree behind which Steig and the others hid. He counted four people on board. They were having an argument. Hands were being waved, and there were voices raised above the running engine. The rear door opened and a tall, burly man with short-cropped hair, dressed all in black, got out. He didn't even glance at the wagon, which was standing not thirty yards from him. Instead, he turned back the way they had come and stretched, as if he had been sitting for some time. Then he turned away from the vehicle and, facing the tree Steig was hiding behind, unzipped his fly and peed.

Steig tightened his grip on the rifle but didn't take aim. He stayed low, loath to show himself, even though the wagon stood in plain sight and they were oblivious to it. Glancing towards the vardo, he checked Beckett, who was standing stock still, not even swishing his tail. Good lad.

"Sbrigati, idiota!" came a call from the vehicle, as the driver wound down his window and remonstrated with the peeing man.

"Non chiamarmi idiota!" he barked back, and continued to argue with the driver as he shook off, zipped up, climbed back into the truck.

As the door slammed, the vehicle sped away in a shower of mud and gravel. The engine noise receded and Steig giggled, relief flooding him; he rolled onto his back and let go of the rifle. Maisie crawled over to him, lay against his side, resting her head on his belly. She was weeping, tears running down her flushed cheeks.

"Hey ... you OK?" Steig asked, his giggles subsiding, concern for Maisie taking centre stage.

"Yes. Tears of relief. I've never been so scared in my life."

"Well, you did great. Stealthy."

"How are you so calm?"

Steig thought about it. He was calm. Why?

"Faith in the neraides, I guess. They seemed to reckon they could outwit the Gratadei. Looks like they were right."

"Of course, we know our magic," said Andion, next to them behind the log, his face sombre. "In the woods, we have the advantage. In the town, not so much."

"You did really well, horse. Here." Steig dealt two mints from the end of the packet and gave them to Beckett, who sucked them in through the side of his mouth, past the bit, and crunched them.

"Easier than Hameltune. Didn't have to gallop."

"Yes, easier than Hameltune. Good lad."

"So, dare I ask what happened at Hameltune?" Maisie quirked an eyebrow upward.

"Probably a story for another time." He turned to Pheoreth. "I have a question, if I may?"

"Of course."

"The Gratadei's armed faction." He waved down the road in the direction the mercenaries had gone. "All-powerful, well-funded, the best equipment and training, yes?"

"That is an accurate attestation."

"Why are they driving around in forty-year-old vehicles?"

"The nature of Khôra is such that some technologies from your world do not work. It is, apparently, an issue of natural philosophy, but I do not know the details."

"So, modern vehicle management systems, microprocessors, stuff like that?"

"Anything that contains a …" She frowned, searching for the word. "Semiconductor, I think is the technology that will not work. It was once explained to me by a physicist, but I freely admit I do not understand the reasoning."

"OK. So, no transistors. No radios. No phones?"

"That is correct." She smiled.

"They have to physically go somewhere to communicate. Excellent. So, what's the plan?"

"One moment." She turned and conferred with Andion, their heads almost touching. She turned back. "I would think the Gratadei are all by now at Ostiarius Lavinia's compound. The Ostiarium will feed them misinformation, lies and falsehoods. That is not xenia, but they are not of this land, so the gods forgive us."

"And we carry on along this road?"

"We do. They are unlikely to come back this way. The direct route is much easier for them. We will make camp in the woods above the road. There is a hidden glade."

"I like the sound of a hidden glade. Better than a patch of grass in full view of the road."

Pheoreth grinned, showing her teeth, but made no further comment. They climbed back into the wagon, released the brake wheel, and Beckett hauled them onward, towards the woods.

Chapter 17

Maisie took a turn driving, as Steig rummaged in the first aid box for pain relief. The misty cloud of the afternoon had dissipated, and the evening was looking clement. The setting sun filled the air with a dimmer glow than she was used to in the "real world", but the colour of the light still lifted Maisie's spirits. The rays tinged the forest's branches and sparse early leaves with a golden hue. Tension ebbed from her neck, her back; driving meant having something to exercise her mind. She had spent so much of the journey worrying about if the search party would see them, and then worrying that somehow the Gratadei would return and catch up with them.

"You can't change the things you can't change, so stop worryin' about 'em."

She turned to smile at the old woman.

"It's true. I was worrying about everything. I'm feeling better now, having something to do." She held the reins up by way of explanation.

Pheoreth materialised next to the vardo, loping at an easy pace, keeping time with Beckett.

"The glade is on the right, just up here. Follow me."

She increased her pace and pulled ahead, then veered off into the trees, slipping with apparent ease between two boles that were too close together for a vehicle. Yet when Maisie pointed Beckett at the gap, the point of view changed, and the gap widened. She wasn't sure if it was a change in perspective or some manipulation of the laws of physics. But either way, they shifted off the track and under the branches of the trees. The sunlight deepened whilst twigs rustled, caressing the vardo's roof.

She drove the vardo as generously as she could around the corners, all the while straining to keep the neraida in sight in the gloaming. Pheoreth walked between towering tree trunks on a meandering path. The vardo bumped over roots, branches, but the way always had enough space, the ground always smooth enough. The trees on either side allowed enough room, the gentle whisper of twigs on the tarpaulin just audible over the loam-deadened thump of Beckett's hooves.

They emerged into a broad glade, the trees crowding in against an expansive circle of short, ratty grass. A smattering of high clouds reflected the last of the day's light in a display of oranges and russets. She parked near one edge, bringing the wagon to a halt with gentle pressure on the reins.

"That'll do, Beckett. Good lad," she murmured under her breath.

Beckett's ears flicked; he had heard. She smiled to herself. There had been a moment, turning off the road, where she was ready to hand the reins to Steig, but she had held her nerve.

"Nicely done, kushti." Bobe Elka touched Maisie on the shoulder, her words soft, gentle.

"Yeah. Accurate driving." Steig was smiling at her from the other ledge, where he had settled before they turned off the road. He had been quiet, not trying to take control. Maisie had seen him, out of the corner of her eye, fidget a couple of times. Granted, they were squeezing through impossible gaps between trees, but he'd kept his faith in her. She felt warm inside.

Pheoreth walked over to them.

"You must exercise caution. This is the Forest of Silentoak. It is an ancient woodland, and the dryads that live here may not be friendly. Be sure to ask before taking firewood. Do not cut any tree. Stay close to the clearing."

Maisie smiled at Pheoreth. "Understood. Thank you."

Pheoreth smiled back, a brief lifting of the corners of her mouth. But her eyes didn't change. Oh, what a cold fish.

Maisie watched the encampment take shape. Steig had untacked and tethered Beckett on the weedy grass and was unwrapping the supplies to see about cooking a meal. Bobe Elka busied herself lighting a fire with the wood they had loaded into the cratch and was boiling the kettle to make tea.

"I'll get more firewood," she suggested, to no one in particular. Steig didn't react. He was busy; Bobe Elka raised her hand, gave a smile, as if to say, "Off you go then." The elves had taken themselves over to the far side of the glade. They were setting up a canvas shelter between two trees, laying out their sleeping rolls and relaxing in that laconic way of theirs.

"Fine." She rolled her eyes and headed for the nearest gap in the trees. Pheoreth's words resonated; she'd go as far as the first windfall and fetch that back, after asking, of course.

As she stepped into the treeline, the noises of the camp muffled to a murmur. The understorey was dense with mould and leaves, deadening any sound. The light dimmed, a thick canopy of new leaves attenuating the setting sun. She stood still, allowing her senses to adjust; her hearing sharpened and her eyes became used to the gloom.

The trees here were medium size, old oaks but not ancient. Mosses and lichens dripped from their bark, and they grew straight, the overstorey high above. It was like being in a cathedral, all greys and browns, very little green at the lower levels, so tightly packed were the trees.

"You really have squashed yourselves in here, haven't you? Did you have to move over to make the glade? Or do you like being this close?"

She reached out and caressed the nearest trunk, felt its rough grey bark, counterpointed with soft moss. Breathed in the smell of old air, musty decay and turned earth. She walked a few yards further into the trees. The light dimmed more; the sounds of the encampment now inaudible. She could hear nothing but her own breath, catching in her throat, and the pumping of blood in her ears as her heart fluttered. Silentoak was a suitable name for this place.

"Maisie, Aedredd's Daughter, Finder of Keys, welcome." The voice was faint, little more than a whisper, and arrived in Maisie's ears from all directions. As if from the trees ranged around her. She froze, her mind racing. Who was it? What was it? How did they know her mother's name?

"Who are you?" she asked.

A thickening of the air between two tree trunks made her eyes dance. The fabric of the air shimmered and shifted, resolving into a figure that simultaneously was a slender young woman, and a moss-and-ivy-encrusted being of immense age. Maisie blinked a few times, trying to clear her vision, and the figure resolved to the young woman. She had sharp-ridged features, pale brown like new bark. Her hair was green tendrils of moss shot through with strands of ivy. Deep brown horse-chestnut eyes regarded Maisie, unblinking. She opened her mouth, revealing rows of sharp, pointed white teeth. Maisie remembered what Steig had said about the meliad: "She had teeth. Lots of sharp, pointy teeth."

"I am Erato, of Arcadia." She smiled as she spoke, her teeth gleaming.

Erato! The priestess and consort of Pan. Maisie dropped to the ground and bowed her head. Although fearful, she managed to speak without too much tremor.

"Erato, f-forgive my intrusion into your realm. I humbly ask for safe passage."

"Rise, child. Do not fear me."

Maisie looked up. Erato had cocked her head to one side, was resting one hand on her hip, and held a bemused expression on her face, a smile twinkling in her brown eyes. Maisie stood up, feeling both awed and a bit foolish. She brushed loam from her knees and hands.

"You will always have safe harbour and passage in Silentoak, on my honour, and by xenia."

"Thank you, Erato. You are generous."

"It is I who must thank you, child. You are the Keyfinder, Inventor Clavis. The Fates have foreseen your actions."

"I fear the Fates have made an error."

To Maisie's terror, Erato instantly grew in stature, doubling, then tripling in height, towering above her. Her feet extruded into giant grey-brown roots that plunged into the earth, throwing loam and twigs into the air. Her fingertips grew outward and turned to strong branches, intertwining with the surrounding trees. The light dimmed yet more, and Erato's voice was so loud and powerful, Maisie felt it in her bones.

"The Fates have spoken an immutable truth," she intoned.

Maisie trembled, cowered as sprigs and leaves showered down from the canopy, dislodged by the resonance. As Erato shrank back to her original size, retracting her roots and branches, she continued at a more normal volume.

"Do not doubt the Fates." The light returned. A smile played at Erato's lips. "I have a gift for you."

Maisie didn't dare say a word. To refuse a gift would go against xenia, and she was in no position to upset the gods. Gods. Plural. Oh my word, what was she becoming? Her attention snapped back to Erato, who was holding her hands over a patch of earth between them. A sapling sprouted, grew from the earth, writhing and casting about in a manic spurt, its bark smooth grey-white. It extended, stretched, grew straight up to the height of Maisie's shoulder.

"Cut the base of the sapling with your knife."

"I-I cannot cut a living tree." Pheoreth's warning rang clear in her head.

"This is your gift. Cut it. Take it. I command you."

Very well, thought Maisie. Commanded by a dryad of the highest order. From Arcadia, no less. Who was she to refuse? She fumbled with the hunting knife at her belt, managed to pull it from the sheath, and held it in her trembling hand. She knelt before the sapling and grasped it. It was warm and moved under her hand, swaying and pulsing. Terror welled up in her. She quailed.

"Cut it! When you cut, hold fast!"

The command in the voice made Maisie's teeth rattle, her bones ache.

She held the knife in her right hand, knuckles whitening with the strength of her grip; she swept up and away from the sapling. In as deft and strong a stroke as she could manage, she brought the blade arcing down through the base of the plant. The knife passed clean through it, her forearm jarring against her left knee where she knelt. The branch jumped in her hand, a pulse of energy jolted and electrified her arm. She cried out in surprise and shock, but held on. As she stood again, holding the sapling, it transformed, writhing like a viper. Maisie watched in abject terror, holding the contorting mass away from her body as far as she could. But she held fast, as commanded.

"Do not release it until its metamorphosis is complete. It will pair bond to you, and only you."

"H-how long will that take?"

"Patience."

And indeed, the sapling seemed to slow its writhing, and straightened, lengthened, became thicker, bulkier. It was moving under her hand, and there was some sort of weird exchange of energy, ideas, information, between her nervous system and this thing. After a minute, or so it seemed, the sapling finished its transformation into a quarterstaff, some inches taller than Maisie. It was straight, an even width all the way along its length, and with a subtle spiral pattern etched into the bark. The bark was grey-white and smooth, as if varnished or polished. It was still warm under her handhold and pulsed in time with her heartbeat.

"This staff of Silentoak is for you, my gift to you. It will assist you in your quest. Take it, go well."

Maisie held the staff, one end on the ground, and bowed so deep she almost doubled over.

"Thank you, Erato. You are most generous."

She straightened from her bow and found she was alone in the trees. Erato had disappeared as if she had never been there. Only the staff held in her hand showed all that had transpired.

Maisie walked back to the camp in a state of confusion, all thoughts of collecting wood forgotten. The staff warmed her hand, vibrating under her touch as if it were alive. As if it had been waiting for her to hold it.

"Stop that," she muttered.

Oh, now she was losing her mind, talking to a stick. And yet, the vibration ceased, the feeling of yearning subsided. Was the staff still alive? Semi-sentient? This was all too much.

Pheoreth was sitting at the fire, staring at her as she approached. When Maisie arrived at the fireside, she scrambled to her feet, alarm crossing her face. Was that … fear? "Where did you get that quarter-staff?" she demanded, her voice raised. "You went into the trees to collect firewood, but return with a staff of Silentoak. You cannot hold that!"

As Maisie stopped, confused, holding the staff at her side, leaning on it, Pheoreth backed away.

Andion and Morwen came running, arriving out of breath, which was a first for Maisie. She hadn't seen the elves break a sweat before. They took up position on either side of Pheoreth, and then as they reviewed Maisie and the staff, they paled and backed away a pace.

Steig stuck his head out of the wagon.

"What's going on? Maisie? Pheoreth?"

He limped down the vardo steps, his hand on the hilt of his knife, and took a stance next to Maisie, facing the elves.

"Yes, Pheoreth, what on earth is going on?" asked Maisie.

"You are holding a staff of Silentoak. It is a powerful magic, and I am concerned that it is you who hold it, you who are leathphór."

"Leathphór?"

"Means 'alf bred, duck. Not very polite."

Bobe Elka came up behind Maisie and stood at her other side, flanking her, holding her own staff before her, firmly planted in the sward.

Maisie frowned. "Half bred? Half bred what? Pheoreth?"

"Explain yourself, Pheoreth. Speak plainly," suggested Bobe Elka.

Pheoreth shook her head, as if to clear her thoughts.

"I am concerned, confused, as to how you come to hold this staff of Silentoak. Please tell me how you came by it."

"The dryad Erato gave it to me. I went into the trees to collect wood. I propitiated the forest spirit. She appeared, and we had a brief conversation, which ended with her gifting me the staff. Why is this such a problem for you?"

"You are leathphór. Only íonghlan may carry Silentoak."

Bobe Elka cackled long and loud. "Oh, are you sayin' she's nay worthy? Ha! You're just jealous, I reckon. Pure bred indeed. Oh, we all know she's half fae, but really. Y'can't go around bein' so ... so bigoted. Look at you! You're fae, yersen. You know, an' I know, worrits like to be discriminated against. An' yet 'ere you are in the holy wood of Silentoak doin' just that. You're no better'n them Nazi buggers in the war."

"Right," commanded Steig, loud enough to turn all heads, including Beckett's. He pointed at Maisie and Bobe Elka. "Sit." He pointed at Pheoreth. "You too. Sit down. And you lot" – he swept his arm towards the remaining elves, now all ranged behind Pheoreth – "bugger off and leave us to discuss this in a civilised manner. Over tea. Maisie doesn't need a-a ... bleedin' audience of elves for this next bit."

He stooped and tossed some more logs on the fire and put the kettle on the hook to boil. Maisie sat down on a stool, holding the staff over her lap. Bobe Elka snagged the spindle-back chair and Pheoreth, with a show of reluctance, settled on her haunches.

"Next bit?" Maisie asked Steig, in a stage whisper. Then, her voice rising, "Hang on. What did you say, Bobe? We all know she's half fae?"

"Oh boy," muttered Beckett.

Steig set out mugs, reached for the kettle and brewed the tea. He fished the teabags out and flicked them into the fire, where they hissed. He glanced around. Bobe Elka sat slumped in the chair, staring morosely at the fire. Pheoreth seemed ready to take flight. Maisie was curling her hand around the hem of her dress, fiddling with it, clearly agitated. She rested her other hand on the staff.

"Well. I dunno. I thought you knew, like," Bobe Elka offered.

"How could I possibly know?"

"Well. I mean. There's your ears, duck."

"What about them? There's nothing wrong with my ears!" Maisie wailed, pulling her hair around her face, covering them.

"Fine staff, you got there," Steig said, trying to change the subject, looking up with worried eyes at Maisie. He offered her a mug of tea. She took it with her right hand, keeping hold of the staff with her left.

"Thank you. This is all a bit much to take in, I must say." She sipped her tea. "So, are you saying" – she turned to face Pheoreth – "that I'm half elf? And my father looked ... well, human. So, it was my mother who was elvish? Daoine sidhe?"

"Yes, that is what I am saying," said Pheoreth, pouting her lips down, and keeping her eyes on the fire.

"And everyone knows? Everyone but me?" Her voice rose a notch. Pheoreth flinched.

"I didn't know. I think you have lovely ears," said Steig, blushing.

"Well. Thank you, I think." She turned back to Pheoreth. "And tell me, how is it you know this? Apart from the ears?" She shot a stern glance at Bobe Elka, who grinned back.

"The Fates foretold it ..." began Pheoreth.

"Not those ... bloody Fates again. If I ever meet them, I'm going to have words, I can tell you."

"The Fates foretold that the Finder of Keys would be leathphór, that her mother is named Aedredd. I apologise for my earlier outburst. Bobe Elka is correct, it was ... narrowminded of me. I was simply confused, surprised, since all I have been told concerning Silentoak is that it is a sacred place for the fae, both neraides and sidhe."

Steig got up and poked the fire with a branch, raising sparks like a swarm of incandescent fireflies. He cleared his throat, gaining the attention of the people around the fire.

He gestured toward Pheoreth with his mug. "I wonder if you would do us the honour of relating your oral history of Khôra, from inception to current times. So that we might gain an ..." He frowned, searching for the word. "An understanding of what we are up against with the Gratadei. Because frankly, at the moment, I don't have a bloody clue what we're doing here. Why does Maisie need to find keys? What's so awful about the Gratadei? You know, stuff like that. Fill in the blanks."

He looked at Pheoreth, the smile on his face not reaching his eyes.

"Very well," Pheoreth replied. "It is the least I can do, by xenia, in this sacred grove."

She stood and moved closer to the fire, allowing the light to play over her features. She closed her eyes for a moment, took a deep breath, and began.

> Many years ago, when the gods and goddesses of Olympia walked the earth, and men and women, fae and all the magical creatures, lived in harmony ...

Bobe Elka snorted down her nose. Pheoreth glared.

> Well. They lived in relative harmony. Heracles, son of Zeus and Alcmene, travelled the lands to the west, until he came to the great Western Sea, that which you call Atlantic. He sailed on Helios' boat to the island of Erytheia, on one of his labours. There he slayed the monster Geryon, and stole his cattle. He now needed to herd a thousand cattle over three hundred miles of ocean. Through the deserts of Mauretania, over the straits known as Jabal al Tariq, through the Iberian Peninsula and Gaul. Over the Alps, and yet more, along the coast of Dalmatia, to return to Mycenae.
>
> However, he was tired of endless travel, endless distances, mountain passes, deserts, all the geography that the continents had to throw at him. He had, frankly, had enough. He slaughtered one cow and burnt it on a huge pyre of oak and ash, offering a sacrifice to Hephaestus, smith of the gods, and to Helios, the god of the sun.

Pheoreth took a drink from her mug, grimacing as she realised it was empty. Steig lifted the kettle back onto the fire.

> Hephaestus, Helios and Heracles worked with each other to devise a way to travel through Europa from

Erytheia to Mycenae. They wanted to avoid all the tedious crossing of oceans and deserts, climbing mountain passes, fighting trolls and so forth. Hephaestus distilled the golden essence, the Chrysí Ousía that powered the dawn, scooped up in a ladle by Helios as he drove across the sky. He poured this into a crack between the worlds, where it grew, with some guidance, into a land that lay apart from the world. Hephaestus called this land Khôra.

Khôra was accessible through a pair of gateways, one at each extreme, west and east. The land was beautiful and yet empty. With clement weather, it had hills and valleys, meadows and woods, but no seas, nor mountains, nor people. The gateways, as I am sure you can now guess, were much closer together in Khôra than in Europa. Hephaestus made keys for the gateways; they were marvellous twelve-sided bronze mechanisms which bridged the old world and Khôra. Heracles returned to Mycenae, walking there through Khôra in just three days, herding the thousand cattle before him. He thus avoided the sea crossings, deserts, mountains and brigands that would otherwise have hampered his progress.

The kettle came to the boil. Steig made more tea, refilling Pheoreth's mug. She settled back on a low stool, sipped her tea, steadied herself, and continued.

> Khôra was born. But it was empty and had but two gateways. Over the centuries, descendants of Heracles rediscovered the mechanism to make more gateways and keys. The perforation of the veil occurred, and Khôra became a shortcut for invading armies, for visiting royalty and for diplomats and spies.

She stopped to catch her breath and allow the story to settle. The fire crackled against the dimness of the glade. Everyone was rapt, eyes shining, watching Pheoreth.

"When did Khôra become populated?" asked Maisie.

"Patience. We will get there." Pheoreth smiled.

> Where was I? Diplomats and spies. Yes. The rise of the Roman Empire led to the formation of the Gatekeepers' Guild, what we know as the Ostiarium. The Celtic fae, Tuatha de Danann, had already appointed themselves keepers of the gateways. They supported travellers and kept an eye out for ne'er-do-wells. The Roman Empire merely added the name and some conformity. And a treaty, of course. The Romans loved their bureaucracy.
>
> As Christianity spread, the Roman Empire became holy, and the papacy rose to power in Europa. The

> effect of this on the fae, hobgoblin, nymph and other creatures was to drive them from Defaltum Mundi ...

She noticed Maisie's confused expression.

> What we call, er, your world. They made their way, over a few hundred years, into Khôra. By the time Christianity was rife across Europa, the fae had left, and were the predominant inhabitants of Khôra.

Pheoreth again paused, to catch her breath. She looked troubled, her countenance dark.

Maisie smiled up at her. "Please, continue, if you can."

> There was a problem with the papacy. It had used a glamour to push its message across the known world in its early centuries. Holy relics imbued with this glamour would entrance entire populations. This was their secret. This was how they became all-powerful in such a fleeting period of time. But the relics were losing their essence. Whatever glamour had been cast was wearing thinner and thinner as the empire expanded. The pope set up a small group of bishops, alchemists, scientists and theologians to solve the problem.

"The Gratadei!" exclaimed Maisie.

"The Gratadei, as you say." Pheoreth inclined her head in agreement.

> They discovered that by siphoning off some of the energy that Helios gave to build Khôra, the relics could be imbued with power once more. They forged a trade agreement between the Gratadei and the Ostiarium. The Gratadei would import goods that are impossible to find in Khôra in exchange for the re-imbuing of relics.

"What can't you get in Khôra?" queried Steig. "It looks self-sufficient. In those areas that aren't a wasteland, at least."

> There is no geology here. So, no minerals. No metals. No salt. Coffee doesn't do well here. The agreement allowed for occasional shipments of bulk minerals in exchange for small, tiny amounts of the Chrysí Ousía. And for hundreds of years, this was the status quo. The Gratadei delivered cartloads of materials, and the Ostiarius Principale allowed the re-imbuing of relics. All this changed a few years ago. We are not sure, but we think the papacy is finding its decline in power in Europa problematic. A surfeit of iron, of modernism, is suppressing the power of the relic.

"So, they have taken more Chrysí Ousía than they should have?" asked Maisie.

"That's not the 'alf of it, duck." Bobe Elka's voice crackled with hatred. "Torn the agreement to shreds. Knackered the Ostiarium. Shut 'em out. Nicked the keys. Taken over. That bloody new boy, the Cardinal they calls 'im."

Pheoreth glanced at Bobe Elka again, and Steig thought he could see an undercurrent of ... what? Annoyance? Guilt? He wasn't sure. He continued to watch, through the smoke from the yog.

"Well, it is true," continued Pheoreth, "that the Gratadei have, um, changed the agreement, and are taking more from Khôra. Hence the desolation, in places at least."

Bobe Elka snorted in disgust.

"OK," said Maisie. "I can see things are bad. But what do I have to do with it?"

Pheoreth smiled, with a hint of solemnity.

"I know you are not fond of hearing of the Fates, and yet they have foretold it. You are she who will find the missing keys and restore the balance to Khôra."

"And to be utterly clear, I'll restore Khôra, how?" Maisie queried, an eyebrow raised.

Pheoreth looked her in the eye.

"I have absolutely no idea."

Steig slipped under the goose-down quilt. The evening air felt chill; the sky was clear, and he thought there would be a frost. The staff was wedged against the coaming along the edge of the bed. It was a beautiful object but radiated a tangible aura that warded him from touching it. He guessed it was a magic thing. And not touching it was fine by him.

Maisie climbed the steps and shut the vardo door after her, holding the stoneware jar of salve in her left hand. Steig could smell it, like a potent antiseptic. She put the jar on the table and wiped her right hand with a cloth.

"This stuff is sticky and smelly."

"How was Beckett with it?"

"He complained, and then mugged me for mints."

"So, he's fine, then? His cuts were quite red this afternoon when I checked them."

"Yes, he'll be OK. Now. Your turn."

Steig sat up in bed, offered his arm, and Maisie unwrapped it, the self-adhesive veterinary bandage making a ripping noise as it unglued.

"Ow, bloody hell, that's tender."

"Sorry," she muttered, dipping the cloth in a pan of water that she had placed on the stovetop to heat.

She dabbed at the angry cut, cleaning away the dried blood and pus. Steig watched her work, a smile playing at his mouth.

"What are you grinning at?" she asked, eyes down, concentrating on his arm.

"How do you know I'm grinning?"

"I can feel it radiating from you."

"I'm smiling at you doing the whole nurse thing. Wondering how you feel about that. I can do my own arm, you know."

"Why didn't you, then?"

"Just forgot."

"Hmm." She applied the salve and re-bandaged his arm. "OK, knee."

She repeated the process: unbandage, clean, salve, re-bandage. Steig felt his knee was healing well, considering the depth of the thorn. Certainly, the pain had subsided since that morning, which he reckoned must be a positive sign.

Chapter 18

"Right, the trick with kathalyog is to find your yog. Obviously, there's a yog 'ere, like," Bobe Elka waved her staff at the campfire by the vardo, where Steig was sitting, drinking his morning tea. "But the thing is to find another yog, to travel from one to the other."

Maisie was dubious. "OK. How do I find the other yog?"

"Well, there's a spell, see. You get your staff to start it, and once it starts, you sorta peer into the mist, like, and you can see the other yogs. Choose one, walk towards it. Easy, like. Here, we can do it by stages. Cast the mist, 'ere, like this."

She waved her staff and intoned, just loud enough for Maisie to hear.

"Sikker sa yogs, lasta sa yogs."

The fire dimmed a fraction, as if the magic had tamped it with earth. A mist enveloped them. Maisie let out an alarmed squeak.

"Dun't fret, lass. You say it, too. Think them words into y'staff. One spell, one person, see."

The staff was becoming warm, vibrating in Maisie's hands. She held it in front of her, as if to ward off a spell, not cast one. She repeated the Romani that Bobe Elka had uttered. The campfire dimmed a notch more, and the mist thickened. Steig shuffled backwards, away from them, cupping his mug of tea.

"Walk into the mist, slow, like ... Follow me." Bobe Elka took a couple of steps into the mist that was shrouding the fire and disappeared. Maisie stepped forward. The cold and damp of the fog froze her exposed skin, beaded her hair with droplets of water. She took another step, and the campfire faded to a distant yellow pinprick, receding whilst staying in place. She was in a world of flat grey monochrome all the way to the diffuse horizon. The glade was no longer visible. Just the yellow flickering dot where the fire had been, and Bobe Elka standing on a swirling grey nothingness.

"Welcome to the Betwixt. S'wot I calls it, anyway."

"It's freezing." Maisie's breath clouded in front of her. Her voice was flat and monotonic, the fog swallowing reflections.

"Aye ... Cloaks are useful for that." Bobe Elka lifted the heavy material of her green cloak, allowed it to fall again. "Right. Trick is to keep an eye to your own yog, like. That there ..." She pointed at the glimmer of light where the fire had been. "And then 'ave a cast around for another one. Once you get your eye in, it's easy."

Maisie peered into the swirling haze. She could just discern other dots of light if she squinted and concentrated.

"I can see them!"

"Right, choose one, walk towards it. Nice and slow."

Maisie did as Bobe Elka bid, took two steps, maybe three, and the orange glowing dot she had chosen resolved into a campfire, next to a small tent, as viewed from above. Though obscured by the dense fog, she thought there was a person, a form, sitting by the fire.

"Shall we visit?" asked Bobe Elka.

"How?"

"Step towards the fire. Slow, like. You need the other 'alf of the spell, and all, like this: kathal yog, adala yog."

Maisie stepped forward, intoning the spell, holding her staff before her, and the mist dissipated. The figure by the fire, she could now see, was a tatty, ragged hob, sitting before a many-patched dome-shaped tent, in a small glade surrounded by fir trees. The hob gave a start, squeaking and scrambling backwards, whimpering, holding their hands over their face. They came up hard against a tree trunk, and peered between their fingers at Maisie, who tried her best smile.

They looked beyond her, at something over Maisie's left shoulder.

"Well, bless me, tis Bobe Elka. Thou gave us a right thrash, me ticker's fit to bust."

"Hello, Kurra. Are you keeping well? This is Maisie, she's—"

"Oh! I know thee!" Kurra's eyes shone, turning to Maisie. "Thou art the Finder of Keys. Come to save all us!"

Maisie felt herself colour from her toes to her hair.

"Oh, well, um ..."

"Don't embarrass the girl. She's still learnin' the ropes. Stick kettle on, lass."

The hob scampered at hob speed, and in a blink, the kettle was on, and three mugs stood ready with loose herbs in each of them.

"Now then, Kurra, tell Maisie 'ere, where are we?"

"This be Mockminnis woods, on the northern side of Khôra. North of here be the Cold Wastes, and south of here be the Fenis mountains."

Maisie calculated their rough location.

"So, not near Silentoak, then?"

"Ho, she is new, ain't she, Bobe?" screeched the hob, slapping her thigh with delight. "We be two days' fast walk from Silentoak."

Maisie wasn't sure about Kurra's tea. It was bitter with tannin, and gritty, and there was no sugar. But she drank it down, and they prepared to depart. Kurra was fidgeting, wringing her hands and hopping from foot to foot.

"What's wrong, Kurra?" Maisie asked, squatting down on her haunches to be level with the hob.

"I 'ave something for thee, My Lady, if it pleases thee?"

"Um. What is it?" Maisie wasn't sure she wanted a gift, if it was like the tea. Though the hob seemed pleasant enough, if a little shy. Kurra darted to her tent, blinking away and back. She extended her hands to Maisie. Cupped in them was a clavis, the bronze polished to a lustre that made its facets shine like a beacon in the dim of the forest.

"Tis the clavis of Witcerce. Well, one of 'em. I 'ave kept it for near on ten years now. It is for the Finder of Keys, as told by the Fates. Thou *must* take it." She held her arms out further, and jiggled up and down, willing Maisie to take the object.

"Oh! Thank you." Maisie took the clavis from Kurra's outstretched hands and slipped it into her messenger bag. She glanced over at Bobe Elka, who was regarding them with her usual toothy grin. Looking back at Kurra, she saw the hob had relaxed her jiggling, and had a serene expression on her face; she had fulfilled a pledge ten years in the making.

"Best be gettin' back, like. Good to see you again, Kurra," said Bobe Elka. They each cast the first half of the spell and so returned to the Betwixt. "Now's the trick, y'see. Which is your yog, with your Steig?"

"Oh! He's not my Steig. He's just Steig."

"Well. That's not 'ow it looks to everyone else!" Bobe Elka showed all her teeth again. "So, can you find yourn?"

Maisie squinted. She could see tens, maybe hundreds of pinpricks of yellow and orange flickers, laid out on a misty grey carpet, stretching to the fogged horizon. She concentrated on the staff, warm in her hands, and formed the question, the command, in her mind.

"Staff of Silentoak, show me my home hearth."

Almost immediately, a nearby dot of light flared brighter than the rest for a brief second. She smiled and stepped towards it.

"Ho, you 'ave the gift of it, right enough," cackled Bobe, walking behind her.

Maisie stopped by the light and leant in. The scene appeared to her, as if through a haze of fog or cloud, seen as a bird's-eye view. Steig was pacing up and down by the fire. His mug of tea, half-finished, was on the front vardo shelf, forgotten. His face was a mask of fear and worry. Pheoreth was standing opposite him, on the far side of the fire. Her face was grim. Arms folded, one finger tapping. Oh no! They hadn't been gone that long, had they?

She intoned the second half of the spell and stepped from the Betwixt into the welcome warmth of the fire. Curling fingers of tendril-fog clawed at her clothes as she passed, her hair once again beading with dew.

Beckett let out a deep whicker of greeting, at the same time as Steig almost bowled her over with a bear hug.

"Where the hell …? Fuck's sake, I was worried sick. You just disappeared!"

She beat her hands against his back.

"Let me go! I can't breathe," she said, though she was laughing as she gasped it out. Laughing at having succeeded in kathalyog, and laughing at being back in the warmth, in one piece.

"I am glad you are back. We were worried." Pheoreth's face held a stern cast, a frown creasing her otherwise perfect dark skin.

"Well, that was quite the adventure. We went to Mockminnis woods!"

Pheoreth's face changed; she allowed amusement to lift the corners of her mouth.

"That is a four-day journey, there and back. You made excellent time."

"I'm really sorry I worried you, Steig."

"It's one thing having Bobe Elka coming and going like that – but you could have warned me! I thought you'd just step in and back out?"

"We stopped for a cup of tea … oh …" A wave of fatigue descended on Maisie like a waterlogged blanket. Her arms and legs turned to jelly, and she toppled over. "Oh! Oh, I don't feel too good …" she managed, as Steig caught her up in his arms, staff and all.

"I forgot t'say, you'll be right washed out ferra bit after that, takes it out of you. You get used to it, though."

"I got you," said Steig. He supported her shoulders, and steered her to the vardo and up the steps before pivoting her onto the bed. She lay in a rag-doll heap, her legs sticking out off the side of the bed platform. Steig took her boots off and arranged them by the stove. He lifted her legs onto the bed and covered her with a blanket that smelt of Beckett.

"I'll bring you some hot sweet tea. Just rest."

Maisie woke from a dark, deep, dreamless sleep. Her bones ached. Such exhaustion! But she had cast a spell, and travelled through a netherworld to a distant place, and come back. It was ... well, it was magic. Incredible, but it had really happened.

Sudden panic filled her. She felt around in the duvet, her movements rushed, fervent. There! Her hand grasped the warming, steadying presence of the staff. She had slotted it into the gap between the duvet and the coaming that ran along the edge of the bed platform. She opened her eyes, the vardo roof as usual inches from her nose. Sounds of cooking and the hubbub of camp life outside, all calm in the wagon. Thin diffuse light filtered in through the windows. The stove was at embers, a steady gentle heat. She snuggled down in the luxury of rest.

She needed to think. So much had happened so quickly. Erato had gifted her a magic staff. She had learnt magic. She had discovered she was half fae. Or sidhe. Or Tuatha de Danann. Whatever. And they still had this whole quest ahead of them? She was the Finder of Keys;

it was her destiny. She wasn't sure how she felt about predetermined actions. The bible, theology, had plenty to say on predetermination. But she wasn't sure she liked it as a concept.

If she turned around and said "Take me back to the real world", would they? Steig couldn't make that happen, even if he wanted to. And he seemed happy here. Bobe Elka might help, but she had an air of unreliability about her. She supposed that was the question: how to get back, should she want to? Where were all the claves to transport people back and ... oh. Yes. Of course. That was her job. Apparently. Oh, it was too much!

She let out a sob, rolled onto her front and buried her head in the pillow.

"Hey, you awake?" Steig called. The wagon shifted on its springs as he climbed the steps.

"Yeah." The pillow muffled her voice.

"Food in a bit, lunch. One of the neraides hunted a deer, so it's venison stew."

"I want to wallow in self-pity for a bit longer."

"Venissson sssteew," his voice whispered, inches from her ear, drawing out the sibilance of the words.

She giggled. "Alright. Alright. I'll get up. Give me five minutes."

The stew was remarkable. It was replete with huge chunks of venison, tender and almost dissolving in the mouth. Root vegetables and tinned tomatoes from the vardo's store cupboard. Wild garlic and some chanterelle mushrooms from around the glade. Finally, it seemed, the cornucopia was, well, bearing fruit. Bobe Elka had returned from foraging the mushrooms and had set to making an enormous pile of chapatis on a metal skillet over the fire.

"This is even better than that pheasant at Stirwood," Maisie enthused through a mouthful of chapati and meat.

"Stirwood! I've not heard that name in quite a while," remarked Andion.

"Oh! Do you know it?"

"Aye. It was my father's domain, before the Departure. Back then, it was a forest to be reckoned with. Full of deer and wild boar. You could travel in the shade of the trees along the silver paths from Cestre to Northantone. Now, tis but a tiny patch of dimling."

"How long ago was that?"

Andion wrung his hands, shifted his weight. "It's not best dwelt on, this old history. Not by the likes of ... by newcomers to Khôra."

"By the likes of leathphór, you mean?"

Andion had the decency to look abashed. "My Lady, you are the Finder of Keys. But this is all very new for us. I ask your forgiveness."

Maisie did another internal calculation. Andion had said his father, assuming he didn't mean ancestor or great-great-times-twenty grandfather, was alive and walking the forest when it stretched across half the country in an uninterrupted sweep. When was that? Henry VIII's shipbuilding spree? Enclosure? The Norman invasion? The Roman invasion? Her history of Breotonlond was a little rusty, but she had a feeling it was between a thousand and two thousand years ago. It seemed the fae must be exceptionally long-lived.

"Hold still, Beckett."

"It stings."

"Well, you'll get really sick without it, so be brave."

"I'm a horse, a flight animal. I don't do brave."

Maisie rolled her eyes. Sometimes Beckett was more horse than she realised. The salve Vilicus had given her certainly smelt foul, astringent, and it was of a thick, gluey consistency, but that just meant it stuck to the blackthorn scratches on Beckett's chest all the better. They were red and raised, but not the hot, angry cuts they had been the day before.

"There. All done. You can do brave, after all."

Beckett swished his tail, left his ears flat on his neck. He was sulking.

"Your turn, Steig. Into the vardo; get your clothes off."

Steig grinned like a Cestrescire cat.

"There's something I didn't think I'd ever hear you say."

Maisie gave him a look. A look that said don't push your luck. He held up his hands in surrender.

"OK, OK, I'm going."

"OK, that's you done. Brr, I'm cold."

She turned the wick of the lantern down before divesting herself of most of her clothes. In her underwear, she slipped into bed. "Warm me up, Mr Sturluson."

"My pleasure, Ms Hanson." He held her around her shoulders, and she snuggled into his side. The night air had cooled her skin. He held her close.

"So. I've been thinking."

"Uh oh." He shifted around so he could face her. "What's up?"

"How do you know something's up? You're infuriating!" She balled her fist and thumped his chest.

"Ow!"

"Well. Serves you right. But I am worried. Everyone seems to think I'm this great saviour. Even Kurra said—"

"Who?"

"A hob we met in Mockminnis woods. Even she knew my name, knew me by sight. 'Thou art the Finder of Keys, come to save all us,' she said. She was camped in the middle of nowhere and yet she still knew me."

"The Fates have seen it," he declared, his voice low and ominous.

"Don't you start. I'm sick of hearing about the Fates. Whatever they are."

"You should know, right? They'll be like the Norse Fates, the Norns? Three of them, past, present, future, something like that? Maiden, mother, crone? Surely the classics have them?"

Maisie glanced over at him, exasperation pursing her lips. "Clotho, Altropos and Lachesis, the Moirai. Just ... this isn't Hellenic Mythology for Beginners, this is ... well, real. And as real as it is, I worry that I'm not the great Keyfinder General everyone seems to think I am. I mean, we don't know anything about the clavis network. We know hardly a jot about the Gratadei. For all we know, they might be the good guys in all this, despite Bobe Elka's obvious dislike of them."

"Well, from the brief interaction we had with them, I would rather side with the neraides and Ostiarium than a bunch of mercenaries."

"Mercenaries?" Her eyes went as big as saucers.

"Well, yeah. Not that I consort with mercenaries as a rule. But they had that look, you know? Ex-military, built like a brick shithouse, tactical-black clothing, wraparound shades even in the gloom, you know the sort?"

"No, thank God. I do not 'know the sort'."

"Well, I do. And they are. So, my money's on this being the good side. Until further data is available."

"OK, granted, we're on the right side. But we don't know what we're doing!"

"We will, though, won't we? You'll learn magic stuff. You have that staff, right? We're travelling slowly, getting the feel of the land, meeting people, gathering information. You heard Pheoreth's oral history. It differed from Lavinia's in quite a few key details. That's more data points we gathered. We're in no great hurry, even if the Gratadei seem to be."

"But what if we want to go home?"

"You mean, what if you want to go home? I am home."

She thumped his chest again. "You know very well what I mean, Steig. What if we want to go back to the real world?"

"Real. That's a joke. This place feels ten times more real than Breotonlond. Did you notice that people here call the other world Defaltum Mundi? The default world. I think that's a better term than real. This place is real, as well."

"OK, what if we want to go back to the default world?"

"I honestly don't know. Calix was telling me that the Gratadei control the Mediolanum gateway into the default world. But we have a clavis, don't we? Can't we use that?"

"Bobe Elka said we could, but that it needs to be in the right place. I really have no clue."

"Essentially, we don't know. So, ask. Ask Bobe Elka or Pheoreth, in the morning. See what they say."

"Mmm, excellent plan." Maisie yawned, stretched, settled to sleep. "Yes ... good plan ..." she murmured. "G'night."

"Goodnight, Maisie."

Steig lay still, his arm around the woman, listening to the sounds of the forest outside, the sound of the wagon inside. An owl hooted. The neraides were murmuring and rustling on their sleeping mats across the glade. Beckett was quiet, having eaten most of the grass available. The fire had burnt down, and the embers fell silently to ash. Maisie's breathing relaxed, became more even, deeper, as she drifted to sleep.

Steig thought over the day's events. The week's events. Running away had seemed like a good idea, though he suspected Bobe Elka's hand in some of it. He thought about this, and discovered he didn't mind Bobe Elka manipulating him, in this instance. It was an adventure, and hopefully they would make a difference to many people. Creatures. Beings. He shut his eyes and drifted, but sleep was a while coming.

Chapter 19

"Best get up. Moving on day."

"Nooo ..." Maisie snuggled under the duvet like a burrowing animal. "Five more minutes."

"Gotta move, time to go, get shifted, moving on day!" Steig sang in a lilting voice. "Come on, shake a leg."

Maisie stuck one bare leg out from under the duvet, shook it in a desultory fashion, and withdrew it again.

"Brr, cold out."

"Up, now, or you'll miss breakfast. The elves have made magic porridge."

Maisie sat up, forgetting once again the proximity of the roof.

"Ow!" She rubbed her forehead, tousled hair falling from her face as she did so, her brow furrowed in confusion. "What? Magic porridge? How? Also, why?"

"No, just normal porridge. But we're on the road in an hour, and I could do with a hand getting Beckett ready."

"Oh, false pretences!" She found a dirty sock on the bed and threw it at him.

"Got you up, though."

"Huh. How's your arm, by the way?"

"Yeah, the salve is stinky, but seems to work. No pain so far today."

"Maisie, gorra min?" Bobe Elka asked.

Maisie thought she sounded nervous. Unusual.

"Of course, Bobe. What's up?"

"Got a coupla things for you. Come on, we best step into the forest for this."

Curiosity piqued, Maisie finished packing the pan box with the cooking ironware, grabbed her staff, and joined the old woman at the glade's edge. Bobe Elka glanced around like a cautious, furtive fox, then nodded with her head, indicating they should step through the treeline.

As before, Silentoak was living up to its name, the sounds from the camp muffled and attenuated. Maisie turned to Bobe Elka, smiling, expectation on her face.

"I'm off, y'see, when we gerroff here. Goin' north. Things to do there. Seein' a man about a dog."

"Oh! I see. Um ..."

"Dun't fret, lass. I'll be back, sure as eggs is breakfast. Only I wanted to give you summat, like. Out of pryin' eyes. Here."

She reached inside her tunic neckline and pulled out a small pendant on a leather cord. She ducked her head and pulled the cord over; held it out for Maisie.

"Oh, no, Bobe, I can't possibly ..."

"Now, don't make me tell you. I'm offering, like, as you will need it more than me. It's a tatchapen amulet. Means y'can see through a fae's glamour."

Maisie examined the amulet. It was a small stone, circular, possibly made of flint. There was a hole in its centre, into which was set a clear, colourless crystal, held with a lattice of fine golden wires. The wires looped up into a ring, with the leather cord threaded through it. It had a peculiar, primitive feel about it.

"Take it, put it on."

Bobe Elka thrust her hand at Maisie, who took the amulet with care, weighed it in her hand, then came to a decision, and slipped it over her head.

"You'll need the spell. It's like this: Garav okkapen, sikker tatchapen."

Maisie repeated the spell, memorising it. She held the words in her mind and grasped the staff, which responded with a gentle pulse of energy, warming her hand and her forearm. The amulet, resting on her chest, also pulsed a gentle warmth.

"You got it, I can feel it. The fae can't tell if you use it or not, so you can just think the spell an' it'll show you what's what without the glamour, if there is one, like. But keep it hid. They'm not keen on us mere mortals usin' the cloch sióg."

Maisie's confusion must have shown.

"Cloch sióg, it's a fairy stone. Stone with an 'ole in it," Bobe Elka explained.

"Thank you, Bobe. You are truly kind." Maisie went to hug the old woman, who took a step back.

"Nah then. Norra hugger, me. But you're welcome. Use it well." She smiled, her toothy grin beaming from ear to ear. Maisie returned the smile. "Ah, also, you'll need to learn the clavis spell, like. You got that one from Kurra? Cos I'm takin' the Wayland one with me."

Maisie rummaged in her bag and pulled out the dodecahedron. She held it by the vertices between thumb and forefinger, peered at it slantwise.

"I don't even know how to make them work."

"Well, that's easy. You just need the intent, said in old Rom or ancient Hellenic. It dun't mind the lingo, just the intent."

"Ancient Hellenic, then. I know that. What are the words?"

"I command you to open. Or summat."

"What, like, Open Sesame?"

"Yeah. It's the intent-shun, see?"

Maisie regarded the clavis, thought about the phraseology, and after a moment's hesitation, said, "Anoígō thúra."

The air around the clavis shimmered and a dull blue glow shone through the holes in the dodecahedron's surfaces. She looked around. No magic gateway. The blue glow faded.

"Aye, you need to be near the gateway for the key to work, like. This one's for the gateway at Witcerce. Won't do nowt here 'cept that grufty blue stuff."

"And presumably 'I command you to close' when you're done with it?"

"That's right. See, you got the 'ang of it straight away!"

"Um, so, katálēxis thúra!" Nothing happened. "Well, I suppose if it didn't open, it doesn't need to close. Cool! Thank you, again, Bobe."

"Well, hope you find a way to sort they Gratadei buggers out, that's all I ask."

"I'll do my best, Bobe."

Though doubt assuaged her.

Steig sighed, searching the edges of the woods with his eyes. He had finished tacking Beckett up, and he had backed the horse into the shafts. He could see Maisie had put the pans away. Where on earth had she got to after that? He hoped she wasn't off in the mists again. Kathalyog, she had called it.

Beckett's ears swivelled to the edge of the glade, where Maisie and Bobe Elka emerged from the gloaming. He let out a rumble of acknowledgement. Steig rolled his eyes. Maisie had come out of her shell since the whole staff-gifting event. Quite a different woman, all things considered.

Pheoreth walked over from where she had been conferring with her troupe.

"Once we are on the road, we will keep the glamour on the wagon, to keep from prying eyes as we travel. But when we get to the highway, we cannot hide you. Hopefully, there will be enough traffic there that you will not be so obvious."

"OK," replied Steig. "Are we going to stop for supplies anywhere?"

"Yes, I was going to suggest at Autissiodorum we stop at the market. It's very busy, so we will blend in. It is two hours away."

"And where are we stopping tonight?"

"We will stop before Fenis Pass. That is a choke point, so we will recce it first thing in the morning for Gratadei. If it is clear, we will go on to a farm at Pont Romain, near Mediolanum, where you can leave the wagon, and Beckett."

Steig was aghast. "I don't like the sound of that at all."

"The farmer is a friend. He will be in safe hands," Pheoreth assured him.

"Well. I'm not sure. Let's see when we get there?"

Pheoreth's face darkened.

"Very well." She turned on her heel and stalked away, back to the rest of the elves. Beckett turned to watch her go. His ears flicked.

"What? I'm not keen on leaving you in the tender care of some random stranger, horse."

"It's in the future. Let's deal with the present."

"You've been spending too much time with Maisie. Didn't know you had the concept of future in that apple-sized brain of yours?"

"There's lots of stuff in my head."

Steig laughed, rolled his eyes. "OK, then." He raised his voice. "All aboard. Let's get on."

Steig helped Bobe Elka up, as she set her feet with care, climbing from the stirrup step to the shafts, and in. Maisie leapt like a mountain goat, straight to her seat on the right, pulling her staff after, sliding it inside, along the wagon floor. *Her* seat. Steig grinned to himself.

"What?" An open-faced enquiry from Maisie.

"Nothing." All innocence. "Can you drive while I lead him off?"

"No problem."

She reached down and took up the reins.

Maisie drove them out of the woods. The route out followed a different path, but with the same weird changes in perspective and track width, the same mysterious smoothness of the way, barely a root or branch to interrupt them. Again, Pheoreth led, and Maisie peered after her into the gloom, trying to keep her in sight. After some minutes they emerged onto what Maisie presumed was the same road that led from the junction in the west to the mountain pass at Fenis in the east.

As they trundled past a farmstead, one of the farm labourers, or maybe the farmer himself (Maisie wasn't sure how you'd tell), waved at the phalanx of elves.

"Good day to you," he called.

His gaze slid from the wagon, as if it wasn't there. Maisie supposed all he could see were a group of elves walking the highway. She wasn't engaging the cloch siόg, but presumed that inside the glamour, you couldn't see the glamour. Otherwise, they would be invisible to each other. Perhaps. It made her brain hurt thinking about it. She would ask Pheoreth how it worked at the next opportunity. After all, if she was half sidhe, she should perhaps be able to cast a little glamour herself?

They had started early, and it was well before midday when they reached a junction on to a more substantial road with more traffic – donkey carts taking produce to market, a horse-drawn wagon similar to their own, and a whole range of other carts and flatbed drays, laden with produce.

"It is market day today. Turn right. We will take the glamour off for now, otherwise you might have someone drive into you."

Maisie applied gentle pressure on the right rein, and Beckett obediently changed direction, walking out onto the broad roadway and turning to the right.

"Thank you, Pheoreth," said Steig. "Maisie, perhaps stay in the back for now? It's you the Gratadei are looking for, isn't it?"

Maisie frowned at Steig's statement. It annoyed her, almost scared her, but deep in her heart, she knew hiding was sensible. For now.

"Dun't take it to heart, lass. Here, I can 'elp you. Come on."

Bobe Elka got up from her seat and shuffled into the dimness of the back of the vardo, rummaging through her knapsack that she had placed on the bed earlier. "It's in 'ere somewhere. Ah! Here we go!" With a triumphant flourish, she pulled a dark, forest-green cloak from the recesses of her pack. "It's me summer cloak, like. You can give it me back in a month or so. S'gorra hood, see?"

She held up the garment, demonstrating the voluminous hood, the ornate brass clasp inlaid with moonstone.

"Oh, Bobe, it's lovely! Thank you!" Maisie took the cloak and swept it over her shoulders, fastening the clasp and pulling the hood over her head. From within, she felt protected and hidden.

"There you go! Can't see your locks now! Disguised, so y'are." Bobe Elka nodded in satisfaction. Lowered her voice. "Don't you go pretendin' to be me now, when you're kathalyog, eh?"

She cackled, nudged Maisie in the ribs. Maisie's fierce blush burned her cheeks. The cackle turned to hoots of laughter.

Pulling on to the edge of the marketplace in Autissiodorum, Maisie could see why Pheoreth was less worried that they might stand out. From her quick count, she saw seven other vardo-type bow-top wagons parked along the perimeter of the marketplace. Also, the market heaved with people and animals. Sellers had laid out stalls of all shapes and sizes in a haphazard, higgledy-piggledy manner. Throngs of people of all ethnicities and species jostled to examine the goods on sale, bartering the prices. The air was heavy with the smell of animal dung, stale sweat, spices, cooked meats and perfumes. The market area, a flat field outside the town itself, was noisy with the shouts of vendors, the braying of animals and, from somewhere, what sounded like a blacksmith repeatedly hitting metal. Maisie struggled to take it all in, pulling the hood tighter up over her head. She stepped down from the wagon, holding her staff before her.

"Wow, you look like ... you look like a witch," commented Steig with a grin, as he turned from putting a head collar on Beckett. "In a good way," he added, seeing Maisie's face darken in the deep recesses of the cloak.

"What are we getting?" she asked. The coffee stocks were low after supplying the neraides at the glade with two days of the beverage. "Oh, and what are we paying with?"

"Lavinia has given me funds with which to finance your expedition," said Pheoreth, jingling a leather pouch that was heavy with coins.

"I think mints, or at least apples," Beckett interjected.

"Well, first you've got to stay here and be sensible. No wandering off. The brake's on," said Steig.

Leaving a brace of elves to tend Beckett and the wagon, they split into two groups, elves and humans, and headed into the hubbub. Bobe Elka and Maisie were like twins, all in green, hoods up, quarterstaffs at the ready. Steig walked between them, smiling but clearly also on edge, his eyes darting everywhere.

Maisie sniffed coffee, and veered off to a smaller stall that displayed paper bags of coffee beans. An ancient hand grinder was set on the counter, with full-sized hessian sacks arranged along the front, each one filled with beans of different shades of brown. The human vendor – an elderly man with greying hair, a reddening cauliflower nose and round wire-frame glasses – sat up at their approach. He wiped his hands on a leather apron and reached for a kettle that was bubbling on a small paraffin stove.

"Seigneur et mesdames, puis-je vous intéresser au meilleur café?"

"I'm so sorry. Do you speak Breotonish?"

To Steig's ear, Maisie sounded contrite.

"But of course. My lord" – he bowed to Steig – "and ladies, might I interest you in a taste of the most excellent beans from Araby? Fresh and direct from the Mediolanum gateway itself!"

"Where are these from, sir?" Maisie asked, pointing at a sack of beans by her feet.

"Why, they are the finest, the most valuable beans; they come from Aksum, grown on the Abyssinian Highlands, imported through the southern gateway at Byzantium," he declared.

"Oh? Is it not the case that the gateways are all closed to trade? This is what I had heard?"

The vendor's face clouded. He checked left and right, then leant forward over his counter and pulled close to Maisie's hooded face. His accent dropped, became more Breotonlond.

"I don't mean to speak out of turn. An' I can see you, My Lady, are of strong and clear character. However, it is the case that the Gratadei have closed the Byzantium gateway. Those ..." He bit back a curse. "The Gratadei have seen fit to limit our trade. These beans are all I have left from my stores. That's why the price has gone up. The Gratadei have strangled the supply. I don't know what I'm goin' to do ..."

His eyes welled with tears, and he turned away from Maisie, sniffling.

"Well. That is the news I was expecting. I'm sure the situation will resolve itself in due course. Meanwhile, I should like two kilos of the Aksumian, fine ground, if you would be so kind."

They continued to walk through the market, stopping here and there to peruse goods, to chat with vendors, and to buy supplies. Steig kept a weather eye on the proceedings, allowing Maisie and Bobe Elka to do the talking. He watched the people as he walked. Predominantly, they were elvish – their pointed ears and long, sinuous bodies were a giveaway. But he also saw occasional humans, and the flit of hobs, and some odder-looking characters passing by. One he was sure would be classed as a troll. It was enormous and slow moving, arms reaching to the ground, with a ridged forehead you could plant potatoes in.

Steig was relaxing into the ambience of the market when a pair of travelling folk approached them. The look, he guessed, was universal. He held back, interested to see how things would play out. They were both young, little more than teenagers, with a swagger to their step and a sneer to their lips. They dressed in greens and browns, clean shirts, leather waistcoats, moleskin flat hats, black leather boots. Their weathered faces held sharp, small eyes.

"Bobe Elka, kushti divvus. Y'takin' on 'prentices? Or is this your dui tiknas? Cos she dun't 'alf look like yer!"

The taller of the two youths gestured to Maisie, who had her cloak hood up over her hair.

"Nah then, Cutlight, no need to be rude. This 'ere's May-Shee, and y'know I don't take 'prentices, so hold your tongue."

Bobe Elka held her staff at her side as she addressed the traveller. Cutlight turned to Maisie, raised an eyebrow.

"May-Shee. Kushti divvus. Not seen y'round before?"

Maisie didn't curtsey, nor bow. From the shadows of her hood, she spoke, her voice modulated and deep, like a fey creature.

"Kushti divvus, Cutlight. I travel the dimling ways by moonlight. You'll not have seen me, nor will you."

She held her staff before her as she spoke, then tapped it on the ground between them. Steig wasn't sure, but he thought he felt a dull thump, a slight shockwave.

Cutlight took a step back.

"Och, Bobe, she's a harsh one, nay?"

Bobe Elka grinned up at him. "Aye, she can be, so, well, watch yersen, Cutlight, when the Goddess glows full."

Steig watched from a couple of paces away. The smaller of the two travellers, a young lad with a mop of greasy black hair, tugged on Cutlight's sleeve.

"C'mon pal, she's messin' with yer. Y'know as 'ow she be?"

"Aye, see you round, Elka." He nodded at Bobe Elka, cast a wary glance at Maisie and pushed between the two women, his friend trailing in his wake. He went past Steig almost at a run, and Steig heard him muttering something about bloody chivani, witches, under his breath.

"So, a spooky accent, and some sort of eldritch staff-work?" he enquired, half joking.

"I-I didn't mean to scare him. Just didn't like him. The staff … sort of thumped." Her voice was quavering.

"It's awright, lass. It's Silentoak. It's linked to you, can feel your mood. Y'should probably practise more. Only, somewhere less crowded, like."

Back at the wagon, after they had loaded the supplies into the cupboards, Bobe Elka took Steig and Maisie to one side, around the front of the wagon, next to Beckett.

"Nah then, you three. I'm off up north this ar'ternoon. You'n come a long way since Roteslund and that bloody Wayland mess. You needs to keep your wits about you, but I reckon you've got that in hand, eh?

You with your staff, and you" – she turned to Steig – "not much gets past you, I reckons. Just look out for each other. And thou, Beckett, just keep doin' what you're doin', horse-like. It will see thee well."

"Oh, Bobe! I'll miss you so much. When will we meet up?" Maisie was crying. She put her hood down to wipe her face with the back of her hand. Her cheeks were blotchy with tears and emotion.

"Well, I need me cloak back, dun't I? So, a month or so, I'll come find you in Mediolanum, or wherever you end up. Once I've been and sorted me affairs up north, I'll be back, like, and I can kathalyog to wherever you are."

Steig put out his hand; Bobe took it and shook it, a firm handshake. She held her other hand over his as she looked into his eyes. He shifted, uncomfortable under her scrutiny.

"You'd best look after her, look after each other. If you die, I'll kill you."

"We'll do our best to stay breathing while you're away. And, the feeling's mutual; don't die."

"Right, well, I'll be off. Kushti bok!"

"Kushti bok, Bobe Elka!" they both called after her departing back.

They watched her as she marched, green cloak flowing, staff striking the ground in cadence with her walk. She approached a nearby campfire and became enveloped in mist and faded from sight.

Chapter 20

The road out of Autissiodorum meandered, leaving behind the river valley and climbing towards a distant col between two higher hills. A small stream bubbled over rocky soil to the left, forest rose up the steep hillside on the right.

The road was busy, with occasional horse-drawn traffic overtaking them as Beckett plodded up the incline, with Steig and a neraida assisting the horse. One four-wheel-drive lorry came grinding up the road, belching exhaust, its engine rattling and roaring. As it passed, the sweet tang of burnt diesel fuel trailing in its wake wafted into Maisie's wrinkling nose. She coughed.

"That will be the Gratadei supply lorry from Lutetia," opined Pheoreth. "They run the lorries daily between Londinium, Lutetia and Mediolanum. We will pull in on the right, up ahead."

The turning was narrow and half hidden, the woodland they climbed into opening out into a bowl of a valley with a level floor big enough for the camp. Ancient alpine woodland surrounded them on three sides, grey and foreboding, the understorey bare but for brambles and pine needles. The fourth side opened to a view over the valley below, back to Autissiodorum. A strip of woodland did a fine job of shielding them from the road.

"Kushti pull-up, very secluded," commented Steig as he untacked Beckett.

"We will add the glamour around the wagon, just in case anyone comes in from the road," Pheoreth said.

"About that," said Maisie. "How does it work?"

"I do not know. We just … think it. Think the thing we want someone to see. You push the image. And they see it. I cannot really explain it. Like here, I would think, 'No wagon here, just trees and elves.' And that is what people see. Come, watch."

She led Maisie away from the wagon to the other side of the clearing and raised her hands as if conducting an orchestra. After a few seconds, Maisie felt what she thought must be the push. It made her scalp tingle. The wagon faded from view; the trees behind showed through, and then the wagon was gone.

"That's incredible."

Pheoreth smiled. "It is very useful, I will admit." She shook back her long hair and half-glided over to where the elves were setting up the tarpaulin tent.

Maisie leant into her staff and cast the tatchapen spell in her head, felt the pulse of energy, felt the amulet grow warm between her breasts. The wagon fuzzed back into view again, Steig untacking Beckett and pegging him out. There was a shimmer in the air around where, she guessed, the glamour's limit lay.

"Oh wow. It really works," she muttered. Then, with a thought, shut the spell down. The warmth faded from the cloch sióg, and the wagon faded from view.

As she walked towards where the wagon had been, it sprang back into visibility. At the same time, she felt that push again, a feeling almost like her ears popping, only all over her body. The edge of the glamour.

"Tea's on!" called Steig.

Steig watched Maisie, across the glade, through the smoke and heat haze from the fire. He leant over to stir the stew, which was simmering in the cast-iron pot on the trivet over the yog. Maisie was practising with her staff. He wasn't sure what, exactly, but he could feel occasional dull thumps through the ground, as she tapped it to the earth. Beckett had his ears back, and was at the limit of his chain, against the edge of the clearing, as far from Maisie as he could get.

Maisie set out three empty tomato cans on the ground, which she had filched from the rubbish bag. She stepped back a few yards and stilled herself. Steig watched with interest. She was concentrating, or communing with the staff, or something. Then she raised the staff, pointed at the tins one after the other. With a muffled report and the raising of a divot, she flattened each can, the twisted remains hurtling away over the clearing.

Pheoreth was also watching from the elvish camp. Steig wondered what she made of Maisie the half-elf, learning her own magic.

Half-breed? Leathphór, they had called it. Well, she was just fine, as far as he was concerned. Self-assured, strong, at home on the road; she had travelled a long way from the bookish, timid Christian of twelve days ago.

Maisie picked up the remnants of the tin cans and walked back to the yog, a beaming smile plastered over her face.

"Looks like you got the hang of it," he called as she approached.

"I taught myself a new spell!"

"Colour me impressed. How did you do that?"

"Well." She collapsed onto a folding chair by the fire, lay the staff at her side and pushed a wayward tangle of blonde hair back from her face, which had the sheen of exertion across it. "I sort of explored the possibilities of the power from the staff ... I can do that thumpy thing quite easily now."

"Yes, we heard."

She grinned. Steig felt there might be a slight air of the manic about it.

"So, I kind of felt around the thumpy thing, and directed it outwards. I wasn't even trying, and it really flattened those tins, did you see?"

Steig laughed at her enthusiasm.

"Yes. Though I'm not sure Beckett is a fan."

"Oh! Oh no! Beckett, are you alright? I'm so sorry."

Beckett lifted his head from his patch of sparse grass.

"It was scary."

"Would you like a scratch?"

Beckett rumbled a whicker of encouragement.

Pheoreth sat on one side of Maisie, and Steig on the other as they ate the stew. Firelight and a lantern lit their features and those of the elves ranged around the yog.

As they consumed the last of the meal and the sky darkened to full night, Maisie sat back with a sigh.

"Excellent food, as always, thank you. Thank you, Andion, for the hunting, and Steig, for the cooking."

Andion bowed. "Tis a simple thing to hunt. Cooking, that is a skill." His smile was broad as he regarded Steig.

A wave of heat rose to Steig's face. He finished his mouthful of food. "You're welcome," he said at last, as he swallowed, trying to cover his embarrassment. "Should have a crack at those flatbreads that Bobe Elka made; they would have added a bit of starch to it."

"Yes, they were excellent," murmured Pheoreth. She turned to Steig, her brow questioning. "You know Bobe Elka, do you not?"

"I've met her before this journey, if that's what you mean."

"It is. Would you tell the tale?"

Steig shifted his weight, glanced around at the gathered audience, all of whom were watching him, either openly like Maisie and Andion, or in a guarded fashion, like Morwen and the others.

"There's not much to tell, really ..."

Pheoreth smiled. "I imagine it is almost a folk tale. I may have heard it told before, following an aural tradition. A tale around a fire much like this one. Let me see." She paused, thinking, a frown on her usually smooth-skinned forehead. "It went from you, or probably you, someone in Roteslund, at least. To George Boswell, and thence Falomar the dwarf, then to my cousin, Findir, and so to me."

"George Boswell? He's known to your kin?"

"Yes. The travelling folk who wish for a better life than Defaltum Mundi's squalid transit camps often end up here. He came through many times, visiting, sharpening knives, mending tinware and farm equipment. I met him once, in Bolerum, at the horse fair."

"Outstanding. Very well, I will tell the tale." He put the kettle to boil and stoked the fire, then sat back, waiting until all eyes were on him, paused a few more heartbeats, and began.

> This is the tale of Bobe Elka, whom you all have met, and you will surely agree that she is a wise woman. But not a young woman. She grew up living a nomadic lifestyle. Some reckon as she is Romani – descended from the Sinti who travelled from Sindhu to Eastern Europa in the sixth century. Some quietly suppose she is Irish – maybe a descendant of the Tuatha de Danann. Others whisper she is of Norse stock, and her ancestors were the Aesir, the warring Viking gods, Freyr chief amongst them, with her cats.
>
> But when I met her, and let me tell you, friends, that was a long time ago, when I met her, she was older than old, wiser than wise. She had a spark to her soul that shone out through her grey-blue eyes.
>
> Now, let me set the scene. Bobe Elka, frail and

hunched, sits on an upturned apple crate, seeking warmth from a bright yog fire as the cold east wind from the steppe sweeps in. You can see her vardo parked nearby. Its wheels are rotten, the tarpaulin faded and tatty, the once bright paint and gold-leaf scrollwork peeling and diminished. Bobe Elka hasn't moved from this pull-up in a long time. She is finished with travelling the lanes and byways, done with healing, and helping. She is waiting for the Old Dark to claim her.

She takes a sip of her steaming herbal tea, places the mug on the table made from another upturned crate, and contemplates the fire for a moment. Then she rubs the round birthmark on her forehead. It itches.

"Ah. One last journey then. You have to help yourself, to help others." And so Bobe Elka picks up her walking staff, carved years ago from a stout ash bough. Now age has darkened it, made it old and stiff ... she stands with difficulty, pulls a worn, dark emerald-green cloak over her shoulders. She fetches a flask, bound in dark leather, from a high shelf in the vardo and slips it into her cloak pocket.

She mutters some words in an elder language – was that High Romani? Old Norse? Gaelic? As she speaks, she gestures with her staff at the fire, and it seems to

> burn dimmer, flickering, for a moment.
>
> She looks around at her camp, and walks out, past the yog, into the encroaching night, where a light mist envelops her, like a silken glove on the hand of an old, old friend.

Steig leant over and poured boiling water into his mug. Some of the elves presented their own mugs, so he busied himself with tea.

"What happened next?" asked Maisie.

Steig smiled. She was irrepressible. "Oh, well." He settled back again, cupping his tea in his hands.

> That was the bit I made up, from supposition and superstition. After all, there was only Bobe Elka sitting by her own yog.
>
> One person who met her on that journey was me. I was sitting by my yog, in front of my vardo, waiting for the kettle to boil. It was a chill evening, not yet fully dark, but a deep, blue-tinged twilight had settled under the trees where I had camped. It was an old forest in Roteslund called Stirwood.

"You know the place," he said, smiling at Maisie.

"I do!"

As the kettle boiled, and I reached for it, there was Bobe Elka. She stepped into the firelight, tendrils of fog and mist clinging to her cloak. All the travelling folk knew of her, of course. An elderly hedge-witch who would appear as if out of nowhere, walk past your yog with a friendly nod, and melt into a mist, departing as mysteriously as she had arrived.

I stood, and said, "Bobe Elka, I presume?"

"Sturluson. Kushti divvus," she replied. How did she know my name? Witchery!

A smattering of laughter. Steig grinned, continued.

"Kushti divvus. May I assist you?" I asked her.

"A cup of tea would be grand, on my way back. Tis a cold night." A smile, a lilt to her voice – Irish? Rom? Norse? Hard to tell. Then she walked into the misty evening and was gone.

So, I pulled the other mug out of the kitchen box and dropped a teabag into it, ready. I looked at Dog, who had slept through the whole thing. He was old, and deaf, and smelly, and enjoyed warming his paws in the ash around the edge of the fire ...

"You had a dog?" Maisie asked, eyes shining.

"Yes. Hush."

So, how do I know what happened? I stitched it together by asking Paul, the travelling farrier, who had spoken to Felix, the wagon-signwriter, who had it by good authority from his partner, Hayley.

Felix had poached a roe deer, and Hayley'd skinned it and jointed it and chucked it in the pot, with some onions and a carrot or two. Tatties were just going in, and it boiled on the yog. Yes, Hayley was sitting in front of her yog. It was a different evening, a different county. The weather was mild. Night had fallen. And there, mist-enshrouded, walked Bobe Elka, green cloak, stout stick, twinkly blue eyes.

"Bobe Elka! May I assist you?" squeaked the startled Hayley, not used to witches materialising on the flat Nordfolc plains.

"Kushti divvus. A bone from the stew would be a fine thing. And a mug of broth. But on the way back. Tis a cold evening, where I'm heading."

"Kushti bok, Bobe!" Hayley called to Bobe Elka's retreating back, and she was gone.

Steig gave a pause then, stretched, looked around. It was full dark. The firelight radiated from his audience's faces.

"Don't stop!" gasped Maisie.

"Very well."

> Now then. Any fine folk tale has three sections, so I won't disappoint. But you need to stretch out the imagination here. There's a different yog, you see. This one is not a bright blazing cooking fire. It's humbled and weak and almost out of wood. The three ragged travelling men hunched around it on their heels are gaining no warmth. Their faces are grim. There's a wailing and a screaming coming from one of the nearby wagons. A birthing isn't going so well. The men feel helpless, powerless, uncertain. The women in the vardo are likewise well out of their depth. No midwife. No nearby farmstead. Miles to the nearest road.
>
> Bobe Elka swirls into the midst of the men, takes in the scene, rubs her forehead.
>
> "Bobe Elka?" One stands, reaches as if to touch her cloak.
>
> "Kushti divvus. No time." She speaks in broad eastern Romani. "There's firewood ... there! In that ditch, hidden in the briars." She points with her staff. "Get

the yog going strong. Boil water. You!" She points again, at the man still sitting on his heels. "Git up and find some mugwort. It's just along the verge there, under that elder tree." The man scrambles to his feet, does as he is bid. Bobe Elka walks to the wagon and enters. She has work to do here.

How do I know this? Well. I did some research. Chirchedele University has a fine section in their library about Rom culture and language. I found an entry in a compendium of folklore, how a hedge-witch came to the aid of a group of Roma. The regime had hounded them, and they were hiding out at the back end of nowhere in ... oh, well before the war ...

He smiled at the glowing faces. "Shall we get back to the action?"

I'll spare you the details; the mugwort was burnt; the baby was born, they all survived, the hot water from the yog used to wash and coddle and refresh. Bobe Elka held the child for a moment, a stout girl with a circular birthmark on her forehead, shaped like a wagon's wheel.

Hayley starts from her reverie – Bobe Elka is here again! Whisper-quiet, she appears from the dark. Silently, Hayley hands her a mug of steaming broth.

And a bone from the stew. She sips the broth, standing.

"Won't you sit?"

"Nay. Me old bones – I don't bend so well. But this broth is welcome. Thank thee."

And the story winds itself back out again. I'd poured the tea, and added honey to mine – then Bobe Elka was there, silent as death with a knife.

"Honey? Lemon?"

"Aye." A smile. "Here, Dog, I got a bone for thee." She tosses the bone to Dog, who snags it with his teeth, and settles in the fire ash to have a good gnaw.

And so, the story ends. Bobe Elka arrives back at her own yog – it has barely burnt down, but she throws on a couple more logs to keep the chill away. For her, it has been a long, cold, exhausting night.

She rubs the birthmark on her forehead, the one shaped like a vardo's wheel. It itches no more. With a wry chuckle she thinks to herself, "It's no good being helpful if you've not helped yourself first, and last."

A smattering of applause pattered around the fire hearth, and Steig bowed his head. It was a fine story. And some of it was, as far as he was aware, true.

Later, as he was washing up the pot, heating soapy water in it to remove the burnt-on food, Maisie made more tea for them. The elves had retired to their tarpaulin shelter across the glade.

"Did you really research Bobe in the Chirchedele University records?"

"I did. They don't mention her by name, but she's in there, in a book of folklore. Also in a couple of 'first-hand accounts' in a narrative by one of the Gypsy Lore Society's archivists."

"So ... the child she helped, was that her?"

"How could it be her?" He smiled. It was the same question he had asked himself. How, indeed, could it be her? An old hedge-witch and a newborn girl, the same soul, in the same place, at the same instant. It made his head reel.

Chapter 21

Maisie collapsed back onto the bed in the vardo. They were due to pull off to the pass, then Pont Romain, in a few minutes, but she wanted time to think. The weirdness at the market the previous day had shaken her up. Her voice had changed all on its own. Because she had thought about it? Was that the glamour? It differed from the thumpy spell – she needed a better name than that – but the automatic glamour that affected her voice was just freaky. Well. Like the thumpy spell, she'd just have to explore it and see.

With a sudden excitement, she sat up and went to the tiny mirror on the cupboard door opposite the stove. Looked at her face – it was terribly grubby. She sighed, went to wash it. Then thought about what she was going to do. Well. It was a test. She held her staff with a gentle pressure and pictured herself in her mind's eye, with long black hair like the neraides. And pointed ears. Well, more pointed ears. And a clean face. Nothing happened. She scrunched up her chest in exasperation, screwed her eyes closed, and pushed. The staff responded.

She opened her eyes and almost screamed in shock. The elf that stared back at her in the mirror had her face, but …

"Well, goodness, I look like a neraida. A clean one! Now then …" She relaxed the push, and nothing happened. She remained as a dark-haired elf. "Oh. Fiddlesticks. Um …"

She thought for a moment. Reversal spell? She imagined the glamour draining away, her face returning to normal, her hair back to its tousled, unbrushed, scraggly blonde. Holding this in her mind, she pushed again, feeling that tightness in her chest rising, the warmth from the staff responding. Like the vardo appearing through Pheoreth's glamour, there she was, fading into view. "I mean," she said to herself, "it's nice to have a clean face, but it's better to be me again."

"You talking to yourself?" asked Steig, as he climbed up the steps. "We're off in a minute."

"Yes, I am," she smiled. "First sign of madness. I'm hiding in the back, am I?"

The final few hundred metres to the Casermetta at the head of the Fenis Pass were hard going, Steig had to admit. He was on the road, pulling at the breeching strap, hauling the wagon up the last incline. Beckett was puffing and gasping as much as he was. They had Maisie hidden on board, plus all the supplies and food. Pheoreth was on Beckett's other side, assisting with the pull. They managed a fair pace, but Steig could feel the strain on his hamstrings and calves, his back muscles and biceps. A hundred metres. Fifty.

"Almost there, Beckett. Keep going, lad."

"Yeh. Got it." His voice came in gasping bursts.

As the road levelled off, they pulled into a space at the front of the Casermetta, an old wooden outpost for travellers caught out in poor weather. It was a basic shack with a water trough fed from a hillside stream tinkling down into the col. Beckett immersed his nose in the water and started gulping it down.

"Hey! Stop that. Take it steady." Steig jumped down.

"Thirsty," Beckett bubbled from underwater.

Steig grabbed his reins and pulled his head up.

"No! You'll get colic. Take it slow."

"What about an apple while I wait?"

"You're impossible!"

"I can smell them." Beckett curled his nose towards Steig's pocket.

"You can have one when we get down the other side. Drink slowly."

"'Kay."

A movement at the unglazed window of the shack caught Steig's eye. He peered into the gloom, and could make out a figure, grey, thin and ethereal with inordinately long arms. Its face was an ugly visage of hair and teeth and age. It shuffled into the shadows when Steig looked. He racked his brains. Bogle was the closest he could come up with from folklore. Turns milk sour, lames dogs, steals children. Unpleasant. He'd best avoid going in the shack, then.

The view from the col was long and clear in both directions. He could just make out Autissiodorum on the distant horizon behind them. He guessed that the black smudge on the plain before them, a cloud of sooty smoke lingering over it like a crown of blowflies, was Mediolanum.

"All OK to move on?" he called to the elves, who had availed themselves of the water once Beckett had drunk his fill.

"Aye, ready to go," came the chorus of replies.

Steig jumped up onto the ledge and clicked Beckett on.

"OK, horse?"

"Yeh. Bogle in that house. Good to be going."

"Yeah, I saw it, too. It's behind us now, no problem."

"A bogle?" Maisie called from inside the back of the wagon.

"Yeah, sort of like an old hairy hob with really long arms. Pretty nasty. I can't imagine what it must be like to get stuck up here in a blizzard with that thing lurking in the only safe shelter for miles."

"Well, I'm very glad it's spring. Or whatever spring is trying to do in Khôra."

Steig wound the last of the brake off with the wheel under his seat. The road levelled out from the long, slow descent from the col. The afternoon was drawing on and the road traffic had diminished. Pheoreth and the others were looking twitchy, Steig thought. He guessed there was less in the way of cover, this side of the hills.

The plain spread out all around them. A pair of deep drainage ditches bounded the road, and rows of cabbages marched into the distance on either side. The grey and the mud were creeping back in, at least in places, and the cabbages seemed stunted to Steig's untrained eye.

Pheoreth loped alongside.

"How long to the farm?" Maisie asked, poking her head out to peer at the landscape.

"We are almost there. It took longer than I thought to descend from the pass. We will have to get into Mediolanum in the dark."

"Is that bad?"

"No, not really. It is better with the darkness to cover us. Down this track, Steig."

She pointed to a farm track running away to the right, with stunted cypress trees crouching alongside it. As the wagon rumbled over the median of the road and onto the track, Steig glanced behind, back along the road. Nothing coming, nothing to see, though he had a prickle in his neck, like something was watching him. Weird.

The farm, when they came to it, was careworn; not quite dilapidated, but clearly in need of some tender loving care here and there. Its red roof tiles were uneven, some missing. The farmhouse windows were dirty, the paint on the door peeling. The yard itself was untidy, with scattered wisps of hay and straw on the muddy ground, a broken bucket discarded in a corner. A desultory, threadbare brown hen pecked at something foul in the grey ooze, and the plaintive bleating of sheep came from a long, low barn along the far side.

"Oh, well, this is nice," muttered Steig. Maisie shot him a glance. "It's OK, don't fret," he offered. "Hold up, horse, let's see what's what."

"You said apple at the end of the hill."

"So I did." He hopped down and fished around in his coat pocket, pulling a small green apple from it. "Here you go, good work, lad."

Beckett snatched the apple and crunched it, chewed it with gusto.

A man appeared from the farmhouse doorway, pulling on a voluminous tweed coat against the early evening chill. He was tall and gangly and balding, traces of short, greying hair around his head, and an open countenance, the beginnings of a smile.

"Buonasera, amico," he began.

"Parla Anglese?" asked Steig. It was all the Calabrian he had.

"Sì, yes, of course. Hello. I am Savio Russo. Pleased to meet you. I am expecting you." He held out his hand; Steig shook it with a firm grip.

"Steig. Well met. This is Maisie." He gestured to Maisie, who was climbing down from the wagon. "And this is Beckett."

"Ciao, ciao." He turned to the elves as they approached. "Ah, Pheoreth, è bella vederti. Come, we will hide the wagon in the barn. Follow me."

Steig led Beckett, who plodded through the mud of the farmyard, hauling the vardo. They rounded a corner of the house in time to see Savio opening a pair of tall wooden doors set into the end of a stone building. Inside, bales of hay and straw were stacked against the far wall. At the side, various carts and pieces of farm equipment, all wooden and horse-powered, were parked in a tidy row. There was a space at the end for the vardo.

"Please, you put it 'ere." Savio gestured towards the space.

Steig and Beckett worked together. Steig gave commands, holding the reins loose at Beckett's head. Beckett shifted his weight sideways to move the shafts and front wheels. He manoeuvred his heavy body forward or backward inch by inch to perform a three-point turn.

"OK, lad, we're all lined up. Back now, slow and easy. Back, back, back." Steig placed his hand on the horse's broad chest and pressed, little more than a touch. Beckett shuffled backwards, the weight of the wagon across the breeching, as it rolled into place alongside the barn wall, facing outwards.

"Molto bene! Well done, like, er, il balletto!"

Steig untacked Beckett where he stood, putting the tack under the wagon to be sorted later. Maisie walked Beckett out of the shafts. She watched with obvious interest as Steig unclipped the shafts, removing a long metal rod that attached them to the wagon. He put the shafts under the wagon as well, clearing the way for the barn doors, which Savio closed.

"I 'ave a stable for the 'orse. Come, follow me."

Beckett's stable was large and clean, with plenty of hay and fresh water in a wooden pail. Beckett tucked into the hay with no hesitation.

"You OK, then, Beckett?" Maisie asked.

Two flicks for yes. Flick. Flick. Maisie smiled at Steig.

"He's fine."

"Yep, seems so."

"Come to the 'ouse. There is, er, stufato? Eh ... stew."

The three of them walked across the farmyard to the house, where they found the elves already sitting at a long table in a low-ceilinged room. It was all beams and dim lamplight, with warmth from a huge open fireplace at one end. A plump, short woman with black hair shot through with grey was serving bowls of stew from a substantial iron pot that was warming on a shelf in the hearth.

"Please, sit, sit," commanded Savio, then waved at the woman. "Maria, prendi un po' di stufato per il cercatore di chiavi."

"Cercatore di chiavi? Madonna mia!"

The woman bustled up with two bowls. She blushed as she passed one to Maisie.

"Miss. I please ... see you ... to find ... er ... keys," she managed, her Breotonish halting and heavily accented.

Steig's face darkened. Maisie was right. Everyone knew about her. This might be a problem if they were supposed to be incognito.

"Grazie mille, signora," Maisie replied, taking the proffered bowl.

Steig took his bowl and sniffed. It smelt amazing. They hadn't eaten since breakfast. This was just what he needed, he thought. He'd worry about incognito later.

Savio followed Maria with a wineskin, pouring out generous measures of a bitter, light yellow wine into earthenware cups.

Maisie sat on the long bench with Steig at her left and Andion at her right. The farmer, Savio, and his plump ... wife? Housekeeper? Savio and Maria were being excellent hosts. The stew was delicious, and the wine was welcome and warming.

But. There it was again. The Finder of Keys legend preceding her. It was, she realised, getting a bit irritating. She sighed, staring gloomily into her half-eaten bowl of stew. Was this the life the Fates had predestined her to lead? Were the Fates toying with her? Would she ever get back to Defaltum Mundi, and if she did, would she be happy there? And what of God? If she was here, then should she be looking to a different pantheon? She felt as if she was at a crossroads in her life. An important one, probably in a glade in a forest with 'This way be dragonnes' on one signpost and 'Here be elves' on another. Just as she's about to decide on the direction of her life, along comes a gorgeous neraida and ...

"Maisie!" Steig's voice cut through her reverie.

"Uh? What?" She came back to the low-ceilinged room, now stuffy and over-warm with so many people crammed together at the table. Steig gestured to Pheoreth, who was sitting further up the table, leaning forward, looking expectant. It was clear Pheoreth had just asked her a question.

"I said," began Pheoreth, enunciating, "can you get ready to go in a short while? As soon as we have eaten, we should leave for Mediolanum."

"Oh! Yes, of course. I'll need ten minutes to get a bag together, and we need to split up the supplies to carry. Or is there food there?"

Pheoreth smiled. "Yes, there is food there. But your coffee is better."

"I can be ready shortly."

"I'm going to come to Mediolanum tonight, but then back here tomorrow. Unless you need me?" asked Steig.

"Oh! I thought ... I don't know what I thought. I presumed ... it's always a bad idea to presume, isn't it?" Maisie felt she was gabbling. The thought of both Steig and Bobe Elka abandoning her, all within two days, was deeply disturbing.

"You'll be busy with ... with whatever it is, finding keys, and I'll be a spare part. I'll come back here, check on Beckett, and then have a scout around the area, see what's what, you know, gather intel. We're only a mile from Mediolanum as it is. It's not like I'm going back to Autissiodorum or Silentoak."

She rested her forehead on his shoulder. He put his arm around her, a gentle touch, but reassuring nonetheless.

“I-I’m not sure. I don’t know what to do,” she stuttered.

“Hey, Maisie.” He peered at her face, close enough that their noses almost touched. “I’ll not be far away. We’ll be alright. Let’s go in tonight, and if you are uncomfortable staying, we’ll come back out tomorrow, together. How’s that?”

She smiled, but still felt like she was a small cog in a very much bigger and scarier machine. “I-I guess.”

“Come on. Eat up. We’ll get on the road. I’ll go check on Beckett and we’ll be off.”

“Oh, I need to split the salve. Make sure Savio knows to apply it to Beckett’s cuts.”

“It’s alright. I’ll get that done.”

Chapter 22

Maisie pushed the worries she had about Steig leaving her alone, about the Gratadei, about, well, everything, to the back of her mind. She'd deal with all that when she had time. Right now, she had a job to do. A disguise to craft. She smiled to herself. Stared in the mirror in the vardo as she pulled the tingle of the glamour from the staff. She pushed the image of a dark-haired, clean-faced, pointy-eared Maisie. With more ease than the previous time, her appearance changed. Once again, she was an elf. Well. More elven. She considered adding some embellishments – a torc, a tiara, a flowing robe of silver thread, but stopped herself. Baby steps, Maisie my girl. Don't overextend yourself.

She reassessed the image in the mirror. The cross that she wore at her neck, that she had worn for as long as she could remember, was now out of place. The tatchapen amulet remained hidden, but the cross, a sign of Christianity, shone out, incongruous. Before she had second thoughts, she unclipped the chain and took the necklace off, wrapping it in some paper and slipping it into her washing bag.

She packed her rucksack with a few books, the coffee, a couple of changes of clothes. Toiletries. Shoving it all down to make it compact. Oh, I do hope there's a bath, she thought.

Staff in hand, cloak fastened at her neck, and with her walking boots on, she stepped down from the vardo to the barn floor. Steig walked around the corner, holding the pot of salve, and stopped dead, a look of first surprise, then incredulity on his face.

"Oh! Well. Wow. Um ..."

"I don't think I've ever seen you actually tongue-tied before?"

"That is so weird. It's your voice, but elven everything else. I'm impressed."

"Hang on, I can fix that ..." She pulled a bit more glamour from the staff. Felt her throat tingle. "How's tha—" She stopped, surprising even herself. Her voice was sibilant, like Lavinia's. She cleared her throat. "How's that?"

"You sound like one of them. Very cool. Name?"

"Maisie ... oh! You mean my elven name? Um ..."

"May-Shee is a bit ... well ... obvious. How about ... Fanwen?"

"Fanwen it is. Fanwen, daughter of Fildaerae, from Silentoak." She shook her head in wonder. She truly did sound like an elf. Getting used to that was going to take some time.

Pheoreth was, Maisie decided, far too cool an elf to react. Which was a shame, as she had been looking forward to making her at least do a double take. All that happened when she walked into the farmhouse was Pheoreth gave her an appraising glance, a nod, and said, "That will do."

That'll do? Huh. Well, they would see, she supposed, when they met any Gratadei searching for the blonde human. Having full elven ears was weird, even if they were just an illusion. She had spent so much of her childhood covering up her elongated ears, and here they were, poking out of her hair for all to see! She wasn't sure whether it was a good thing or bad. Again, push it to the back, think about it later.

The walk to Mediolanum itself was uneventful. They said their goodbyes and thank-yous to Savio and Maria, then headed along the road, into the gloaming of early evening. They left the cabbage fields and wound between what had once been orchards and vineyards. Now, though, they were little more than desolation, stunted trunks of dead trees, grey soil and the stench of decay.

Emerging from the serried ranks of dead vines, they passed the first houses. They could see smaller hamlets lit in the distance. Dogs barked at their passing, from within walled courtyards or behind doors, but not a soul was abroad.

Turning the next corner, crossing a stone bridge over an unseen watercourse, at what she supposed was the proper start of the town, they met a roadblock, of sorts. Three bulky figures were standing by a steel barrel, in which a feeble fire burnt in fits and starts. They moved out into the road at Maisie's party's approach.

Maisie recognised the look. Black tactical, Steig had called it. Synthetic fabrics, shiny black boots, crewcut hair, modern pistols in holsters on their hips.

"Fermati!" The middle thug, short ginger hair and a scar down his cheek, held up his hand, palm out, in the universal command for "Stop".

The elves spread out, taking what Maisie presumed was a defensive formation. She stuck herself on the end of the line of elves and ended up opposite a short, ratty man who sneered at her, showing yellow teeth. She saw Steig hanging back, out of the corner of her eye.

"Chi sei e dove stai andando?" Ginger Scar asked.

Pheoreth was opposite him and she answered in what Maisie thought of as "best elvish sibilant hauteur".

"We are neraides. Where we go is our own business. Stand aside, human."

Maisie felt the push when it came – stronger than before. The three men appeared confused for a heartbeat, then wandered back to the brazier. They gathered around it, warming their hands and complaining about elvish brigands and the stupidity of the Gratadei. Or so it seemed to Maisie, who lacked the Calabrian language to catch the nuance, even if the overall direction of their muttering was obvious.

The phalanx of elves moved forward with care and silence. When they reached the next corner without the alarm being raised, Maisie breathed out a sigh, trying to relax her internal tension.

"The sooner we get off the streets and to the safe house, the better," commented Pheoreth. "Come, it is this way." She headed off along a side street, dark timber and wattle buildings rising on each side of them, a dog's incessant barking in the distance.

As Pheoreth faced off against the ginger mercenary, Steig held his breath, his hand hovering over the handle of his kukri. The rifle remained wrapped in its cloth, slung over his shoulder with his pack. No time to make it ready. Pheoreth didn't have her hand on her knife, nor had she unslung her bow from where it rested on her back.

"We are neraides. Where we go is our own business. Stand aside, human."

Without warning, a wave of confusion washed over him. What was he doing here? Who were these three hard cases standing opposite him? He stood silent, still, barely breathing. The three men who he now remembered were Gratadei mercenaries, wandered back to their brazier and started cursing under their breath. They chatted, complaining like soldiers everywhere. Steig shuffled, making as little noise as he could, to the deeper shadows of the building opposite. Once there, he backed away to the corner, slipping around it and out of their sight.

His thoughts cleared. Was that a glamour? Had it caught him in the backwash? Damn it. Now he found himself separated from them. He had no idea where he was going or what he was supposed to do. Of course, Pheoreth hadn't said where they were going. What would Maisie do when she realised he was missing?

He weighed up his options. Wander the streets of Mediolanum, asking in Breotonish for directions to the Ostiarius Principale's secret residence? Sure to attract the attention of those aligned with the Gratadei. Head back to Savio's farm, check on Beckett, and spend the night in the wagon? Wait there for further instructions? That seemed the most obvious course of action. Or wait here and see if Maisie came back for him? That was a good plan, too, in the short term.

He looked around. The side road he stood at the mouth of was narrow, with single- and two-storey housing on either side. The housing was all behind walled courtyards or through locked gates that offered no hiding place. He walked as if he were in the woods stalking a deer or outwitting the gamekeeper, with silence, forethought, stealth. Halfway down the street, he found a gateway set back from the road, its solid, iron-banded wooden doors firmly bolted. But it provided a level of cover from anyone glancing down the street, and the shadows within its archway were dark and deep.

He laid down his pack, untied the covering on his rifle, and checked the breech. Settling in on his haunches, he faced the way he had come, and waited.

"Here we are," announced Pheoreth, stopping at a dark, heavy door set into a long, stone wall, hidden down a narrow alleyway, somewhere in the centre of Mediolanum. The twists and turns they had taken had disorientated Maisie. Street lighting had been sparse, and once in the centre of the town they had passed only a few people, and they all seemed to move in fear. Maisie could sense the sour mood of a country under totalitarian rule.

Pheoreth rapped on the door, three times, then a pause, then once. Code. A hatch in the door opened and a hob's small, wizened face peered out. It gave a squeak of surprise; the hatch slammed and there came the sound of many bolts and latches being undone. The door swung inwards on well-oiled hinges. Pheoreth led, followed by Maisie and then the rest of the elves.

Inside, there was a small, flagged courtyard with a covered walkway around its perimeter and doors leading off.

The hob turned up a lantern that hung by the door and said to Pheoreth, "I will fetch Aelene. Ostiarius Rosalia is ..." He gulped, as if he had been crying. "They took Rosalia."

Maisie noticed the dampness of his cheeks. An icy hand clenched in her stomach. She turned to speak to Steig. "This can't be good ..."

But Steig wasn't there. She had been so intent on the route through the streets, the dark, the unfamiliar architecture. Panic took up residence in her stomach alongside the cold, sinking feeling.

"Where's Steig?" she asked, her voice sharp.

Pheoreth stared at her, eyes widening in alarm. Checked the other elves, who were all doing much the same. A counting of heads. Seven.

"Skatá," she swore. She glared at Andion and Morwen. "How? And where did he go?"

"I know not, Pheoreth." Andion cast his gaze to the floor, abashed.

Pheoreth hissed, a sound like a viper.

"Search for him. Try the thugs at Via Severiana. Go!"

Andion slipped out of the door and was gone, making no more fuss than a warm evening breeze. Pheoreth turned to Maisie, who was starting to feel panic rising. Pheoreth's face softened.

"He will turn up. As a traveller and a woodsman, he will have found a place to hole up. Andion will find him. He is like a bloodhound in that respect."

Maisie didn't like to rely on Steig; she didn't, in truth, like relying on anyone. People were, she felt, wholly unreliable. However, she sensed their relationship extended beyond keeping warm in bed. She was … safer, more able, supported, when he was at her side. Without him, she was lopsided, unbalanced. Oh, it was too much. She tried her hardest not to cry, but could feel tears welling.

A door on the far side of the courtyard opened, spilling out a warm light. A willowy elvish figure walked through and approached them along the covered walkway. As the figure came closer, Maisie could make out what she now knew to be classic androgenous Celtic Tuatha de Danann of the same mould as Lavinia. Long blonde-white hair, green eyes, an elongated face, high cheekbones, simple silken robe in a light cream.

"Aelene. Well met. What happened to Rosalia?" asked Pheoreth.

Aelene gave Pheoreth a dismissive glance, ignored her question, and turned to Maisie. She let her gaze linger, appraising her. Then sneered. Maisie guessed what Aelene saw didn't impress her. How rude.

"You must be Maisie Hanson, Finder of Keys." Disdain dripped from her words. "I am Aelene, Rosalia's assistant. I am assuming her duties whilst she is … otherwise engaged."

Maisie found Aelene's voice, her whole haughtier-than-thou elvish attitude, instantly irritating. And she had been so rude to Pheoreth. Well. Two could play at hauteur. Subconsciously, she gripped her staff and pulled the tiniest bit of power from it. Or fizz, or whatever it was. She channelled it into her voice, lending it, she hoped, an even tone and a level of command.

"Well met, Aelene. Tell me, what happened to Ostiarius Principale Rosalia?"

The effect on Aelene was immediate. She took a step back, flinching, shock on her face. Out of the corner of her eye, Maisie saw Pheoreth covering her mouth to hide her grin, her shoulders shaking.

"You dare, you *dare* command me, like some ... some child?" Aelene raised her voice, her face colouring with fury.

"It is but a simple question. If you're too rude to answer it the first time, maybe being asked with more vigour is required. And yes, I dare. Now. Where. Is. Rosalia?" She tapped her staff on the flagstones in counterpoint to each word. Shockwaves reverberated around the courtyard. The tiles on the roof shook. At the last tap, the flagstone under the staff split with a sharp report and a puff of powdered stone. In the silence that followed, a tile slid from the roof and smashed on the pathway behind Maisie. Everyone except Maisie jerked at the shock of the noise. A calculating look passed, fleetingly, across Aelene's face; she recovered her composure.

"Very well. Let us talk in the parlour. I'm sure you are all hungry and thirsty after your journey. Come."

She swept away, swirls of silk rustling as she went back to the open door.

The parlour was a long room connected to the kitchen with a hearth in between. The kitchen used one side for cooking and the parlour used the other for warmth. They sat themselves down at another long table, similar to Savio's, but this time with less homely geniality and more ceremony and hidden agendas.

Pheoreth, sitting next to Maisie, leant in to whisper, their foreheads touching with warmth, whilst the hob served wine and pastries.

"It is considered rude to use the glamour on each other, you know. At least as unsubtly as you did. I would be happy to teach you a more ... acceptable way to employ it."

She stared into Maisie's eyes. Maisie blinked, self-conscious. Up close, Pheoreth smelt of summer rain, with an earthy undercurrent.

"Oh, I thought that was quite subtle. If I'd gone with my first thought, the roof would have been down. And yes, I would be delighted if you could help me."

"Very well then. I shall." And she smiled. This time, the smile reached her eyes. Maisie felt warm inside for a moment before remembering Steig. The icy hand of dread returned to her stomach.

Aelene stood at the head of the table.

"So. As I said earlier. It is with regret," she began, her face impassive, "that I must inform you that yesterday the Gratadei came here in force and searched for you, Maisie. They 'arrested' Ostiarius Rosalia and took her away. I presume to the Citadel. We have heard nothing from her, or them, since they departed yesterday."

The elves muttered to each other. Maisie glanced at Pheoreth, who appeared upset, close to tears, but also angry. She looked back at Aelene. Gripped her staff, which was leaning against her side, propped under the table. Invoked the tatchapen spell, an invocation she managed with silence and care. The last thing she wanted was the elves knowing what she was up to. But Bobe Elka had said the fae folk could not sense it. So, let me see the truth, thought Maisie. The amulet warmed her chest where it lay, concealed.

At first, everything seemed the same. Maisie tried to look closer, beyond the edge of the glamour ... Pheoreth appeared a little older, a touch dishevelled. Crow's feet around her eyes. Wrinkles at the corners of her mouth. More real, Maisie thought. Beautiful, with her dark skin and brown-black eyes, the imperfections that were now visible made her more alluring ... Maisie tore her eyes away, before Pheoreth could turn her head to notice.

The rest of the elves were a similar story. Their perfect skin and freshly washed hair appeared slightly less perfect, a tad mussed. Then her roving eyes settled on Aelene, still standing at the head of the table, a glass of wine in her hand. She stared back at Maisie, appraising her. Maisie, in turn, managed to not react to the sight; Aelene's face was completely different. Still a Celtic blonde-haired Tuatha de Danann, unmistakably so. But she was clearly a different person under her glamour. Older, with a more yellow-blonde colour to her hair, which was long yet wavy. She had dark rings under her eyes and a scar above one, uneven and white on her forehead against her skin, running into her hairline. Blue eyes. Blue eyes that were narrowing as she stared at Maisie. Without reacting or breaking the stare, Maisie unwound the tatchapen spell and let it settle, the power flowed back down her arm to the staff; the amulet seemed to shrink in size as it cooled. She smiled at Aelene, nodded once, and reached for her drink. Oh, she wished Steig were here. They had much to discuss.

A thought struck her, and she turned back to Pheoreth.

"If the Gratadei know I'm coming here, is it safe for us to remain here?"

"That was exactly what I was just considering. We will leave shortly. I know a place where we will be safe."

Maisie didn't know whether Pheoreth was trustworthy, but at least she wasn't pretending to be someone else. And she had kept them safe from the Gratadei with her glamour. She'd just have to trust and hope.

She leant forward, so once again their foreheads were almost touching. Pheoreth looked at her, raising an eyebrow in question.

"Can we find somewhere where no one else knows us? Or at least, somewhere that the Ostiarium and the Gratadei don't know about?"

"As I said" – she smiled, with a warmth that made Maisie's stomach fluttery – "I know a place where we will be safe. We will wait another five minutes. Let us see if Andion finds Steig, then we will go."

Steig's calf muscles were complaining. He'd been sitting on his haunches too long. He stood, slow and careful, rifle at ease, watching both ways up and down the alley, all his senses straining for signs of approaching danger. Which made the appearance of Andion, out of the gloom, a complete shock. Andion stood, smiling in that measured, infuriating way that the fae had, whilst Steig gathered his wits and tried to calm his hammering heart.

"How do you do that?" he gasped.

"Years of practice." Andion's voice held amusement.

"Did you glamour me?"

"I didn't need to. You were looking the other way."

"Huh. Well, thanks for coming back. I got zapped by the glamour when you did the roadblock."

"Yes, we assumed that was what happened. Please accept my sincere apologies. I should not have lost sight of you."

Steig felt awkward. The fae, apologising?

"Hey, no problem. I was going to go back to Savio's if no one came by midnight-ish."

"We must not tarry. I suspect Pheoreth will move Maisie to a hidden location, since the Gratadei have compromised the house at San Allessandro. They have taken the Ostiarius Principale prisoner."

"Oh, that's not good. Is Maisie alright?"

"I know not. Pheoreth despatched me as soon as Maisie noticed you were apart."

"Well, shall we go, then? And are you going to glamour the guards, or find a way around?"

"They are sleeping."

"Huh. Fine. Lead on." He slung his pack on his back, with the rifle across his front, on its sling, at port arms.

The two of them wended through the streets, down the side road, down the alleyway. They arrived at the doorway to the house at San Allessandro just as the hob was bolting it; the neraides and Maisie were standing outside the door, letting their eyes adjust to the gloom.

"Steig!" Maisie almost shrieked, flinging herself at him. He hugged her close. She felt warm and supple. "Oh, I'm glad you're back. Um ..."

Pheoreth stepped towards them. "We must go. Please, Steig, try not to get lost this time."

Maisie took his hand, stretched on tiptoes, and whispered in his ear, "She's tetchy because things are falling apart a bit. Don't be angry." Her breath was warm and sibilant in his ear.

"I'm not angry ..."

"That look you gave her ..."

"Well. It's a bit much, being zapped with the glamour and then being blamed for not keeping up."

"Like I said. You're here, now. Come on." She tugged his arm, and they trotted to catch up with the departing neraides.

As they walked, Steig thought of what he wanted to do. Yes, being with Maisie was pleasant. Sometimes a challenge, but in a positive way. But she was all fired up for this thing, and he ...

"I'm not overly comfortable in towns," he said under his breath.

"What are you thinking?" There was worry in Maisie's voice.

"Dunno. Gonna go back to Savio's, stay in the vardo."

"Oh, Steig. Come on. Be here tonight, do it tomorrow."

"I dunno. See where we end up. Where are we going, anyway?"

"We are going to a friend's house. He is a baker. My cousin, by marriage." Pheoreth spoke over her shoulder as she walked along the narrow, dark road.

After more twists and turns, which Steig tried to track and remember, they came to a commercial district. At least, he presumed it was commercial. There were a number of buildings with expansive front windows displaying wares of diverse types – feed merchant, haberdasher, clock repairs and a bakery. "Findir's Bakery" declared the sign above the door. It had a painted picture of an elvish baker, ears sticking above his puffy white hat, pulling loaves from an oven. No lights showed at the front.

"Down here," Pheoreth said, leading them to a wooden gate. She clicked the latch and led them all into a small courtyard. Morwen lit a lantern and held it aloft. They found the side door to the bakery, a light showing yellow in the window, and a courtyard with a kitchen garden beyond. A narrow wooden stair led from the courtyard up to a door on the first floor.

Pheoreth rapped on the side door, and a gravelly voice from inside asked, "Chi è?"

"It is Pheoreth. And some friends."

The occupant unbolted the door with a series of metallic clunks and flung it open, revealing a short, not so elvish, figure. He sported an enormous ginger beard, a broad nose and hooded eyes, a large forehead. He was wearing grubby baker's whites.

"Pheoreth! Welcome. How were the western lands? And you brought friends. Come in, come in." Pheoreth hesitated. "Come! I will excavate a bottle of the finest vintage." His voice had the power and magnitude of a coastal foghorn.

"We need somewhere to stay."

"Of course. And we will discuss that, over wine! Inside! Now!" He held the door, and the elves trooped in like schoolchildren. Steig cast around then shut the gate to the road and settled down on a handy empty barrel in the courtyard. He dug around in his bag and pulled out a blanket. Maisie looked at him, a question forming. He held up his hand.

"I'm going to stay out here. Been quite a night so far. You go in. It's late. I'll wrap up, get some sleep."

"Steig! We need to talk!"

"Well, go sort out your digs. We'll talk after. I'm more comfortable here."

"You're impossible!"

"No, I just ... I don't like being told what to do and where to go. That's the whole point of running away to an enchanted realm. For me. So please, bear with me. I'll be here when you know what's what."

Maisie squatted down on her haunches, so her face was level with his. She put her hands on his shoulders.

"Hey. You OK in there?"

"Yeah. Sorry. Bit overwrought. Elves and faeries and things that go bump in the night."

"I'm here, you know?"

"Yeah. I know. Go on, Findir's waiting." He indicated the door, still held by the short ... was he an actual dwarf? So, how could he be Pheoreth's ...? He shook his head. "Go on. See you in a bit."

Maisie stood, rested a hand on his shoulder for a moment, then turned and headed for the open door.

Findir set out eight cups on the tiny kitchen table and sloshed a deep ruby wine into them from an oversize bottle.

"Here's to health, happiness and absent friends!" He beamed at the attendant elves and Maisie. Lifted the cup and drained it in one. Set it down with a thump. Wiped his mouth and beard, which had collected some of the wine, with the back of his hand. "So. You've been to the western lands. You have returned with the Finder of Keys. Remarkable. Come, tell all."

He smiled at everyone again. Maisie watched the elves' faces; they were not a cheerful bunch. Findir was at least trying. She picked up her wine and sipped it. Actually, not bad.

Pheoreth sat back in her chair. She clasped her hands together in front of her, her thumbs twitching.

"There is not much to tell. We stopped at Ostiarius Lavinia's villa on request and picked up these two ..." She looked around. "Where is Steig? Again?" She directed the enquiry at Maisie.

"Oh, he's ... not comfortable in towns. He's in the courtyard, getting some rest."

"So, picked up Maisie here and Steig, who is in your courtyard, apparently. The Gratadei pursued us. They are interested in Maisie, but not in a positive way. We lost them in Silentoak. They found where Ostiarius Rosalia was residing and have taken her prisoner. So, we cannot stay there, as they will surely be back. Then, I thought, Findir has that room, above the bakery ..."

"Ah, so you want to hide out here, eh? Subterfuge. I like it. Of course, you may, but it's not" – he glanced at the morose elves around his table – "not ... spacious."

"I think it would be best if we disbanded for a few days," said Pheoreth. "I will stay here with Maisie and Steig. For the rest of you, I suggest Cleofair's farm out at Mediglia. It is close enough to get there in an hour and far enough out that the Gratadei will not bother looking. However ..." She paused, looking into the eyes of each elf in turn. "No one, and I mean no one, is to know Maisie's location, my location, or any mention of Savio's farm. We are compromised. Someone is feeding information to the Gratadei. So, we keep where we are strictly to ourselves. Is that understood?"

A chorus of acknowledgements and affirmatives rippled through the group.

"Good. Drink up, get out to Cleofair's. Andion, send a runner back here twice a day for information. Go!"

The mustered elves, muttering, drained their cups and set them on the table, then took their leave, each thanking Findir with a bow as they departed.

Findir looked at Pheoreth and Maisie. "So, you're not going to give me any hot gossip?" he asked, grinning as he refilled his cup, bushy eyebrows twitching.

"No, you just heard; we are trying to keep a lid on everything. So, please, Findir, not a word. It will go badly for all of us if the Gratadei come here."

"Oh, you don't need to worry about me, Pheoreth. You are my father's brother's wife's daughter. Or something. Anyway. You have my word and bond." He thumped his breast with one heavy fist.

"Very well. You will appreciate we are not able to fill you in with the details. Yet. When this is all over, then we will have tales to tell, yarns to spin, late into the night over many bottles of this fine wine." She poured another cup for herself and Maisie. "Until then, please, just show us the room."

"Of course, of course. Come now, it is up the steps outside."

He picked up a lantern hanging by the door and lit it, then went out into the fading night. Maisie followed, startled by the approaching dawn. They had been up and about all night! She yawned. No wonder she was worn out.

Findir stamped up the steps and opened the door at the top; Pheoreth followed. Maisie walked over to Steig's bundled form, and shook his shoulder.

"Steig, wake up. We're going up there." He was wrapped in his blanket, stretched out on the ground. His eyes opened to slits.

"Is cold. Freezin'."

"Come on."

Mumbling and grumbling, Steig staggered up, wrapped the blanket about his shoulders and clambered up the stairs after Maisie.

The room, Maisie thought, was homely, but tiny. A small bed took up most of one wall. The opposite wall held a washstand with a basin and a jug of water. A cracked mirror. A dusty window opposite let in the faint glimmer of the dawn. A tiny pot-bellied stove sat against the far wall with its chimney pipe fed out through a space where a windowpane used to be. Pheoreth unslung her pack, dropped it on the bed and slid the bow and quiver of arrows out of the way.

"Well, I am off to light the ovens and get the day's bread baked. Come down when you are ready, and we can have a proper breakfast."

Findir thundered down the stairs, singing a tuneless baritone song as he went.

"Eurgh, I am exhausted." Maisie flung herself on the bed, wrapping the cloak around her. Steig was pacing up and down by the door.

"Er ... I'm going to head back to Savio's farm," he said. "I don't think I can cope with this space."

That cold hand clenched in her stomach again. She opened her mouth to speak, but Pheoreth beat her to it.

"Very well, but have a care that you do not fall foul of the roadblocks."

"I'll skirt around them, take back paths to the edge and work over the fields. It's not difficult to stay off the roads."

"As you say. Kushti bok."

Steig bowed to Pheoreth. "Kushti bok."

Maisie sat up on the bed, went to speak again, but Steig held up his hand.

"Hey. I'm only a mile or two away. You can find me by yog, no?"

"Oh, yes! I suppose I can. I hadn't thought of that." Then she realised the journey Steig would undertake in daylight. "But what will you do? How will you avoid the Gratadei?"

"I've moved around the countryside in stealth mode enough times. Those thugs won't see me. It'll be fine."

He seemed confident, and Maisie supposed he was competent at moving with stealth. And she could find him by yog. Though that would need practice if she weren't to exhaust herself every time.

Chapter 23

Steig shut the door to the tiny room at the top of the stairs. Shouldering his small pack and the long gun, he headed down into the yard and out through the wooden side gate. The smell of baking bread came from the bakery, along with the atonal singing of Findir, the dwarf-elf. A wan, misty light seeped into the streets, pushing to dispel the night. Steig was bone-cold from sleeping on the floor. A brisk walk would see him warmed up. He glanced toward the glow of the dawn, and headed directly away from it. West would take him towards the side of Mediolanum that he needed. Once he was on the outskirts, he could work along ditches and hedgerows, such as they may be, to avoid the busy thoroughfares.

As he walked through the streets, the dawn lightening with every step, he took stock of the town in the dim light. Wooden wattle and daub timber-frame houses, red pantile roofs, many with enclosed courtyards secured by imposing, solid gates. The few people around so early were what he was coming to recognise as the usual demographic of peoples in this realm. Fae, blonde Celtic or dark Hellenic, with a smattering of humanity, and a couple of dwarfs. Also, the vague sight of a hob or two, fleeting past at hob speed, no doubt out erranding for their masters.

The route he took down the narrow streets ran roughly in the same direction as what he suspected was the central street, Via Quintana. He avoided that, sticking to the lanes and backyards. He scaled walls and fences where needed, navigating by the sun. He avoided leaping dogs that barked inside their yards by balancing along the tops of walls. Thankfully, there seemed less in the way of spikes on wall-tops in the town.

After half an hour of busy weaving to and fro, Steig arrived at the same narrow lane where he had waited the previous evening. Slightly out of breath, he paused for a moment. Remembering the walk in from the farm, he knew there was a river bridge to cross. Which would be in sight of the roadblock.

Along the lane was the entrance to a snickleway, running at right angles.

"Well, it's worth a try," he muttered, creeping his way down the tiny alley between kitchen gardens. The end of the alley opened into a small, sparse covert, bordered on one side by the road and bridge and the other side by the river.

No one was on the bridge. No one around at all. He sneaked to the corner of the covert and, from within the understorey, checked back along Via Severiana. Sure enough, he spied the brazier, with the heavy-set, ginger-haired mercenary looking sleepy but upright. The bridge, therefore, wasn't an option, since they would see him. He crawled backwards and made his way down the steep slope to the riverbank.

As if in answer to his needs, the river was at a shallow ebb. Whilst wadeable, it was sludgy and disgusting, edged with foul, yellow scum. Someone had made a crossing with stepping stones and old planks. With a reasonable amount of balance, he tight-roped over to the far side without slipping into the turbid muck.

Scrambling up the far bank, angling away from the road, he came out at the edge of a tatty vineyard. The vines were dead and brown, but they began greening up the further he walked along the rows and away from the town. After half a mile, he came to the road. Checking for traffic, he sauntered across, thinking that anyone looking along the road would take him for an itinerant or a labourer, not a fugitive.

He carried on walking through scrubby woodland on the far side of the road until he came to the turning for Savio's farm. The morning air was utterly still. Pausing for a breather, he heard a woman's scream, truncated.

Steig dropped to the ground, concealed in the scrub, and shrugged off his pack and rifle. He checked the magazine, pulled a spare from the side of his pack and stuffed it in his back pocket. He crawled forward towards Savio's farmhouse, using the spindly bushes along the lane as cover. After a minute, he came to a slight rise that gave him a view into the farmyard.

"Oh, no, no, no, this isn't good. Fuck's sake," he whispered.

In the farmyard, parked at an angle, was one of the dark-green four-by-four trucks used by the Gratadei. One thug was standing over Maria, a handgun pointed at her head. She was lying on the ground, crying, sobbing.

Another mercenary was holding Savio with his arm twisted up his back. There was a lot of shouting.

From what Steig could make out, the conversation was going along the lines of "Tell us everything or we kill her."

"Fuck. No."

Steig fumbled with the bolt of the rifle, chambered a round, clicked the safety off. Actions he had done a hundred times before, hunting deer, rabbit, muntjac. But when he brought his eye to the telescopic sight, and the reticule centred on the chest of the Gratadei standing above Maria, he hesitated. His father's words, one of the very few sayings he took to heart, came back to him. "If you are going to aim a gun at someone, do it so you kill them. If you don't want to kill them, don't point the gun."

"Damn it, Dad. Them or us."

He let his breath out, tried to calm his hammering heart, relaxed his hands, and squeezed the trigger. The silencer muffled the report, but the bullet's supersonic progression ripped the air with a sharp crack.

As the rifle kicked back into his shoulder, he worked the action, moved the reticule to the other Gratadei holding Savio, who was just reacting to the report. Taking care to keep the reticule away from Savio, he squeezed again.

He felt sick.

"Fuck. Fuck-fuck-fuck."

But he had to be patient. No jumping up. No running in. There could be others. He worked the action again, a third round chambered in the breech, the brassy tumble of the empty round muffled by the grass. The tang of cordite, astringent in the still air. He remained hidden, motionless, scanning the ground, the vehicle, the barns. Nothing.

Savio went to Maria, and she sat up, and they hugged, and stayed, still sitting on the muddy ground, hugging. Shock, Steig thought. He'd be the same soon enough.

Movement. The vehicle. A door opened. A hairy grey foot appeared, followed by the disgusting, grey, patched torso and ugly head of the bogle. His arms were longer than his body and snaked out of the vehicle after him, two terrible appendages on a terrible being.

The rifle kicked again. Steig wiped his eyes, tried to hold back the sobs. Kept watching. No more movement.

After ten minutes, Savio and Maria stood up and hobbled to the farmhouse. They skirted around the two bodies in their yard, not looking at them. Steig finally allowed himself to relax, shock overcoming him. He vomited bile, which spattered, steaming and yellow and acrid, onto the grey soil. Sobs turned into wracking heaves as he cried onto the cold, unforgiving ground.

"I've moved around the countryside in stealth mode enough times. Those thugs won't see me. It'll be fine." The door shut, and Maisie heard Steig's boots clumping down the steps. Then, after a pause, the click of the gate latch shutting. A tear rolled down her cheek.

She pulled herself together enough to uncast the glamour of her disguise. Took off her boots and outer clothes, which she discarded in a heap by the bed. She'd left the staff lying along the wall, in reach, in the bed, as was now her habit. She was so tired. It was musty, yet warming underneath the blankets and sheets. And soft. Steig's behaviour worried her. He was acting quite oddly. No one was telling him what to do, were they? Was she? He had agreed to come to Khôra, back, oh so many days ago it seemed, by the Wayland, by Beckett.

A wave of loneliness washed over her. She missed the big horse and his pithy one-liners. She missed the vardo and its curved roof. And Steig. Yes, she missed him, and worried about him. Oh, her thoughts were all over the place. She tried to push her worry to the back of her mind. It wouldn't change anything. Bobe Elka was correct in that respect. She looked over at Pheoreth; the slender neraida regarded her with serious, dark eyes, but with a hint of a smile. Maisie's stomach fluttered.

Pheoreth, having removed her boots at the door, turned her back to Maisie and stripped off her jacket, tunic, utility belt, pantaloons. She was naked underneath. Her dark skin and gentle curves caused the same stirring in Maisie that she had felt earlier, when she had used the tatchapen spell and seen Pheoreth for her true self. So had she? Had she undone her glamour now?

Pheoreth turned back to Maisie, and she saw the crow's feet at her eyes, the less-than-salon-perfect hair. She was breathtakingly beautiful.

"Would you mind if we share the bed?" she said. "I am tired. And you are warm."

Maisie stuttered, "Y-yes, of course, please."

She pushed herself over in the narrow space, the staff a comforting presence where it pressed into her back. She turned the cover down for Pheoreth, who slipped in with the grace of a ballerina.

As Pheoreth's skin touched Maisie's, a tingling electrical shock and goosebumps coursed up her arms and legs. A warmth in her breast and groin spread to her face as she blushed. Pheoreth was leaning on one elbow, regarding her with a raised eyebrow.

"So, you have removed your glamour," Maisie whispered. "And yet, you are more beautiful than I could have imagined."

"I use a tiny glamour, like all the fae folk. It is just something we do. My true self, I only show to those I wish to get to know more ... intimately."

"Intimately?" breathed Maisie.

"Yes. Intimately ..." Pheoreth leant closer to Maisie. Her heady scent was wood smoke and sweat, rain on meadow grass.

Maisie woke to a rumbling noise. She sat up in bed and looked around, startled. Golden sunlight flooded the tiny room. Pheoreth was a tangle of sheets, long black hair, pointed ears and luxurious dark limbs, stretched, elongated like a cat, lying next to her.

"Good afternoon. I think your stomach is saying something," she purred.

Maisie blushed a deep, beet red.

"Morning. Oh! I'm famished. Oh gosh, did you say afternoon?"

"We have slept for much of the day. Well, we have travelled, and adventured, and ... loved. We needed the rest."

Maisie lay back down, snuggled into the curve of Pheoreth's hip.

"One question. How come you wanted to ... sleep with me, if I'm leathphór?"

"I am eternally sorry for my words in the Silentoak glade. I spoke them in haste, with no thought. That you are leathphór is of no consequence to me other than in relation to the staff; since Erato gifted the staff to you, your ownership of it is not in question. As for wanting to 'sleep' with you, as you so eloquently phrase it, I think you are brave, beautiful, bold, clever, articulate. You have a natural affinity with the fae glamour and the traveller lore, and you have stood up for yourself and for me. Really, what is there not to admire? Who would not want to experience more intimacy with you?"

"Oh. I see. Gosh." She sniffed the air. "Ew, I stink of sweat and … and sex, and …"

"You smell wonderful to me."

"Stop that." She smiled. A guilty memory of waking in Steig's bed entered her mind, unbidden. "Oh no, what am I going to do about Steig?! Have you bewitched me?"

"I did no such thing. I have dissipated my glamour. What you see is just me." Pheoreth's brow creased with annoyance.

"Uh. I was joking. Sort of. I can tell when you use the glamour. Um. I have this spell …"

"It is not a joking matter. So, this?" She reached over and touched the amulet that rested on Maisie's chest. Her hand lingered there, then brushed against the inside of Maisie's breast. Electricity surged through her skin from nipple to groin and she gasped.

"Aaahah, not fair! Behave." She batted Pheoreth's hand away. "Yes, that. I can see through glamour. And you must know. Aelene isn't Aelene."

Pheoreth looked up, her body tensed, all languor snapped away.

"What?"

"I used the spell when we were drinking in her parlour. I saw your face as you are now, um, exquisite." She blushed, looked down for a second. "And when I saw Aelene, she was completely different. A different face, a different person."

"Oh. Well." Pheoreth's hands fluttered in panic for a moment, then she calmed, became thoughtful. "Well. This changes the perspective of things. I have known Aelene for many years. I do not understand." She cast her eyes down, furrowing her brow in deep concentration. "If she is not Aelene, we can assume that whoever she is, she is a powerful sorceress. To cast that level of glamour without the rest of us noticing. And furthermore, we can assume she is our leak to the Gratadei."

"It does look like that, doesn't it?"

Footsteps sounded on the stairs, light and fast. Maisie started with fright and reached for the staff. Its touch calmed her, and she drew power from it in preparation. Pheoreth put her hand on Maisie's arm.

"It is Morwen, come with news."

A knock at the door.

"One minute!" shouted Maisie and started pulling on clothes.

Maisie stoked the pot-bellied stove, so it burnt hot and bright, the bowl of its base glowing a cherry red. She shut the stove door and closed the air vent, so it wasn't roaring with such frenzy.

"Please keep the fire burning until I am back. Otherwise, I'll be stuck, or lost. Lost in the Betwixt isn't something I want to try. It's cold in there. Freezing."

"I will keep the fire burning until you are back, of course."

Maisie stood, adjusted her cloak, took up her staff. Turned to Pheoreth, who was looking on with a frown on her face.

"I'll be back in an hour or two, if I can find him. If he's not by a yog, I'll just have a cast around and explore, see where I get to."

"This course of action sounds perilous. Unwise."

Maisie stepped closer to the elf and inclined her head, touching foreheads.

"I'll be back tonight. I'll be careful. I promise."

Pheoreth wrung her hands.

"What's wrong?"

"It is not a magic I can perform. So, you will be gone from me, and I will have no way of finding you."

"Well, you understand I need to see Steig, to check in on him like I said I would?"

"Yes, I understand that. I just dislike the idea of you disappearing into the mist all on your own. I-I want to protect you." She stared down at her feet.

Maisie grabbed her by the shoulders and pulled her face close, kissing her on those beautiful, dark red lips, snaking her arms around her neck and hugging her close. She whispered into her ear, "I'll be back tonight, I promise." As she released her, she remembered performing almost the exact same hug with Steig only a couple of days ago. Her chest tightened with conflict.

Without thinking twice, lest she decide against this "perilous" course of action, she invoked the first half of the kathalyog spell and stepped into the Betwixt. The chill air penetrated her bones within seconds, and she started shivering. She pulled the cloak close around her, and thought to the staff, "Show me Steig's yog."

Nothing happened. The mist enveloping her was grey and dark and unpleasant. She tamped down the rising panic. Then squinted, trying to find the pinpricks of light. They were there, but very faint. Something was pulling the energy from this place. She guessed it was whatever the Gratadei were doing at Mediolanum.

She asked again, pulling power from the staff, hoping that the local Gratadei disturbance didn't affect the staff's power, linked to Silentoak and Erato as it was.

One of the dim pinpricks of yellow light, a few metres from her, flared, just a tiny flicker. But a difference. She kept her eye on it and walked forward. Peered in on the light, waited for the mists to clear and her eyes to adjust. There she saw Steig, sitting by a yog. She let out a sob of relief. Cast the other half of the spell and stepped through.

Beckett rumbled a greeting.

"Shit, you scared me." Steig scrabbled to his feet. Maisie had materialised, standing by the yog, in her cloak, with her staff, fogged air falling from her in waves. "Are you alright?"

In reply, Maisie launched herself at him and clung on, a hug that almost knocked Steig over. She wrapped him in her arms and cloak, dropping the staff, and held on as if Steig were the only solid thing in the world. Steig wrapped his arms around her as well, welcoming the contact, her warmth. He stroked her hair, which was dew-soaked from the Betwixt.

"Hey, I missed you, too. How have you been?"

Maisie sniffled. "I'm fine, thank you. I'm better now that I'm here. It's been … difficult."

"I shot three people." He felt her freeze, her body going rigid.

"You did what? Shit. Are they dead?"

"Two Gratadei thugs and the bogle from Fenis Pass. They were about to kill Savio and Maria. And yes, they are dead."

Maisie unwound her arms and held Steig at arm's length, looking into his face, into his eyes.

"Shit, Steig. Shit. I mean. Shit."

"Yeah, I know. I keep getting the shakes. Savio was grateful, of course, but then we had to move the bodies before anyone came. It was awful." He felt the welling of tears, the shaking of his body that he couldn't halt, the tightness in his chest. He couldn't breathe. Maisie hugged him again. The hug seemed to go on forever. He leant into it, allowing her to support him. Having someone support him helped. The shaking subsided. His legs were jelly weak.

"Here, I'll put the kettle on. Sit you down. We'll sort it out," she said.

He sat on his haunches and stared into the fire.

"Where's the kettle? Hang on. Where's the vardo!" She looked around the wooded clearing with sudden consternation.

"Oh, yeah, well, I moved the vardo from Savio's after we got rid of the bodies and their vehicle. I hid the vardo in some woods. I asked the local dryad, and they did this weird thing with moving trees. Like Pheoreth did at Silentoak."

"You spoke to a dryad, and they did what you asked?"

"I invoked the name of the Finder of Keys."

"You didn't?" Her mouth fell open in shock.

"Yeah, the dryad was very accommodating after that. So, I've hidden the wagon. And Beckett and I are travelling light, sticking to the highlands and the woodlands. Well, that's what we did today. I was hoping you'd turn up so I can find out what we're all up to. And here you are. Oh, here, this is the travel kettle." He handed her a small, blackened metal kettle with a partially singed plastic handle. "There's water in that water container, and there's a stream a ways away, so no need to ration it. That satchel" – he pointed at a battered, faded, tan leather bag – "is the travel kitchen box."

Maisie smiled. "I love that, as a traveller, you have a travel set of stuff as well as the normal set of stuff that you travel with. Tea?"

"Yes please. Oh, it's so good to see you. It's been a really tough day."

She squeezed his shoulder but had a strange look on her face. She set about the tea and soon passed him a steaming mug.

"Thanks."

"You're welcome. So. What happened? Please tell, if you can."

"After I left you two, I sneaked out of Mediolanum with no major problems. When I got to Savio's, Maria was about to be executed. I couldn't let that happen. Afterwards, Savio and I loaded the bodies into their own truck and drove it back up to Fenis Pass and ran it into a ravine. We think what happened is that the bogle followed us to Savio's farm, then flagged the Gratadei down on the pass and brought them back. Um. Then I took the vardo and Beckett and we hid the vardo with the dryad and headed north and uphill, until we got here, and that's how I came to be here." He realised he hadn't taken a breath, and gasped for air. Maisie hugged him again, but her face wore a strained expression. "What about you?"

Maisie breathed a deep sigh.

"Well." She stopped and fiddled with her cloak. "So. Um. At Aelene's parlour, I used a spell to see through the glamour. And Aelene isn't Aelene. She's a Gratadei witch. A powerful one. Also. Um." She glanced up at Steig, and he saw tears brimming.

"Hey. Whatever happened, it's OK, you know? Elves and faeries, right?"

"Yes. So. When I used the spell to undo the glamour, Pheoreth was ... well, all the fae, it turns out, use glamour all the time, just a bit. Like make up. Just to tweak their looks. Without the glamour, Pheoreth appeared slightly older, but so much more real. Incredibly beautiful." She looked up, eyes shining.

Steig thought he knew where this was going. "And so?"

"And so. When you left. We were in the room above Findir's bakery. And." She stopped again, fiddled with her cloak some more. She had distress written across her face.

"You slept with Pheoreth and now you're conflicted because I'm not with you and you want to be with me, but you're attracted to Pheoreth as well. Is that it?"

"Oh Steig. I'm so sorry." She flung herself at him again, burrowing into his neck, tears wet on his skin. He hugged her, held her as she sobbed.

How did he feel about Pheoreth? About Maisie? Complicated. But not so complicated that Maisie's feelings didn't come first.

"I like you a lot, Maisie," he said, his voice soft, speaking into her hair. "Which isn't something I would have said about you two weeks ago. I've grown to enjoy your company, and I hope that feeling is mutual."

"It is," she whispered from his neck, nodding.

"But we are all free spirits. When we first met, I said that it's a free country. Well, free-ish. That still holds. We are independent individuals, and we're grownups, and we can make life decisions for ourselves. What I'm trying to say is, there's no judgement here from me. You've got a thing with Pheoreth. I applaud that. I hope she doesn't hurt you. I hope you have a fun time, and a friendship or relationship blossoms, if it works for you. And I would hope to remain friends and to share a bed when there's a need. Whatever that need might be."

Maisie tightened her grip around Steig's neck. Her sobs had subsided, but she sniffled, still. He held her, quiet, watching the flames dance in the light breeze. After a while, he shifted his weight, hugged her closer. He had something to say that had been weighing on him.

"Seems to me this whole adventure is turning out a bit too real," he said, his voice low and even. "We are reacting all the way along. No actual plan. No contingency. Here I am, in the middle of the woods. You're stuck in a tiny room and travelling by yog. Goddess knows where or what the Gratadei are at. I'm feeling like we should keep our own counsel, and really trust no one. That is, if we trust each other?"

Maisie raised her face from his neck, red-eyed.

"Don't you trust me?"

"Yes, I do trust you. Just no one else. I mean, do we trust Bobe Elka, if she reappears? She helped to get us to Khôra. Who's to say she's not doing it for a Gratadei kickback?"

Maisie bridled. "I'm saying. She's solid. I trust her completely."

"Because?"

"Because if she weren't trustworthy, she wouldn't have given me the kathalyog and the tatchapen spells. And shown me the gateway commands. She'd have let me flounder around getting nowhere if she was on the Gratadei side."

"Well, I'll take that with a pinch of salt. What about Pheoreth?"

Maisie sucked her teeth, making a hissing noise. "What about her?"

"It's not a criticism. I'm trying to be objective. Try to think beyond what, eh, happened between you. What has she done for us or against the Gratadei that is irrefutable?"

"Oh. I see. Well, she hid us from the Gratadei before Silentoak. She led us to the Silentoak glade. She got us through the roadblock. Well, except you got lost, but she sent Andion back for you."

"But that's not actual proof, is it? Of course, I'm not sure what would constitute proof."

"Maybe we just have to trust and have faith. Oh! It's hurting my head thinking about it. Why can't people be straightforward?"

"I'm hoping that was rhetorical, otherwise we may be here a while." He smiled at her. "We have each other. Hold on to that."

"Yes. Literally." She wound her arms around him and hugged tight. Then sat up, remembering something. "Oh! I brought you fresh bread. From Findir." She rummaged in her messenger bag, withdrew a slim loaf. "Here."

"Thank you, this is welcome." He balanced the loaf on the satchel. "So, can we try to be proactive? What should we try to achieve in the next twenty-four hours?"

"We need to rescue Rosalia."

"Why?"

"Why? Because the Gratadei have taken her, of course!"

"Are we sure of that? We only have Aelene's word for that."

"Argh, my head! Well then. How about we eavesdrop on people and find out what's going on? All the actors in the play who are involved. Aelene. The Gratadei leader, this mysterious Cardinal. And maybe Lavinia?"

"Now, you're talking sense. Any idea how we can do that?"

"Oh. I thought, kathalyog. Before I drop into the fireside, I can see you, as if from above. Maybe I can tune in the sound as well?"

"So, you can just peer in on people's firesides without them knowing? Outstanding. Yes, you should definitely try to get the sound."

"Yes, I'll do that. Aelene, or the Cardinal, if I can find him, I'll try first. So, I'll report back on that tomorrow."

"Awesome. I'm a bit stuck out here, but I'm going to go into the next town along, tomorrow. I'll try to get a sense of who likes the Gratadei and who doesn't, see if there's a resistance organisation. See if anyone knows Aelene. Oh! Do you have any local currency?"

"Yes, of course; I got some from Pheoreth. Here." She rummaged in her bag, extracted a leather pouch that chinked with the sound of coins. "I'd better get back. It's really murky in the Betwixt around Mediolanum. The magic is definitely suffering. So, I'm hoping my yog is still lit. If not, I'll come back here."

"Did you bring any apples?" Beckett called from where Steig had tethered him to a picket line slung between two trees.

"Oh! Hello, Beckett." Maisie walked over to the horse, unearthed an apple from the depths of her bag, and fed it to him. He crunched it up and chewed with obvious enjoyment. "I'm sorry, I should have come and hugged you sooner, but ... it's all complicated at the moment," she said into the horse's ear. Beckett whickered a gentle response. Maisie leant against him, gave him a groom on his neck, under his shaggy mane, with her fingertips. "I've missed you."

He responded with another whicker.

"Alright," she said to Steig. "I really must get back. I'm worrying about my yog."

"Travel safe. Come back here if you get stuck. I'll keep the fire burning hot for another hour or so."

"Thank you." She flung herself around his neck again, squeezed hard. Steig hugged back.

"Send my regards to Pheoreth. Just ... just don't get blinded by her glamour."

"I won't. Right. I must go. I-I miss you."

"I miss you, too. Be careful! See you tomorrow, same sort of time? Kushti bok."

"Yes!" She walked towards the yog. She held up her staff; the katha-lyog mist rose from the ground. "I'll bring bread. Kushti bo—" She dissipated into the mist, before Steig's eyes.

"Huh. And she's gone."

"She brought an apple."

"Aye, that she did, horse." Steig walked back to the yog and heaped on another log, sending up a cascade of sparks into the branches above. "Just don't get blinded by her glamour," he murmured to himself, confusion clouding his thoughts, worry twisting his gut.

The Betwixt was as cold as ever, but less murky; Maisie guessed that was because of her current distance from Mediolanum. She once again wrapped the cloak tight.

"I'll need to get a better cloak. Something heavy and fur lined, at this rate," she muttered to herself. Gripping the staff, she asked for her home hearth, and a flare of yellow light some way off was her reward. "Well, at least that works."

She strode to the light and peered in. The last thing she wanted to do was walk in on the Gratadei, or the wrong yog. Also, she needed practice at spying. She wasn't sure how she felt about spying, but Steig was right; they needed information, and it seemed they could trust no one but each other.

She leant in, peered, and saw Pheoreth, sitting back on the bed, propped on her elbows, head back, eyes closed. Was she asleep? The stove was running hot, glowing red. She'd kept it going, as requested.

Could she get sound? She increased the acuity of her hearing, a trick she had commanded since adolescence, but the surrounding mist seemed to dampen all noise. It muffled even her own movements and heartbeat. Again, she leant into the power of the staff, asked that it might enable sound. The image flickered; the wood burner dimmed its light. But now she could hear the fire's crackle and the suck of air through its flue, could hear Pheoreth's gentle snores. So, sound was an option, as long as no one linked the dimming of the yog to the spell being cast. She released the pressure on the staff, then intoned the second half of kathalyog and stepped into the room.

A tangible wall of heat struck her. As she took her first breath of the air in the room, Pheoreth's eyes flickered open. She turned her head and her mouth parted into a broad, beautiful smile.

"I am glad you are back."

"I'm glad too. It's rather warm in here. But welcome after the Betwixt."

Pheoreth stood and sashayed over, unfastened Maisie's cloak from about her throat.

"Let me assist you with your clothing," Pheoreth said with a straight face and undertones of need.

As she leant in to do the catch, Maisie smelt her hair. That scent of … lust, birdsong, golden light … Pheoreth hung the cloak on a peg on the door, turned back and looked at her from across the room, her eyes an intense black; her face was the most exquisite countenance Maisie had ever seen. Pheoreth took a step closer. She wasn't using the glamour. Another step. Pheoreth was so very attractive, Maisie could feel the lust rising in her. Surely, it must be some form of sorcery. But she couldn't prevent it, didn't want to prevent it. With a deft movement, Pheoreth covered the last stride to her, held her in her arms, and was kissing her mouth as urgently as Maisie kissed back. Their hands fumbled with a carnal excitement at buckles and clasps, tearing at underclothes. They fell onto the bed in a tangle of hair and limbs and delight.

Chapter 24

Maisie woke with a pang. Not hunger, but longing. For the wagon. For the curved roof, the open air, the yog, the space. Being in a building was suffocating, like being incarcerated. She wondered when her psyche had undergone that change. And what had caused it?

Taking a deep breath to calm her claustrophobic feelings, and warm in the bed, she considered the previous day. Steig. He had killed people. How did that make her feel? Soldiers killed people in wars, and weren't held up as monsters. Well, not by most in society. That didn't make it right. And yet. If he had watched and waited, and the Gratadei had killed Maria and Savio, what would that make him? It was Scylla and Charybdis. And like the conversation with Steig the previous evening, it hurt her head.

He was still, essentially, Steig. Would he have trauma and nightmares from his actions? Undoubtedly. Would she comfort him when that happened? Of course. If she was there. Which she wasn't. She felt guilt for her absence, and to a certain extent she felt guilt for having a physical relationship with Pheoreth.

She pushed the guilt and the angst and the worry to the back of her mind, to be considered later. Line it up at the back of her subconscious with all the other traumas and worries. Good plan.

Sighing, she stared up at the mottled plaster of the ceiling and the dust-stained walls, sniffed the frigid, musty air, wood smoke, the tang of unwashed bodies.

"Eurgh, I stink."

"Mmm, smells good ..." came the mumbled refrain from Pheoreth, somewhere buried under the covers.

Maisie nudged the elf with her knee. "Budge over. I need to pee and wash."

As she stood, she realised the kathalyog hadn't exhausted her, as it had the first time. That was encouraging.

The wooden floor was rough on her bare feet, but she enjoyed the feeling of the chilled air on her skin. She put on her cloak to cover her nakedness and slipped out to use the toilet in a small outbuilding in the yard below. From the top of the steps, she could see the eastern sky, brightening, but it remained dim outside, still some time until the town would wake. Findir's awful singing emanated from the bakery, along with the smell of fresh bread.

When she returned, she found Pheoreth sitting on the bed, brushing her hair. The stove was alight, but not yet throwing much in the way of heat.

"Be warned, the water is akin to ice."

"Yes, if there was one thing I'd miss, living on the road, it would be baths." She disrobed and poured some of the frigid water from the jug into the basin. As she sponged herself, she let out small gasps of shock as the water sucked the last of the warmth from her skin. "Worse than the Betwixt."

"Are you thinking of becoming a traveller, then?" Pheoreth's face was open and interested.

"I don't know what I want to do with my life. If this is a turning point, there are few signposts. I love living in the wagon; I completely get Steig not wanting to stay in a building. But bathing. Warm water and lots of it. Oh, a dream."

She finished with the sponge and dried herself on the one small towel that had been in the room, still damp from Pheoreth's wash. She hung it on a chair-back next to the wood burner.

"Yes, being far from home and dirty from the journey is uncomfortable." Pheoreth sounded wistful.

Maisie sat on the bed next to the elf. "Where is your home, Pheoreth?"

Pheoreth's face became guarded.

"It is far in the east. Well, not far, really. Nowhere is far in Khôra. My real home is near the village of Balat, in Anatolia, in the Defaltum Mundi. I dream of returning there as a free person, some day. But alas, for the time being, I am restricted to Khôra. So I have built my home in the east, in a position as close to the Balat gateway as I can get. We call it Miletus."

"Why can't you go to Balat?"

"How many of us" – she indicated her ears – "have you seen in Defaltum Mundi in your lifetime?"

"Oh. I see. But why do your kind ... oh! Our kind ... why would we, you, not return?"

"You are young. And I am not ... so young as you. I remember the fear and the burnings and the pogroms of the neraides, when we lived in Defaltum Mundi. We made Khôra our home. Away from tyranny. Away from fear."

Maisie considered this. She was privileged to live in her world without fear and spite. Leaving aside the incessant teasing she had endured at school because of her ears. That had been difficult, but not as bad as being hounded from your home country. As she ruminated on Pheoreth's life, her home in the east, a thought occurred to her.

"You were in the far west. And on your way back to Miletus. Lavinia asked you to collect Steig and I and accompany us to Ostiarius Principale Rosalia. And yet, you are still here? Have we not interrupted your journey?"

"Yes, and we will resume our journey after you have completed your quest. Assisting the Finder of Keys is an honour and a privilege."

"So. About that. How will I complete my quest? What even is my quest?"

"All I know is that there are many claves missing, and you can find them. That is the foretelling from the Fates. With more claves, we can, um, defeat the Gratadei."

"That makes little sense. Having more gateways open will just mean the Gratadei can carry on pulling the power from the land. You've seen the state of the land here, and other places, like Lavinia's. It's as if there has been a war. Grey mud and sludge everywhere, nothing growing. The Betwixt is the same, here. It's grungy and withered and ... and sick."

"What, then, is your counsel?"

Maisie saw the curve on her lip. "You're mocking me."

“I am not. But you are extraordinarily beautiful when you have a cause in which to shine.”

Maisie coloured red.

“Um. Never mind that.” She fiddled with her cloak where it lay on the bed. “I don’t have any suggestions. Fresh out. One thing I do need is a better cloak, if I’m going to spend any more time in the Betwixt. This is Bobe Elka’s, for a start. Do you know of a cloak vendor in Mediolanum?”

“I do. We can go there this morning. In disguise. I will show you how to use the glamour in a subtle way. You need not break any flagstones or roof tiles.”

Steig watched the bivouac canopy above him, backlit and dappled by the rising sun. It was a lightweight camo tarpaulin, pegged out over a rope stretched between two trees. It was open at the sides but, as long as the wind wasn’t a gale, it afforded waterproof cover, though the wind was now getting up, and the tarp was billowing and filling. He rolled over and looked through the gap under the tarp. Beckett was standing with his behind to the wind, one back leg resting as usual. He seemed to be asleep, but as soon as Steig sat up, he let out a low whicker of greeting.

“Mornin’.”

“I like this wood,” Beckett replied.

Steig agreed. The trees were reasonably spaced, and plentiful grass grew between them. Beckett, on his picket line between two trees, away from the camp, had eaten down a strip of grass to almost nothing.

"Good eating?"

Two flicks for yes. Steig rolled his eyes, scrabbled around in the yog to kindle a flame for coffee.

He washed, breakfasted on cold traveller's ish stew from the previous day, then packed down the tarp and gear into two large leather saddle bags. Once these were loaded onto Beckett, Steig climbed aboard, grabbing a handful of dreadlocked mane to assist. He didn't have a saddle, instead using a small felt blanket that was held on to the horse's back with a surcingle. With the rope, tarp, sleeping kit, rifle and saddle bags strapped on to this, he was like any other itinerant worker. He had seen quite a few on the roads and felt he wouldn't stand out. After all, the Gratadei were hunting for Maisie, not him.

"Heddup then, lad, we'll get back to the road and keep heading north, see where we get to."

"Downhill. I like that."

"Hey, we're both getting fitter! Remember that first hill out of the Catmouse Vale? Almost killed us."

"I remember I was pulling the wagon, and you were walking alongside."

"Touché."

They picked their way through the woods, and soon met the dirt road that led up from Mediolanum to points north. Traffic was light. They waited and watched, just at the edge of the road. A pair of itinerant elves, all elongated frames and pointed ears, pushed a handcart loaded with their possessions. They glanced at Steig but said nothing. Next came a man in fine clothes on an impressive, gleaming black gelding. The gelding snorted and reared as it passed the elves. Finally, a dwarf with a huge beard and a leather cap, driving an ox-cart, passed in the other direction. The cart was laden with barrels of beer poorly covered by a greasy brown tarpaulin.

Steig asked Beckett onto the road, and they headed north at a steady walk. Steig relaxed into his seat, enjoying the warmth from Beckett's sides and back, Beckett's dorsal muscles moving under him. Quite different from driving the wagon. He suspected he'd be sore and stiff by lunchtime.

After an hour, they came to the edge of the woodland, and the last of the hills, a long escarpment with a track running along its length. The land dropped away to a broad plain; hills or small mountains smudging the far distance. A town lay in the crook of two hills, bridging the broad sweep of a deep river. He steered Beckett off the ridge and down a narrow track that led to the town.

A hand-painted wooden sign declared the town as Grauplenk. It had a distinctly Frisiian feel to it. Canals and small waterways bisected streets running from the river, with as many craft on the water as on the roads. It had a bustle and a vitality to it that was sorely lacking in Mediolanum. Steig suspected that was because of a lack of Gratadei interference.

"Huh. Long may it continue," he muttered.

The market square in the centre of the town was tight-packed with stalls and people. Steig dismounted and led Beckett to a substantial building at the side of the square; he hoped it was a coaching inn or livery stables. It boasted a wide arched entranceway to an enclosed courtyard, with busy stables beyond that. A sign above the archway, swinging in the freshening breeze, announced "Valken Hotel – Stalhouderij". It sported a picture of a bird of prey in stoop above the writing, and a pictogram of a horse and carriage below.

Steig wasn't sure about the formalities of parking a horse – he usually just tethered Beckett out on the verge or tied him to a railing or lamp-post. But then, he didn't usually go into the larger villages or towns, where Beckett might meet ne'er-do-wells. Towns made him twitchy. Just as he was about to give up in fear and abandon the idea of some food shopping, a hob appeared at his side. It wore what Steig assumed was the hotel livery – a burgundy jacket and matching pill-box hat.

"Take yer 'orse for yer, sire?" he squeaked.

"How much for an hour? I just need to get some supplies."

"Half a florin an' I'll clean his tack an' check his shoes an' that."

"Very well. Your name?"

"Kangrim, sire."

Steig prevaricated for a second, but his empty belly reminded him of the need to purchase supplies.

"OK, horse, behave, don't go anywhere else. I'll get apples." Two flicks for yes. He passed the reins to Kangrim. "Just hay, no oats or anything."

"Very good, sire."

He watched as the hob led Beckett through the archway, through the courtyard busy with horses, coaches, footmen, a real bustle, and into the stables. Kangrim tied him into a stall. With Beckett's black-and-white rump the only part of him visible, Steig went in search of victuals.

Maisie tried again. Gentle, she had said. Subtle. Twice she had tried, and each time Pheoreth had raised her arm when Maisie had cast the glamour, even though the neraida was facing the wall. A new experiment was in order. She didn't touch the staff, didn't lean on its magic, didn't pull fizz from it. She felt foolish and strangely exposed, almost naked. But she pushed at the thought of the glamour with as little conscious effort as she could. To her surprise, the features of the woman in the mirror changed as she watched. Her face belonged to a generic neraida, dark-skinned, dark-haired, pointy-eared. Brown eyes. Attractive.

"Well?"

"Well, what?" Pheoreth turned around. "Oh, Great Goddess! You did that without me feeling a thing! Third try. Bobe Elka was right, you do have a natural ability." Pheoreth turned her hair a deep red, lightened her skin, added freckles. "This will keep them guessing," she said, smiling.

They stepped out into the morning sunshine; the wind playing with the edges of Maisie's cloak. On the street, foot traffic was busier than she'd seen it. But then, she'd spent the previous day hiding away. She linked arms with Pheoreth, and they set off, just two elves out on a shopping trip.

As they approached the centre of the town, there was a larger structure, like a small castle, on a slight rise on the north side. A broad, well-paved road ran up to the imposing gates of the fortress.

"What's that place?" Maisie asked, nodding towards it.

"That is the Citadel. It is the seat of the Gratadei's power in Khôra. It is in the same position as Castello Sforzesco, the castle in Milano. Your world Milano, in Calabria. The Mediolanum gateway is inside, strongly guarded. That gateway was the route taken by heavier vehicles, back when we had trade with Defaltum Mundi. Now, only Gratadei trucks use it."

Maisie regarded the gates, a tremor of fear crawling up her spine.

Once on the central thoroughfare through the town, Via Quintana, Maisie kept a lookout for Gratadei soldiers. Despite the bustle, the people who were out and about appeared subdued, as if walking in fear. The shops lining both sides of the street were doing a brisk trade, with carts stopping and loading up or delivering. Humans, elves and dwarves walked on foot or rode on horseback. Hobs flitted past. But no watchers, nothing suspicious. No one in tactical black.

If I were the Gratadei, she thought, I'd have watchers hanging around everywhere. Then a thought occurred to her, and her heart chilled. With a cold sweat prickling her back, she gently, oh so gently, pulled some power from the staff and cast the tatchapen spell. A shimmer rippled around the end of the street, catching her attention. Two mercenaries stood in the shadow of an overhanging first-floor balcony. They looked on with obvious attention to every single person who passed their position.

Without reacting, though every fibre of her soul was screaming *run*, she turned to a haberdasher's shop window. The window was leaded, small warped glass panes, but with the angle of the bay, she could see behind herself in the reflection. The amulet burnt hot on her breast. Another Gratadei mercenary was at the other end of the street, also watchful.

"See anything you fancy?" asked Pheoreth.

"I ... uh ... cloak, we need the cloak shop." She could barely talk. Her heart was beating out of her chest.

"Are you alright? You look like you've seen a bogle."

"I ... Yes." She smiled, put on a brave face. Tried to ignore her inner voice, that was screaming, *Get off the street! We're all going to die!* "Bit tired. Um. Cloak shop?"

"Come on. Down here." She led Maisie down a narrow road that let off the street. The cobbled lane was dim and smelled of boiled cabbage. As they walked, the sounds of busyness faded. The amulet had cooled somewhat. It appeared to get hot when it had a glamour to deal with, so, hopefully, nothing much was hidden down here. At least not with magic.

The shop was what Maisie considered a proper, old-fashioned tailor's establishment. Double fronted with dusty leaded glass in two deep bay windows. A bell tinkled, a bright, welcoming noise as they opened the door. She gazed down the length of the shop. Was there a back entrance?

"Oh, is that you, Pheoreth? What a lovely glamour. The colour suits you!"

The speaker was a tall, thin man. He was balding, distinguished, wearing an elegant but vibrant purple suit, complete with paisley cravat and waistcoat.

"Hello, Michael. Nothing gets past you, now, does it?"

"Oh, don't be silly, I can tell by your jerkin, dear. I made it, after all. Now, please introduce me to your exquisite friend."

"Ah, yes, this is Fanwen, daughter of Fildaerae, of Silentoak. She is ... travelling with me for a while."

"Delighted," he said, taking Maisie's fingers in a gentle hold and bowing, brushing his lips to the back of her hand. He stood, looked Maisie in the eye and asked, "And how is dear Elka Morgenstein?"

"E-Elka?" stuttered Maisie.

Michael smiled. "You're wearing her cloak. Though I can't see her taking apprentices. How is she?"

"Last I saw of her, she was as crotchety as usual. It is, in fact, about the cloak that Pheoreth brought me here. Elka will need this one back. Do you have one like this, but winter weight, in dark blue? Perhaps fur lined?"

"Well, I can certainly make one to your specification. It will take but a moment. Korex!" He raised his voice, and an elderly hob dressed in a beautiful three-piece suit of pinstriped grey appeared at his side. He was wearing round wire-frame eyeglasses and had a tailor's tape measure draped around his neck.

"Sire?"

"Would you be so kind as to measure the young lady? I shall fetch the material."

"Sire. My Lady, please remove your ... cloak," he said the word with such disdain ... but then, it was a grubby garment, well worn, mended in places, wearing through in others. "And I shall measure, if My Lady assents?"

"Of course." She removed the cloak, placing it on a nearby seat. The hob flitted in and out of sight. Maisie felt the air moving around her, the occasional tug at a hem or seam, and then the hob was once again stationary in front of them.

"I have measured you. We may be some time whilst My Lord selects the materials."

Was there an undercurrent of ... amusement, Maisie thought? Korex had almost rolled his eyes.

While they waited, Maisie took in the displays of suits and bolts of cloth. Pheoreth simply lounged in that disdainful elvish way of hers. Though Maisie thought she knew Pheoreth better, now. The disdain was perhaps more front. Before she could think on this further, Michael reappeared, carrying a roll of heavy, deep-blue cloth and a sample swatch of fur.

"Here we are. Is this the sort of thing you were thinking of?"

Maisie felt the cloth between thumb and forefinger, lifted a section, and felt the heft. It was a dense, plain weave, heavyweight, almost like a canvas. But not as stiff. It appeared slightly worn, as if stonewashed.

"The cloth is a sandstone duck cotton mixed with Leithon wool. Waterproof, but flexible and comfortable. Exceptionally durable. The Weavers have imbued it with a hint of glamour. Here, the fur, it's ..." Michael paused, frowning. "I'm afraid it's synthetic, made by the Weaver-Dwarves in Dyvenvorde. But, again, waterproof, lightweight, very warm, and, well ..." He glanced at Bobe Elka's grubby cloak. "Washable."

"It's perfect! Thank you. Should we come back in a while, or ...?"

Truth was, Maisie was getting twitchy. She cast a nervous glance at the door. Pheoreth caught her look, reached for the leather money pouch she wore at her belt.

"I'm sure Korex will assemble this in a blink. Is that not so, Michael? We are ... keen to be moving along. How much do we owe you?"

Korex took the cloth and his measuring tape and disappeared into a back room. Maisie could hear the sounds of cutting and sewing and muttering, only sped up a hundredfold. It was like the flutter of a sparrow's wing.

"Oh! I was hoping you might join me for a cup of tea. No? Well. Let me see now. Cloth, four yards, the fur, three yards, lining, the labour, brass clasp, let's call it a round hundred florins, shall we?"

"A hundred? You are not getting any cheaper in your old age, Michael. Call it fifty."

As the banter and arguments ticked back and forth, Maisie kept a lookout from the bay window, up and down the alleyway. Keeping the tatchapen running was tiring her, fraying her nerves. But she didn't want anyone to sneak up on her.

"My Lady." The voice made her start, her heart palpitating. Korex was at her elbow with the freshly stitched cloak. He stood on a set of steps to help her on with it. The fit was perfect, the feel of the fur glorious. And the colour – such a deep blue that it seemed to suck the light from around it. As Michael had said, it had a hint of its own glamour. The brass clasp at her neck was ornate but strong, the hood deep and enclosing, and ...

"Pockets!" she squeaked.

"Yes, My Lady."

"It's perfect! Thank you so much, Korex, Michael. But ... Pheoreth, we must not tarry."

"We are settled. Let us be away," Pheoreth declared, shaking Michael's hand. Maisie bundled the old cloak in her arms and, gripping her staff, leant against the paint-flaked door jamb, peering both ways before leaving the shop.

"Problem?" Pheoreth asked as they walked away from Via Quintana, towards the back streets.

"I felt very exposed, on the main street. Let's take a detour," she replied.

She didn't feel like she wanted to share her reasoning with Pheoreth. That the Gratadei were employing their own glamour had set alarm bells ringing in Maisie's head.

"It will only be three hours. I need to check in with Steig, and I want to recce the Citadel."

"I must protest. This course of action is still perilous. I do not think you should go." Pheoreth was pacing, as best she could, up and down in the tiny room. Three paces, turn, three paces, turn. It made Maisie dizzy.

"Well, I'm not sitting in here cowering like a frightened doe anymore. Time for action." Before Pheoreth replied, Maisie cast the spell and stepped into the Betwixt. The grey dimling was sludgy and dark, as it had been before.

"Show me the hearth of Cardinal Baroffio," Maisie asked of the staff. It vibrated, warm, in her hand. A faint flare of light, but enough to guide her. She stepped over, peered in, pulling the new cloak around her shoulders. Its warmth was revelatory, its very fabric supportive, like being wrapped in a semi-sentient duvet.

The Cardinal was standing by a cluttered desk in an expansive study. His fireplace held a roaring fire. A rotund, elderly man, he was wearing – Maisie chuckled to herself – cardinal red robes and vestments. Heavy gold signet rings adorned his pudgy fingers. His overlarge jowls shook as he talked to, or perhaps berated, a minion. His secretary, in all probability.

The supposed secretary was a tall, angular human. With thinning black hair cut short, he was middle-aged with a worn down, hunted cast to his features. Maisie pulled on the staff for power, opened the "sound channel", as she was coming to think of it. The fire flickered.

"... so don't bring me news that I already know. I want them found. We can't afford to lose men like this. I mean, they can't have just disappeared into thin air. This forsaken country just isn't that big."

"I will have the men redouble their search, Your Eminence."

"Do that. Now. I have an appointment with that elven banshee. Goodness knows what she will have to tell me this time. It's never anything positive."

The Cardinal swept from the room, leaving the secretary wringing his hands. After a moment's hesitation, he also departed.

Maisie continued to watch the fire, listening to its crackle. Missing men? The ones Steig shot. Elven banshee? That would be Aelene. So, she had a few minutes. Dare she? Nothing ventured, nothing gained. Pheoreth's voice sounded in her head: "This course of action is perilous." Well. Where had careful ever got them? She invoked the other half of the spell and stepped into the Cardinal's chambers in the Citadel's heart.

Chapter 25

As she stepped into the office, Maisie froze, scanned the room with her eyes, increased her hearing's acuity and listened. Her heart was beating so fast she thought she might have a seizure. Never in her life had she been so frightened. Apart from the last time, she corrected herself, with chagrin.

The room was empty, the loud crackling fire the only noise. Apart from the Cardinal's overlarge desk, piled with papers, the room was bare. No sofa, no furnishings or decorations, no pictures. A simple wooden crucifix adorned the wall above the fireplace.

Maisie checked the documents on the desk. Most were in Calabrian, and wholly unintelligible. They seemed to be financial records, notes of transactions, receipts; nothing that would be of any use.

She tried the drawers. Locked. Felt around under the edge of the desk. There! A tiny key. It fit into the central drawer, and she slid it open to reveal a rolled-up document; some sort of map.

"Maps are always useful. I'll have that," she muttered, slipping the roll into her voluminous cloak pocket.

"It's in his office, just a moment," came the voice of the secretary, and the door to the study opened.

Maisie ducked under the enormous desk. No time for the kathalyog spell. It would leave a trail of mist lingering. She pulled in her cloak edges, held the staff as far in as she could, hoping the angle of the desk and chair sufficed to hide it. Footsteps, the secretary approaching the desk. She tried to slow her breathing; the ringing in her ears from terror was disorientating. The footsteps stopped on the far side of the desk. A shuffle of papers. She looked up towards the chair. The drawer! Still open. She could hardly breathe.

After a moment, the footsteps retreated. The door opened and closed again. She dared not move. But she had to get out of there, before a hob turned up to tend the fire or the secretary came back.

She crawled out of the desk space on all fours, glanced over her shoulder towards the door. All clear. She slid the drawer closed and locked it. Quick as blinking, she had the spell done and fell back into the Betwixt, panting and gasping with the aftereffects of her terror.

Taking a few breaths of the rank, frigid air brought her back to her senses.

"Show me the hearth of Aelene," she asked of the staff.

A brief flare of light showed her the place nearby. Leaning over the point of light, she allowed her sight to stretch into the hearth. The parlour at Rosalia's villa, with the fire bisecting the room from the kitchen. Aelene was sitting in a high-backed armchair pulled up to the fireplace. Next to her was a similar chair, empty.

The hob who had opened the gate for them two days before – or was it three? – stepped into the room, leading the Cardinal, in his swirl of crimson robes. The Cardinal, scowling, seated himself in the empty chair.

"Bingo," breathed Maisie, pulling energy from the staff to allow the sound to come through.

The fire wavered, but neither person seemed to notice. They were intent on each other. The hob, however, glanced at the fire, stared up at the ceiling, gazed directly into Maisie's eyes. A tiny smile. The hint of a wink. Maisie realised she had stopped breathing. The hob looked away from her, bowed to Aelene and the Cardinal, and left the room. Maisie let her breath out in a whisper. Well. Hobs can see into the kathalyog. Something to remember. She hoped this hob was on the side of Rosalia, and not Aelene. She turned her attention to the conversation, which had just begun, the Cardinal not mincing his words.

"... very disappointed with the progress so far," he was saying, his mouth pursed in a moue of distaste.

Aelene set her ornate cup of wine down on the small table between them.

"We know exactly where she is. I have someone watching her. She won't be able to evade us."

"Well, just bring her in, then. What, exactly, are you waiting for?"

"Cardinal Baroffio, you know very well that if we move too soon, we risk scattering her followers and supporters to the four winds. We must wait until all the relevant people are present; then we can dispose of the pawns, and the queen." She paused, picked up her glass, and took a sip. "The queen can be interrogated, coerced, retrained, whatever it is you have in mind. But we can do that without the interference of her friends, as they will no longer be a problem."

Maisie's head reeled. Dispose of the pawns. Oh no. That sounded final. Fatal. We know exactly where she is. Surely they could not? The tatchapen spell would have shown her the watchers, as it had on the central street. Her head was spinning. She was missing something.

And the cold persisted, insidious, despite the cloak. She listened in some more, but was keen to find Steig, or return to Pheoreth.

"What news from the western provinces? Èirinn and beyond?" asked the Cardinal.

"The Tuatha de Danann have no argument with us; they will not prevent us looking to Mundus Novus. Witcerce, as the westernmost gateway, is ready as soon as we can locate the clavis."

"Or persuade her to repurpose an existing clavis?"

"Indeed. When we capture her. When she agrees. When we have, um, trained her."

"Do you see any problem with that?"

"No. We have leverage, or will have. The pawns, as I mentioned."

"Good. Well, I will leave you to this task, but my patience is not boundless. You have a week to deliver the repurposed claves for Breotonlond and Mundus Novus."

The Cardinal got to his feet with some difficulty, his age and bulk taking their toll. The hob reappeared and opened the door for him. Maisie withdrew her view from the room and straightened up, back in the freezing Betwixt. Her shivering and shaking were not entirely due to the pervasive cold. She was trembling in fear. Leverage. Pawns. Capture. She tried to rally her thoughts. Get to Steig. Between them, they could come up with a cohesive plan.

"Show m-me ..." She was shivering so much now she could hardly speak. She put the thought together, leant on the staff. A more distant speck of fire flared. She staggered through the mist towards it, her legs like rubber bands. Every step was an effort, each one more difficult than the one before.

When she arrived at the spec of fire, she didn't bother leaning in to look; she was too cold, too fraught. She needed to get out of the Betwixt. In here too long. Losing concentration. She uttered the spell and stepped through, crashing into a sudden searing heat and deafening noise.

"Hoi! Wat de fuk?" a deep, resonant voice called.

She fell forward onto the floor, one hand clutching her staff, the other protecting her face. The floor was flagstones, dirt, metal filings, straw. The stink of smoke, hot metal, horse dung assailed her nostrils.

Large, powerful hands grabbed her arms and hauled her to her feet. She tried to struggle, but the cold had sapped her strength. She sagged, and the man, a huge, sweating Viking of a man, held her upright.

"Gaat alles goed? Waar kom je vandaan?" he demanded, his face shiny with sweat and soot, his beard brushing her face.

A whicker from a horse. She recognised that.

"Beckett?" she called. The whicker came again, more insistent. Then Steig was there.

"She's with me," he said to the giant, who shrugged, nonplussed.

"Ze verscheen uit het niets? Er, she ... one second, shoe horse. Next, she here?" He mimed her appearing next to the fire. A set of three

Beckett-sized iron shoes was set before the forge on a brick ledge, and one in the fiery coals, glowing orange. The heat was incredible. There was a hob, stripped to a loincloth, pedalling a pair of bellows behind the furnace.

Steig took her from the blacksmith, supported her, led her away from the noise and heat into a yard busy with horses, wagons, hotel hob-porters in burgundy livery. Her head was swimming.

"Here, sit on this bench. Gods, you're freezing. It's mid-afternoon. How did you find me? Never mind that. What do you need? Hot sweet tea? Hob! Kangrim!"

She sat on the stone bench, wrapping the cloak around her, shivering uncontrollably. A hob in the hotel livery appeared.

"Kangrim, please fetch this young lady a hot drink of something restorative. Quick as you can."

"Sire."

Maisie blinked, or so it seemed, and Kangrim was back, with a substantial earthenware jug that was steaming, smelling sweet and alcoholic. He poured a generous measure into a cup.

"My Lady."

"Thank you, er ... Kangrim," she said, managing a smile.

It steamed, but was not scalding. She gulped it, spilling some down her chin. The drink at once warmed her from the inside out, the heat spread through her chest, and calmed her frayed nerves.

"Oh, that's superb. Oh, I feel better now. Remarkable. Hello Steig. Hello Beckett!" she called to the horse, standing in the farrier's forge, which was set in one corner of the yard, behind her.

Another whicker from Beckett. Her heart flipped over with an abundance of love for the horse.

“And then I didn’t know what to do. I was so panicked. I just came to find you. Lucky you were having Beckett shod, next to a forge fire, really, or I’d have lost my way.”

“You’d have gone back to Pheoreth, I guess.”

Steig led Beckett, with Maisie astride the horse, holding on to his mane to keep from slipping. They were almost at the top of the escarpment, heading towards the scrubby woodland that ran along the lee slope.

“We’ll set up camp in the woods and try to work out what to do next. Though it sounds like your proactive approach has paid dividends.”

“It certainly has provided us with much-needed information,” she replied, nodding.

From the road along the escarpment, they forked down to a copse that provided shelter and cover. Its distance from the road meant that passers-by wouldn’t see or hear them. Steig unpacked the tarp and rope and showed Maisie how to set it out between two trees.

There were plenty of windfall branches around the camp, and they soon had a fire going and the travel kettle on. Maisie reached into her cloak and pulled out the roll of parchment, or vellum, or thick paper – Steig wasn’t sure what to call it. It was yellow with age and hefty, like card, but flexible, like leather. She undid the red ribbon that held it closed and spread it out on the grass next to the fire. Steig leant in to look.

"That's all of Khôra, by the looks. See, Western Lands, the Cold Wastes, Mediolanum in the middle here."

"What are these symbols? A circle with a dot in the middle?"

"Gateway. See, one in Mediolanum. Some others, without the dot? Look, Wayland, no dot. You found it in the river. So, missing gateway. And Miletus, no dot – didn't you say Pheoreth can't get back there? And see, some have crosses. Maybe those are the ones that the Gratadei have stolen?"

"But there are ..." She pointed, counting, and gave up at ten. "Twenty? Thirty missing gateways. Even one here, see? Grauplenk? But far more with crosses. So the Gratadei have, what, over a hundred, hidden away?"

"Yes. I guess if you could find them all and reconnect them, it would give the Gratadei leverage over the land. They would control all the import–export trade. With that they would be all-powerful, could continue to leach the magic for their relics?"

"I think that was the inference from the conversation I overheard. They said, 'looking to the western lands and Mundus Novus.' Also, they said, 'find the Witcerce clavis or persuade her to repurpose an existing clavis.' What does that even mean?"

"Can you make a clavis work with a different gateway? Or just any location?"

"Bobe Elka said no, that it will only work if it's next to the gateway's physical location."

"Well, sounds like the Gratadei think you can make a clavis open anywhere. That would be ultimately powerful. They could have gateways to all the major population centres in Defaltum Mundi and use Khôra as a shortcut. Or a free trade route, without customs or taxes.

Or weapons of mass destruction. Goddess, the possibilities are endless. Frightening. I'm guessing that is why they are so keen to capture you." Maisie's face reflected his own fears, lines of worry etching her skin. "You have the Wayland clavis? Or the one from Kurra?"

"Bobe Elka took the Wayland clavis with her. The other is back at the bakery."

"Alright." Steig was thoughtful for a moment; he prodded the fire with a twig. "What else did they say? That they know exactly where you are?"

"Well, I'm hoping they don't know I'm here with you, or the jig is most definitely up. But they seemed to think they knew where I was, yes. 'We have someone watching her,' they said. I used the tatchapen spell, and could see the watchers on the main street, but they weren't looking at me. A glamour was hiding them, though."

"Presume that would be Aelene's handiwork?"

"I would think so. But don't you see? There were no watchers near the bakery."

"So, what's the obvious inference?" Steig could see Maisie's thoughts as if she were writing them out in bubbles above her head. Thinking. Realising. Dismissing. Thinking some more. Concluding.

"Oh no, she can't be on their side! Surely not? She hates them. She can't be acting. Can she?"

"I don't know. But it seems weird that no one else is watching you. What did they say about the western lands?"

"Umm ... hang on." Steig could almost feel her remembering, the air of concentration was so intense. "'The Tuatha de Danann have no argument with us; they will not prevent us looking to Mundus Novus,' is what they said."

"So, they would need an envoy to the Tuatha de Danann, a recent one. Where was Pheoreth, before she picked us up?"

"Oh, fiddlesticks."

Steig thought for a moment.

"Well, there is one way we can be sure. Tell her where I am."

"But if she's on their side, then the Gratadei will find you and capture you, maybe even kill you!"

"Not if you tell her I'm somewhere else. Somewhere I can watch from afar and see if they turn up."

"Genius. Then if they go there, we know Pheoreth is a turncoat. If they don't, we can examine other possibilities."

"It's a plan, at least. Also, I reckon you should get out of there. What if the Gratadei ambush you early morning when the fire's out?"

"How about this? Look, come here." She got up and walked to the edge of the copse, where there was a view into the broad valley in which Grauplenk nestled. "Can you see that barn down there, the one near the curve of the river, with the broke-back roof line? That's quite distinctive."

Steig looked. The barn was a half mile distant, on the edge of a field of spring crops. It sat, isolated, near the road leading into the town. And it seemed deserted, at least from here.

"Yes, that's a good plan. I'll go down there after you go, and light a campfire, leave some mess as if I've been there. Hoof prints. That way, when they search, they will assume I've moved on."

"I feel like we're getting somewhere."

"Well, there is the elephant in the room. Well, in the small, wooded hilltop." She turned to him, a quizzical expression flitting over her face. "You need to find some keys. See if you can repurpose them. We can open a gateway, drop through, at will, anywhere. That way, we could break into the Milano castle, or wherever, steal back the claves, rescue Rosalia."

"Um, but I don't know how to—"

"No, you don't," he interrupted, "but a week ago you didn't know how to kathalyog with sound, or tatchapen, or use the glamour on yourself, or, I don't know, flatten tomato tins. Seems like a week is a long time in Khôra."

She smiled at that. "You're right, of course. Alright, I'll sow the seeds of disinformation with Pheoreth, and we'll see how long until the thugs turn up here. There, I mean." She pointed to the barn. "Oh! Please don't shoot them."

"I won't shoot them, I promise. I'll set up a hide and watch from afar."

The journey back through the Betwixt was challenging. She struggled with the cold, then the cloying polluted mist around Mediolanum, finally the difficulty in getting her home hearth to show. On top of all this, she was dreading lying to Pheoreth. She hated lying. What if Pheoreth had her own tatchapen spell, and could see a lie? What if she wasn't the watcher Aelene had spoken of? What if the Gratadei were waiting for her? What if. What if. What if?

She leant in and took in the stove, the tiny room. It was empty. She tried to pull her viewpoint out to the stairs and the yard, but the magic didn't let her see beyond the boundary of the room. She stepped in with a sigh and warmed herself at the stove, before opening the door a crack and peering out into the late afternoon.

Pheoreth was sitting on the top step of the stairs.

"You are back! I have been worried. You have been gone for hours!"

"I'm sorry. I got caught up in discussions with Steig."

"How is he? Where is he?"

Maisie stepped out and sat on the step next to Pheoreth, feeling the wan warmth of the sun on her face.

"Oh, he's alright. He wants to know what's going on, what the plan is. I told him there wasn't a plan. I mean, we're all in the dark here, right?" She looked at Pheoreth, who was nodding in agreement.

"So how far has he got? Did he pick up Beckett and the vardo?"

"He's got Beckett with him. Travelling light. He's up near Grauplenk. He found a broke-back barn near the river to camp in."

"But he is safe?"

"Yes, I think so. I'll check in with him tomorrow night. Right now, I'm exhausted." She started a mock-yawn, which ended in a real, full yawn. She was tired. "I'm gonna get some sleep. Could you perhaps get some of those pastries, like we had last night? A couple of them should see me right for ... um ... any exertions we might decide on later."

Pheoreth gave her a wicked grin, her eyes twinkling.

"Of course. I think I will need to go into the centre to get them though, at this time of day."

"Oh, take care, please."

"Always." And she headed away down the steps.

Maisie estimated the time it would take for Pheoreth to get to Aelene's ... well, Rosalia's villa. Without thinking too far ahead, for fear she would balk, she put her cloak back on and slipped Betwixt, and was soon looking in on the parlour, as she had before. Both armchairs were empty.

As she waited, she tried to push back dark thoughts, tried to ignore the creeping chill gripping her heart. After a minute, the door opened and Aelene and Pheoreth walked in. Maisie's heart sank like a cold stone in her chest. Tears welled, and she wiped her face before they froze on her cheeks. She leant on the staff for sound.

"... up near Grauplenk, in a broke-back barn near the river. With the horse. But no wagon."

"Excellent work, Pheoreth."

"I'm extremely unhappy with this. Maisie is our own kind."

"Maisie is leathphór. She is not like us. You would do well to remember that. Also, keep in mind what the Gratadei are offering. I need to have people on the ground to take advantage of that offer. People like you. Don't throw away this opportunity on some ... lovelorn fantasy."

Maisie had seen, heard enough. Tears froze on her cheeks, and her nose was dribbling snot, which was also freezing. She stumbled back to her hearth and warmed herself at the wood burner, stoked it up, disrobed, and fell into bed, exhausted and miserable.

Half an hour later, Pheoreth returned. Maisie had dozed and was muzzy with sleep when the neraida sat on the bed next to her and stroked her hair.

"Hey ... wake up ... I brought pastries ..." Pheoreth murmured, her voice sibilant and soft.

Maisie rolled over and pushed hair from her eyes. Gazed up at Pheoreth's wonderful, beautiful, sensual face.

"How could you do this?" The words came out before she realised what she was saying. Her face was still blotched from crying in the Betwixt, and fresh tears welled, rolling down her cheeks.

Pheoreth's body stiffened. "What? How could I do what?"

"Sell us out to Aelene. To the Gratadei. Steig. Me. How?" Her voice rose in volume and pitch, and her anger rose with it. She struggled to sit up, but Pheoreth pushed her back, using her weight to hold her down. She was angry, her movements sharp, panicked.

"I-I did not. It ... it is not as simple as you think."

"Let me go," Maisie modulated her voice with command. She realised the staff was touching her back. Pheoreth sprang away as if electrocuted. Maisie sat up, rubbing her arm where Pheoreth had held it. "Tell me why."

Pheoreth's shoulders slumped.

"Aelene. She persuaded me that this would be a good thing. To get more claves, more gateways. We would reintegrate our kind, the neraides, all the fae, back into the world. We would be in charge of our own destiny. Have our own towns, enclaves, land. Even trade routes. The Gratadei promised Aelene this."

"Have you not seen the damage the Gratadei are doing to this land? Leaching the magic for the Church's ends? Are you so blind to that?"

Pheoreth cast her eyes down.

"I am not blind—"

"Oh, and let's not forget the marvellous track record the Church has with integrating minorities. I mean, you're female and gay, never mind the tiny issue of being a different species. You really think they'll allow you anything once you've delivered me?"

"I pledged loyalty to Aelene. Before she ... before she became so obsessed with this ... this plan. I cannot ... I will allow nothing to happen to you." Her voice cracked as she entreated Maisie with her dark eyes. Maisie snorted in disgust.

"Do you know what Cardinal Baroffio said about me? What Aelene said?"

"No," she whispered, as she dropped her head.

"Look at me."

Pheoreth looked up. There was pain, anguish in her eyes. Maisie's heart melted a tiny fraction. But her resolve remained.

"They said, 'Dispose of the pawns. Then we can interrogate, coerce, retrain the leathphór. We can use her friends as leverage.' Who do you suppose will be their leverage? Steig? You?"

"I-I did not know that was their plan." Sobs racked Pheoreth's voice.

"Oh, for goodness' sake! Open your eyes!"

"Oh, Great Goddess. I have been so stupid." Pheoreth drummed her fists against her face, hitting herself hard, the impact making a fleshy smacking sound. Maisie caught her wrist.

"Stop that. Good grief."

Pheoreth slumped, staring down, tears flowing freely and splashing onto the dusty floorboards. Her nose dribbled crimson blood where she had punched herself. Maisie got up and started dressing.

"I'm leaving."

Pheoreth's head snapped up. The bright blood from her nose spotted onto the sheets, her lips.

"No! You cannot!"

A jolt of panic struck Maisie's stomach. "Why not? What have you arranged?"

"Oh, no, I'm so stupi—"

"Tell me what you have arranged." The floorboards gave a slight shudder and dust fell from the rafters. Maisie had, without meaning to, used the command tone again. She realised, with surprise, that it worked with no aid from the staff. Pheoreth was utterly distraught.

"I said I would keep you here tonight. I told them where to find Steig. Once they have him, they will come here for you. If I renege on that, Aelene will ... I do not know what she will do, but ... you have not seen her angry. It is terrible. She becomes as if possessed by a demon."

"They won't find Steig." She noticed Pheoreth's face, tutted and shook her head. Searched in her messenger bag for a tissue. Handed it to her. "Clean yourself up."

Pheoreth took the tissue, dabbed her nose. "Thank you."

"Do you know where Rosalia is being held?"

Pheoreth slumped. Her eyes were red-rimmed, her nose a mess of dried blood, her cheek smeared with mucus. Yet she was still beautiful. "Tell me?" asked Maisie. She didn't need to use the command. Pheoreth had capitulated.

"I-I think she is in the castle in Milano. The other side of the gateway. It is a fortress. Impossible."

"Nothing's impossible." She finished dressing, pushed Bobe Elka's cloak into her rucksack. "You need to decide where your loyalties lie. With Khôra and its inhabitants, and that currently includes Steig and I, or the Church and Aelene, and her insane, naïve plan."

"Please ... do not leave me," Pheoreth implored, sobbing.

Maisie shook her head, turned away as she shrugged into her rucksack straps and slung her messenger bag over her arm. She grabbed her staff from the bed. The mist rose in the room as she cast the kathalyog spell, and she walked into its icy embrace. All the while she was trying not to fall apart. She listened to Pheoreth's sobbing fade, as she slipped with anger and sorrow into the Betwixt.

Steig drained his cup of tea, set it down next to the travel kitchen satchel.

"Now then, horse, we've got some subterfuge to employ. Let's get to it."

Beckett gave a whicker of agreement.

Steig packed up the campfire things – fire starter kit, kettle, kitchen bag. He had his kukri at his belt, along with a snub-nosed handgun that used to belong to one of the Gratadei. Positioning the long gun over Beckett's back in its oilskin wrap, he packed the rest of the kit around it. He left the camouflaged bivouac set-up, hidden in the woods, with the sleeping mat and bedding.

They picked their way out of the strip of woodland, taking care to join the road on a gravelly patch; Steig jumped down and scrubbed the hoofmarks out, hopeful that the camp would remain undiscovered.

They trotted down to the broken-back barn, and found it empty, draughty, with a muddy floor. There was a jagged hole in the roof that let through some light, and a host of sparrows had taken up residence in the eaves.

Steig lit a small cooking fire, boiled the kettle, made a cup of tea, discarded the teabag on the floor next to the fire. This rankled him, but it was necessary to leave a false trail.

Beckett joined in, stamping around in the mud with what Steig felt was more delight than was strictly required. He even left a pile of dung in one corner.

After half an hour, they packed the kitchen satchel and headed back up to the escarpment. Arriving at the camp in the copse, Steig tethered Beckett, hidden in the trees, on a running picket line with fresh grass. The sun was approaching the horizon.

"I'll be back in the night, or in the morning, latest. Don't wander off. No talking to strange hobs."

"Will there be apples?"

"Come on. Of course."

"Good."

Steig put on his stockman's coat over a thick jumper, slung the long gun over his shoulder and headed down the hill, over the fields.

Two hundred yards from the barn, he found a dip in the ground surrounded by bushes. He crawled into the undergrowth, facing the barn. The last bush acted as cover, under which he propped the rifle's matt-black barrel on its built-in bipod. He wasn't planning on shooting anyone, but the sight on the rifle would help see in the dimling night.

"Well, at least it's not raining," he said to himself, then settled, shifting around to move errant twigs from under him. As he brought the stock of the gun to his shoulder, a memory paralysed him. The mercenary at Savio's, blood blooming, falling back. An image indelible in his mind. He felt a welling of grief, and let out a sob. Wiping his eyes on his sleeve, he did his best to muster some control, pushing the grief and guilt down into his soul. "Fuck. Focus, Steig."

Looking through the sight, he blinked tears away, getting his breath back under control. He had a clear view of the barn, side on, and the approach lane from the road. He could also see a sweep of the river, and the faint lights of the town in the distance, becoming visible in the gloaming.

Night had taken hold, the stars and a waxing crescent moon dim through the high wisps of cloud, when he heard a vehicle in the distance. It rattled along the road from the direction of Mediolanum. One of the now familiar four-by-four trucks hove into view, slowed at the junction with the barn's lane, and stopped. The lights and engine shut off.

Steig had been looking away from the headlamps, dim and yellow as they were, keeping his night vision amped. Now he used the gunsight. Three figures got out of the vehicle, a fourth remained hunched over the steering wheel. They didn't make any noise, but spread out in a fanned line, walking up the lane to the barn. Two went to the front entrance, one went around the back.

There was a flash of light, which speared out through the open doorway, and through the hole in the roof. A fraction of a second later, the sharp report echoed over the hillside. The birds in the eaves departed at speed, shrieking their terror. Stun grenade, Steig thought. No messing.

The two figures at the front lit up with torches, attached to stubby machine guns. They entered the building, and Steig heard a faint call of "Chiaro". He guessed that was the all clear. The third man appeared from behind the building and entered.

Steig could see the play of torches flashing here and there within the barn. Then the three mercenaries came out, guns at ease, torches pointing at the ground. They walked back to the vehicle. Two of them stopped to light cigarettes from a lighter. Steig could see their faces through the gunsight, lit from below, then the glow of their cigarettes. Ginger Scar and Ratty, from the roadblock.

After the vehicle's engine noise had died away, Steig remained motionless. If he were leading the search party, he'd have dropped someone off to come in on foot behind the vehicle, and left them there for half an hour to see if Steig was watching. He wasn't sure whether these fellows would do that, but he wasn't in a hurry.

The night quietened around him. An owl called from down the valley, the long sharp rasp of a barn owl. Or at least, that's what he thought. Never could tell with owls. A dog put up a barking volley from the outskirts of the town. Nothing else.

Satisfied the unknown Gratadei would not ambush him, he backed out of the bushes, showing no light and leaving no trace. He walked back up the hill in the full dark, navigating by the terrain, and finally by Beckett's munching noise and greeting whicker.

"So, horse, looks like we fooled them. I'll get the yog going, reckon Maisie might be along. She'll want to know whether Pheoreth is on our side."

"Pheoreth is complicated. She smells sad."

"Well, she's an elf, so ... maybe that's just how they smell?"

"No. The other elves don't smell sad."

"Huh. Fair enough. I'll light the yog." He kindled the fire, which had been out for hours, and filled the kettle. As he turned to put it on the flames, a mist sprang up, Maisie materialised, and flung her arms around him, almost knocking him over with the weight of her and her rucksack.

"Oh ... where have you been?" She thumped him on the chest, then clung on tighter, burying her face in his neck. She started sobbing, little hiccups of grief.

"I-I've been watching the barn. Like we agreed? They came and went. What happened? Are you alright?"

"No, I'm not alright," she whimpered. "I followed Pheoreth in kathalyog. She went straight to Aelene. It was awful. Then when she came back, I just blurted it out, like a ... like some sort of idiotic teenager. Then I had a fight with her, then she beat herself up, then I couldn't stand it any longer and left without saying goodbye." This last, she rendered in a heartfelt wail that dissolved into tears and sobs and more hiccups.

Steig didn't question, he just held her. She was here. She was safe; they had evaded the Gratadei. And the kettle was on. As far as he was concerned, the evening was a success. Tomorrow would, as ever, bring its own problems. But that would be tomorrow, a whole night distant.

Chapter 26

Maisie woke, but kept her eyes closed. She wanted to keep this feeling for just a moment longer. It wasn't comfortable. Steig's sleeping mat wasn't very thick, and the ground was uneven. She suspected a tree root had moved in the night. But she was warm, wrapped in her cloak and Bobe Elka's, and with Steig's sleeping bag, unzipped and opened, covering both of them. And with Steig's body heat. And with Steig. That was the thing. She sighed. The sex with Pheoreth had been amazing. Pheoreth was inventive, and athletic, and gentle, and kind, and ...

And had sold her out to the Gratadei. Her eyes welled, and she blinked them open. She knew Steig had no side to him. He said what was what. Yes, he could be blunt, but at least he was honest.

She looked up at the tarpaulin shelter roof. The morning sunlight dappled, slantwise, the browns and greens and leaf patterns. She heard Beckett snuffling in the understorey nearby, the crackle of leaves as he clumped around, the munch of grass. Birds were weaving their melodies through the treetops; the wind was gentle. She let out a heartfelt sigh, settled into the surroundings.

"So," Steig said in her ear, "we pass through the unknown gateway to Milano. Break into the impenetrable castle fortress. Rescue Rosalia, then forcibly evict Aelene and the Cardinal and all the mercenaries from Khôra. Without killing anyone. Without anyone shooting us. Is that about right?"

"Eurgh. You really know how to douse the moment, don't you?"

"Sorry. Just thinking out loud." He sat up, rubbed his face with the palm of his hand. "Huh. It's all well and good camping like this, but I miss my home comforts. Give me wagon-living any day."

"Yes, I have to agree; the bed in the vardo is super comfortable. And this hillside, well, it isn't." She smiled at him. "But my word, it's wonderful to be with you." Then her face clouded. "I still can't quite believe Pheoreth sold us out."

"Beckett said she smells sad. Maybe she was being coerced, or acting out of a misplaced loyalty."

Maisie looked at him with incredulity. "Are you taking her side?"

"No, of course not. I'm just stating what Beckett said. He thinks she's complicated and sad." He got out of the bedding, stood, and stretched. "I'll get the coffee going. Do you have a plan?"

"Not yet." She watched Steig walking off to pee on the lee side of the hill, in the bushes. What was her plan? All she could think was that the task seemed impossible.

Steig returned, untied Beckett, and led him to a nearby stream. Beckett slurped at the meagre water. "Tastes funny," he declared, spitting most of it back out.

Steig nudged a stone into the stream with his boot. "Are you being fussy?"

"Yeh. But still, tastes funny."

"OK, well, back to your grass. We'll stop at the next stream. You can compare and contrast."

While Beckett grumbled to himself at the difficulty of being a horse in a magical kingdom, Steig fried up some dried sausage and flatbreads.

"Delicious," declared Maisie, through a mouthful of bread. She wiped her chin with her sleeve. "So, I think given the scale of the problems facing us, we must decide item one on the agenda: do we carry on or do we run away?"

Steig regarded her with an impassive face, but with one eyebrow raised.

"Bear with me," she said, holding up a finger, chewing and swallowing. "Or, item two on the agenda: do we try to recruit some non-duplicitous helpers to the cause?"

"Well, I'm not for running away. Apart from anything else, people like Savio and Maria, Lavinia, Calix, all the people who have been kind to us. They are all in danger if the Gratadei carry on here. This country could be a paradise if the Gratadei allowed it to flourish. I want to give it that chance."

"OK. Item two?"

"If we assume that Pheoreth's followers are as ropey as she is, if you'll excuse the expression ..." Maisie waved the comment away. "We can't rely on Andion and his cohort, even if they are above board. What about Bobe Elka?"

"I trust her. I don't know if she's in Khôra, though."

"You could try to find her in kathalyog? Ask her for help?"

"I ... could, I suppose."

"What's the problem?"

"Actually? No problem. I was just doubting myself. But, as you rightly pointed out yesterday, I'm more capable every day, at handling the magic. Yes, I'll search for her. Right after I've had a wash in the stream. I'm a grubby urchin."

Steig washed up the single plate and cup that they had been sharing, while Maisie splashed water on her face from the stream, eventually stripping off in the frigid morning air to wash fully.

When she came back to the fire, Steig had built it up, so it kicked out a decent heat.

"Thanks, bit chilly," she muttered, warming her skin by the flames.

Once she had dried off, she dressed in her warmest clothes, with her new cloak comfortable over her shoulders.

"I'm actually sweating now. Oh, I'll take Bobe's old cloak. She can have it back." She grabbed the cloak from the bedding, picked up her staff, and turned to Steig. Took a step closer to him, and another. He stood, so their faces were inches apart. Time slowed.

"Um. I'll try to find her, and if I do, I'll be a while, because I'll need to fill her in on everything. So please keep the fire going. I'll find you, then."

"I know." He smiled at her, but she could tell something was on his mind.

"What is it?" she asked.

"Be careful. I've become quite attached to you."

She reached up with her hands and pulled his face down, and kissed him, a brief brushing of the lips. He smelt of wood smoke and leather and horse.

"I'll be careful. And the same goes for you."

With that, she turned and, forming the spell in her head, slipped Betwixt.

"Show me the hearth of Bobe Elka," she asked of the staff, pulling power from it. The Betwixt here felt fresh and clean – as fresh and clean as a grey, misty, cold netherworld could be. A thousand times better than around Mediolanum. And yet, nothing happened. Maisie tried again, pulling harder at the power, so much so that her arm numbed with pins and needles, and her vision swam. But far in the distance, at the very limit of the fog-enshrouded world, or so it seemed, a single flare sputtered, then died.

Maisie kept her eyes on the spot and walked towards it. This was the furthest she had travelled by yog, and the energy was draining from her as she walked. Lifting her foot for every step was an effort. Putting it down again seemed to sap more heat, more vitality from her. Her home hearth, Steig's hearth, was pulling at her, that slim, nebulous umbilical, stretching ever thinner. The pull, ever more insistent. Every step, harder than the last. She leant forward as if into a gale, though the air was still and dank and frigid.

When she came to the point of light that was Bobe Elka's hearth, or so she hoped, she peered in. The fog was more dense and opaque than normal. She could only make out indistinct shapes. Figures around a campfire. Nothing more.

"Oh, fiddlesticks. Well, here goes nothing."

She formed the second half of the spell and stepped into the camp.

Maisie stood by the fire, letting the mist dissipate, letting the heat warm her bones. She was panting for air, frozen through and wary. She had stepped into the middle of a circle of people sitting around a substantial campfire. A rangy, biscuit-coloured dog put up an incessant barking, snarling with salivating jaws and very white teeth. Its owner was holding it back by the scruff of its neck.

"Scally, hoy, shut-ther-fuck-up, it's a chivani," said the man holding the dog.

He had a missing tooth at the front, a scraggly ginger beard, dreadlocks and dirty white skin. He was dressed in raggedy, stained denim jeans and a biker's leather jacket. A tweed flat cap with a greasy peak topped him off. The dog quieted but was still growling. The man kept a hand on his scruff.

"Don't mind 'im, lass, he's just surprised. Weren't expectin' sudden company."

"Uh," began Maisie, trying to get her breath back, leaning her weight on her staff.

She looked around at the other faces peering at her from the circle. All human, or recognisably so. No fae. No dwarves. No hobs. All dressed the same, with crew cut sides to their heads, dreadlocks, beads, facial piercings, tattoos. A fearsome group, to be sure.

"I'm, uh, terribly sorry to just, well, arrive like this," she said. "I-I'm looking for someone."

"Dun't fret, lass," said a rotund woman, sporting a knot of blonde dreadlocks under a tatty bowler hat. She was dressed in voluminous skirts and a careworn stained jumper. "Sit yersen down. Kettle's almost boiled. Cuppa tea'll set you right. Reckon as you're after Elka. She's kippin'. We was up late."

"Oh! That's truly kind, thank you. Yes, I was hoping to speak with Bobe Elka."

She sat down on a proffered, upturned wooden milk crate. Glancing around, she took in more of her surroundings. An open plain of stubbly grass, sparse trees, some dead. There was a dusting of snow on the nearby hills. A wind as sharp as a honed blade whipped over the land. She pulled her cloak closer. Arranged around the fire were a couple of bow-top wagons, a flatbed horse-drawn dray. Tucked between were some dome-like tents made from tarpaulins and bent poles. Tethered beyond the wagons stood three or four black-and-white horses, similar in size and shape to Beckett.

"Here you go, lass. Plenty of sugar in it." The blonde woman thrust a large mug of strong, dark tea at her. It steamed in the chilly air.

"Thank you. I'm Maisie."

"Jeannie. That's Del." She pointed at the man holding the dog. "An' the ferocious hound is Scallywag. He's harmless really. And that's Nick, and that's Lara, and that's ... 'ere, fellah, what's your name again?" She pointed at a man with short, dark hair shaven at the sides and a black beard, with a spider's web tattoo over one side of his face. He was wearing a red check padded shirt and dirty jeans. "He's new, he is," she said in an aside to Maisie, who smiled.

"John the Skip. Pleased to meetcha," said John, holding his hand up in greeting.

Jeannie introduced Maisie to the whole crew, about ten people, but she knew she would forget their names almost straight away. She could always ask again.

"Jeannie, I know this is probably a silly question, but where are we?" she asked after the introductions were done and she had sipped her tea, warming up slightly.

"Oh, sorry, thought you'd know. This is the Cold Wastes, north of Skiri. Last place the Goddess made, I reckon."

"This is Khôra?"

Jeannie regarded her with a questioning expression. "Yeah, course. Where else?"

"I thought ... I don't know. I thought it was so far, I might have travelled over to Defaltum Mundi."

Jeannie let out a peal of laughter.

"Oh no, lass, you can't travel out of Khôra by yog! Or else I reckon all you chivani'd be off in a twinklin'. You need a clavis for that. You savvy that, right?"

"Leave her be, now, Jeannie. She's new to the lark, like."

Maisie spun around at the sound of the familiar voice.

"Bobe Elka!" Then, remembering her manners, she stood and said, with a curtsey, "Kushti divvus."

"Aye, well, yer kerfuffle woked me, thought I may as well gerrup. And don't start all that curtsy rubbish. I'm too old to do it back. Kushti divvus to you, though. Bright blessin's, merry meet, merry bleedin' part." She looked her up and down. "O-ho, nice cloak!"

Maisie blushed. "Thank you. I brought yours back. I'm sorry, I haven't washed it, it's a bit ... well, I've been living in it a bit." She proffered the garment.

"Don't fret so, lass. Now, sit yersen down again and pukker yer chattle."

Maisie settled down. Jeannie got up and offered her seat to Bobe, who took it with a nod of thanks. Jeannie handed Bobe a fresh mug of tea.

Maisie spun her tale, from Fenis Pass, through all her adventures. She told of Steig's travails and Pheoreth's betrayal. She had the travellers around the fire rapt with wonder. The telling was a great unburdening, a catharsis she hadn't realised she needed.

"And so last night I left Pheoreth and camped with Steig and Beckett under a tarp in the middle of nowhere. This morning I came to find you, in the hope you might have a plan, or a pointer of an idea, or, well, anything," she finished.

"Well. That's a right kaerdi an' no mistake," Bobe Elka mused. A murmur of assent circled the fire.

Jeannie made a huge saucepan of porridge, which all the travellers lined up for with their bowls. Jeannie leant over to Maisie and handed her a spare bowl.

"Oh! I had breakfast already, thank you."

"Second breakfast. Go on."

Maisie's stomach rumbled. Lunchtime was approaching, she supposed. "Alright, then. Thank you." She smiled, taking the bowl.

Bobe Elka turned to her as she wolfed down the porridge.

"Hungry, lass?"

"Yes! I don't know why, but I'm famished."

"Kathalyog. It does that. Fair takes it out of you. Did you come straight here from Steig's yog? Grauplenk? Heck of a way. The trick, y'see, is to stop off at other yogs on the way. You drop in like, scrounge a cuppa, then carry on. Breaks the journey. Or else you end up knackered."

"Ah. Of course. Steig told me your story. You drop in on people's yogs, just along the way. It makes sense now. It felt like there was a thread pulling me back to Steig's yog. The further I got, the harder it was to carry on."

"That's it. You drop in, and the thread is sorta reset, see? Makes it loads easier."

"Yes, I see now. Thank you. I'll try that on the way back."

Bobe Elka finished her bowl of porridge and ruminated for a moment before turning back to Maisie.

"If you needs some help with the Gratadei, you could look no further than the travellin' folk. No love lost between them and them, if you know what I mean. There's a gang of them in Milano. Reckon as they would like the gateways free and open to all, again."

"Oh! Do you have a name?"

"Well ..." Bobe Elka took a moment, considered the request. "Well, I s'pose it can't hurt, like. Y'need to find Damocles, north-west end of Via Triboniano. Bang on the big gates, he might help you. Dun't tell him I sent you though, he's a mardy bugger. He's still sore cos the Gratadei closed his operation down, stranded him in Milano. He's from up north. Well, you'll see when you meet him."

Maisie concentrated, memorised the instructions.

"OK. Got it, I think," she said with an uncertain smile.

"First, we should fix up some clavises, mind."

"Fix up a clavis?"

"Make it work any old place. That's your skill, apparently. The Fates hinted at it, but the Cardinal seems to think that's the thing, so ..."

Maisie's face darkened, but she held her tongue. Those pesky Fates again.

"Well, if you have any ideas on how that might work, I'm all ears."

"Do you have the clavis that Kurra give yer?"

"I do, actually."

Maisie opened her messenger bag and rummaged for a moment. Pulled out the bronze dodecahedron. The travellers around the fire had gone silent and still; everyone was staring at her in anticipation.

Bobe Elka waved them all away.

"Yous lot, mind your own butsi, this be chivani business." She turned back to Maisie. "Right, lass. Open it up. Let's see where it goes."

"How?" Maisie asked. "All it will do is glow and go out again."

"Well, how about, use your staff, put a bit of fizz into it? Force it, like."

"You're just guessing, aren't you?"

"Guessing, aye. And a bit of old lore. Try it. Can't hurt."

Maisie was dubious, but stood with the clavis in her right hand and the staff in her left. She faced away from the fire, out towards the distant hills. Closed her eyes, thought of the words to open the gateway. She asked the staff for power, felt it vibrating up her arm, and her whole body tingled.

"Anoígō thúra!" she intoned. She felt a shift, the power running down her right arm, the tingling evaporating, the clavis putting out a slight radiant heat into her palm. There was a ripping noise, like linen being torn, and a collective "Ah!" from the travellers around the fire. She opened her eyes.

The clavis was putting out a steady blue glow from its centre. A few feet in front of her, the vision-bending silver-grey misted surface of the gateway shimmered. It had a blue cast to its light and was big enough to drive a wagon through.

"Um. Bobe Elka, where does it go?"

"Dunno, lass." She turned to the watchers around the fire. "Any volunteers, yous lot? Nip through, see what's what, nip back?"

John the Skip stood up.

"Yeah, what the hell. I'll give it a go. Don't close it though, afore I'm back, for fuck's sake. All me stuff's here."

He walked up to the glimmering gateway, took a last glance around at the campsite, and stepped through. It swallowed him with scarcely a ripple.

"Um, how long do they stay open for usually, Bobe?"

"Usually, til you close them, like. With the command. You remember?"

"I remember." Maisie was especially careful to not even think about the close command, let alone verbalise it. She placed the clavis on the ground to one side of the gateway, where it continued to put forth its cobalt glow.

Jeannie brought them both another cup of tea whilst they waited, and stood for a moment, watching the gateway's mirror-rippled surface.

"Where d'you think it opens out?" she asked.

"Well, either Witcerce Abbey, which would be mighty odd, or ... I dunno, somewhere north of Aquincum, in Pannonia, I reckons," suggested Bobe Elka.

The silver mist parted, and John reappeared, strolling as if on a country walk, rather than travelling between realms. Everyone cheered. Even Bobe Elka had a grin plastered on her face.

"So, lad? Where'd you end up?"

"It's woodland, a steep hillside, smells clean and fresh. I could see a village in the distance, in the valley. Could have been Slavoria, somewhere like that? Eastern Europa, for sure," said John. He also had a huge grin on his face.

Maisie picked the clavis up from the ground.

"OK, I'm going to close it now," said Maisie. "Katálēxis thúra!"

With a pop like a cork being pulled from a monstrously huge bottle, the gateway collapsed in on itself and disappeared. The clavis' radiance subsided.

"Bobe Elka, can you open it again, see if it's stuck to the new place for all users?"

"Aye, lass, good plan." Bobe Elka muttered her own opening spell in Old High Romani, and the gateway sprang back into existence.

"John, would you be so kind as to 'ave another dekker? See if we're still in Slavoria?"

John nodded, walked through, and came back out a few seconds later.

"Same place."

Bobe Elka muttered, and the gateway popped out of existence.

"You knows what this means, dun't you?" she said to Maisie.

"Yes. I can reprogram claves to work away from their original location. This is the game-changer we need. Only ..."

"Yes, lass?"

"Where can I find more claves? I'm supposed to be the Finder of Keys. I've only found one."

"Well, can't help you there, I'm afraid. Beyond me ken."

Steig put another log on the fire. Maisie had been gone most of the day, and he was growing concerned. She had said she might be some time, but the inability to know what was going on was a nagging worry for him. Though he couldn't do anything about it, so there was no point worrying at it. A conundrum, as Beckett would say. He lay back on the ground mat and stared up at the sky, watched the clouds, listened to the skylark's song and daydreamed about what he wanted from the future. Which, to his surprise, included being with Maisie, as well as the obvious, living in Khôra.

Beckett's whinny brought his attention back to the present. A mist had sprung up, and then Maisie arrived, looking tired but happy, cheeks rosy pink from the cold.

"Hey, welcome back. How's Bobe Elka?"

"Hello. Gosh, it's been a busy time. Yes, she's fine. Says hello." She knelt down and embraced him. "Good to be back," she murmured into his neck.

"A yogic trance?" Steig asked.

"It's worth a try." Her voice held embarrassment and exasperation in equal measure.

"Like a Hindu yogi?"

She sighed. Rolled her eyes. "Yes. Just like that."

"Where did you learn that?"

"I had meditation tapes to help me sleep. Now. Do be quiet."

Steig sat back on his heels, settled in for the evening. Beckett was back at the camp on the escarpment. They were below the town of Grauplenk, near the stone bridge over the river, hidden by the dimming light and the trees and bushes that grew along the riverbank. Steig had with him a small lantern, currently extinguished, and a folding spade. They were at the river because if there was a clavis lost nearby, then it had probably once been on or near the bridge; this seemed to be the pattern, according to Maisie. He was there to keep watch, and dig, but mainly to prevent Maisie from jumping in the water. Neither of them wanted a repeat of the Wayland adventure.

Steig listened to the sounds from the town – the muted hubbub of voices from a tavern, the occasional shout or call, horses' metal-shod hooves on cobblestones. The splash of a boat on the canals beyond the bridge. Though secluded, he tried to keep alert, in case someone came walking, or rowing, along the river. He was confident that the Gratadei would not bother looking here, but an overabundance of caution seemed like a promising idea right then.

He glanced at Maisie, who was lying down on the bed-mat on the grass, arms at her sides, eyes closed, her breathing slow and even. Her staff lay alongside her, and she had her left hand on it. Nothing was happening. The evening rolled around to full dark. Steig was almost dozing when Maisie shot upright, bending at the waist as if pulled up like a marionette. Her eyes were wide.

"Follow me," she hissed, grabbing her staff, scrambling to her feet, and walking downstream along the riverbank. They stumbled and fumbled their way in the dark until they came to a bend in the river with a pebble beach on the lee side.

"Down here!" she called, scrambling down onto the beach.

Steig followed, taking care not to tumble onto the pebbles. He lit the lantern, safe now they were around the corner from the bridge. Maisie ran to one end of the curve, where a natural overhang, almost like a small cave, had formed in the eroded wall. She dug with her hands into the soft mud and soil. Her breath came ragged, her face flushed.

"Here, let me dig." Steig took up the spade and gently excavated the riverbank. After a few seconds, the spade hit something metallic with a dull click. Maisie leapt in and scrabbled at the pebbles and mud, before extracting a small angular shape from the muck. She took it to the water's edge and rinsed it, revealing the now familiar twelve-sided bronze shape of a clavis.

"Well! We found it!" She smiled at Steig.

"You found it. And I am impressed. Does the clavis work?"

"Let's take it back to Savio's and try it there. I'll need to repurpose it, otherwise it won't do anything away from the bridge at Grauplenk."

Chapter 27

The morning dawned damp. A steady drizzle had arrived in the night, the rain a susurration on the tarpaulin. Maisie snuggled in closer to Steig, spooning into his back, listening to the sounds of the world as she woke. When she opened her eyes, the light was stealing in through the trees. Water dripped in glimmering droplets from the tarp's edge. Beyond that, Beckett was standing patient, his back slick, shiny with rain. Her breath misted as she breathed.

"Brr, cold. Don't want to get up," she asserted under her breath.

Steig stirred, rolled, stretched, groaned. "I miss my bed. This camping out lark is definitely no fun after day two. Come on, let's get to it." He sat up.

"How?" began Maisie, leaning on one elbow and looking over at him. "How can you be so completely asleep, then completely awake, from one breath to the next?"

“Don’t know. Just, y’know. Things to do. Dictatorial religious zealots to overthrow, captive elves to free, stuff like that.” He smiled at her. “Ready?”

“As ready as I’ll ever be, I suppose.”

“It’s at least ten or twelve miles to Savio’s. We could walk it easy in half a day. But I’d like to take a line along the ridges. There’s more cover, so we’ll move slow. So, best get to it.”

“Yes, sir!” Maisie saluted, rolling her eyes.

They struck the camp, wrapping everything except the long gun in the tarp. The rain fell in bigger droplets from the overhanging branches.

Steig led Beckett over to the camp, now just a ring of flattened grass and the dying fire, and tied him to a tree while they tried to organise what went where. He had the felt pad and surcingle on, and a strap from that to his tail, what Steig called a crupper. The panniers – stuffed with cooking kit, bedding, the tarp – lay over Beckett’s rump. There wasn’t much room for two riders.

“Are you going to be OK carrying us both, Beckett?” Maisie asked, worry creasing her brow.

“Yeh. Easy-peasy,” he replied.

“Are you boasting?” Her forehead wrinkled as she raised an eyebrow skyward.

“Yeh. Bit.”

Maisie grinned; the horse had actually managed to look bashful.

Steig half-leapt, half-hauled himself onto Beckett, the long gun rattling on his back. Then he put an arm down for Maisie.

“Sort of take a run at it, swing on my arm, grab my waist and leap ...” he suggested.

Maisie wasn't sure, and her first attempt resulted in her sliding off Beckett's side with all the finesse and elegance of a sack of potatoes. Putting more effort in the second time and using her staff as a vaulting pole with one arm, she managed to at least get her foot, then leg, hooked over Beckett's back. With a heave from Steig on her jeans' waistband, and a fair amount of laughter, she arrived on the horse, sandwiched between Steig and the packs.

"Bit snug," she commented, wriggling to get comfortable. Beckett was deliciously warm on her legs. Steig was deliciously warm on her belly. She put her arms around his waist and rested her chin on his shoulder.

"All good? Ready?" he asked.

"Tally-ho!" she responded with more laughter. Beckett set off, and they headed out of the woodland at a slow walk.

"Mind out for branches, Maisie," Steig said, as they ducked under a low bough.

They crossed the road and wound around, up onto the ridge opposite, following the road's general direction towards Savio's. Though they passed along the edge of copses and small woods, following shallow valleys, fording streams, dropping in and out of view from the road.

"You alright back there?" Steig asked.

"Yes, thank you! It's lovely to feel the movement of Beckett's muscles. How are you managing, Beckett?"

"Yeh. Busy," said the horse. He was negotiating a stream, splashing through the shallow water. He stepped to avoid the small boulders and stones that littered this section of the valley floor. Then vaulted up the far side as Maisie squeaked and clung on.

Once on the flat again, Maisie squeezed Steig around the waist. She gazed out; the land around here was rolling hills, reasonably verdant. They would soon enough come to the desolation towards Mediolanum. For now, she breathed the still-fresh air, took in the view of the green vegetation, and was content.

Beckett halted in Savio's muddy farmyard. Steam rose from his flanks, and he hung his head, tired from the day. Maisie slid off from behind Steig. She landed on the ground and almost toppled over into the mud, grabbing Steig's foot at the last moment.

"Good grief! My legs! I can't walk!"

Steig chuckled. "The feeling will come back soon. You'll acclimatise after a few days of riding." He leant forward and rubbed Beckett along his neckline. "Well done, lad. Wash down and some hay?"

"Yeh. Bit tired."

Steig swung his leg over Beckett's neck and slid down from his back. He helped Maisie to limp over to a low stone wall along the edge of the yard by the house, where she sat down with a sigh. Maria came bustling out of the house.

"Mia povera ragazza! Sembri sfinita! Entra e bevi un po' di vino!"

She hauled Maisie to her feet and helped her into the house. Savio appeared from around the corner of a barn.

"Ciao, Savio. How are you?"

"Ah, Steig. Is ... good to see you. Yes, good, here. Come, I have a stable, like before."

Steig followed Savio, leading the weary horse. They installed Beckett in his old stable, untacked him, washed the sweat and mud from his flanks, put a stable rug over his quarters. Beckett tucked in to a substantial pile of hay.

"All good now, horse?"

Two flicks for yes.

"Good lad." He turned to Savio, who was hovering by the stable door. "Did any more Gratadei come looking?"

"No, it is ... quiet, 'ere."

"That's a relief."

"Yes. Come, we have wine in the 'ouse."

Maisie sighed, stretching out in the bed. Maria had taken her grubby clothes and bustled off with them before supper. She had been wearing clothes borrowed from Maria's grown-up daughter, who had been stranded in Defaltum Mundi since the Gratadei arrived. She was almost the same size and shape as Maisie, and a belt had cinched the slightly-loose trousers at her waist. Maria had looked at her with wistful tears in her eyes. Without the gateways, her daughter had not been home, or in touch, for a number of years. Maisie hoped they could rectify that soon.

But in the meantime. A bath, with hot water. Clean sheets on a proper bed, with pillows. She felt spoilt. And fragrant. She thought back to the evening; it had been companionable, another delicious stufato at the big table in the smoky long room, barely half-filled with the four of them. Gentle chatter about the day, the week, their plans for after the Gratadei were gone, the opening of the gateways. Everyone seemed to think these things were inevitable. Maisie hoped she would live up to the hype.

And there was no mention of the shooting, the dumping of vehicle and bodies, the rescue of Maria and Savio from the mercenaries. Steig hadn't said any more about those events, but she had felt the tension radiating from him as they approached the farm earlier.

The bedroom door opened, Steig ducked in under the lintel, a towel wrapped around his waist, his hair wet from the bath. He closed the door after him, the latch clicking shut with a muted snick.

"Hey, you," Maisie said. "Clean?"

"Yeah. I was stinky. Sorry."

"I like the way you smell. But it's wonderful to be clean. Luxurious."

"Yeah." He pulled the towel off and hung it on the end of the bedstead, turned the wick on the bedside lantern down and slipped into bed. "Ooh ... so much better than that thin ground mat. But I miss the vardo."

"Me too. Very much. Come here," she reached over and pulled him close, wrapping her legs around his, her arms around his neck; she closed her eyes. She felt entwined, like ivy on an oak tree. Inhaling his scent, she smelt soap and damp skin and an underlying hint of wood smoke. "Mmmm," she sighed.

Steig shifted in her arms.

"So, tomorr—"

She put her finger to his lips.

“Hush. Tomorrow, we will discuss tomorrow. Now, we are just us, just here.”

Chapter 28

Maisie walked into the kitchen, off the long smoky room. It was, she was relieved to see, exactly what a farmhouse kitchen should be. A huge age-blackened range took up one wall, with bread ovens and a water heater and a hotplate on which you could fit eight pans, should the need arise. It gave a gentle, even heat into the room. Hung from the darkened oak beams were several haunches of what she presumed was air-dried ham, and a couple of enormous salami. Tied on a rack above were sprigs of drying herbs.

Sitting at the table, Savio was tucking into a plate of eggs and doorstep slices of bread from a rustic loaf.

"Come, sit," he said, through his mouthful of food. He gestured at the empty chairs around the table.

"Thank you." She pulled out a chair and sat. Maria came in, full of energy and smiles as usual, from the adjoining pantry; Maisie could just make out shelves laden with storage jars and wrapped bundles in the cool darkness.

"Ora abbiamo uova e pane, eh, eggs, and err ... bread!" she said, her accent thick, her smile broad.

"Oh, yes, thank you. And thank you for laundering my clothes," she plucked at her blouse by way of explanation. Maria's Breotonish was a good as Maisie's Calabrian.

"Non fa niente," Maria replied, busying herself at the stove, breaking eggs into a pan and stirring with vigour. She poured a mug of coffee from a pot that was warming at the edge of the hotplate. "Caffè per chi trova le chiavi," she said, placing the mug and then a plate of scrambled egg in front of her.

"Grazie, Maria," said Maisie, blushing. She had worked out what trova le chiavi meant, now. Finder of Keys. Fates!

"Mmmm smells good. Mornin' all. Buongiorno!" Steig announced as he strode into the room.

Maria had a grin spread over her face. She nudged Savio, who smiled, but gave her a look, Maisie thought, as if to say, 'leave our esteemed guests alone'. Maisie blushed beetroot, the heat travelling up her face. Steig sat down next to her.

"Mornin' Sturluson. You're chipper. You were snoring when I got up."

"Well rested." Maria placed a plate of eggs in front of him. "Mmm, thank you, grazie mille!" Steig said, smiling at the Calabrian woman.

"In 'ere." Savio opened the doors to a stone stores set back from the rest of the farmyard. Sunlight filtered through the slit windows and illuminated dust, old farm machinery, wooden crates stacked in a corner.

"The ... er, porta, er ... door is 'ere. Was 'ere." He pointed at an archway in the back of the stone building. It looked like a doorway, but they could see it had never had a door fitted. Just a doorframe made of stone, set in a stone wall, and filled with the same dressed masonry. "See ... the, er ... key, is here. Was here." He lifted a stone slab set into the floor, revealing a small inset chamber. Steig peered in. Some spiders, cobwebs and spilt grain filled its corners.

"Where is the clavis, the key?" asked Maisie.

"My, er ... grandfather, he took it, he go to Defaltum Mundi ... er ... he never come back."

"Oh, I'm sorry."

"We will try to get you a key for this, when all this is done," said Steig.

"Thank you. We, er ... we hope is soon." He smiled, but Steig could tell he was nervous.

"Maisie? Shall we?" Steig asked. She seemed distracted, thoughtful.

"Oh! Yes, sorry. Here goes." She pulled out the clavis from Grauplenk, muttered some ancient Hellenic that Steig couldn't catch, and the weird blue light flared from within. He heard a sound like newspaper ripping, and there in the stone doorway was the gateway, iridescent and, if he was honest, just a bit unsettling.

"Savio, look after that horse!" Steig said, putting mock ferocity in his voice.

"Of course. Good luck!"

"We'll be back in a few days. Hopefully," added Maisie, and hugged the farmer, before stepping into the swirling silver pool of the gateway.

Steig waved to Savio and followed her, closing his eyes as he immersed himself in the electric, shifting meniscus.

Part III

The triple joys of living on the road: A crackling yog,
a well-shod horse and a prize worth taking.
– Traveller proverb

Chapter 29

The odd sideways shift disorientated Steig. He stumbled as he stepped through the gateway, bumping into Maisie's back where she had stopped on the far side.

He looked up at the archway of an ancient bridge over a river. They had emerged onto a stone terrace below the bridge. The sunlight shone brightly after the dim barn, and the noise of traffic was an immediate impingement on his hearing. And the stink of vehicle exhaust assaulted his nose. Another, more modern bridge spanned the river away to the right from where they stood in the blinding sunshine.

"Oh! We're back! I can't quite believe it!" exclaimed Maisie.

"Yep. Pretty odd. Don't forget to close the gateway."

"Yes, good point." She muttered another phrase in ancient Hellenic and the gateway, which was set into a stone archway in the wall behind them, popped out of existence. The archway, like that in the barn, had been back-filled with blank stone.

Steig examined the ground. Sure enough, there was a square of stone in the pavement, another hiding place for a clavis.

"I'm guessing we're not going to leave a clavis here 'just in case'?"

"Gosh, no, absolutely not. Not until we've dealt with the Gratadei, and we have more than two, anyway!"

"So, is there one already in there?" He tapped the square stone slab with his boot.

"I don't know. We'll check on the way back. Mm, warm in this sunshine." She smiled up at the sun, shielding her eyes with her hand. Then she put the clavis into her messenger bag and took off her cloak.

"Here," said Steig, and took the cloak, squashed it into the ruck-sack. "We may have to get some clean clothes, try to blend in a bit. We're both, um, conspicuous."

Maisie grimaced as she brushed at her stained jeans and jumper, the warm clothes against the chill days in Khôra. Maria's best efforts hadn't been able to remove the worst ingrained muck from her jeans. And here, the full Alpine spring burst around them; the sun was blazing hot.

"Come on," he said, and took her hand.

"Do we have any money?"

"I have a load of sterling, but we probably need to get euros. I'm assuming we're in Calabria. So, a bank or cambio is probably the first port of call."

"Well, let's try up here."

They turned up some stone steps that led from the terrace by the river, up into a busy town square, choked with cars and tourists.

Steig did a double take when Maisie walked out of the changing room in the department store. Apart from the intricately carved staff, she was very chic, in a new cream blouse, a long sky-blue skirt and sensible flat-soled espadrilles. He had gone for jeans and a plain green T-shirt, keeping his stockman's coat and lace-up ex-army boots. They both had bought dark sunglasses. Also, he had chosen a baseball cap; Maisie had gone for a broad-brimmed alpine walker's hat. Steig stuffed everything else into the large rucksack, folding Maisie's cloak over the top, and shrugged it onto his back.

"Well, we're a bit more blendy-in," he said with a smile. "Let's get a taxi to Milano, see if we can find this contact of Bobe Elka's."

"Isn't Milano a hundred miles away, or something?"

"Yes, but I don't want to hang around in train or bus stations. We're alright for money for a bit."

"Um, alright. Um, I should probably see if my phone works. I need to let work know I'm not coming back. And I should let my father know I'm alright. I did just disappear with you, literally into thin air."

"You're not going back to work?"

"I don't know what I'm doing, but after seeing what I've seen, and knowing now what I know, I don't think accountancy is the career I want to pursue."

"Well, fair enough. You should probably keep your phone off when you're not using it, though. I mean, I don't know, but maybe the Gratadei could track it?"

"Crikey. I hadn't thought of that. Well, I'll send a couple of texts from the taxi, then turn it off. That way, even if they track it for a few minutes, it will do them no good."

"Excellent plan. Let's go!"

Chapter 30

By the time they arrived at Via Triboniano in Milano, the evening was drawing in.

Maisie got out of the taxi and looked around. What she saw did not fill her with confidence or delight. Steig paid the driver and got out as well, hefting the rucksack.

"Lovely neighbourhood," he muttered, his tone sarcastic, as the taxi pulled away.

"It's not what I was expecting," Maisie agreed.

With the sun set, and the evening cooling. Maisie held her staff close, wishing for the comforting embrace of her cloak – not just for the warmth, but also for the anonymity of the hood. But it was still folded up in the top of the rucksack.

The street was long, straight, and bordered along one side with a high concrete wall, daubed and smeared with faded graffiti. Beyond the wall, glimpsed through cracks and gaps in the crumbling edifice, was a huge shunting yard full of railway rolling stock. Graffiti also embellished most of the railway trucks. Tall, forbidding warehouses, boarded-up industrial units and gap-toothed open lots butted up against the road on the other side. Piles of rubbish, rotting and stinking, lined the edge of the street. A three-legged dog hobbled past, gave them a wary glance, and carried on down the roadway, slipping into an alleyway between two buildings.

"What did Bobe Elka say about finding this character?"

"She said, er ... 'go to Via Triboniano, the north-west end, bang on the gates, ask for Damocles'."

"North-west is that way," said Steig, pointing down the road. "Come on."

He started walking. Maisie tried to tamp down her welling despair. Why was everything so difficult? She clung to her staff and followed Steig, catching him up.

"Don't abandon me."

"Not a chance."

He held out his hand for her. They walked the length of the street. It didn't improve – more industrial units, more graffiti tags. Hardly any people around; those that were abroad kept their gaze averted.

The end of the street came with a petering out of the paved roadway, giving way to a gravel roadbed between metal hoardings and the railway wall. At the end of the roadway, in a rutted, dusty turning space for lorries, stood a pair of enormous iron gates. Vertical bars made a forbidding barrier, plastered with guarddog warning signs. Beyond the gates, Maisie could see a deep lot stacked high with shipping containers.

"This one, d'you think?" asked Steig.

"No idea. 'Knock,' she said."

Steig picked up a short plank of wood that was lying in the dust and banged the bars of the gate. They resonated, a low, dull clang.

"Hello! Damocles!" he yelled.

A dog started barking from deep within the compound. But nothing else happened. They stood in the encroaching dark; a single nearby streetlight flickered to life as they waited, casting a desultory orange glow.

"Hellooo! Da ... Mo ... Clees ...!" Steig yelled again, banging the wood on the gate in counterpoint. The barking rose into a crescendo.

"Shut it, Deefer. Awright, awright, ah can fookin' hear you, yer tosser. Stop makin' that bloody racket. You'll 'ave the 'ole of Milano's coppers on me arse at this rate. Twat."

The voice was gravelly, broad Mamecestre. A wiry, short, balding man in his forties emerged from the gloom behind the gate. A huge black-and-tan Alsatian dog trotted at his side, ears pricked and eyes alert, mouth open, showing long fangs. It growled under its breath, a low rumble. The man arrived at the gate and leant on the bars, looking up at them. Maisie stepped back, eyeing the dog.

"Who the fook are you two?"

"Hello. I'm Maisie. This is Steig. Are you Damocles? Bobe Elka said you might help us." As the words left her mouth, Maisie silently berated herself for mentioning the hedge-witch.

"Aye, I'm him. But, well, fook me. If that witch said you need 'elp, then who am I to argue, eh?"

He continued to stand, staring at Maisie with open hostility. She tried staring back, and the silence extended into the realms of discomfort. A different tack, she thought.

"Steig, would you explain to Mr Damocles here what we need?" she asked.

"Hey up, pal. Kushti divvus. Elka reckoned that you're wanting the Gratadei off the land and sorted, once and for all. We're in the middle of doing that, but we need some help with a small matter. Prize is your own gateway. You in, or do we go elsewhere?"

"Well. Kushti divvus yourself. Now you're talkin' the right sorta language. Me own gateway. Hmm. Steig, was it?"

"Yes. And this is Maisie."

"Oh, aye, 'ang on a minute." He put his hand to his temples and screwed his eyes shut, concentrating. "Maisie ... Maisie ... well, bugger me. Not the Finder of Keys?"

"Hello! That's me!" said Maisie, smiling and raising her forearm, waving her hand.

"Fook. Awright. Come on in."

Damocles pulled back an iron bar that locked the gates and swung them inward far enough for Maisie and Steig to squeeze through.

"Don't let the fookin' dog out, whatever you do. He's a right pain to catch again."

The Alsatian nuzzled Maisie's hand and whined. His rubbery nose was broad and wet in her palm.

"What's his name?"

"Deefer."

"Deefer?" asked Maisie.

"Deefer Dog."

"Oh. Ha ha. Yes, funny." Maisie wasn't sure if it was an entirely appropriate name for a dog. At least, in a literary way, it made sense. She wiped her hand on her skirt.

Damocles took them through a yard of towering shipping containers, through to the back of a large warehouse stacked high with crates and boxes, where he'd kitted out a shipping container as an office. There was a spartan reception area, complete with a tatty sagging sofa, a watercooler with no water in its bottle, and a robust desk at the far end, piled high with the detritus of a busy workplace.

"Sit," he commanded, pointing at a pair of chairs in front of the desk. They sat. "Deefer, gerronyerbed." Deefer whined and slunk to the sofa. "So. What do you need from me? An' what are you payin'? You said me own gateway. A gateway to where?"

Before Maisie started talking, she cast the tatchapen spell, just in case there was an elvish glamour around the place. Nothing obvious changed. Then she pulled some power from the staff and added the tiniest bit of command to her voice.

"Well," she began, "we need information first. And as Steig said, we can give you your own gateway, anywhere you want. I'm guessing here it would come out in the middle of Mediolanum."

"Aye, well, not much use doin' that if the Gratadei are still there. Guaranteed to just bring me grief, that is. But y'say you're on the way to kickin' them out? How d'you propose to do that?"

"That," said Maisie, "is what we need the information for."

"What information?"

"The castle, here, where their gateway is. What it's like, how many guards, a floor plan if you have it. Also, whereabouts they might hold a prisoner, stuff like that." Damocles went to speak, but Maisie held up her finger. "And, any information on how long they open their gateway for, and how often? Where they keep the clavis when it's not in use. If they have any of the missing claves."

"Do you want the Cardinal's fookin' shoe size an' all?"

"We need this information by tomorrow," added Steig. "The clock is ticking."

"Well, bugger me. You're not askin' much. I'll see what I can do. Anything else?" He spread his hands, palms upwards.

"Well, yes, actually," said Maisie. "We'll need some fighters. A squad of six, by preference. Able to handle automatic weapons, work as a team, that sort of thing. And obviously, we'll need them fully equipped."

"Obviously. I'm bloody sorry I asked. Alright. Day after tomorrow for the squad. I'll 'ave the info tomorrow night. Come back 'ere for it."

Maisie stood up, leant across the desk, and shook Damocles' hand.

"A pleasure doing business with you." Her face was serious, unsmiling.

They walked out of Damocles' compound, into the street-lit Milanese night. Via Triboniano was quiet, deserted. They stopped at the first junction. Steig checked up and down both streets. He wasn't used to cities or towns, but he was used to looking out for trouble. Everything seemed calm.

"That was tense. Did you think that was tense?" Maisie asked, her voice pitched high with stress. "Goodness, I'm shaking. Could you pass me my cloak?"

Steig set the rucksack down and rummaged for the cloak, shook it out and held it up for her, moved closer to clip the catch at her throat. He encircled her in a hug. Leant towards her ear.

"You used a glamour on him, didn't you?" he asked, his voice barely above a whisper.

"Oh! Was it obvious?"

He smiled in the dim light. "No. But he agreed to sort out the info and squad far too quickly. We'd best be wary. He might work out what just happened."

"I hadn't thought of that."

"Come on. Let's find a hotel for the night. Unless you want to gateway back to Mediolanum? Though I'm guessing this close to the city centre, we'd be right in the Citadel."

"It's weird how the scale works. Everything is so much closer together in Mediolanum. But yes, it seems risky. We might come out in the moat, or inside a wall, or in a locked room. I should practise and see if I can find a way to tune it, see where it comes out."

Steig took her arm in his, and walked towards the distant busy road, where traffic was constant. He talked as he walked.

"Could you combine the gateway with the kathalyog, sort of look at the Betwixt between realms?"

"I have no idea. I wouldn't like to get stuck somewhere." She shivered. They walked in silence for a while.

"There." Steig pointed. A few hundred metres away, a dim, yellow sign advertised a hotel. It was a small, seedy-looking affair. They walked in and a young man at the reception desk looked up from the textbook he was reading. College student, Steig surmised.

"Posso aiutarti?" he asked.

"Parli Anglese?" Steig countered.

"Ah, yes, how can I help you?"

"Can we get a room please for two nights?"

"Of course. Twin or double?"

He glanced at Maisie. The question had thrown him. She was impassive, her mind elsewhere.

"Uh ... twin, please."

"Certainly. Er, passport numbers please, in the register." He slid an open book over to them, which had columns laid out for name, address and passport number.

"Shit. Er, we don't have passports. We, er, lost them."

The man frowned. Steig opened his wallet and withdrew a hundred-euro note.

"Would this help?"

This startled the man, who checked around the reception area to ensure they were alone. He slid the note from the counter.

"Put your name and home address in the register, please, sir. And it's forty-five euros for the room, per night."

Steig smiled, signed his name "Tom Smith", and made up an address in Roteslund. Found another hundred-euro note and handed it over.

"Thank you. Keep the change."

The room was small, but clean enough, with a tiny shower room ensuite.

"Two beds?" asked Maisie.

"I asked; you were preoccupied."

"Oh. Fiddlesticks."

Steig raised an eyebrow. "Really?"

She coloured red. "Well. Yes. Really. Also, you didn't need to bribe him. I could have just, you know, um, glamoured him a bit."

"Well. He's bribed. I have been wondering if coercing people with the glamour is morally acceptable?"

"It's the end justifying the means. But yes ..." She cast her eyes down to the scruffy carpet. "You have a point. Sorry."

"Hey. You're OK." He hugged her. "Just, y'know, not everything needs the fae touch." He squeezed her closer, and she sniffled a bit, then hugged him back.

"You're right, of course. I'll try to find a different way next time. It's just so easy!"

"With great power comes great responsibility," he intoned, keeping his face straight. Maisie looked at him with incredulity, and rolled her eyes. He grinned and heaved the rucksack onto a bed. "Anyway. What were you preoccupied with?"

"Your idea of trying to see where a gateway comes out. How I might do that without trapping myself between realms."

"Do you think the Hephaestus magic and the traveller lore will work together?"

"When I cast a spell, for a clavis, or fae glamour, the traveller lore, or even the power from the staff ... it all feels similar. So, I think it will work in harmony. I just need to find the right buttons."

"OK. Do you need to practise that?"

"I always need to practise. But we're sort of constrained by time."

"We have a day or so. Come on, let's find a takeaway, I'm starving."

Steig put his empty takeaway container on the bedside table.

"OK. Are you sure this is a good idea?"

"No. But I want to try. If I can see where a gateway opens, I can direct it. And I have an idea how to do it."

"OK. Well. What do I need to do?"

"I'm going to open the gateway in this room. It will end up somewhere in the middle of Mediolanum. But I'll make it tiny. Hopefully. Then ... this is the tricky bit that might not work." She wrung her hands. "I'm going to use the gateway to power my kathalyog spell, rather than a fire. Like you suggested. If that works, I might be able to kathalyog through the gateway to Khôra ... and if that works, I might be able to see where it comes out ... hopefully."

"I'm hearing a lot of 'might be ables'. It sounds dangerous."

"It's fraught. Hah," she scoffed. "Pheoreth would say, 'This course of action is perilous.'" She mimicked Pheoreth's sibilance perfectly. Sadness flickered over her face.

"I can only agree with her sentiment." Steig took a sip from a bottle of water.

Maisie stood up, grabbed her staff, shrugged into her cloak.

"I need to try. If I stop to think about it, I'll go mad." She picked up the clavis that they had found in Grauplenk, and after a couple of seconds, it glowed blue from within. Steig stood from the bed and backed up against the far wall behind Maisie.

Maisie appeared to be having a conversation with herself. She screwed her eyes shut, and her lips were moving. The ripping noise, when it came, was more like crepe paper, not newspaper. A small square of blue-tinged silver light, little bigger than Steig's palm, opened in the middle of the room, floating at head height. Maisie looked over her shoulder at Steig, her face grim, but with an edge of triumph.

"Well, it's not wagon-sized. That's a start. Back in a minute, just hang on to the clavis, OK?" She handed the glowing brass key to Steig, who held it by the knobbly vertices, between thumb and forefinger.

"Be careful."

"I will. Here goes nothing."

She turned back to the gateway, then all at once dissipated into a haze that had filled the room. Steig remained, holding the glowing clavis, with the gateway hovering between their two beds. The faintest crackle of static electricity discharged from its edges.

Maisie stepped into the Betwixt.

"Well, this is different," she commented to herself. The usually dull, grey mist was brilliantly lit, from one distant horizon to the other, by an intense, shining, cadmium yellow plane. It stretched from the floor and rose straight up to the far mists overhead. It was like a thin, translucent, glowing yellow wall.

"What are you, weird yellow wall?" Maisie knew that she was thinking out loud, but it calmed her nerves, and she was definitely nervous. And it wasn't like she would be overheard.

She held up her staff and prodded the yellow plane. It didn't move, but when her staff touched it, ripples spread out along it, like a vertical glowing golden pond. She felt a push back along the staff – resistance, and something else. Like a back pressure in the ether.

She said the kathalyog ending spell and stepped out again. Back to the hotel room. Steig was still standing where she had left him, holding the clavis. She realised she was overheating.

"It's warm in there. I-I'll just take my cloak off."

"Warm? That sounds different."

"You have no idea. There's this odd yellow glowing wall. Right!" She dropped the cloak on a bed. Took a deep breath. "Once more unto the breech." She stepped back into the Betwixt, was once again presented with the yellow plane.

Knowing she could drop out back to the hotel boosted her confidence. The test would be when she tried to "look into" the wall. If the wall was an analogue to the glowing yellow points made by the yogs, then she should be able to see into it. She closed her eyes in fear, then leant forward. A wave of vertigo washed over her. Leaning on her staff for balance, she opened her eyes.

The view, when the mist had cleared, was from halfway up a wall, out over the central street of Mediolanum. Thirty metres to one side, the walls of the Citadel rose, implacable. The narrow roadway leading to Michael's shop was opposite, just visible if she twisted her head and peered. She had an idea, and, pulling power from the staff, pushed the edges of the gateway with her mind, visualising it sliding along the wall. Her viewpoint changed. Was the far end of the gateway moving as well? When she stepped out of kathalyog, would she come out in the shunting yard, squashed by a train? No time to stop. She kept pushing, guiding, visualising. Took more power from the staff. Her arms and shoulder went numb. She felt sick, dizzy. Kept pushing.

The gateway moved to the narrow road on the far side of the street. Despite the dim light, she could make out that the wall had an old doorway that time had bricked up. Perfect. She pushed, teased, tempted the gateway until she felt it nestle in the doorway. It liked it there; she felt a sort of sigh, in the ether, and an expansion, as if the gateway had found a home. It filled the doorway.

She pulled her head back, and her viewpoint returned to the golden yellow Betwixt. Now to see if the other end had moved. She cancelled the spell and found herself back in the hotel room. Steig hadn't moved, though his face wore a concerned expression.

"Alright? It got bigger." He waved his hand at the shimmer, which now filled the opposite wall and was the size of a door.

"Yes! I moved the far end of the gateway. Hang on for two minutes. I'm going to test it."

Without waiting for Steig's reply, she stepped into the shimmer. She was getting used to the brief sideways disorientation, so stepped out into the alleyway in Mediolanum without stumbling too much. She checked around. No one had seen her. She turned and stepped back through.

Steig grinned at her, but it seemed more like a rictus. Nerves? Terror? She couldn't tell. She said the ancient Hellenic to close the gateway, which shrank down and disappeared with the customary pop.

"I moved the gateway from the central street in Mediolanum to a bricked-up doorway in an alleyway next to the shop where I bought the cloak," she explained. "It was difficult to move it far, so I think that means when I open up a new location, I can fine tune it, then it's set. If we move this clavis from this room, I'm certain it will need to be set up again."

"Well, I'm just glad you're back. Though I guess this means we can open gateways at will?"

"Exactly. We're ready for the next step."

Chapter 31

Steig looked at the castle, Il Castello Sforzesco, from across the square, past the enormous fountain. It was, he had to admit, rather imposing. The outer walls were fifty feet high, with formidable round watchtowers looming at the corners. The entrance gateway was only accessible over a narrow bridge overlooked by battlements, studded with murder holes.

He turned to Maisie, who was standing beside him, also looking at the castle.

"Are you ready?"

"No. But we need to do it. If I stop to think about it, I'll fall apart."

"Alright then. Disguise?"

"Yes. One minute." She held up her hand. As Steig watched, her staff shrank down and morphed into a hospital-issue walking aid, which Maisie leant on. She affected a limp, and her hair, under her alpine walking hat, turned a dark shade of auburn, growing down her back.

"I'm still utterly amazed when you do that. Such a neat trick."

"Well, let's hope they don't have a way of checking people."

Steig squeezed her hand. "You worry too much."

They sauntered, Maisie still affecting her limp, up to the castle gate and ticket office. Just another tourist couple come to gawk at the castle, the museum.

Earlier, at the central Milano railway station, Steig had checked their rucksack into the left luggage department. The previous day they had gone shopping, and had bought two sturdy canvas roll bags, which Steig now carried, one inside the other. Maisie had her messenger bag, which was heavy with Steig's handgun, two spare clips of ammunition, and the claves, one from Kurra and one from Grauplenk.

At the castle, after buying a pair of tickets, they came to a security station with a metal detector. Steig, then Maisie put their bags on the conveyor belt. They walked through the metal detector portals. Heat prickled down Steig's spine as the stress and worry kicked in. He scanned the room. Easy enough to run fast, back out again. But security cameras watched their every move. The jig would be up.

"Scusi, signora," called a guard, waving Maisie over. "Questa borsa è tua?"

Maisie understood the question. It was her bag. "Si," she replied.

"Guarderò dentro."

"Er ... Anglese, per favore."

"Er ... I need to search your bag."

"No problem."

The guard opened the bag and peered in, then stiffened, his face going white.

"There is no problem. Close the bag," commanded Maisie, leaning on her walking stick.

The guard folded the flap back over the bag and passed it to Maisie. He had a peculiar look on his face, as if he had forgotten something, but he was smiling at her.

"Er ... Enjoy your visit to il castello."

"Thank you."

As they walked, hand in hand, through the door from the security area and out into the castle grounds, Steig whispered, "You're getting really accomplished at that command thing."

"My heart's beating so fast I think I'm going to pass out," she replied, her voice little more than a murmur. "Keep walking, but the first bench we get to, I need to sit down. My legs have turned to jelly."

They walked through the formal gardens arrayed between the outer wall and the imposing keep in the centre. In one corner, which was off the direct track from one to the other, they found seclusion on a bench under an orange tree. They sat side by side.

"OK, next step. Hang on." Maisie's face changed as she concentrated. Her hair grew long, became white-blonde, very straight. A green cast suffused her eyes, her face lengthened into classic Tuatha de Danann, complete with prominent cheekbones. Her ears became pointed, and she jammed her hat down to cover them, morphing it into an off-white fine cotton headscarf. Her clothes changed to a cream silk dress in a plain style. The staff grew from the walking stick back to its former glory. To Steig's eye, it stretched out with more expression than something made of wood should have been able to manage.

"How does that look?" Maisie's voice was the sibilant whisper of Aelene and the other sidhe.

"Well, it would fool me. Hopefully, the guards won't be looking too closely. May I?" He put his hand on Maisie's bag, which under her glamour looked like it was new, made from soft, light tan, designer leather. She glanced around. All calm.

"Yes, go for it."

Steig reached in and pulled out the gun. He took care not to show it more than necessary and tucked it into his waistband, covering it with his long shirt. He stuffed the ammunition into his front pockets. They had bought some heavy-duty cable ties the day before, and he pulled these out, threading them into his back pocket.

"Time?" asked Maisie.

Steig checked the cheap plastic watch on his wrist. They had found it in the same hardware shop as the cable ties.

"Twenty to. Twenty minutes to get into position," he replied.

"Do you have your crib sheet?"

He held up his left palm, on which he had scribed various Calabrian phrases in indelible ink.

"OK, shall we?" she smiled at him.

He hoped he appeared as confident.

They stood, shouldered their bags, and walked around the edge of the gardens to the tourists' entrance to the main part of the building. As they passed through the portico, Steig constantly scanned for signs of detection. Checking for guards, Gratadei mercenaries, security cameras. He was in a state of high alert, and very jittery.

"Calm down, you're jiggling."

"Sorry." He tried to still his inner tremors. It wasn't working. They joined a queue of tourists to get into the café.

"There, you see? Exit the café to the toilets and the door to the Gratadei side is off that hallway," she murmured. She nodded towards the toilet sign near the entrance to the café. They swung away from the queue, walked down a short, spartan passageway past the toilets and arrived at the end of the corridor.

There was a thick red rope slung across the passage between two chrome stands, with a sign on the rope that declared "Privato". Steig moved one stand, and slipped through, holding it for Maisie. He replaced it, all the while looking up the passageway. No one had seen them. They stood for a moment.

Steig had memorised the route from the map provided by Damocles. Around the next corner would be one or two guards, preventing people who did what they had just done from progressing into the private section of the building. The section run by the Gratadei.

"Time check?" hissed Maisie.

"One minute to go," he murmured back.

"We'll wait here?"

"Yes."

Steig's watch clicked past the hour. He listened. Sure enough, despite being muted through the enormously thick walls of the castello, he could hear the distant, percussive report of semi-automatic gunfire.

"Damocles has started. Let's go."

He strode with feigned confidence around the corner, moving rapidly along a carpeted corridor lined with office doors. There was a Gratadei mercenary, clothed in tactical black, standing at the door at the end of the corridor. He had his hand to his ear, listening to a hidden earphone, his head turned, and hadn't seen them. When they were three metres from him, he startled, turning.

"Fermati!" he shouted, but then noticed Maisie. "Mi scusi," he said with a flicker of recognition.

"Apri la porta," commanded Maisie.

The guard seemed confused, but opened the door and stood to one side. He had some fingers missing from his left hand, which hooked the door handle with one finger and thumb as Steig and Maisie walked through.

"Grazie," said Maisie, smiling at him.

"Prego, Aedredd," replied the guard, frowning.

The door closed behind them. Steig paused, scanned this new corridor for threats. Nothing. The same long, carpeted corridor. Same potted plants, office doors, muted wallpaper. He knew the route in his head. All was going to plan. Damocles' distraction at the rear entrance had taken the guards' attention and would keep most of them busy for the next five to ten minutes. He started walking, then stopped and turned.

"What is it?" he asked.

Maisie had gone chalk-white, even beyond the glamour of Aelene's pale features, and was frozen in place.

"He called me Aedredd."

It took Steig about a second and a half to compute what that could mean. "Aedredd's daughter, Finder of Keys." His mouth fell open, then closed. He shook his head to clear it.

"No time. It's probably a common name. We need to get to Rosalia before they realise Damocles' attack is a diversion."

Maisie was rooted to the spot, her face pallid. Steig stepped up to her and shook her shoulders, his face close to hers.

"Now! Let's go! No time!"

"Alright. Wait. Eh." She wavered, gasping for breath.

"Don't pass out on me," Steig said in a terse whisper, taking her arm and leading her along the corridor. An office door ahead of them crashed open and two mercenaries ran into the corridor, and straight past them, giving them not a second glance.

"Looks like Damocles has them riled. Come on!" He pulled on her arm.

"Er ..." Maisie was muttering to herself, but at least she was keeping up.

Steig followed the route in his head, left, through double doors, through a hallway, through next double doors, right down narrow stairs. They clattered down the metal steps into a service area. He pulled his gun out of his waistband and chambered a round as they went. At the bottom of the stairs, there was a desk with a mercenary sitting behind it. He gave a shout, went to stand, but Steig had the gun pointed at him.

"Fermo!" he shouted. "Mani in alto."

The guard put his hands in the air. Steig kept the gun pointed at him.

"Maisie! You're up."

"OK. Sorry."

She shook her head as if to clear it, then pulled a cable tie from Steig's pocket, moving to one side as they had practised in the hotel room the previous evening. As she cable-tied the man's hands behind his back, she seemed to be regaining some composure. He glanced at his left palm, keeping the gun steady with his right hand.

"Sdraiati!" he ordered, hoping that meant lie down. The man slid off the chair and onto the floor, where Maisie arranged him face down. She took another cable tie and bound his legs. She pointed her staff at the man, muttered something unintelligible, and watched as he went limp.

The gun back in his waistband, Steig stood over the guard and removed the pistol from the holster at his hip.

They pushed through the doors beyond the desk area, which opened out onto storerooms and corridors. Beyond was a light-grey-painted utilitarian space. It was all heating pipes, open trays of wiring suspended from the ceiling, grilles and hard edges. Their information was that the Gratadei had converted one storeroom to a cell for Rosalia. Steig ejected the magazine from the guard's gun and threw it under some pipes against a wall; the empty gun he slid along the opposite wall.

"Time?" asked Maisie.

"Eight minutes. We need to hurry."

Maisie closed her eyes and stilled her body. Steig waited, watching the stairs through the open doors behind them, listening for the clatter of feet.

Her eyes flew open.

"This way." She jogged through the open area, took the first right between two huge vertical heating pipes, and disappeared down a narrow, pipe-lined corridor. Steig ran to keep up. He skidded around the corner to find Maisie pointing her staff at a solid metal door blocking her way. As he arrived, there was a dull thump, and the lock hasp shattered. Maisie pulled the door open. As she did this, her appearance reverted to the Maisie that Steig knew so well.

Maisie piled into the cell, which contained a camp bed, a stinking bucket, and, Steig presumed, Rosalia. He crouched in the doorway, gun ready, watching and listening. Maisie was explaining what was going on to Rosalia, in an urgent but low voice. Then there came the tearing silk noise of a gateway forming. He risked a glance inside the cell. Rosalia was tall, svelte, androgenous, with long brown hair and pale skin. She was standing in one corner, worry and confusion crowding onto her cut and bruised face. Her blood stained the front of her once-cream robes; she had received a beating, that was evident.

The gateway hovered, small and crackling, in the far corner. A slight hazing of the air showed where Maisie had been.

Steig peered out again. Still no noise from the stairs.

There was a gasp from the cell and he glanced in again. The gateway had grown to the size of a door. So far, so good. Maisie reappeared, red-faced from her recent exertion.

"Rosalia. Listen to me. This gateway goes to the road at the back of the Citadel. Go through, then hide yourself somewhere that no one knows. Remember, Aelene knows most of your friends and contacts. Good luck."

Rosalia was on the point of breaking down in tears. She couldn't move.

"Go!" said Maisie.

Steig felt the command, an urging that almost made him walk to the gateway himself. With a conscious act of will, he remained by the door.

Rosalia moved and was gone.

The gateway closed with a pop. Maisie scooped up the clavis from the floor.

"Time check," she called.

"Ten minutes. Damocles will be retreating now. Hopefully."

"Give me a minute. Quiet."

"OK."

Steig walked to the end of the pipe-lined corridor and shuffled around the end, gun ready in both hands, risking a glance across to the desk and the stairs. Still no noise. The inert form of the guard lay, half hidden, under the desk. He tried to calm his nerves. They were in a dead end, underground, and sure as horses eat hay, once the Gratadei realised the subterfuge, they would check in down here.

The soft patter of Maisie's shoes brought him back to the job in hand.

"Found them! Come on." She ran past him, sliding on the grey-painted concrete floor, headed further down the maze of corridors and rooms that let off the service area. Steig followed, checking behind, gun ready.

Another pipe-lined corridor. Another metal door. Once again, the shattering of the hasp. Steig heaved the door open. Maisie slipped through the widening gap.

"Bingo!" she cried from within the small room.

Steig stepped in; his eyes adjusted to the gloom. Metal racking lined the walls. And on the metal racking, arrayed in serried ranks, were tens, perhaps over a hundred claves.

"Bloody hell. OK. Start packing."

He pulled out the second bag from the first. They started shovelling the claves into the bags as fast as they could, the metal objects clinking together as they tumbled, the bags bulking out.

Steig zipped the second bag closed, and looped the handles through his arms, staggering under the weight. Maisie was panting and leaning on her staff, her bag pulling her to one side with the sheer uneven mass of the bronze.

"We're not going to run far with this," she muttered.

A shout from the stairs, and the sound of clattering feet descending. More shouts came from the desk area.

"We're not running anywhere. Gateway, now!" urged Steig, pulling the metal door into the corridor closed.

He cast around for something to wedge it with. A section of racking shelf sort of fit against the handle, but it was a temporary fix.

The sound of newspaper ripping filled the dim space, the blue glow eerie on the walls.

"I don't know where it goes!" shouted Maisie, her voice cracking with stress and fear.

"No time, go, go!" Steig countered, as the door handle rattled against the shelving, and a series of metallic thumps rang through the room.

Shouts sounded from beyond the door, a string of furious Calabrian expletives. Maisie, with a look of abject fear, threw herself into the gateway and disappeared. Steig cast a last glance at the door. As the shelving snapped from the repeated impact of the hammer blows from outside, he too dived, as best he could, with the bag on his back, into the azure meniscus.

As soon as Steig staggered and fell onto the flagged floor beyond the gateway, Maisie closed it down with a pop. They collapsed against a stone wall, lying next to each other, their backs propped by the heavy bags of claves. They were in a long, dark, damp corridor. Silence enveloped them.

"Oh. My. Fucking. God," breathed Maisie.

"Yeah. Intense," agreed Steig.

She checked along the corridor in both directions. Slit windows on one side provided a dim illumination. She slid her arms out of the bag's handles and, standing on tiptoes, peered through the slit.

"Oh, no! We're in the Citadel. I can see the central street over there."

"Not ideal. Can you open a gateway again, or I dunno, kathalyog to somewhere with the claves?"

"If we walk westwards about ten metres, we'll be clear of the castello and the moat and gardens. The ratio is on our side. Remember, a metre here is, what, a hundred in Defaltum Mundi?"

Steig popped open the leather flap of a pouch on his belt and pulled out a small compass. He studied it for a second.

"This corridor is north–south. North's that way." He pointed up the corridor.

"OK, well, north, that puts us in Parco Sempione. It's huge; we should be fine going there." She walked to the far end of the corridor, one hand clutching the clavis, the other dragging her heavy bag along the ground.

Steig struggled to his feet with his own bag, heaving it onto his back. There was a noise behind them, from the other end of the corridor. Footsteps, and a voice, sibilant, familiar from Maisie's glamour.

"This ends now."

Time almost stopped. He turned, noting in slow motion that Maisie was also turning, had dropped the clavis, was raising her staff. An express train hit Steig's body, hammering him along the corridor and into the far wall, beyond Maisie, who shrieked in terror.

Maisie shrieked in fright and surprise as Steig, his arms still looped into his bag's handles, flew past her and smashed, bag first, into the end of the corridor with a noise like a car crash. She felt the backlash from the spell, had already pushed down into the ether to counteract it. Her feet slid along the ground, and she felt as if she were, for a moment, in the path of a hurricane, yet she was still upright.

Aelene was standing at the far end of the corridor, vibrating with rage, hatred contorting her features.

"I should have strangled you at birth," she spat, and raised her hands.

Maisie felt the surge of magic. She tried to raise her staff, but found the witch had paralysed her. As if a gigantic snake was coiled around her. She lost her balance and toppled over, landing with a thump on the stone ground, winded, knocking the side of her head. Her vision filled with actual stars.

She watched in horror, lying helpless on her side, as Aelene walked along the corridor, taking her time, as if deciding which spell to cast next.

"Steig?" Her voice trembled.

No answer.

"Your gypsy scum boyfriend won't help you now," Aelene mocked.

"But ... but wait." Cold realisation swept Maisie like iced water from a pail. "You're Aedredd, aren't you? You're my mother! Why are you doing this?"

Aelene was standing over her. She let her glamour go, and she morphed into the blonde-haired, older woman with the scar over her eye, who Maisie had seen at Rosalia's.

"Yes. I am Aedredd," she said with a sneer. She rolled Maisie onto her back with her foot. Maisie struggled, but could not move. As if her muscles were not listening. She thought she'd been frightened before, but now she was beyond terrified. She felt her bladder empty, and shame added its serpent's head to the maelstrom of emotions battering her.

Aedredd knelt, one knee on either side of Maisie's torso, trapping her arms. The pain was intense.

Aedredd sniffed the air.

"Pathetic, you've pissed yourself, you leathphór vermin."

"I-I'm your d-daughter!"

"Oh, I should have known that useless excuse for a human would beget me such a worthless, whimpering quim." She spat phlegm at the corridor wall. "Look at you. I'm doing both worlds a service by ending you."

She reached to her belt and pulled out a long, curved knife from a scabbard. She held it to Maisie's nose, the tip an inch from her eye.

The edge cut into her cheek, and the warmth of her blood flowed down her face.

"P-please ... you don't have to do this ..." Maisie recoiled at the gleam of madness in the woman's eyes.

There was a fleshy noise, and Aedredd shuddered once, then sat up straight, taking the knife away from Maisie's face. Something pointed and bloody had erupted through Aedredd's left shoulder, through the cloth of her robes. A patch of bright crimson expanded from her armpit, staining the cream silk.

Aedredd shrieked, stood, turned, and flung the knife down the length of the corridor, a powerful overarm throw. The spell binding Maisie loosened, and she frantically scrabbled for her staff. Pheoreth stood at the far end of the corridor, the knife hilt protruding from her chest, another arrow already nocked. But as Maisie watched, horror filling her, Pheoreth sagged, unable to draw the bow.

An arrow, flight feathers white against red, protruded from Aedredd's shoulder blade.

Aedredd turned, stamping on Maisie's arm, kicking the staff away. She sank back onto Maisie with her knees, and grabbed her throat.

"You ... just ... need ... to ... die ..." she gasped, pushing at Maisie's throat with each word.

This is it, thought Maisie, mortality arriving in her mind. This was the end. Killed by her own mother. Failing Khôra. Failing Steig. She'd never hear Beckett's whicker of greeting again. Strangely, that hurt her most.

Another shudder, another arrow, this one in Aedredd's other shoulder. Aedredd was like a demon, would not stop, would not cease, continued to strangle the life from Maisie.

As her vision was fading, there was a noise so immense, she thought it must be the Citadel falling around her. Something threw Aedredd backwards. Blood and brain matter fountained from her head and sprayed over the walls and ceiling. The pressure on Maisie's neck ceased, as did the magic binding her body. She heaved a ragged breath through her bruised larynx.

Steig held the handgun, still pointing at where Aedredd had been. He had bruised his back when he impacted the claves in the bag, and the stone wall. His head was muzzy with concussion. And now he was deaf from the report of the gun in an enclosed space. Maisie moved, retching and gasping for breath. Still alive. Good. Though he had just shot her mother in the head. Not so good. Given the circumstances, perhaps she'd forgive him.

Deal with that later, he thought.

Looking along the corridor he saw Pheoreth, slumped against the far wall, a spreading stain of blood around the knife hilt. He de-cocked the gun and stuffed it in his waistband. Standing with difficulty, he shuffled to Maisie. His heart jumped when he saw the blood on her face, smeared across her cheek, dripping onto her neck.

"Help Pheoreth!" Maisie wheezed, waving her arm along the corridor. "I'm fine. Go!" She struggled to sit up.

Another figure appeared at the end of the corridor, leaning over Pheoreth. Andion. Steig had the gun up, and pointing, in an instant, though his back screamed pain and his vision swam.

"Do not be stupid, Steig," said the neraido, as he knelt by Pheoreth. "If I wanted to harm you, I would have turned you in to the Gratadei when you were lost in Mediolanum."

"But ... you do know what Pheoreth did?" asked Steig, as he put the gun away again.

"I do. I find it as reprehensible as you do. However, she has comprehensively changed sides. Now, help me, or she may die."

"Fuck's sake," Steig muttered. He knelt next to Andion, taking in the broken body of the fae woman. "What should we do? Gateway to a hospital in Milano?"

"No. We have a healer in Mediolanum. We will take her there."

"She's got a probably fatal chest wound. Surely a full modern Accident and Emergency department is what she needs?"

"We are neraides. We have specific medical requirements. Trust me, Carmenta is her best option."

Thonwen and Morwen arrived at the end of the corridor.

"We will assist Maisie," Thonwen reassured them, as they filed past. Steig grabbed Pheoreth's shoulders and Andion took hold of her legs. They carried her limp body to the open courtyard at the end of the corridor, where one of the Gratadei's four-wheel-drive trucks was waiting. Five Gratadei mercenaries were lying dead, in pools of blood, in the courtyard. Arrows protruded from their bodies, their jaunty angles and white flight feathers a counterpoint to the grim spectacle.

"How far is the healer?" Steig asked.

"About half a mile outside town."

"Put her in the truck, in the back," Steig ordered, and they heaved her onto the flatbed. Andion climbed in next to her.

"Keep a pressure on her wound with your hand, but don't remove the blade. I'll drive. Shout directions," Steig called, as he got in the cab and started the engine.

He shook his head to clear his blurred vision. It didn't really help. He would need to deal with the concussion. But, Pheoreth first.

The enormous iron-bound gates of the Citadel that Maisie had described were standing ajar. Steig nudged them open with the truck's bumper and headed out onto the main drag of Mediolanum.

"Left, down that street!" came a call from the flatbed.

He drove with exaggerated care, his vision still blurry, mindful of the blade in Pheoreth's chest. The truck rolled over the cobbled street, towards the healer.

Chapter 32

Maisie finally rolled onto all fours, coughed, retched and spat red-tinged phlegm onto the stone floor. Blood, running in a constant flow from the cut on her cheek, joined it.

"Ew. Eurgh," she exclaimed, as the coughing fit receded. "Oh … yuk." Her underwear was wet. She reached under her dress and pulled her pants off, balled them up, crawled to the roll bag and stuffed them in with the claves. "Hah. No knickers. Least of my worries."

She used the back of her sleeve to dab at the cut on her cheek, but it continued to pour blood, dripping down her chin. Footsteps approached. She grabbed the staff and swung with it, drawing energy, ready. Thonwen and Morwen, the twins.

"We have come to assist you," said Thonwen.

"The Gratadei in the Citadel are dead," said Morwen.

"Wait, what? How?"

"We heard from … sources in Milano …" began Thonwen.

"... that you were planning on liberating Rosalia," finished Morwen.

"Stop! Stop-stop-stop. Just one of you speak."

She glanced at the crumpled corpse of her mother, and without warning, rolled and vomited copious yellow bile onto the flagstones. It mingled with her bloodstained spit, gathering in the cracks. She retched again, but nothing more would come up. The pain in her chest spasmed with loss, guilt, longing, woe.

"Fuck. Would someone please cover my mother with something?" She waved towards the corpse without looking at it. Sobbed once.

"Your ... mother?" asked Thonwen. Then realisation arrived. "Oh, Goddess. I am so sorry. Of course. A moment." He stood, cast around, then pulled a dull blue hanging from the wall and used it to cover the corpse.

"Thank you," said Maisie, wiping her mouth. Dabbing her cheek. "Ouch. My throat really hurts. Ow, ow, fucking ow." She thumped the floor, then glanced up at Thonwen through tears. Groaned. Reached inside herself and pulled strength from ... somewhere. Took a deep breath.

"Please. Tell me what happened. Just you, Thonwen." She forced a smile of apology at Morwen, though her cheek stung and bled freely.

"We heard from sources that you planned an attack today. We ..."

"Sources?" she asked, raising an eyebrow.

"Someone who works for Damocles. A neraida."

Morwen opened a leather pack at his belt and pulled out a tiny jar of salve, which he set about dabbing onto Maisie's cheek using a square of cloth. Maisie sucked in a sharp breath at the sting of the astringent salve, trying not to cry out.

"Pheoreth thought it would be a suitable time to mount an attack on the Citadel," continued Thonwen. "We timed the attack to coincide with yours. We used hooks and ropes to scale the walls, whilst the gateway to Milano was open, and news of your attack was reaching here, distracting the guards. The Cardinal and some men left with the clavis, closing the gateway. We attacked from above. Only Aelene escaped our arrows."

"So, it was Pheoreth's idea?" Maisie asked. Another tide of loss rolled over her and she gulped air.

"It was. She has renounced her association with the Gratadei and Aelene. We fought with her today, but I do not know what the future of our band will hold, even if she survives. We are all uncomfortable with her duplicity."

Waves of fatigue and grief assailed Maisie. She pulled some strength from the ever-present staff, Erato's forest providing her sustenance. Her thinking cleared. A critical point was presented to her.

"Er ... What is to stop the Cardinal from reopening the gateway?"

"Other than the likelihood that we will shoot his men as they walk through it? Nothing."

"So, if they drive an armoured car through, we're sunk, right?"

"Ah. I do not think Pheoreth had thought that far ahead."

Maisie couldn't quite believe what she was about to say. She took a deep breath. Reached in for more inner strength. Pushed the image of Aedredd's corpse from her mind. She would need to face that, but not right now.

"OK. I'm going to Milano. We need to get the Cardinal's clavis."

"How are you going to do that?" asked Morwen, his face creased with worry.

Maisie pulled back from the yellow, glowing, inter-planar kathalyog, as she called it. Back to the Citadel, in a storeroom in the furthest point to the north-west, towards Damocles' yard. Once again, the scale difference between the worlds was in her favour. The gateway was open, sitting against a wall, filling the space with its eldritch silver-blue shimmer. Morwen stood by the door to the storeroom, watching, attentive.

Taking a moment to organise her mind, her thoughts jumped to the moment her mother died, flying backwards, blood spurting ...

"Maisie, Inventor Clavis, how can I assist you?" Morwen asked her, as he knelt next to her.

She had collapsed into a shivering heap. Lying on the dirty floor of the storeroom, tears streaming, shaking uncontrollably, spasms of sobs racking her, she pressed her hands over her face. Oh, this would simply not do.

"Th-thank you, Morwen. Help me up, please." She struggled to her feet, feeling foolish and drained. She used the back of her sleeve to wipe the tears from her face. Her cheek stung as if someone had rubbed salt into the cut, but at least it had stopped bleeding. She dug around in her bag for a tissue, blew her nose. Morwen stood by, looking uncertain, head on one side, fidgeting.

"I'm alright, thank you, Morwen. Just ... a lot has happened today. As you know."

"Indeed. May I accompany you on this last quest?"

"N-no. Thank you, though, for the offer. I must do this myself."

Her mother's voice echoed in her mind. She bowed her head, tried to steady her breathing. Reached into the staff, drew some power just to feel it in her veins. Whimpering quim, indeed. She put her head up, smiled at Morwen, but knew she looked a touch manic.

"I won't be long." She turned and stepped through the gateway – just her, her staff and the clavis.

The other side of the gateway let into an open shipping container, placed at the back of Damocles' lot. It filled the far end of the container. Maisie closed it and slipped the clavis into her bag.

As she strode out of the container and around the corner of the yard to the warehouse, Deefer put up a couple of barks, then realised it was her and started wagging his tail, whining and yelping. He ran around her in excited circles.

"Fook me, it's the witch," the gravelly voice of Damocles echoed around the warehouse.

He and a half dozen hard-case men, who Maisie took to be gangsters, were sitting around a table made from a huge wooden cable drum. The men could have been brothers, or at the very least, close cousins. They had a similarity of feature and build – all were broad, heavy, muscular, with short black hair, dark olive skin, brown eyes and broad noses. They were drinking beer and smoking evil-smelling Anatolian cigarettes.

"Bloody hell! You been fightin'?" Damocles looked at her with raised eyebrows.

"Hello, Damocles. It's lovely to see you as well. Thank you so much for your help earlier today. The operation was an almost complete success."

"The operation was fookin' outstanding!" he exclaimed. "We peppered the castle with automatic fire, scared the shite out of the castle guards, and buggered off before the polizia even showed their hairy arses. But what the fook happened to you?"

"Well. Let us not dwell on me. I thank you for your efforts to date. There is a gateway in that shipping container," she waved behind her, "which opens into the Citadel. As payment for the earlier operation. Here is the key."

She tossed the clavis to him, which he caught in one hand, without taking his eyes from her.

"Thank you. Good business."

The gangsters let out a collective sigh as they caught sight of the clavis. Maisie suspected the Ostiarium would need to inspect the goods passing through that gateway now and then, to keep Damocles in line. A problem for another day, and really, a problem for Rosalia, not her.

"I have a favour to ask of you. If you would be so kind?"

"I'm fookin' quakin' in me boots. What now?"

"Could you light me a small fire, perhaps in an old oil drum?"

"What, here? Now?"

"Please." She beamed her best smile.

Damocles looked at her as if she were mad, but said something in an Eastern Europan tongue and two of the gangsters got up. They were frowning in confusion, but headed off into the yard, where they collected some old pallets. They also found an oil drum that had seen use for this purpose before, its burnt sides and rough air holes a witness. After a few minutes, and with the help of a diesel-soaked rag, a strong blaze was burning in the barrel.

"You must keep this fire burning for the next two hours, without fail, whether or not I come back. Do you understand?" said Maisie.

"Oh, fookin' *must* I?"

Maisie internally rolled her eyes. Using the command was so much easier. She sighed.

"It is in your interest. If you were to lose the Finder of Keys on the eve of her successfully retrieving the final Gratadei clavis, how welcome would you be in Khôra?"

"Fookin'ell. Awright. Two hours. No problem."

Maisie looked around at the watching gangsters, and Damocles and Deefer, and invoked the kathalyog. She stepped into the Betwixt by the oil drum fire. It was the usual dull, grey, misty uniformity, the same as in Khôra. So far, so good. Now, she thought to herself, the tricky part.

"Show me the hearth of Cardinal Baroffio."

A flare of light some distance away. But manageable in one stretch, she felt. She strode over to it, feeling the gentle pull from the oil-barrel fire. She leant into the Cardinal's fire and peered. The view from the hearth resolved into an enormous office, the huge slate grey fireplace holding a modest blaze. The spring day in Milano was warm; Maisie supposed the thick castle walls took a while to admit the heat.

The Cardinal was sitting behind an imposing oak desk, which was topped in green leather and piled with papers, letters, agreements. Much like its counterpart in Khôra.

In this room, there were sofas and chairs beyond the desk. A more comfortable, homely office. Again, a wooden crucifix hung above the fireplace.

The office was empty except for the Cardinal, who was busy writing in a ledger, opened out across his desk. Perfect.

Maisie applied glamour to herself, holding Aelene's appearance in her mind. Invoked the second half of the spell. She materialised and stood by the fireplace, silently watching the Cardinal, who hadn't noticed her arrival. He was busy with pen and ledger, muttering to himself.

"Cardinal Baroffio."

Her voice held the sibilance of Aelene's. The Cardinal jumped, holding his hand to his chest.

"Good God! You scared me half to death!" he shouted.

"I will be brief. Your tenure in Mediolanum and Khôra is at an end. Give up the clavis to me now, and I will allow you to live."

The Cardinal's face turned puce, and his body shook, his jowls wobbling with fury.

"You dare threaten me? Have you forgotten your place? Heretic! Banshee!"

He stood and started towards her.

Maisie used the same spell she had used on the tin cans and knocked the Cardinal over. She had used little power, but he banged his head as he fell, and sprawled on the floor, moaning. Maisie walked over and patted down his pockets. Nothing. She tried the drawers of his desk. Nothing.

Sighing, she thought about entering a yogic trance from which to search for the clavis, but the Cardinal's moans grew loader, and it was clear he was regaining his senses. She waited until he sat up, then she approached him again. Although she heard Steig's voice in her head warning of great power and great responsibility, she felt this was for the, well, greater good.

"Where is the clavis?"

She put a lot of command into the words. A paperweight rattled off the desk and shattered on the marble floor. The command physically shook the Cardinal, and he clutched at his chest. Oh, good grief, don't have a heart attack.

"In the safe."

Maisie rolled her eyes. "Get it for me."

The Cardinal managed, with a lot of huffing and sweating, to heave himself upright. He walked to a panel on the wall opposite, which hinged back to reveal a small safe, complete with dial and handle. He opened it and took out the clavis, which was wrapped in a purple cloth. When he offered it to Maisie, she faltered. She wasn't sure how comprehensive her command was, so took no chances.

"Put it on the desk and step away, to the corner of the room."

After he was far enough away, Maisie picked up the clavis. She turned to him, reached for more command from the staff, from herself.

"Tell me the truth." Her voice rattled the windows in their frames. The Cardinal stepped back as far as he could, edged into the corner of the room, cowering like a cornered rat. "Is this the only clavis that the Gratadei possess, apart from the ones in the storeroom under the castello?"

"You have all of them now, you witch. I hope you rot in Hell."

"I have news for you, Baroffio. I'm already there."

With that, Maisie invoked the kathalyog and stepped back into the welcome Betwixt. She removed her glamour and made her way through the greyness to Damocles' barrel fire.

Deefer was more excited to see her than the gangsters and Damocles, who had moved their afternoon drinking session to the fire. They barely started when she materialised. Deefer, however, tried to turn himself inside out with wagging at her arrival.

"Damocles, please open the gateway to Khôra. I wish to pass," she asked.

"Did you get the fookin' clavis? Did you off the Cardinal?"

"The Gratadei no longer have a clavis to, nor a presence in, Khôra. The Cardinal yet lives, but I suspect he might find that state uncomfortable after I have spoken with His Holiness."

"Fook me, you don't fook around, do you?"

"I've found it's best to be direct. The gateway?"

Damocles walked with Maisie and Deefer to the shipping container, where he opened the gateway back to Khôra. Maisie stroked Deefer's head, scratching between his large, pointed ears.

"Be a good boy, Deefer."

He whined his assurance to her. She turned to Damocles, who was grinning.

"A pleasure, as always, Damocles," she said, smiling back, stepping towards the gateway.

"Oh, yeah, by the way," he called after her, "you do know there's a pile more ..." But she had already stepped into the gateway, had already gone. He shrugged, looking at Deefer. "She'll find out about all the fookin' Gratadei mercs hiding in Khôra soon enough, eh, dog?"

Author's Notes

First of all, without the help and support of the following people, this work would never have been started, let alone have made it to publication. My thanks to Myszka Fox, for her suggestion that I turn the ending of Steig Sturluson's *Tales from the Road* into the beginning of a fantasy novel, and for a whole host of other assistances, edits, encouraging words, brainstorming sessions, amazing Foxy dinners and, oh yes, a novel writer's course.

My thanks to the Foxes' Retreat Writing Group, and all the marvellous writers who attended in one aspect or another. Your positive and helpful suggestions and feedback have helped shape this novel. Also, those writers who attended the Get It Written sessions; again, knowing you're out there is a great help.

Thank you to Manda Waller, my editor, for her encouraging remarks and her skill at steering me gently in the right direction.

Thank you to my beta readers, Zen Akhtar and Elizabeth Raikes especially, for their useful feedback.

Thank you to the creators of Dabblewriter and Atticus software for making the authoring journey slightly less bumpy.

Thanks to the travelling folk, the Rom, Irish and New travellers who I have met on the road over the years. You are a magical tapestry whose weave and weft becomes more intricate the closer you look. Specifically, thanks to Janet, Paul the Farrier, Hayley and Felix the Sign-writer, who got me into being horse-drawn. And thank you to George the travelling man, sadly now departed from this realm, who spent many an evening sitting by my yog, in Roteslund, spinning yarns late into the night.

A special mention has to be made to my horses, characters who I have known over the (many) years of equestrianism: Saffi Bobbles, who is the basis of Beckett, and had a penchant for mints, and Lucy, my Appaloosa mare, who carries the flag for talking horses everywhere. And a herd of others, all now ranging in Elysium.

If I have missed anyone out of this section, please accept my apologies.

Travelling Folklore

The Romani folklorists of the Gypsy Lore Society of Chirchedele University and beyond, will have a frown upon their undoubtedly large and wrinkled foreheads, as they look upon the tales herein and declare, 'but! But! This is all made up!' Yes, it is. Mostly.

Anglo Romani language (amongst others)

If there are grammatical or linguistic mistakes in the text of this novel, around the Anglo Romani, ancient Hellenic, Latin and other languages, then please understand I have made my best effort at getting it right, but I'm not a linguist. It is, essentially, all Hellenic to me.

Names of Creatures

A certain fantasy author published a series of somewhat successful books about a boy wizard from 1997 onwards; in these books, the full pantheon of northern European folklore appears to have been ~~hijacked~~ gracefully repurposed. If you find creatures in these pages that sound familiar, they are not stolen from that book series, but taken from the earlier folklore. Though I have changed their names slightly to make them less familiar, and to protect the guilty.

Betwixt and Khôra and Dodecahedrons

The idea of the Betwixt is a nod to the *Dragonriders of Pern* series by Anne McCaffrey. Imagine my surprise, literally days before publication, when I discovered the idea of 'looking from between' in Charles de Lint's excellent *Juniper Wiles and the Ghost Girls* novel. I suppose it is a trope. Or at least, it is now.

The original idea of Khôra came from the intriguing book *The Ancient Paths* by Graham Robb. Whilst his pseudo-scientific approach, in my opinion, might be a little shaky in terms of academic rigour (Oh, I'm going to get letters, aren't I?), the idea of a proto-Celtic network of pathways across Europa, built by Heracles, beguiled me enough to use it as a starting point for the clavis network of gateways.

Roman-age dodecahedrons have been found all over northern Europa. No one knew, until now, what these odd bronze objects were for. At least *that* mystery has been cleared up for the archaeologists. You're welcome.

Roteslund

I grew up in Roteslund, the smallest county in Breotonlond. Many of the places in Part I are places I have stopped at when either horse-drawn or living in a converted lorry. It is a marvellous jewel of a county. If you visit, please take your rubbish home with you.

About The Author

Adam is a neurodiverse author of fantasy novels and historical fiction-non-fiction novels.

When he's not inventing stuff or wiring stuff up, he's writing, or out and about on Lucy the horse, exploring the hidden byeways and the deeper wooded sections of the Peak District.

Bibliography:

- Vardo Witch (Kurra's Story) (Vardo 0.5)
- Vardo Path (Vardo 1)
- Vardo Moon (Vardo 2) Publication date October 2024

His website is:
https://adamfoxauthor.co.uk/

About The Publisher

Foxes' Retreat is a writing retreat, offering counselling, coaching and bespoke retreats.

Website: https://www.foxesretreat.com/

Printed in Great Britain
by Amazon

40002690R00239